Early Dawn

Catherine Anderson

Early Dawn

**Doubleday Large Print
Home Library Edition**

A SIGNET BOOK

SIGNET
Published by New American Library, a division of
Penguin Group (USA) Inc., 375 Hudson Street, New York,
New York 10014, USA
Penguin Group (Canada), 90 Eglinton Avenue East,
Suite 700, Toronto, Ontario M4P 2Y3, Canada
(a division of Pearson Penguin Canada Inc.)
Penguin Books Ltd., 80 Strand, London WC2R 0RL, England
Penguin Ireland, 25 St. Stephen's Green, Dublin 2, Ireland
(a division of Penguin Books Ltd.)
Penguin Group (Australia), 250 Camberwell Road,
Camberwell, Victoria 3124, Australia (a division of
Pearson Australia Group Pty. Ltd.)
Penguin Books India Pvt. Ltd., 11 Community Centre,
Panchsheel Park, New Delhi - 110 017, India
Penguin Group (NZ), 67 Apollo Drive, Rosedale, North
Shore 0632, New Zealand (a division of Pearson
New Zealand Ltd.)
Penguin Books (South Africa) (Pty.) Ltd., 24 Sturdee
Avenue, Rosebank, Johannesburg 2196, South Africa
Penguin Books Ltd., Registered Offices: 80 Strand,
London WC2R 0RL, England

First published by Signet, an imprint of New American Library, a division of Penguin Group (USA) Inc.

ISBN: 978-1-61523-986-3

PUBLISHER'S NOTE
This is a work of fiction. Names, characters, places, and incidents either are the product of the author's imagination or are used fictitiously, and any resemblance to actual persons, living or dead, business establishments, events, or locales is entirely coincidental.

The publisher does not have any control over and does not assume any responsibility for author or third-party Web sites or their content.

This Large Print Book carries the Seal of Approval of N.A.V.H.

Years ago, when Keegan's Lady was published, the book was supposed to have been dedicated to my great-niece, Wendy, who was my inspiration when I created the character Caitlin O'Shannessy. Sadly, my mother passed away, and at the last minute I changed my mind, dedicating Keegan's Lady to her instead. Wendy understood, and I assured her that Eden Paxton's love story would be dedicated to her. At the time, I had no idea that I would get locked into writing contemporary novels for so long! Now, finally, Eden Paxton is making her appearance in Early Dawn, and my wonderful great-niece is getting the promised dedication.

This book is dedicated to Wendy,
who has brightened our lives with her
gorgeous red hair, laughing blue eyes,
indomitable spirit, and most wondrous
of all, her baby boy, Lucas.

Joseph Simon Paxton, Sr. (1824–1866)

Dory Sue Jesperson Keegan (1831–1920)

Ace Keegan
(1855–1932)
Married 1885
Caitlin O'Shannessy
(1863–1952)

Little Ace Keegan
(1888–1976)

Dory Sue Keegan
(1890–1979)

Keegan's Lady, 1996

Joseph Paxton, Jr.
(1858–1953)
Married 1889
Rachel Hollister
(1867–1954)

Summer Breeze,
January 2006

David Paxton
(1860–1949)

Story Yet to Come!

Esa Paxton
(1862–1933)

Story Yet to Come!

Eden Paxton
(1867–1954)
Married 1890
Matthew James Coulter
(1859–1943)

James Matthew Coulter
(1901–1986)
Married 1920
Sarah Beth Johnson
(1902–1989)

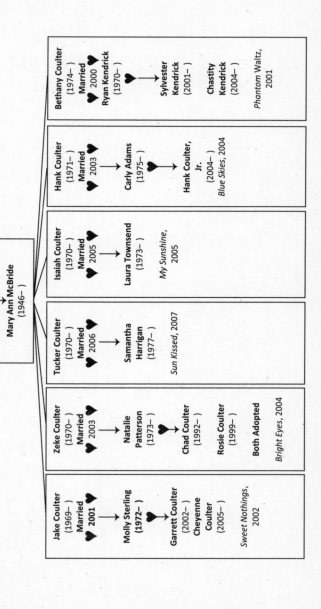

Prologue

June 1887

Matthew Coulter awakened to a soft hissing sound, the faint smell of kerosene, and the dim glow of lantern light. A nearly blinding pain knifed from his left eyebrow into his temple, and as he struggled to focus he was filled with a terrible sense of dread. When his eyes had adjusted, he realized that he was abed in his childhood sleeping nook, a rectangular space with rough plank walls that was barely large enough to hold a cot, battered dresser, and small wardrobe. *Strange.* He'd been married five years ago and hadn't stayed overnight at his folks' place since. But there was no mistake. The familiar scent of his mother's Irish stew drifted in from the kitchen to tease his nostrils, the air redolent with pan-browned lamb chops simmered to perfection, and the unmistakable fragrance of thyme, a spice his wife, Olivia, seldom used.

Matthew yearned to slip back into the darkness of sleep that had so recently enveloped him, but that niggling sense of dread grew stronger as he came more awake. Something was wrong, horribly wrong, but his head hurt so badly that he couldn't remember what.

"Ma?" he croaked, and pushed up onto one elbow with a low groan because a sharp stitch in his side nearly took his breath away.

The room spun around him, the shadows that lurked beyond the sphere of light seeming to dance and sway. He wrapped a hand over the mattress edge to keep from pitching off onto the floor. *What in Sam Hill?* It felt as if every bone in his body had been broken, and the pain in his temple throbbed with each beat of his heart.

"Ma!"

A blurry female figure dressed in blue

appeared in the archway. "Matthew! Thank God!" The lilt of her faint Irish brogue was as familiar to Matthew as his own voice. "We were starting to think you might never wake up."

Matthew lay back against the pillow and closed his eyes as his mother sat beside him and placed a cool, soothing hand on his right cheek. The gesture reminded him of the early days of his childhood, when she'd checked him for fever or fussed over him when he was sick. He let himself enjoy the sensation for a moment before prying his eyes open again to fix his gaze on her face. Even at fifty-six, Hattie Coulter was a lovely woman, with black hair and eyes the deep blue of a summer sky. The years had lined her skin, but on her the traces of age were like the tiny cracks on the surface of an old oil painting, only adding to its beauty.

"Where's Livvy?" Matthew asked hoarsely.

She withdrew her hand from his cheek and brought it to rest on her lap in a tight fist. Matthew knew then that something really was amiss. The thought that it might involve his wife filled him with panic.

"Ma?" he pressed. "Where's Olivia?"

Hattie pushed to her feet. "I'll be back in a moment, dear heart. I need to tell your father that you're awake."

Matthew watched her hurry from the room. Something dark hovered at the back of his mind—something so ominous and unthinkable that he didn't want to acknowledge it. He flung his forearm over his eyes to shield them from the light and immediately regretted it when pain exploded in his left temple. Gingerly he explored with numb fingertips to discover that his head was wrapped in gauze. An injury of some sort? He couldn't recall having an accident, but after working with horses most of his life, he knew he might not remember if he'd been kicked in the head.

Matthew had almost convinced himself of a horse's kick when he heard the heavy tattoo of his father's boots on the kitchen floor. An instant later, Matthew Coulter Senior filled the doorway, his weather-bronzed face creased with worry, his blue eyes shadowed with sadness. He slowly approached the bed, his wife hovering behind him.

In that no-nonsense way of his, he

wasted no time hemming and hawing. In a brogue much more pronounced than his wife's, he said, "Your ma says you don't remember what happened, son, that you been askin' where Olivia is." He cleared his throat. "You need to brace yourself, boy, 'cause I can't think of no easy way to say this, and I ain't good with words at the best of times. Your Livvy was kilt by a gang of ruffians. Happened nigh onto three weeks ago now."

"What?" Matthew couldn't wrap his mind around the words bouncing inside his head. He pictured Olivia's precious face, her soft brown eyes and gentle smile. Dead? She was so young. That couldn't be. His father had to have it wrong. "No," Matthew grated out. "No!"

His father shook his head and sank heavily onto the edge of the bed. "I'm sorry, son. It pains me more'n you can know to be the one to tell you such a thing. We loved her, too, your ma and me. She was like a daughter to us."

Though the discomfort was excruciating, Matthew shook his head in denial. "No."

Even as he whispered the word, Matthew knew by the dark sorrow in his father's eyes that it was true; Olivia was dead. The ensuing silence drove that home to him. His ma didn't interrupt to say that his pa had it wrong, nor did she offer Matthew any assurance that everything would come right in the end.

"How?" Matthew forced himself to ask. "Ru-ruffians? We don't have . . . It's safe hereabouts."

"The sheriff says it was the Sebastian Gang." Matthew Senior cleared his throat. "You've heard tell of 'em. We read about 'em in the *Crystal Falls Courier* a few months back. A couple of days after the attack on you and Livvy, they struck again over near Medford. Shot a boy dead for tryin' to stop them from stealin' some horses. Them Sebastians are wanted damned near everywhere west of the divide. A posse out of Sacramento was hot on their heels, and the gang took a detour through here, tryin' to shake 'em off." The elder man's voice had gone almost as hoarse as Matthew's. "You and Livvy—well, near as we could tell, you was on the way home from a picnic by the crick. The gang must've come out of the trees, all of a sudden like, and surrounded your wagon. You wasn't armed, and there wasn't much you could do. Livvy . . . she was—" He broke off as if the words had stuck in his throat. Then he passed a gnarled, work-roughened hand over his craggy face. "Well, we can only pray she went quick and didn't suffer over-much. Doc believes you was already unconscious by the wagon when it happened. Pistol-whipped, kicked after you went down, and then shot in the chest and left for dead. Doc did all he could, but you was in sorry shape with busted-up ribs, a hole near your heart, and an injury to your head he couldn't fix. If not for your ma's prayers and nursin', we might've lost you, too."

Wringing her hands in her apron, Matthew's mother moved closer to the cot. "It's true, dear heart. I've barely slept a wink since they brought you in. It's been touch and go. We were afraid you might never come back around."

Matthew wished he hadn't. His sweet Livvy, dead? He didn't want to believe it. How could something like that have happened and he had no memory of it?

Embarrassed to lose control in front of his father, Matthew rolled onto his stomach and pressed his face into the pillow to stifle his sobs, even though the pressure against his temple hurt like hell.

"Have a care, Matthew," his mother cried. "You'll reopen your wounds."

But Matthew was beyond caring about his wounds. He hoped they'd break open so he could bleed to death. *Livvy.* On their wedding day, he'd vowed to keep her safe from all harm, and he'd failed her in a way no husband ever should, all because he hadn't taken a weapon with him on a stupid picnic.

He felt his father's hand come to rest on his shoulder. "We'll leave you be for a bit. There's times when a man needs to be alone, and I reckon this is one of them for you."

Matthew held his breath until his parents left the room. Then he released a sob that shook his whole body. *Livvy.* He'd loved her since boyhood. How would he face the rest of his life without her?

From the hallway, he heard his brother Hoyt murmur something he didn't quite catch.

Matthew Senior replied, "I don't think he remembers much, and I didn't think it was a good idea to fill in the blanks just yet. No point in hittin' him with too much at once."

"But, Pa!" Hoyt protested, louder now. "You gotta tell him. If you don't, somebody else will say somethin' without thinkin'. Better to break it to him gentle-like."

"Shh. Hush, you two," Ma urged.

Matthew rolled onto his back to better hear the conversation taking place in the hallway. What had his father neglected to tell him? Livvy was dead. What the hell could be worse than that?

Lowering his voice again, Hoyt said, "His wife was brutally raped, for God's sake, and then the sons of bitches carved on her with a knife before they slit her throat! You can't keep that from him. He's bound to find out sooner or later, and it'd be easier for him to hear it from you."

"Maybe," his father agreed, "but not this minute. That boy needs to heal some first."

Matthew squeezed his eyes tightly closed. *Oh, God.* The memories of that afternoon were coming back to him now, fast and hard. The unthinkable darkness at the back of his mind had slipped into the light of day. He tried to block the pictures that swirled through his mind, but they just kept coming.

Livvy. He could see the sunlight slanting down through the tree limbs to dapple her sweet face, hear the sound of her laughter. During the picnic, she'd told him that she was finally in the family way, and they'd been so happy, anxious to get home so they could share their joy with his parents and hers. Then six men on horseback had spilled from the nearby woods and encircled their wagon. *Oh, God.*

The thugs had been armed. They had demanded valuables, and neither Matthew nor Olivia had had anything to offer them. Matthew's gold pocket watch had been at the jeweler's for repairs, and Livvy's wedding band hadn't been worth much. Those bastards had retaliated by dragging Olivia from the wagon. When Matthew jumped in to defend her, two of the no-account polecats had held his arms while a third man beat him senseless with the butt of his revolver.

Afterward Matthew had lain by the wagon with his face in the dirt while they kicked his torso, burying the toes of their boots as deeply as they could into his flesh to do as much damage as possible. When they'd grown weary of that sport and turned their vile intentions on Olivia, Matthew had tried desperately to move, but his body refused to cooperate. He hadn't been able to lift his head. As if from a great distance, he'd heard Livvy screaming his name, over and over, until finally there was an awful silence. Seconds later, one of the ruffians had returned to Matthew, rolled him over onto his back with the toe of one boot, and shot him in the chest.

It was all Matthew could remember. After that was only blackness.

Matthew stared through a blur of tears at the ceiling rafters, wishing with every fiber of his being that he had died, too. He'd lain there in the dirt while his wife was raped and murdered. What kind of man was he?

No kind of man, he decided. No kind of man at all.

It took Matthew three more weeks to recover enough to get out of bed, and even then, he wasn't anywhere close to being healed. His broken ribs hadn't mended quite right, so it still hurt to breathe deeply. The bullet wound, which had done more damage to his shoulder than his chest, had left him barely able to use his left arm. He also had a hitch in his gait caused by an injury to his right hip.

When Matthew first gained his feet, he staggered around like a drunk, his head spinning, his stomach lurching with nausea. At the mirror by the wardrobe, he saw why. The gash at his temple had been deep and nearly six inches long. Though his hair was growing back to cover the scar, it was still a vivid red and visible through the half-inch stubble. Yet another scar slashed from above his left eyebrow to the upper part of his eyelid, the line puckered from Doc's lack of finesse with a needle and thread. Another jagged, crimson line angled along his cheekbone.

With trembling fingers, Matthew traced the marks. His ma had shaved him yesterday, but she may as well not have bothered. His face had never been pretty-boy perfect, and now it bordered on the grotesque. The man who'd worked him over with the pistol butt must have been right-handed, Matthew decided, a fact that he filed away for later. Little wonder he felt dizzy on his feet. Head injuries like these could have killed him. The temple wound had been severe enough to affect some of his gray matter. It might take a while for his brain to right itself completely, and until then, he would probably feel dizzy and sick to his stomach more times than not.

Even so, Matthew was determined to be up and about. While lying helpless in bed, he'd had a lot of time to think, and he'd kept coming full circle to the undeniable fact that no man worth his salt allowed a bunch of low-life bastards to cruelly rape and murder his wife. It was too late now for Matthew to undo the events of that terrible afternoon, but as God was his witness, it wasn't too late to avenge Livvy's death.

Matthew managed to saddle his horse, Smoky, that first day and ride into Crystal Falls to stock up on ammunition for his .44-caliber Winchester rifle and his Colt revolvers. Before heading back home, he stopped at the jeweler's, where he'd left his gold pocket watch for repairs a couple of weeks before the attack.

The proprietor, a balding, middle-aged man of considerable girth who wore a black bib apron over a white shirt, the bosom and collar of which were polished to a high sheen, looked startled when he first saw the marks on Matthew's face. Then he nodded solemnly and placed his plump hands palms down on the wooden counter.

"Matthew," he said by way of greeting. "Glad to see you on your feet. You look like you tangled with a grizzly bear and lost the battle."

"Wasn't a grizzly, and there wasn't a battle. I wish to hell there had been."

The jeweler nodded again. "The wife and I attended the services. I can't begin to tell you how sorry we are about Livvy. Known her since she was no bigger than a grasshopper. Such a pretty little thing, always ready with a smile to cheer people up. She'll be sorely missed."

Matthew touched the brim of his Stetson, his only response. He couldn't speak of Olivia without his voice shaking.

"I reckon you're here for your watch." The jeweler opened a small wooden drawer behind him and plucked out a manila packet. "Just needed a good cleaning. There'll be no charge."

Matthew met the older man's gaze. "Us Coulters don't take charity, Paulson. Your time's worth something."

"A dime will do it, then."

Matthew fished in his left hip pocket, wincing at the pain in his shoulder. He handed over the dime and grabbed the packet with his right hand. "Thanks for not sellin' my watch. Took me a spell to come back for it, and I know your policy is to keep things for only thirty days."

"No worries. I inscribed that watch for Livvy right before your wedding. I know how precious it must be to you."

Matthew's throat went tight. He touched the brim of his hat again and exited the shop. Once on the boardwalk, he opened the envelope and tipped the watch out onto his palm. The gold gleamed in the late-summer sunlight like a puddle of freshly churned butter. His heart hurt as he flipped the watch over to read the inscription on the back. *Love Always, Matthew. Forever Yours, Livvy, 1882.* Tears blurred his vision as he slipped the timepiece into his watch pocket. Forever, he realized now, was a very long time, and he had to face it without her.

With difficulty, he remounted the horse and rode slowly home, trying not to jostle his shoulder or ribs. Hoyt, two years his junior, met him at the ranch gate. The younger man's sun-browned face bore the Coulter stamp, a bladelike nose, Irish blue eyes, a strong jaw, and a squared, stubborn chin. In a rugged, lean way, Hoyt was a handsome man, but like Matthew, he could never lay claim to having fine features.

"You're goin' after 'em, aren't you?" Hoyt asked.

Matthew nodded. "Have to. What they did can't go unpunished."

"I'm goin' with you, then." Hoyt jerked off his battered hat and raked thick fingers through his dark brown hair. "Us Coulters stick together. It's how Pa raised us. I can't let you do this alone."

Matthew sighed and rested his crossed wrists over the saddle horn. "Pa needs you and the other boys here, Hoyt. I appreciate the offer, but I can't accept."

"You can't take on six outlaws by yourself!"

"I'll brush up on my shooting before I light out, and every day after. By the time I catch up with them, I'll be as good with a gun as they are. I'll be fine." In truth, Matthew didn't care if the bastards killed him. Without Livvy, he had nothing left to live for. "You've got to stay here, where you're most needed."

"Pa can do without me for a few weeks. Zed and Gareth can do my share of the work for a spell."

"The Sebastians have stayed one step ahead of the law for good long while, Hoyt. What makes you think I can catch up with them in only a few weeks? It may take a lot longer than that. I'm hoping not, but there you have it."

"You shouldn't go after 'em without somebody to watch your back, big brother."

The way Matthew saw it, their mother already stood to lose one son. There was no point in doubling her grief by putting Hoyt's life at risk.

"Should or shouldn't aside, I'm not taking you with me." Matthew reined his horse to go around his sibling. "The family needs you here."

As Matthew rode toward the log stable, he trailed his gaze over the ranch, which had been dubbed the Lazy J. The name had never made a lick of sense to Matthew. There was nothing lazy about raising beeves and horses. His pa had sweat blood to clear enough land to support his growing herd of cattle, and that wasn't to mention all the hours of labor it had taken to build the roomy log home, the outbuildings, and all the fences. Even now, at almost sixty, Matthew Coulter Senior worked from the first crack of dawn until well after dark, and all four of his sons did as well.

At the door of the stable, Matthew swung from the saddle, supporting the bulk of his weight with his right arm until his feet settled on solid ground. A mere stone's throw away sat the little log house that he had built for Livvy. He didn't allow his gaze to wander in that direction. He hadn't walked over there yet, because he dreaded going through the empty rooms. They would be just as he and his wife had left them on that fateful afternoon, her Bible resting on the nightstand, her Sunday shoes tucked toe first under the bed, her church dress draped over the back of the rocker. He didn't know if he could handle that.

He would have to soon, though. A man couldn't hit the trail without a few changes of clothes. He'd give himself a couple more weeks to heal, target-practicing the entire while, and then it would be time to head out. His wife had endured a terrible and painful attack, and he had a score to settle with the Sebastian boys.

Matthew wouldn't rest until either he was six feet under or every last member of that gang was dead.

Chapter One

Three years later
May 1890

Weak, rain-drenched sunlight filtered through the lace curtains at the window of the Pacific Express passenger train, casting a dappled pattern on the white sheet of stationery that Eden Paxton clutched in her hand. As the luxury car chugged along the track to crest yet another steep grade on its way to Denver, she reread the words written on the paper for at least the tenth time in a week. Assimilating their meaning gave her the same sense of vertigo she often experienced when she looked down from high places. In short, her whole world had been tipped off its axis, all her hopes, dreams, and plans drifting away from her like pollen in a high wind.

Her fiancé, John Parrish, had ended their engagement, not because he no longer loved her but because his highfalutin parents, San Franciscans of considerable social prominence, disapproved of Eden's lineage. According to them, she lacked a "purebred" pedigree and therefore was unsuitable to be John's wife or the mother of his children. John hadn't even had the courage to tell Eden in person but instead had sent her this dreadful letter.

Five years of my life, she thought bitterly, *wasted on a pampered milksop who lacks the backbone to defy his father and mother.* Even more telling to Eden, John had failed to stop his parents from vilifying her reputation in order to gain public support for him. It was unseemly for a man to end his engagement to a respectable young lady without just cause, so the Parrish family had whispered the ugly truth about Eden's illegitimate birth to anyone who would listen, not caring a whit about the embarrassment they might cause Eden or her mother, Dory. Every time Eden thought about it, she burned with anger.

Yesterday morning she and her mother had left the city in disgrace, scorned by lifelong friends, snubbed in places of business, and turned away from houses they'd visited for years. They were now pariahs in San Francisco, a place they had both considered home. The humiliation had been complete and as sharp as a stiletto.

How could John have allowed his parents to behave so shabbily? Eden didn't care so much about the consequences for herself. All the fussiness of city life had set her teeth on edge at times, and she'd grown impatient more than once with her flibbertigibbet friends who cared more about their appearance than anything else. But it had broken Eden's heart to see her mother mistreated. A stiff-necked butler at the home of one prominent family had glared down his nose at Dory Paxton as if she were a cockroach and ordered her off his employer's porch. Dory had handled this dismissal like a grand lady, holding her head high as she quit the property, but Eden would never forget the pain she'd glimpsed in her mother's eyes.

As if guessing her daughter's thoughts, Dory curled slender fingers over Eden's wrist, forcing her hand and the letter to her lap. "Please, darling, no more fretting on my account." A delicate blonde with gentle blue eyes, Dory flashed an overbright smile. "I've wanted to live closer to your brothers for *years*. Truly I have. Every time we've visited them at one of their ranches, my heart has broken a little when it came time to leave. I thought about relocating. The only reason I never acted on it was because I couldn't bear the thought of leaving you behind. You were so in love with John. Your future seemed to be all mapped out. I couldn't be in two places at once, so I decided to stay put."

Eden no longer felt certain that she had ever truly loved John. She'd shed a few tears after receiving his letter, but then anger had taken over. Where was the heartbreak that she should be feeling? Why wasn't she devastated and filled with despair? When a woman truly loved a man, she surely felt something besides outrage and secret relief when he walked away.

The thought troubled Eden. How could she have misread her own feelings so completely? Even more worrisome, why had she never seen how weak and spineless John was when it came to displeasing his parents? She considered herself to be a fair judge of character. With four older brothers to educate her, she'd learned at an early age that not all men could be trusted. And yet she'd trusted John, accepting all his flimsy excuses for postponing their nuptials, never once suspecting that he no longer wanted to marry her. Perhaps that was why she felt only anger—because he'd made a complete fool of her. If Eden possessed one trait in goodly measure, it was pride. Being made to look ridiculous didn't sit well with her.

"Everything will work out fine," Dory went on. "You'll see. Remember how wonderful it was when we lived on the ranch in California before Ace started winning big at cards? Despite the struggles, we pulled together after Joseph Senior died, and we all became so close—a real family."

Privately, Eden couldn't help but think the term *ranch* was a little too grandiose for the scraggly patch of land and three-room shack that they'd been forced to call home when they finally reached California. But her mother was right otherwise. As a family, they had made many wonderful memories during those lean, trying years—target-practicing, going on hunting trips for meat, playing games in the yard after the day's work was completed, and then gathering for evening meals, grateful to have food, no matter how simple the fare. Later, when Ace began winning at cards, their circumstances had drastically improved, a rags-to-riches story, but when Eden revisited some of her fondest childhood memories, she often recalled the shack and the wondrous love that had warmed every drafty room.

Sticking to her subject, Dory chattered away. "Ace has made some very sound investments on my behalf over the years, you know. Soon I'll have the proceeds from the sale of the house in San Francisco. There will be plenty of capital to start over fresh. No Name is such a friendly little town. I'm sure we're both going to love it there."

Eden hoped that would be the case, but deep down, she doubted it. For one, her mother was accustomed and well suited to living in a city where she could enjoy art museums, a well-stocked public library, shopping opportunities galore, and a variety of social activities. No Name, Colorado, offered few of those amenities. There was also the fear that Eden's remarkable resemblance to her sister-in-law, Caitlin, would raise suspicion. People in No Name might snub Dory once they realized the truth about her past—that their town drunk, Connor O'Shannessy, Caitlin's father and now deceased, had taken wrongful advantage of Dory twenty-four years ago and left her pregnant with Eden, his bastard daughter. The fine citizens of No Name might not dress as richly as Dory's faithless friends in San Francisco, but under the homespun, they could be just as self-righteous and narrow-minded. None of them would want to associate with Eden or with the woman who had given birth to her.

Keeping her thoughts about that to herself, Eden stuffed John's letter back into her beaded reticule and snapped the bag closed. Over the last week, Dory had endured insult after insult, and Eden didn't have the heart to deal her yet another blow by playing devil's advocate. Besides, maybe Eden was wrong, and the good people of No Name would welcome them into their midst with open arms. If not, Eden would deal with the problem when it arose. For now, it felt good to see her mother smiling again.

"I'll love being able to see my brothers on a daily basis," Eden said with forced cheerfulness. "Little Ace is over two years old now! Can you believe it? I'll bet he's absolutely darling."

"About the age of our little towheaded traveling companion," Dory replied.

At mention of the child seated behind them, Eden glanced over her shoulder to smile at his mother. The slender brunette had done a remarkable job of keeping the toddler entertained during the journey from San Francisco, reading him stories, playing games with him, and helping him to draw pictures. Occasionally, though, the little fellow escaped into the aisle and raced madly back and forth to burn off excess energy. Whenever he stopped near Dory's seat, the older woman plucked interesting objects from her reticule and allowed him to handle them. He was particularly fond of her little mirror and heavily laden ring of house keys.

Returning her attention to her mother, Eden said, "As much as I've missed my brothers, I'm excited about seeing the little ones. I have a niece I've never clapped eyes on! In Ace's last letter, he said she's already smiling and trying to make sounds. It'll be so much fun to play with her." Born in December, Dory Sue Keegan was the newest addition to Ace's growing family. Eden didn't approve of parents naming children after living family members. To her way of thinking, the practice created unnecessary confusion for the children. But she was pleased that it made her mother happy to have the baby named after her. "If she's as beautiful as Ace claims, she'll be a delight to behold. Do you suppose her eyes may change from blue to brown when she gets older?"

Dory nodded. "It's possible. But I'm hoping not. With Caitlin's fair complexion and Ace's black hair, she'll be truly breathtaking if her eyes remain blue." Dory studied Eden's face, a slight frown furrowing her brow. "If the baby resembles Caitlin as much as Ace says she does, she also looks exactly like you. How are you going to feel about that? The first time you met Caitlin, I know it gave you a start."

Meeting Ace's wife the first time had given Eden far more than a start. It had been like seeing her own reflection in a mirror and had shocked her to the marrow of her bones. Caitlin was a bit shorter than Eden, but otherwise, they looked enough alike to be twins, sharing the same fine features, wide blue eyes, and flame red hair. Until meeting Caitlin, Eden had accepted on a superficial level that Connor O'Shannessy was her biological father, but the reality of it had never been driven home until she stood face-to-face with her sister-in-law and saw the undeniable evidence of her parentage with her very own eyes.

"I'll be fine, Mama. I've come to love Caitlin. You know that. She isn't to blame for what her—for what *our* father did." Eden patted her mother's hand to reassure her. Immediately after being told the truth about her real father, Eden had been furious with Dory for lying to her for so many years, but over time, she'd come to understand that her mother had meant well. Bastards weren't welcomed into polite society, and Dory's deception had spared Eden untold heartbreak during her childhood. If people in San Francisco had known of Eden's illegitimacy and that her father was a land swindler and murderer, they would have made her life a living hell. "I'll enjoy having a little niece who looks like me."

Settling back in the plush leather seat, Eden turned her mind to other possible topics of conversation. Revisiting the past always upset Dory, and little wonder. The poor woman had lived through trials that many females wouldn't have survived. "I'm feeling a bit parched. I wonder if they have any lemonade on board."

Dory glanced at the gold watch pinned to her pleated silk bodice. "It's nearly midday. We could adjourn to the dining car a little early. I'm hungry already."

"That is a grand idea." Eden reached up to straighten her hat, an awkward creation bedecked with a riotous fan of red feathers and a fake canary. One nice thing about moving to No Name was that she would no longer have to follow fashions she felt were absurd. Her brothers would have a good laugh when they saw her with a bird perched on her head and wouldn't hesitate to poke fun at her high-necked choker collar and bell-shaped skirt. Pushing to her feet, she offered her mother a hand up. "If we're early, we can have our choice of tables."

"And perhaps we can save a place for that young woman with the towheaded little boy," Dory suggested. "He is such a sweet child."

Eden glanced over her shoulder to smile at the young mother again. The toddler was squirming in his seat and rubbing his eyes with one plump fist. Eden sympathized. The train ride from San Francisco to Denver was always fun and exciting at the start, but the novelty soon wore off, even for adults.

"Would you and your little boy care to join us for dinner?" she asked the brunette. "My name is Eden—Eden Paxton. My mother's name is Dory. We'd greatly enjoy the company."

"Helen Rodericks," the brunette said, leaning forward on the seat to briefly clasp Eden's outstretched hand. "And we'd love to join you. Thank you so much for the invitation."

Eden chucked the little boy under his chin. "And what is your name, young man?"

The child muttered something indecipherable. Helen clarified with, "Timothy."

"Hello, Timothy. I'm delighted to meet you." To Helen, Eden added, "Perhaps over lunch, we can keep him entertained so you can enjoy *your* meal for a change."

Helen laughed and flashed a grateful smile. "That would be *fabulous*. He's getting very restless, and I'm running out of ideas to keep him distracted."

"I'm getting restless, too," Eden sympathized. "According to *The Little Giant Cyclopedia of Ready Reference*, modern-day trains travel at an average speed of just a little over forty-eight miles an hour, but this one definitely isn't."

The brunette laughed again as she set Timothy off her lap and vacated her seat. "If only we *were* traveling that fast. We would have reached Denver sometime early this morning."

"Instead we won't be arriving until late tonight." Eden smoothed her silk skirt. "My traveling costume will be hopelessly stale and wrinkled when we finally reach our destination. After we get to Denver, we have to take another train south from there to No Name."

"It's all these steep grades," Dory inserted. "No train on earth can consistently travel at forty-eight miles per hour up all these inclines."

Just as Eden turned to collect her reticule, the passenger car lurched violently. The sound of tearing metal filled her ears as she was thrown against the back of the seat in front of her. The impact snapped her forward at the waist, and she barely managed to catch herself from becoming airborne. Her blasted hat, securely anchored to her head with pins, went flying, taking some of her hair with it. Concerned for her mother, Eden groped for Dory's elbow.

"Timothy, are you all right?" Helen cried from behind them. "Did you bump your head?"

"Dear God!" a man somewhere at the back of the car shouted. "We must have hit another train!"

"Or there's some sort of debris on the tracks," another man grumped. "I swear, as much as I paid for my fare, you'd think I'd get better service."

"Mother, are you hurt?" Eden asked, helping Dory to regain her balance.

Dory collected herself with brisk efficiency, righting her plumed hat and tugging on the cuffs of her leg-o'-mutton sleeves to straighten her velvet traveling jacket. "My goodness, what a fright! I'm fine, dear, just fine." Dory cast a worried glance at the crying toddler behind them. "Is little Timothy okay?"

Bent over her son, Helen replied, "He's got a goose egg on his forehead, but I don't think any serious damage was done."

"I wonder what on earth we hit," Dory mused aloud.

Eden was about to reply when a distant popping sound came from outside the train.

"Oh, sweet Jesus, have mercy," a woman across the aisle bleated. "It's a holdup! We'll all be killed!"

Helen grabbed her towheaded son into her arms. "Perhaps it's only a mechanical malfunction."

Eden had been around weapons too often to believe that. The muted popping sounds were gunfire, no question about it. The train was about to be robbed.

Eden quickly switched places with her mother.

"What are you doing?" Dory cried.

Eden knew better than to confess that she wanted to be in the aisle seat in case the situation became violent. Dory was older and frailer. Eden would recover from a physical injury far more quickly. "I just want to see what's happening." As she spoke, Eden sat down, spread a lace handkerchief over her lap, and began unfastening the diamond pin from her bodice. "Remove your jewelry, Mama. If it's a robbery, they'll want all our valuables. If we cooperate, we should be fine."

Dory clucked her tongue. "Not my wedding band, surely. It's not worth much, and it has a great deal of sentimental value to me."

"Tuck it inside your bodice and give me everything else then," Eden replied. In a louder voice, she addressed the other passengers. "If you want to survive this spot of trouble without any mishap, bundle all your jewelry and money in a handkerchief and stand ready to hand it over without argument."

"Oh, dear God," a woman cried.

Another woman snorted in disdain. "I refuse to hand over my ruby bracelet! It cost a fortune!"

"Is it more important to you than your life?" Eden dropped her timepiece and gold locket onto the handkerchief. Then she reached into her reticule for her engagement ring, which she'd stopped wearing after receiving John's letter. The large emerald, encircled by diamonds, was ostentatious and had never been to her liking, but John had selected it and she'd always worn it with pride. It was one piece of frippery she would never miss. "Hurry, Mama."

Eden heard footsteps on the platform at the front of the car and the faint sound of screams coming from the car behind them where other passengers with less coin were packed together in more Spartan accommodations.

"We must be ready to hand it all over," Eden pressed. "That's why they're here, for our valuables and any gold or cash that may be on board. If we draw no attention to ourselves, perhaps they'll pass us by without a second look."

The door burst open and three disreputable-looking men spilled into the car, all of them wielding Colt .45 revolvers, Eden's own sidearm of choice. As a youngster, she'd spent countless hours learning to handle all types of weapons, a skill her eldest brother, Ace, had deemed highly important, even for a girl. But young ladies in the upper echelons of San Francisco society had no need to carry a gun. Though Eden still target-practiced on a regular basis to avoid getting rusty, she'd fallen out of the habit of keeping a weapon on her person.

Eden took the measure of the robbers and was instantly filled with dread. They were the filthiest creatures she'd ever seen, their clothing rank, their unshaven faces gray with grime. But what truly alarmed her were their eyes. Her brother Joseph had taught her to size a man up by searching his gaze. *Eyes are windows to the soul*, he was fond of saying. *Look hard and look deep, little sister. If you can't see into a man, run like hell.* These men's eyes resembled gray marbles—cold, glassy, and expressionless. The hair at the nape of Eden's neck prickled. Unfortunately, running like hell wasn't an option. She could only send up a quick prayer that no one on board would be harmed. The men seemed well practiced in the art of robbery. One rushed to the back of the car, a second covered the middle, and the third took a stand near the front door, brandishing his weapon as he thrust out a soiled drawstring bag to collect the passengers' valuables.

"Jewelry, timepieces, money!" he barked. "Keep your traps shut and hand it all over if you want to stay alive!"

A finely dressed gentleman at the front of the car pushed up from his seat. "Here, now, there's no need for violence!" he cried.

That was all the poor man had time to say before he was shot dead center in the chest. The bullet's impact sent him careening backward onto his wife's lap. The woman began to shriek hysterically, pressing her hands over the hole in her husband's shirt, which oozed blood.

"Morrison!" she cried. "Morrison?" She looked up at the robber, slack-jawed with shock. "You've killed him!" she screamed. "You've killed him *dead*!"

The bandit leveled his gun at the woman's forehead. "And I'll kill you dead if you don't shut up." He tore a necklace from around her throat and stuffed it in the bag. "Give me the rings. *Now*. Or I'll hack off your fingers to get them. Don't think I won't."

The woman tugged at her blood-smeared rings, trying to pull them over badly swollen, arthritic knuckles. "Morrison, *Morrison*," she chanted softly. "Oh, dear *God*, dear *God*."

Eden sat frozen in her seat. She'd never seen anyone die. Ace and Joseph had always tried to shield her from the ugly aspects of life, and they'd been mostly successful. For a seemingly endless second, she could only stare in horrified disbelief at the murdered man's sprawled legs. How could a life end so quickly?

The towheaded child behind them began to cry again. Eden heard Helen frantically trying to shush him. The bandit who manned the middle of the car waved his gun in a threatening manner.

"Jewels and money, and be fast about it if you don't want no holes in your hide!" He extended a bag toward an older woman two rows forward. "I said *everything*!" he barked when the matronly lady failed to hand over her earrings. Then, without waiting for her to comply, he jerked the gold loops from her ears, tearing the flesh of her lobes in the process. "Your fault, not mine. Stay quiet, hand stuff over, and there'll be no trouble."

The woman's husband surged to his feet. "Dad-blast you to kingdom come, you miserable excuse for—"

The robber fired his Colt, burying a bullet right between the poor man's eyes. And just that quickly, another person was dead. Eden was now trembling violently, one litany repeating in her mind: *God help us, God help us, God help us.*

To her horror, the robber's attention shifted to the shrieking child behind her. *Timothy.* Eden's heart caught. She heard Helen's breath snag in terror.

"Shut that little shit up!" the gunman snarled. "Or I'll plug him, too!"

Glancing back over her shoulder, Eden recognized Helen's paralyzing fear because she felt it herself. Instead of soothing the little boy, Helen clutched him rigidly to her bosom, her eyes as large as nickels, the pupils dilated with terror. Frightened by his mother's stiffness, the child screamed more loudly. The bandit stomped closer, raising his Colt as if to shoot.

"I told you to shut him up!"

Helen began petting the boy, the flutter of her trembling hands frantic, her softly uttered reassurances unconvincing. The child shrank closer to her torso and let loose with an ear-piercing wail. The robber stopped and took deadly aim at the back of the toddler's head.

Eden sprang up from her seat, spun, and threw herself over Helen and the boy. "No!" she cried. "He's only a baby!" Spreading her arms and legs to provide the mother and child with more cover, Eden heard heavy footfalls advancing on her. "Please, no! Don't hurt him. We'll make him be quiet. We *will*. Just give us a moment."

The next instant Eden's scalp exploded with pain as the gunman's hand closed over her chignon and jerked her erect. She stumbled and nearly fell backward into him. As terrified as she was, she shuddered at the stench of his unwashed body, a nostril-burning blend of urine, soured sweat, and whiskey. The force of his grip on her hair inflicted such pain that she turned to relieve the sting and found herself looking up into his unshaven countenance and hard gray eyes.

"Well, now," he sneered, running his gaze from her face downward to take measure of her person, "ain't you a purty little thing. Be nice to me, and maybe I won't kill the squallin' little snot."

Bile surged up the back of Eden's throat. This animal had just killed two men. She wanted to spit in his face, but fear tempered the urge. As if he guessed her thoughts, he twisted his fist in her hair and rammed the barrel of the Colt against her cheekbone. Eden braced herself, convinced that he meant to pull the trigger. In some distant part of her mind, she registered that the little boy had stopped screaming, and thanked God that his mother had managed to silence him.

"Don't . . . hurt . . . her!" Dory pleaded, her words interspersed with sobs. "Please, mister, don't . . . hurt . . . her. She's done nothing to you, *nothing*. Just . . . take the valuables and leave her . . . be. *Please!*"

Eden straightened her shoulders and met the man's gaze. She saw no mercy in those stone gray depths, and in that moment, she knew she was going to die. Fear made her legs quiver, and she almost wet herself. She wished her mother would be quiet. This man would kill Dory with no more regret than he would feel swatting an insect.

"Don't hurt her!" Dory cried again.

Another gunshot rang out at the back of the train. Eden flinched. Some poor woman's wails told Eden that someone else had just taken a bullet. Afraid her mother might be next, Eden cried, "Our valuables are on the floor. They're worth a small fortune. Take them and go."

Tightening his meaty hand over Eden's hair, the bandit bent his head and slurped his tongue over her lips. Only by sheer force of will was she able to keep herself from gagging. His front teeth had rotted into little brown snags. His spit tasted like vinegar. When he straightened, his battered gray hat sat askew, revealing greasy brown hair gone pewter gray at the temples.

"You're more valuable than a handful of trinkets," he informed her with a leer. "Across the border, a little redhead like you will bring top dollar."

The man at the rear of the car yelled, "We gonna keep her, Wallace? Hot damn! We'll have a fine time tonight!"

Oh, how Eden wished for a gun. Ace had taught her well. With her Colts at her hips, she could have taken on all three men and been the only shooter left standing when the smoke cleared. Instead she could only remain there with her neck twisted to ease the pain of the brutal grip on her hair.

"Why not?" her assailant replied with a laugh. "If nothin' else, she'll give us some fun."

Before Eden could react, the man bent at the knees, tossed her over his shoulder, and started back up the aisle. "Collect the rest of the loot!" he barked. "We need to make tracks!"

Grabbing for breath, Eden made fists in the tails of the robber's filthy jacket, her head spinning from the rush of blood to her brain. She heard Dory screaming and could only pray one of the bandits didn't silence her with a bullet. Relief swamped her when no shots rang out. Her rump collided with the door as her captor drew it open. Then the cold May air cut through her clothing, its iciness nipping at her skin.

It hit Eden then. These horrible men planned to abduct her. She needed to do something to save herself. Only what? Physically, she was no match for them, and she had no weapon. Her upper body bounced with each fall of her captor's feet as he descended the steps from the platform. Then she heard gravel crunching beneath his boots.

Oh, God, oh, God. If he got her on a horse, her chances to escape would be nil. Frantic, she pummeled his spine with knotted fists. When that didn't slow his pace, she grabbed hold of his jacket and walked her hands up his back until she was nearly upright. Then she went after his head, knocking off his hat as she cracked him in the temple with her elbow. He grunted and staggered.

"Leave off, bitch!"

Eden's temper, always the bane of her existence, flared hot. *Bitch?* Hissing air through clenched teeth, she clawed at his ear and tried with everything she had to bury the sharp toes of her Dongola kid boots into his groin. He roared with rage, grabbed her arm, and threw her to the ground. Eden rolled and scrambled to her feet, but before she could run, he was upon her. She nailed him square in the eye socket with her right fist and was about to slug him again when he retaliated in kind, his bunched knuckles coming at her so fast that they connected with her jaw before she could duck.

Black spots danced before Eden's eyes. She blinked and staggered, determined to remain on her feet. But her knees turned to water and down she went. The world had gone strangely gray—a swirling eddy of earth, trees, and sky that sucked her into a black vortex.

Chapter Two

The unmistakable smell of blood wafted to Matthew Coulter's nostrils on the cold, rain-washed morning air. Faintly sweet with a metallic bite, the scent rolled over the back of his tongue, putting him in mind of how water from his canteen tasted after he'd been two days on the trail without coming across a stream.

He drew his horse, Smoky, to a stop so suddenly that the pack mule behind them bumped into the gelding's rump. The Sebastians. Everywhere those bastards went, they left a trail of blood. Matthew had no idea whom they'd killed this time, only that the remains lay somewhere nearby. Oh, yes. He knew without a doubt that the Sebastians were responsible. He'd been hot on their trail for several days, and the tracks had led him directly here. No mistake, no maybe to it. Wallace Sebastian rode a horse with a paddle gait that left a track as unique as a man's fingerprint. Matthew would have recognized that odd stride pattern anywhere.

Shifting in the saddle, he reached back to unfasten the strap that held his Winchester in the sheepskin rifle boot. At close range, he normally preferred to use his revolvers, but in rabbitbrush thicker than fleas on a hound's back and billowing four feet tall, he'd be a damned fool to take on five fast guns with his Colts. Dancing and rolling to avoid a slug would be nigh onto impossible with his feet tangled in undergrowth. He'd be wiser to hit the dirt, burrow deep in the foliage, and pick off the brutes with his long barrel.

Smoky snorted, clearly unnerved. Matthew stroked the gray's neck and then nudged him back into a walk. The poor horse had to plow forward through the bushes, every step impeded by the thick snarl of branches. Herman, the mule, balked and let loose with one of his odd-sounding whinnies, a cross between a bray and a neigh. *Damn it.* There went any chance Matthew may have had to catch the gang by surprise. Not that he blamed the mule. Even the dumbest animals on earth recognized the smell of fresh blood, and Herman sensed the danger. All his instincts were probably telling him to turn tail and run.

Grabbing hold of the lead rope, Matthew gave a sharp tug to get the pack animal moving again. As both beasts pressed forward, Matthew made a mental note to slap them on the rump if trouble started. Over the last three years, Smoky and Herman had become Matthew's only friends. He didn't want either of them to take a bullet.

Moments later, they broke into a small clearing surrounded by stands of stunted oak and various bushes heavy with blossoms of pink, yellow, purplish blue, and white that stood out against the gray-green backdrop of brush. What appeared to be a peddler's wagon was parked to one side of the opening, its garishly painted doors yawning to reveal a gutted interior. The team that had pulled the wagon to this spot was nowhere in sight, the poles and traces lying empty. Pots, pans, shoes, clothing, books, farm implements, and other wares had been scattered every which way across the rain-soaked ground. An old man in a brown suit lay sprawled amid the rubble. Even at a distance, Matthew could see that he was beyond help. The poor fellow's throat had been slit, an Arkansas grin curving from one ear to the other under his be-whiskered chin.

Matthew's skin turned as pebbly as a fresh-plucked chicken's. In the sunlight that had just broken through the clouds, the blood on the peddler's neck glistened wet and bright red. He had been dead for only a few minutes. His killers couldn't be very far away.

Jerking the lead rope loose from his saddle to set the mule free, Matthew fanned the chambers of his Colts to make certain they were fully loaded—a purely reflexive gesture, because he always kept the chambers full—and then reined his horse in a circle to scan the surrounding brush. In land like this, the horned larks and prairie chickens normally chirped and flitted in the bushes, and small rodents scampered every which way. Not so in this place. A spooky hush lay over everything. The breeze had suddenly abated. Not even a leaf moved in the clumps of gnarly oak.

Withers twitching, ears cocked forward, Smoky blew and sidestepped, his shod hooves sharply striking a partially buried slab of shale. The tattoo rang out in the hush like rifle shots. Matthew had a bad case of the whim-whams himself. Before dismounting, he rode a wide loop around the clearing to make sure the gang had left. He soon found churned earth, an indication that the fiends had lit out in a northwesterly direction. After studying the tracks, Matthew determined that they'd taken the peddler's two-horse wagon team with them, draft animals, judging by the size of the hoofprints.

Matthew burned to go after them. He'd gotten this close to one of them only once before, a memorable afternoon down Tucson way when he'd belly-crawled through cactuses pricklier than whores on Sunday to sight in his Winchester on the youngest Sebastian brother, who'd been dispatched to the nearest town to replenish the gang's liquor supply. Sadly for Eric Sebastian, the call of the alcohol had been more urgent to him than getting back to his siblings, so he'd stopped off under a mesquite tree to have a few snorts. With no regrets, Matthew had emerged from the cactuses, poised himself to draw, and, after telling the other man why he was there, had sent him off to meet his Maker, making the world a safer place and reducing the infamous Sebastian Gang's number to five.

Since then, though, it had been slim pickings, with Matthew hearing of a horrendous crime and haring off after the wrong desperadoes—or, even more frustrating, joining up with yet another posse composed of an incompetent lawman and a ragtag collection of clod busters who started out strong but lacked the stick-to-itiveness necessary to stay on the Sebastians' trail. In a way, Matthew had understood their lackadaisical attitudes. A man had to lose someone precious and dear—he had to hate and lust for revenge—in order to stay with a chore that seemed endless, paid nothing, and offered few creature comforts.

Now, after so many false leads and bitter tastes of defeat, Matthew was once again right on the Sebastians' asses. He swore he could smell the stench of their un-washed bodies lingering in the air. Unfor-tunately, before he gave chase he needed to properly bury the old man. As hardened as Matthew had grown since departing from Oregon, he still clung to the tenets of common decency that his father and mother had drilled into him. Leaving a dead body out in the open to become car-rion for vultures and predators wasn't in his makeup. He'd even buried Eric Sebas-tian, the devil take his rotten soul, rather than abandon the bastard in the desert to become crow bait.

Once back in the clearing, Matthew set to work with a small spade he carried in his pack. The tediousness of the grim task left him with too much time to think. *Death*. It had a way of creeping up on a person without warning. It troubled him how quickly a life could end.

The rocky ground made for difficult dig-ging. Fortunately, Matthew was able to go shallow and cover the body with the stones he unearthed. Even so, the sun had nearly reached its zenith by the time he finished the excavation. He closed the peddler's eyes and tugged off the old man's jacket to cover his bloodless face before lowering him into the shallow grave. *Jesus, help me*, he prayed as he covered the remains with rock. Since setting out after the Sebastians, he'd seen sights that would haunt his dreams for the rest of his days.

This morning the Sebastians' victim was an elderly man whose life had been nearly over, but that wasn't always the case. Those heartless polecats killed young and old alike. Only a few months ago, Matthew had come across a Spanish family down in Mexico—mother, father, four older children, and a brand-new baby—who had been slaughtered like pigs. Judging by the condition of the woman's body, she'd been repeatedly raped before being sent off to meet her Maker. The memory still made Matthew shake with horror or rage, probably both. Their deaths had been so pointless. But the Sebastians had slain them nevertheless, and with no more regret than Matthew felt over shooting a rabbit for the roasting spit. *Bastards.* They were worse than animals.

Removing his Stetson, Matthew stood beside the old man's grave. Another heavy rain would pack down the freshly turned earth. In only a short while, the peddler's final resting place would look like nothing more than a rock heap. Passersby wouldn't even realize someone was buried here.

The thought sent Matthew back to the perimeters of the clearing with his hatchet. He worked up a sweat cutting two lengths of green wood to form a cross, which he bound together with rawhide thongs. Then he spent a good half hour carving *A peddler killed by the Sebastian Gang* into the crossbar. As he drove the marker deep into the dirt at the head of the grave, he could at least console himself with the certainty that the old fellow's resting place would be recognized as such for a couple of years.

Afterward, Matthew mounted his horse, collected his mule, and went to find the tracks he'd seen earlier. His blood surged with excitement, which he quickly tamped down. The brothers had cut a broad swath through the brush, the trail so clear that a child could have followed it. Matthew was going to catch up with them this time. He felt it in his bones.

Time to ride. If he'd learned anything

over the last three years, it was that the Sebastians had a talent for vanishing into thin air. Matthew wasn't about to let them slip away from him again. Nohow, no way. Not this time. He would make up for the delay and catch up with them again or die trying.

Scanning the horizon every few seconds, he followed the tracks. The Sebastians were shrewd. If they suspected someone was on their heels, they'd double back to pick him off. Matthew flexed his shoulders and released a taut breath. Letting down one's guard was a greenhorn's mistake, and he was no greenhorn, not anymore. Being on the trail had taught him a host of lessons, the most important being that it wasn't always speed with a gun that saved a man's life. Sometimes it was pure, old-fashioned common sense and having eyes in the back of his head.

Determined to stay alert, Matthew settled into the saddle for the long ride that lay ahead. At the start of this mission, he had always been in a hurry, a feverish eagerness burning in his veins even as he slept, but he'd soon realized that only dogged determination would enable him to succeed where so many posses had failed. It was a lonely and often boring endeavor. Except for changes in the weather and coming upon dead bodies more often than he liked, one day was pretty much like the next, a monotonous repetition of riding mile after mile, followed by sleeping along the trail with only his saddle as a pillow and his animals for company. His rare brushes with civilization occurred only when he fell in with a posse, needed supplies, or went digging for information about where the Sebastian Gang had last been seen. He seldom met anyone intriguing during those brief sojourns in a town. Shopkeepers, sporting women, and drifters. After a while, their faces all looked the same and their stories all sounded alike.

In the beginning, Matthew had kept a journal, but after a time, he'd given up on that. His Gaelic-speaking mother, born in the old country, had studied relentlessly to attain a good command of English and insisted that her children do the same. Though Matthew had only five years of formal schooling, he'd developed a good vocabulary and spelling skills, but he still wasn't a great hand at writing. He penned his thoughts pretty much like he talked, simple and to the point. When he wrote home to let his folks know he was still alive, he kept it short. *Hello. I'm fine. Hope you are, too.* He had no way of knowing if his letters reached their destination because he never stayed in one place long enough to get return mail. Hell, so far as he knew, both his parents could be dead by now.

The thought saddened Matthew, but not in the sharp, painful way it once would have. He had trouble remembering his loved ones' faces when he thought of them now, and homesickness had lost its hold on him long ago. The ranch had become a distant memory, the squat little cabin he'd shared with Olivia a blur. Sometimes he almost forgot why he'd undertaken this task. Then a nightmare about Livvy's death would jerk him awake from a sound sleep, and he'd remember with harsh clarity. Bottom line was, he'd set himself a goal, and he couldn't give up until every last one of the Sebastians was dead. He'd failed to protect his wife, and punishing her killers was the only way he knew to make up for that.

Once he avenged Livvy's death, he had no idea what the future might hold for him. Oregon no longer called his name. Too many bad memories waited for him there. Maybe he'd hire on somewhere as a cowhand or broncobuster, saving his wages until he had a stake and could start his own ranch. Montana still had a lot of wide-open country. A man could make a fresh start there and put the past behind him. It'd be lonely, but Matthew had come to accept that as his lot in life. He didn't have what it took to be a decent husband—or father, for that matter. A man worth his salt protected his family.

Guiding his horse through a dense thicket of skunkbrush and mountain mahogany, Matthew followed the Sebastians' tracks to a promontory where thickets of silver buffaloberry clumped around huge boulders. After picking his way through the dense foliage and rocks, he reined in sharply and stood in the stirrups to see over the edge of the cliff, wondering what the gang members had been thinking to take their horses down such steep, treacherous terrain. In the draw below, he saw only brush at first, but then his gaze caught on a glint of steel. *Railroad tracks.* Following their course, he saw a train in the distance. The locomotive appeared to have jumped the tracks. Matthew couldn't determine what might have caused that, but he had a bad feeling it hadn't been an accident. Squinting to see, he counted five cars between the locomotive and caboose, and they didn't look to be the kind that carried freight. Too fancy. A passenger train, maybe?

His chest went tight with dread. Now he understood why the Sebastians had put their horses at risk to go down the steep slope. They'd waited up here to ambush the train. Lips pressed into a tight line, Matthew turned east, hoping to find a safer way down into the draw. To his surprise, he discovered that the Sebastians had ridden this way as well. Their tracks soon led to a gentler slope that looked less dangerous for Matthew's animals. As he began the descent, he realized why the gang had chosen not to launch its attack from this angle. The people on the train would have seen them coming, just as they could see Matthew now. Two men emerged from the locomotive onto its rear platform. They seemed to be looking at Matthew through binoculars. One of them held a rifle at the ready in the crook of his arm.

As Matthew drew closer, he saw piles of broken rock scattered across the tracks in front of the derailed locomotive. Mystery solved. To stop the train, the Sebastians had rolled some boulders into its path. Then they'd ridden back to the promontory to await the inevitable collision. *Bastards.*

Matthew hoped the man with the gun didn't get nervous and shoot. If the train had recently been robbed, as Matthew suspected, tension would be high, and the approach of a stranger might make the rifleman edgy. He wore a brown plaid frock suit and a jaunty bowler hat, pegging him as a passenger and possibly a city fellow. Wasn't that just perfect? Matthew had never met a dandy yet who knew squat about firearms.

The other man, a bullnecked, portly gent, wore a black suit and matching billed cap. Though Matthew had never traveled on a passenger train, he figured the fellow to be the conductor or some other kind of railway employee. He lifted a hand and waved, hoping to let them know he was friendly. Being mistaken for a bandit wouldn't make for a pleasant encounter.

"Howdy!" he called out as he drew closer.

The man in black placed his hands on the platform railing and leaned forward at the waist. "What brings you here, mister?"

Some twenty feet from them, Matthew reined in his horse. The pack mule let loose with a nervous bray-whinny. "I'm after the Sebastian Gang. Their tracks led me here."

"You a bounty hunter?"

"No, sir."

"Well, you sure don't have the look of a lawman."

Matthew fingered the thick growth of whiskers on his jaw. "Stopping to wash and shave isn't easy when you're trying to run polecats to ground. Name's Matthew Coulter. Hail from Oregon."

"You're a long way from home, partner."

Matthew nudged up the brim of his hat to meet the men's gazes. "That I am." He cast a glance at the rock-strewn tracks. "Looks to me like you're in a fine fix."

"Yes, we are." The dandy in the frock coat lowered the rifle to his side, a gesture that indicated he no longer felt threatened. Problem was that the barrel of the weapon was now pointed straight at Matthew. "We've got three dead, and they took a young woman hostage."

A chill moved down Matthew's spine. If the Sebastians had taken a woman, she'd most likely be dead by sundown. If not, she'd be wishing she were. "I'm sorry to hear that. The Sebastians aren't exactly what you'd call gentle with the ladies." He inclined his head at the rifle. "If it's all the same to you, my friend, I'd feel easier if you pointed that gun at something besides me."

The fellow quickly shifted the rifle so the shooting end was aimed at the sky.

"Were any passengers hurt in the wreck?" Matthew asked.

"Mostly cuts and bruises, but one man went flying and busted some ribs. He's been spitting blood and should see a doctor."

"Help is probably on the way," Matthew replied. "The telegrapher at the next station would have sounded an alarm the moment he realized the train was overdue."

"Not in Holden Creek," the conductor countered. "The telegrapher there up and died a few weeks back."

Matthew shifted in the saddle. "So who took his place?"

"Nobody, yet." The conductor fingered open his watch pocket. "After Holden Creek, it's almost five hours to the next stop." He checked the time. "By my calculations, no alarm will be raised for another three hours."

Matthew absorbed that bit of news. "One of you needs to go for help, then. They've surely got a sawbones in Holden Creek. That man spitting blood could have a punctured lung."

The city fellow gestured at the broken boulders. "The train is dead in its tracks, and we have no horse."

Matthew almost asked if they'd ever heard of walking. The injured man could die without medical treatment. *Damn.* Wasn't this just his luck? He knew, without their even asking, that they expected him to head toward Holden Creek. If he allowed himself to get sidetracked that way, the Sebastians would get miles ahead of him, and he'd play hell catching up with them again. He rubbed his jaw, wishing he had it in him to just ride away.

"How far is it to Holden Creek?" he finally asked.

"Ten, maybe eleven miles. That's a long way for a man to walk when he's not dressed for this cold weather and the freezing rain." The conductor eyed Matthew's buckskin jacket, which had turned supple and shiny from repeated applications of bear grease to make it shed water. "You reckon you could get word to the marshal there that we need assistance and a doctor?"

The way Matthew saw it, the rain had let up and the sun was out. Ten miles wasn't that far for a man to walk. He had hoofed it that far a number of times. Maybe they were afraid to leave the relative safety of the train. The Sebastian boys had a talent for putting the fear of God into folks.

With an inward sigh, Matthew went over his options, hating to waste precious time on an unnecessary side trip. But in the end, he couldn't see that he had a choice. There was the injured man to think about.

"How much blood is that man spitting up?" Matthew asked.

"Not much, just a little pink now and again." The conductor arched an eyebrow. "Why do you ask?"

"I hate to press my animals unless it's a matter of life and death. They've come a far piece."

"We won't quarrel with how fast you ride, Coulter, just so long as you go. I think the injured man will be okay until help arrives."

"My horse and mule can go about four miles an hour at a steady walk. At that rate, it'll take me two and a half hours to reach Holden Creek, plus a few minutes to talk with the marshal. With fresh horses, he and his men should be able to make it back here in a little over an hour if they ride fairly hard. That puts help about four hours out. Do you think the injured fellow can hold on that long?"

"We have him bedded down. If he doesn't move and do more damage, he should make it."

Just then a petite older woman came tearing down the platform steps of a passenger car. The most outlandish hat Matthew had ever seen was perched at an angle atop her head, silk flowers, gewgaws, and feathers poking every which way. Hands clamped to her waist, she ran toward them, the leg-o'-mutton sleeves of her blue velvet traveling costume flapping like the wings of a frantic bird.

As she drew up near Smoky's flank, she pushed a strand of graying blond hair from her eyes. "Please, sir, you *must* ride for help at a fast pace! Those horrible men took my daughter! If someone doesn't catch up with them quickly, they might do her serious harm!"

Apparently the lady had heard Matthew say he didn't want to exhaust his animals by pushing them too hard. His mouth went as dry as dirt. He knew the Sebastians would kill this woman's daughter before a posse ever caught up with them. The Sebastian boys wasted no time with their raping and murdering.

"I'm about to leave now, ma'am," Matthew said, his voice thick and hoarse. "I'll tell the marshal to get a group of men together as fast as he can."

She pressed quivering fingertips to her pale cheeks, her blue eyes swimming with tears as she nodded. "Thank you, thank you," she murmured. "She's a good, sweet girl who's never harmed a soul. If something happens to her, it'll break my heart."

Resigned, Matthew nudged his horse into a trot, a pace he set only for the woman's benefit. Once out of sight, he'd slow Smoky to a walk. There was little point in killing his horse and mule in an attempt to save a girl who probably couldn't be saved.

Why was it that every time he almost caught up with those rotten bastards, something went wrong?

Holden Creek turned out to be a one-horse town with a train station only a bit larger than a water closet. As predicted by the conductor, the place stood empty. The main street was little more than a rutted dirt path lined with uneven boardwalks, wobbly hitching posts, and straggly clumps of soapweed yucca. The saloon appeared to be the largest establishment, even larger than the church at the far end of town. What a fine testimony that was to humankind. Not that Matthew begrudged anybody a snort. He imbibed a bit himself. But with the church barely bigger than a sitting room and a school not in evidence, he couldn't help but wonder about this community's priorities.

The marshal's office was no more impressive than the train station, situated amongst a string of businesses with battered doors and CLOSED signs that hung crooked in every dusty window. *Strange.* According to Matthew's calculations, it was Thursday. In most towns, the shops closed only on Sundays, and often not even then. Maybe he had his days mixed up. No big surprise if he did. There had been times over the last three years when he'd forgotten what month it was, let alone the day of the week.

Matthew pulled up in front of the unimpressive law office, dismounted, and tethered his horse to the hitching rail before stepping up onto the weathered wooden walkway. The door proved to be unlocked, creaking open with a light push of Matthew's thumb on the lever. Though a fire crackled in the rust-streaked potbellied stove and a dented blue pot on one of the burner plates emitted the scorched smell of overboiled coffee, the room and single cell at the back were empty. *Shit.* The last thing Matthew wanted was to waste more time trying to find the lawman. Where the hell was he?

Turning and closing the door, Matthew angled a look across the street, settling his gaze on the bat-wing doors of the saloon. Piano music tinkled from within the establishment, and an occasional burst of laughter trailed to him on the afternoon breeze. It struck Matthew as being mighty early in the day for folks to be imbibing, but who was he to judge? One thing was for sure: There was no better place than a local watering hole to get information.

Before striking off across the muddy thoroughfare, Matthew tethered Herman to the hitching post beside Smoky so he could reach the water trough. A little liquid refreshment would do all three of them a world of good. Matthew decided he might even buy himself a jug for the trail. When he killed the Sebastian brothers, there would be cause to celebrate. It'd be a hell of a note if he had no whiskey to mark the moment.

The interior of the saloon was undistinguished, a mirror reflection of a thousand others he'd seen over the last three years, complete with the requisite oil painting of

a nude lady hanging above the bar. Ironi-
cally, the saloon's piano key tapper was
playing "The Fountain in the Park," a romantic ballad with sappy lyrics that Matthew hadn't heard since leaving Oregon.
A sporting woman in a faded red dress
belted out the words, flinging her arms
wide as if she were performing onstage
for a huge audience.

"'While strolling in the park one day, in
the merry month of May!'" She smiled and
homed in on Matthew, her gaze a blood-
shot blue that spoke of too many whiskey-
soaked nights. "'I was taken by surprise
by a roguish pair of eyes! In a moment my
poor heart was stole away.'"

Matthew ignored the invitation. He
couldn't waste time in an upstairs room
right now, even if he'd felt so inclined—
which he didn't. The woman looked like
she'd been ridden hard and put away wet.
Matthew had enough troubles without
catching the clap. He turned his attention
to three older men who sat at a corner table playing poker.

"Can one of you tell me where I might
find the marshal?"

"You've found him." The portliest of the three men turned on his chair, the bulge of his belly rubbing the table's edge. "How can I help you?"

Matthew's heart sank. The man was old, for starters, and to top it off, he appeared to be more than a little drunk. Pulling out a chair, Matthew turned it around to straddle the seat. After three years in the saddle, he no longer felt comfortable sitting the proper way. As quickly as possible, he told the marshal about the train holdup.

"The Sebastian Gang, you say?" The elderly lawman rubbed his balding pate. "How can you be so all-fired sure it was them?"

"Because I've been tracking them for three years. Trust me, it was the Sebastians."

"They're a dangerous bunch, by all accounts."

More dangerous than this old fellow could imagine. "Yes, sir, they're very dangerous. Luckily for you, they're long gone by now, so you won't have to deal with any of them."

"Why you tracking them?"

Matthew found it difficult to talk about what had happened to Olivia. "I've got my reasons."

"You aren't thinking about taking the law into your own hands, are you, mister?"

Matthew ignored the question and pushed to his feet. After glancing at his pocket watch, he snapped the lid closed and said, "If you ride hard, Marshal, you can reach the train in a little over an hour. One of the passengers is in a bad way, so you should take the local sawbones along if you can."

The marshal nodded and swayed to his feet. For an instant, Matthew entertained the notion of telling the lawman about the kidnapped young woman, but he quickly discarded the idea. He didn't want a posse of drunks catching up with him sometime tomorrow and getting in his way. If the girl survived the night, which was unlikely, Matthew stood a better chance of saving her than this inebriated yahoo and a bunch of inexperienced deputies. Matthew had learned that lesson the hard way. Just because men wore fancy stars on their shirts didn't mean they had what it took to face the Sebastians.

Tipping his hat, Matthew strode over to the bar and ordered a shot of whiskey. After downing it, he bought a jug to take with him. Then, leaving the saloon, he made his way up the street to the general store to pick up a few supplies for the trail. In order to get inside, he had to clang a cowbell to draw the shopkeeper's attention. While he gathered what he needed, his ears were pummeled by the old man's small talk—about how slow business was, and how puny profits had forced him to let go of all his help.

"You got a slab of bacon?" Matthew interrupted as he rummaged through a barrel of potatoes. "I need cornmeal and coffee, too."

On the off chance that the captured woman survived, he'd need grub to feed her, Matthew reasoned. Not that he believed, even for a second, that she would. If the Sebastian boys held true to form, they'd rape her until the shine wore off and then slit her throat.

Eden awakened to a stabbing pain in her stomach, a bad headache, and an awful dizziness. Blinking to see, she realized she'd been slung over the back of a horse, her arms and head dangling. *Oh, God.* The events of the morning came rushing back—her struggle to escape from that horrible, filthy man and then sinking into blackness after he struck her.

She focused dazedly on the toe of his dirty boot, thrust through a stirrup only inches from her nose. The acrid stench of his unwashed body was so strong it made her nostrils burn. Moaning, Eden tried to push herself up. With every step of the horse, the saddle horn jabbed her in the middle, and the pain was excruciating.

"Be still!" A hard palm connected with her posterior, delivering a sharp sting even through her skirt, petticoat, and bloomers. "I ain't puttin' up with no sass. You hear?"

To Eden's horror, he cupped his hand over her buttock and gave it a squeeze. She bucked and tried to wiggle away, only to be cuffed on the back of her head with such force that she saw stars.

"Be still, I say. Maybe you was a highfalutin young miss this mornin', but now ye're nothin' but a fine swatch of calico I got plans to enjoy."

"Take your hands off me, you filthy good-for-nothing! My brothers will hunt you down like the dog you are and kill you for this day's work!"

The robber laughed and jerked up the back of Eden's skirt. When she felt cool air slipping in through the slit of her bloomers, she shrieked and jabbed him in the side with her elbow. He snarled and grabbed her by the hair. The sting on Eden's scalp brought tears to her eyes. The next instant, he wrenched her head back so far, she feared he might snap her neck, but at least he let go of her skirt.

"You're a little spitfire, ain't ya? I ain't never had me a redhead afore. You gonna fight me, sweet thing? I like a little spunk in my women. Never lasts, of course. Even the spitfires go to squealin' and cryin' after they get poked a few times. But it'll be fun while the fight in you lasts."

When he released his hold on her hair, Eden slumped over the saddle, her head still spinning from the blow to her skull. Despite the pain in her belly from the saddle horn, she decided to take his advice and be still. Fighting him now, when he had her at such a disadvantage, was a waste of energy. She'd bide her time. Sooner or later, they would have to stop and rest the horses. When they did, she'd run the first chance she got. *Squealing and crying?* He had another think coming. She was no sniveler—never had been and never would be. No matter what they did to her, she wouldn't give them the satisfaction of seeing her cry.

Thoughts of what they might do to her made Eden's blood run cold. Though she'd been sheltered all her life, she was well aware of the danger she was in. Even unmarried ladies shared stories, whispering behind cupped hands of the atrocities that had been committed against other women. If even half of those stories were true, Eden was in big trouble. She might hold her own against one man, but she would be powerless against five.

Only a few minutes later, the men stopped along a stream to water and rest the horses. Eden was tossed from the saddle with no more regard than if she'd been a sack of onions. She hit the damp earth with a bone-jarring thud that knocked the breath out of her. Before she could recover, two of the men grappled her onto her back while a third jerked up her skirts, spread her legs, and knelt between her thighs. As he reached to unfasten his pants, Eden knifed up a knee, planted her traveling boot in the middle of his chest, and sent him tumbling backward with a hard shove.

"Hoo-ee!" a man holding one of her arms cried. "We got ourselves a scrapper!"

Eden spit in his face. "Touch me, and my brothers will kill you!"

They only laughed at the threat. Though Eden struggled with all her strength, she couldn't escape them, and soon the man she'd kicked was in position again, his trousers hanging open. At the sight of his engorged member—the likes of which she'd never seen or even imagined—Eden nearly fainted with fright.

"My oldest brother is Ace Keegan," she pushed out tremulously. "He's a famous gunslinger, and my younger brothers are just as fast! They'll hunt you down and make you curse the day you were born."

"Have to catch us first." The man in position groped for the slit in her bloomers. She felt his filthy fingers touch her private places. "And we got us a fine talent for not gettin' caught. Ain't you never heard of the Sebastian Gang, girlie?"

Eden bucked and shrieked, but he moved forward to impale her anyway. She clenched her teeth, squeezed her eyes closed, and held her breath, knowing it would hurt. But instead, he suddenly fell sideways across her leg. She lifted her lashes to see a fourth man standing over her, feet set wide apart, fists clenched. It was the fellow she'd tangled with right after leaving the train, the one who'd hit her and knocked her out.

"We didn't steal the damned girl so you could ruin her!" he yelled. "We're takin' her across the border to Estacado, I said. That old Mexican loves gringo females. He'll pay a small fortune for a redhead."

"Ah, come on, Wallace," Eden's almost-rapist whined as he rolled onto his knees. "What can it hurt if we have a little fun with her first?"

Wallace was taller and stockier than the other four men. He spit a stream of tobacco juice and wiped his mouth with the crusty sleeve of his jacket. "You can have all the fun you want, little brother, but don't go poppin' her cherry. Estacado likes his women unused, and before he hands over any money, he always checks first to make sure they're virgins."

"What fun can we have if we can't give her a poke?"

"You can play with her all you like, I said. Use your imagination, for God's sake! Just don't let me catch you dippin' for honey. When you get to that point, finish yourself off with your hand." Wallace spit again. His cold gray eyes moved over Eden's body. "And hold off on messin' with her until tonight. Could be we got a posse on our asses. Soon as the horses is watered and rested, we need to make tracks."

The moment Eden was released, she rolled onto her side and curled into a ball to hug her throbbing stomach. Mindless prayers circled in her mind. *Tonight.* The mere thought of those animals touching her made her want to die. *Run.* She needed to get away. Only, the men stayed too close for her to make an attempt. After securing their mounts to nearby trees, they hunkered near her to eat. She could hear one man's jaw popping as he chewed on a piece of jerky. She hadn't eaten since breakfast, but they offered her nothing but a cup of stale water. Eden had difficulty drinking it. Fear had closed around her throat like a brutal fist. But she forced herself to swallow. Then, bruised and shaken, all she could do was lie there, huddled in misery.

Soon the men collected their horses. This time, Eden was allowed to sit upright in front of the cold-eyed Wallace. At first she deemed that to be an improvement, but then he looped the reins loosely around the saddle pommel and cupped her breasts in his hands. Eden jerked and tried to squirm away. He only laughed at her struggles, tweaking her nipples and then rolling the hardened peaks between thumb and forefinger. Remembering her training sessions with Ace, Eden snapped her head back and nailed him in the mouth. He roared with anger, and the next thing she knew, he'd dragged her off the horse by the hair and was slapping her. She tried to duck and avoid the blows, but his hold on her hair was relentless and his strength of arm kept her standing upright. She'd done some damage by butting him in the mouth. Blood dripped from his split lips and collected in the spaces between his decayed front teeth. He swung repeatedly at her face.

"Go, Wallace! Show her what for!" one of the other men yelled.

"Woo-hoo!" another encouraged.

Wallace continued to slap Eden until her face went numb and she could no longer feel the blows. When he finally let go of her, she dropped to her knees, so dazed that her legs had become useless.

"Don't you never pull that kinda shit with me again, little girl. Next time, I'll strip you naked and lay into you with my belt until my whippin' arm gets tired. Then I'll let my brothers have a turn. There won't be a spot on you without welts, includin' those purty little tits you don't want me touchin'."

Eden shuddered and bent her head.

"Git back on the horse," he ordered.

She tried to stand up and couldn't. He caught hold of her hair again and jerked her to her feet. When she failed to mount the horse on the first try, he cuffed her again, then grabbed her at the waist and tossed her up on the saddle. When he swung up behind her, Eden expected him to resume fondling her breasts, but for reasons beyond her, he didn't. She touched her tongue to her puffy lips and tasted blood. One of her eyes was starting to swell shut. Nevertheless she counted herself lucky. Matters would have been far worse if he had used his fist instead of the flat of his hand.

They rode hard until well after dark, which disgusted Eden. Horses couldn't see well during the twilight hours, and most of the horsemen she knew stopped to rest until darkness fell, fearful that their mounts might stumble and possibly break a leg. Not these men. They seemed to care about nothing and nobody but themselves.

Much to Eden's regret, when they finally halted to make camp, they built only a meager fire, no doubt because they feared a posse might be close and see the flames. Eden prayed they were right in that assumption, for it might be her only hope. The train had been robbed west of Denver in the foothills, a good day from the city on horseback, and the gang had been heading north ever since at a breakneck pace, covering as much ground as possible. With every minute that passed, they were taking her farther and farther from home and family. By tomorrow at this time, she would be three days out from Denver and four from No Name, located thirty miles south of the larger town. Even if she managed to steal one of the horses and scatter the others, the men might catch up with her before she could reach safety.

Eden's silk traveling costume offered little protection against the cold, and she soon felt as if she were freezing. When the man named Harold tossed her a piece of jerky and handed her a tin cup of brackish water, she briefly considered refusing the food and drink. Women in such situations often sought death. But Eden rejected the idea. Her circumstances weren't that dire yet. Determined to sell her across the border for a tidy profit, Wallace had made it clear that no one was to lower her value by raping her. Though Eden wasn't certain what "playing with her" entailed, she figured she could endure it until she got an opportunity to escape.

Shivering with cold while she ate her meager supper, she peered through the darkness at the horses tethered to a high line between two stunted oak trees. She'd learned to ride at an early age, and though she was a bit rusty from lack of practice, she still felt confident in her abilities as a horsewoman. Maybe after the men fell asleep, she could make a run for it. If she took one equine and scattered the others, her captors would be left afoot and unable to give chase. She sent up a silent prayer that no one would think to bind her hands and feet.

God had turned a deaf ear. Eden had no sooner sent up that heartfelt plea than the man named Pete advanced on her with two thongs. Though all the brothers resembled one another, Pete stood out in her mind because of the meanness that glinted in his marblelike gray eyes. He jerked her arms behind her back and tied her wrists so tightly that the leather dug into her flesh. Next, he lashed her ankles together.

"There's no need to bind me," Eden tried. "Where have I to flee?"

He ignored her question. Hunkered near the fire, Wallace called, "Bring her over here so we'll have light. Won't be no fun playin' with her in the dark."

Pete grasped Eden's left arm and dragged her toward the flames. Unable to walk with her feet bound, she gasped at the pain that lanced through her twisted shoulder as he pulled her over the rough ground, but Pete didn't seem to care. He dumped her beside Wallace and then squatted to stare at her. "She ain't so purty after the whalin' you gave her."

Wallace's swollen lips twisted in a leer. "Ain't her face we wanna play with."

With that, he grasped the front of Eden's bodice and drew his knife. With three slashes at the cloth, he laid open her dress. Then he went to work on her camisole. He didn't bother with the corset because it didn't cover her breasts. Eden felt the night air nip at her bare skin. Humiliation coursed through her. She strained against the leather that bound her wrists behind her back, but Pete had tied her securely. She was helpless to defend herself.

"Well, now, what have we got here, little lady?" Wallace asked with an oily chuckle. "It's been so long since I seen me any pink tits that I plumb forgot how purty they are."

"I want to go first," Pete wheedled.

"Go ahead. We got all night. All of us will get a turn. Just remember not to mark her up, and don't lose your head and give her a poke. I got plans for the money Estacado will pay for her. He'll take one look at that face and red hair and froth at the mouth like a rabid dog."

Pete jerked Eden to a sitting position, tossed aside his filthy hat, and bent to take one of her nipples into his mouth. The shock of sensation made her body snap taut, but the leather at her wrists and ankles was so tight that she couldn't struggle. A scream welled at the base of her throat. She swallowed it down. She would *not* allow these animals to reduce her to that. She felt a filthy hand groping under her skirts. *Oh, God, no, please, no*. But the hand shoved her knees slightly apart, despite her prayers.

In that moment, Eden came face-to-face with the horror of her situation. All her life, Ace had drummed into her head the phrase *mind over matter*, his theory being that a person could live through anything if he had enough strength of will and a plan for survival. "When life kicks you in the teeth, you hunker down and keep going, no matter what," he'd often told her and his younger brothers. Eden had once seen David walk home from a riding accident with a broken leg. He'd found a tree limb to use as a crutch, and he'd inched his way back for help, every step so painful that he'd almost lost consciousness. *Mind over matter.* Another time, Ace had taken a bullet in the thigh, and her mother had dug it out of his flesh with the tip of a butcher knife. With no coin for whiskey to dull the pain, Ace had clenched his fists around the headboard of the bed and asked Eden to talk to him about pretty things while Dory fished for the slug. In a quavering voice, Eden had described a meadow in springtime, how the wildflowers nodded in the soft breeze, how sweet the air smelled from their blossoms. Though her other brothers had been ready to hold Ace down, it had never become necessary, because Ace had lain there, perfectly still of his own accord, sweat streaming from his twisted face, his glazed eyes focused on nothing while he withstood the agony.

Mind over matter. Eden had grown up seeing others in her family set the example, and now it was her turn. She fixed her gaze on the flames and forced her thoughts to faraway places, picturing her mother, brothers, and that meadow she'd once described for Ace when he'd needed something pretty to think about. *Let these men do their worst*, she thought fiercely. *I'm Eden Paxton. I come from good stock. No one is going to make me whimper and beg, least of all miserable worms like these.*

While they groped and fondled her body, Eden remembered her early days and happy moments on her family's sorry excuse for a ranch on the outskirts of San Francisco—like the time she'd gotten sick as a very small child, and Ace had hired himself out to empty spittoons, his most despised way of earning money, to buy her a doll. And the time David had bargained at the dry-goods store, swapping his only belt to buy her pretty silk hair ribbons as a birthday gift. For months afterward, he'd used one of their mother's sashes to hold his britches up. There'd been sad times, too, of course, like the time her little dog, Sam, had been run over by a farmer's wagon and died in the road. Afterward, her brothers had dug a grave, and then they'd held a regular funeral complete with handpicked flowers—mostly dandelions—and hymns, sung in a pubescent blend of breaking voices and deep baritones that Eden would never forget. Dory had culminated the ceremony by reading from the good book. David had followed the readings by assuring Eden that it wasn't only people who could lie down in still pastures. He had claimed Sam was welcome there, too, and that, after a good rest, he'd be hale and hearty again, racing across the meadows after sticks thrown for him by the angels. As Eden looked back, even the saddest moments in her life now seemed bittersweet because she'd always had her family to love her, hold her, and ease her pain.

The memories calmed her, creating a buffer between her and reality. She thought of Ace's wife, Caitlin, whom Eden so closely resembled, and the couple's boy, Little Ace, who'd been a plump darling with dancing brown eyes and a mischievous grin when Eden had visited No Name seven months ago. Soon, she would get to see her niece, Dory, Ace and Caitlin's baby girl, and she'd also be able to visit at length with Joseph's new wife, Rachel, a lovely blonde with beautiful blue eyes. When Eden's thoughts turned to her younger brothers, David and

Esa, who still weren't married, she had difficulty focusing. So she jerked her mind back to Ace's children again.

Eventually the torture stopped. The younger Sebastian brothers grew so intoxicated that they staggered away to their pallets, leaving Wallace to drag Eden over to a patch of cold earth beside his bedroll. Before falling asleep, he drew a noose over her head and knotted the loose end of the rope around his wrist.

"You move while I'm asleep, and I'll wake up. You hear?"

Eden rolled onto her side with her back to him and brought her knees up to her bare breasts in a feeble attempt to stay warm. Wallace didn't even give her a blanket. Eden could scarcely conceive how anyone could be so uncaring of another human being. But there it was. He'd cut away much of her clothing, and now he meant to cozy down for the night under two layers of wool while she lay exposed to the elements on damp ground.

As the chill of the night air seeped into her bones, Eden stared blankly across the clearing. The small fire had burned down to a mere glow of embers now, providing little light, and the waning moon was hidden behind a layer of clouds that promised more rain. For an instant, tears gathered at the backs of her eyes, but her determination to be strong burned them away. Yes, she had endured the unthinkable tonight, but crying wouldn't undo it or make her feel better. She thought of the wildflowers she and her mother had seen from the train—delicate blossoms surviving in a harsh, unforgiving terrain. She needed to be like those wildflowers. So what if life had brought a storm that threatened to flatten her? Eventually the sun would shine again. She just had to survive until then.

In the meantime, rescue was on its way. She knew that as surely as she knew her own name. Ace had recently gotten a telephone. Their mother could call him as soon as she reached Denver. Eden's brothers would waste no time in riding out to find her. God help the Sebastian brothers. Eden hadn't been lying when she'd told them they would come to regret the day they'd been born. Before this was over, they would be the ones who sniveled and begged for mercy. Her brothers weren't cruel men by nature, but if someone dared to harm one of their own, not even the wrath of hell would hold a candle to their anger.

That was Eden's last thought as she slipped into a troubled, restless sleep.

Chapter Three

For Eden, the next three days passed in a nightmarish blur of brushland. In times past she would have marveled over the way spring had touched the rolling land-scape with such vivid color. In the rocky gulches, Apache plume shared space with chokeberry, both blooming in abundance. The white blossoms of the plumes salted the wispy backdrops of dusty pink, the rosy chokeberry bushes bending under the weight of conical clusters of petals, which drooped from the branches like fronds of snowy grapes. Along the streams, false indigo lay like a fluffy purple carpet beneath brilliant green caps of bushy foliage. Wild plum blossoms filled the air with fragrance as exquisite as any French perfume.

With her pelvis rocking against the saddle horn mile after bruising mile, Eden tried to block out the discomfort by imagining herself on a walk with her mother to collect flowers for Caitlin's table, but exhaustion had her thoughts circling in on themselves in fits and starts. In some distant part of her mind, she recognized the beauty of her surroundings, but it was like the touch of a feather against one's skin, a whisper of sensation that she *almost* felt but couldn't stay focused on.

Every joint in her repeatedly abused body ached. The cold, rainy weather had given way to bright sun, and by the end of the second day her face, hands, and exposed breasts were badly sunburned. At night, the cold returned. After the first evening the men built no fire when they made camp, giving her cause to hope that a posse might be close on their heels, but the lack of heat also left her suffering more intensely from the relentless cold and biting wind when "playtime" finally ended.

She was given no blanket. Her daily rations consisted of one tough piece of jerky and three cups of brackish water. Wanting to conserve her strength in case an opportunity arose for her to escape, she consumed every drop and morsel.

But a chance to escape never came. When the men rested the horses during the day, she was tossed to the ground, ordered not to move, and was watched very closely. Once, when she dared to join the horses at the creek to get a drink, she was beaten for her trouble. Each night when they stopped, Pete, the cruelest one, assumed the duty of binding her hands and feet. After he'd finished cinching the leather so tight that her fingers and toes started to throb, he helped set up camp for the night. Then he returned to drag her over to the others.

After the men bedeviled her and drank themselves stupid, Wallace, the keeper of Eden, Estacado's prize, maintained the precautions he'd established the first night, tying the loose end of her noose around his wrist so he would feel the tug if she moved while he slept. She huddled on the ground, chilled to the bone and filled with despair. Though Wallace had thus far saved her from being raped, he didn't hesitate to take his turn playing with her in the evening. To these men, she was nothing but an object to be sold or used. If anything happened to make them question her eventual worth, she knew she would be raped and then killed.

By the end of the fourth day, Eden felt hollowed out. She was so far from home now, at least five days of solid riding from Denver, plus another to reach No Name. Even worse, the Sebastians were going northwest now instead of doubling back for the border, as law enforcement would undoubtedly expect them to do. She felt so alone—cut off from all that was familiar.

Since early childhood, Eden had clung to the belief, under Ace's tutelage, that nothing could ever take her to her knees. But neither she nor her brother could have foreseen her abduction by these monsters. Her fiery temper and feisty nature had deserted her. All her high-flown ideals about strength and perseverance had become as elusive as dandelion fluff dancing on the wind. Slowly but surely, her primary emotions became terror and a debilitating sense of defeat.

She no longer felt certain her brothers were going to show up. Granted, she knew they were searching for her, but the Sebastians were pushing their horses with cruel disregard for the animals' welfare. They were also clever, riding willy-nilly, first north and then northwest, with no apparent plan of escape. How could her brothers outguess men who didn't appear to have a rational thought in their heads?

While the men set up camp the fourth night, Eden sat in the moonlit darkness with her back to a boulder. The trailing branches of a wild plum brushed her cheeks with its delicate, fragrant blossoms. Though she tried to focus on the softness of the petals and their lovely scent, she found it difficult. The rawhide thongs that bound her hands and feet dug into her flesh, so tight that her fingers and toes pulsated with pain. By now, she knew the discomfort would eventually abate as numbness set in, but until then, the hurting was nearly unbearable.

The men worked in the silvery shadows all around her. James, the youngest of the five, had been assigned the task of unsaddling and rubbing down the horses every night. While he did that, Pete and

Harold strung a high line between two trees where the animals could be tethered until morning. The two oldest brothers, Wallace and Charles, spread out everyone's pallets and blankets, swilling whiskey while they worked.

"I don't understand how come you won't let us give that gal a poke," Charles grumbled. "Don't make no sense, savin' her for Estacado when you ain't even sure he'll buy her."

"Hell, he probably won't!" Pete hollered across the camp. "Anybody looked close at her lately? She ain't so purty now. Who in their right mind would pay good money for a wore-out, sunburned whore?"

"Pete's got a point, Wallace," Harold chimed in. "She was purty enough when we first took her, but she sure as hell ain't so fine-lookin' now."

"I don't think we should even keep her around," James inserted. "She's slowin' us down. You want us to get caught, Wallace, and dangle at the end of a rope?"

"You bastard!" Boots slapping the earth, Wallace advanced on his youngest brother. Thumping James on the chest with a rigid finger, he said, "I been keepin' you safe all your miserable life, you little shit. I'll go on keepin' you safe if you mind what I say."

"I'm just pointin' out that she's a danger to all of us," James replied. "You seen her clothes when we first took her. She comes from some fancy rich family. You think they won't try to get her back? People like that got influence. They'll sic a dozen posses on us, and maybe even come lookin' for her themselves!"

"I do the thinkin' for this outfit." Wallace gave James a final thump on the chest. "You keep your mouth shut and follow orders. Understand?"

"What we understand is that you think your vote carries the day!" Pete's voice rang across the clearing. "It's four against one, Wallace. Seems to me our opinions oughta count for *somethin'*. I'm tired of just playin' with her every night. We ain't none of us had a woman in weeks!"

"And you ain't gonna have one for several more." Wallace tossed a scathing glance at Eden. "She's for Estacado."

"Estacado won't even want her!" Pete insisted. "Take a hard look at her. He'll laugh in your face."

"We'll lay over after we cross the Rio.

Give her some time to heal and clean herself up. She'll be purty as ever again, and Estacado will pay top dollar for her. If you boys is that horny, you can rent yourself a whore down there at Margarita's cantina. Until then, keep your peckers in your pants."

Long after the argument ended, Eden mentally circled everything the men had said. What if Wallace lost control of his brothers, and they raped her despite his protests? Once that happened, she would be of no value to them any longer, and one of them would surely kill her. The thought should have terrified Eden, but after four endless days of torment, fear of dying had lost its hold on her. It wasn't that she wanted to die. No one in her right mind would. It was more a question of what lay in store for her if she survived. Rape, death, or being sold across the border to some filthy old man and enduring a lifetime of servitude and abuse. Wouldn't it be better if her trials ended swiftly?

Her brothers hadn't come. That was the crux of the matter. Until they'd moved from San Francisco to No Name a little over five years ago, they'd always protected her. But now, when she needed them the most, they weren't here. She felt completely lost and indescribably fearful, because nothing they'd taught her to believe about herself was proving to be true. She *wasn't* strong. She *wasn't* invincible. She *wasn't* as good as any man. During all those training sessions, when she'd clung to Ace's every word, believing she could prevail against almost anything, she'd been listening to lies. She was only a woman, pitted against five vicious men. If she had still been able to laugh, she would have. To think that her canceled engagement had been the greatest calamity of her life only a few days ago. She would welcome the ostracism of San Francisco society and count herself lucky—now.

Later, after the brothers tired of toying with her, Eden lay near Wallace on the ground, wishing for a blanket. They were at a higher altitude in steep, rugged, and rocky terrain that sported occasional stands of ponderosa pine. Eden had hoped the hills and trees might provide a windbreak, but instead the cuts and gullies acted as funnels for the icy gusts, making the night miserably cold. How on earth did they expect her to rest when her teeth were clacking? Squeezing her eyes closed, she tried to drift off, but sleep eluded her. So instead she drew in the moldy scent of the pine needles beneath her cheek and thought of her brothers, praying that they would find her soon.

Just before dawn, Eden was jerked to her feet by the noose. The snap of the rope around her neck brought tears to her eyes. Wallace removed the thongs from her hands and feet, which set off a prickly feeling, as if thousands of needles were jabbing her flesh. Then he tugged her along behind him to his horse as if she were a dog. Grabbing the hemp with numb fingers to keep it from cutting into her throat, Eden stumbled behind him on rubbery feet, miserable at the thought of another endless day on horseback stretching before her. Even worse, she knew it would culminate as the last four had, with her providing the Sebastian brothers with evening entertainment until they got so drunk they passed out.

Eden didn't know how much more of this she could endure without losing her mind. With each passing evening, they grew crueler, jerking her back to reality with painful pinches and nips of their decayed teeth. It was as if they sensed that she was separating herself from what was oc-curring, and her lack of response some-how spoiled their fun. So far, Eden had determinedly lost herself in a dreamworld of memories while they played with her, but at this point, she was running low on lovely thoughts.

When the dream well ran dry, what then? Eden wanted to think that she would endure the humiliation with stoic resolve, but a part of her was fast coming to realize that she lacked the steely willpower her brothers believed she possessed.

Hunkered down in front of his horse, Mat-thew peered through the gathering gloom at a patch of churned earth, tracing the edge of one hoofprint with a fingertip. *Fresh*, he decided. After riding hard for five days, he'd finally caught up with the sons of bitches. It had taken him longer than he wished because he'd stopped to rest his animals more often than the Se-bastians had, but constancy and determi-nation had finally won out. He was right behind them.

Matthew knew from experience that the gang would ride until well after dark. Crazy bastards. The five-day journey had brought them into steep, rocky terrain. It wasn't horse-friendly country, even in broad daylight, and no matter how careful a rider might be to guide his mount over uneven ground, an animal could still stumble during the twilight hours when its vision was impaired. Matthew wasn't about to put Smoky or Herman at risk of breaking a leg. He would wait for full darkness, when the gelding and mule would be able to see clearly again.

The Sebastians would stop to make camp in only a few hours. During that time, Matthew would give his animals a much-needed and well-deserved rest. They'd given him their all during this chase, and he would have to demand it of them again before the night was over, not because he wanted to, but because the woman was still alive.

Matthew could barely conceive of that. How she had survived for five full days with those heartless assholes was beyond him, but somehow she had. This morning when he'd come across the place where they'd camped last night, he'd seen her smaller footprints mixed in with the men's. She wore pointy-toed boots with wedge heels, impractical footwear for this terrain— not that she'd ever planned to be here. And therein lay the rub for Matthew, that she'd made it this far.

He didn't wish her dead, never that, but he couldn't help but resent the fact that her presence would ruin his plans. Instead of killing the Sebastians, as he'd dreamed of doing for three long years, he'd be trying to rescue a female he didn't know who might not even appreciate the gesture. After all she'd endured, she probably wanted to die, God bless her, and Matthew couldn't blame her. The memories of these last five days would haunt the poor thing for the rest of her life. Unless she was made of stronger stuff than most, she'd never come right again.

None of that mattered, though, damn it to hell. She was alive, and he felt obligated to rescue her whether she wanted it or not. He would have to postpone settling up with the Sebastians until he got her safely away from them.

Pushing wearily erect, Matthew removed

the saddle from Smoky's back and re-lieved the mule of its weighty packs before leading both animals down to the creek for a drink. Moving upstream, Matthew lay on his belly to scrub his unshaven face and slurp cold water from his cupped hands. *Damn.* He needed an all-over scrubbing. How long had it been since he'd been able to take a bath? Two weeks, maybe even three? He couldn't recollect exactly. He knew only that he stank.

His mother would have conniptions if she could see him now. As a boy, he'd been grabbed by the ear and jerked to his tiptoes more than once for forgetting to scrub his neck. *Soap and water come cheap!* she'd always admonished. *No son of mine is going to parade around with gray skin, you hear? Cleanliness is next to godliness.* Those words had found fertile ground within Matthew. Even on the trail, he normally immersed himself in a creek fairly often for a good wash.

Over the last few weeks, however, gain-ing ground on the Sebastians had taken precedence over personal hygiene, and he hadn't allowed himself the luxury of bath-ing. He'd been settling for scrubbing his face and ears without soap and rubbing his teeth as clean as he could with his finger. Problem was, staying halfway clean from the neck up didn't diminish his body odor.

When all five Sebastians were lying dead in shallow graves, he'd buy a new set of clothes, from the skin out, and treat himself to a tub bath, he vowed. And once he was squeaky clean, he'd order himself a sit-down dinner at a restaurant and rent a room so he could sleep in a real bed. Ah, to rest his bones on a down-filled mattress. He hadn't felt that kind of softness since leaving Oregon.

When the horses had finished refreshing themselves, he ground-tied them near the gear where they could graze on tufts of grass, while he spent nearly an hour rubbing them down with burlap. They'd been working their hearts out for him, damn it. The least he could do was show a little appreciation. He'd purchased a bit of grain for them in Holden Creek. He finished off the grooming session with a handful for each of them. Herman, the mule, let loose with one of his silly-sounding nickers that always made Matthew want to smile. Poor creature didn't know for sure what he was, donkey or horse. Matthew could sympathize. He no longer knew for sure if he was a decent man or a dyed-in-the-wool killer. He'd been thinking murderous thoughts for so long that they had started to overshadow everything that had once been good within him.

He left the animals to munch on serviceberry and switchgrass while he stretched out beside them for a short nap. He had no fear that either animal would step on him. Herman and Smoky had become his trusted friends. He watched out for them, and they returned the favor.

The wind picked up, whispering through the canopy of pine boughs above him. He breathed deeply of their scent, which reminded him of home and Olivia. Once again, his plans to avenge her were delayed.

He stared at the swaying boughs for several minutes, hating himself for his meanhearted thoughts. It wasn't the woman's fault that she'd been abducted, wasn't her fault that she had survived. He needed to stop thinking, If only . . . and deal with the situation handed to him. Determined to do just that, he closed his eyes, forced his mind to go blank, and drifted off to sleep.

When the men finally decided to make camp, they'd been riding in complete darkness for nearly three hours. Eden pitied the animals, even the draft horses that carried no riders. Despite the lack of weight on their backs, the poor things were exhausted. Her sympathy for the beasts was fleeting, though, because evenings were her torture hours.

As the men set up camp, Wallace pronounced that it should be safe to build a fire tonight. No posse had caught up with them yet, and he had decided it was unlikely that one would. Eden had given up on anyone rescuing her, so instead of allowing the news to depress her any more than she already was, she thought of how wonderful it would be to feel warm for a little while.

When Pete delivered her meager supper a few minutes later, she briefly considered refusing both the water and jerky. If help wasn't coming, she needed to die, and the only way she could accomplish that was to stop nourishing her body. Only she couldn't make herself do it. As far back as she could remember, her mother had taught her that life was a precious gift. As long as Eden still drew breath, there was hope. Maybe the Sebastians would relax their guard in the days that followed, allowing her to escape, or maybe her brothers would finally show up to rescue her. Instead of seeking death, the coward's way out, she had to stay focused on surviving.

After guzzling whiskey with his brothers, Pete returned to bind Eden's hands and feet. As always, he jerked on the rawhide until it dug into her flesh. He smiled into her eyes as he snapped the leather taut, knowing it caused her pain. Eden locked gazes with him but uttered no sound.

He looped the noose over her head. Then instead of grabbing her arm to drag her over to the others, as he always had before, he tugged on the rope.

"Crawl for me, bitch." He leaned down to leer at her. "Show us boys how eager you are to play."

Eden yearned to spit in his face, but fear of him squelched the urge. "I can't crawl with my ankles bound."

"You sassin' me, bitch?" He drew his

knife and thrust the sharp edge against her throat. "I told you to crawl!"

The glint in his eyes told her that he wanted to cut her. If she didn't at least try to obey him, he might actually do it.

So she attempted to crawl. With her feet lashed so tightly together, it was impossible to inch one knee in front of the other, but she made an attempt anyway, only to topple. Unable to break her fall with her hands tied behind her, she fell face-first in the dirt. Pete grabbed her by the hair, jerked her to a kneeling position, and yelled at her to crawl for him again.

"I can't!" she cried.

He pressed the knife against her throat. "You're a haughty little bitch and need to learn your place. I said crawl."

Eden tried, again and again. The last time she tumbled to the ground, Pete rewarded her efforts by burying a boot in her side. Pain lanced through her ribs, robbing her of breath. Black spots danced before her eyes as he dragged her by the hair the rest of the way to the fire.

Matthew lay on his belly in a copse of bitterbrush, watching the Sebastians abuse the woman. The bastards had built a fire, enabling him to see clearly. It was all he could do not to draw down on the sons of bitches when she was ordered to crawl and repeatedly fell face-first to the ground. When the toe of a boot dug deep into her ribs, he came close to jumping up yet again. But, no, now wasn't the time. If bullets started flying, the girl might be hit. His aim was to rescue her, not get her killed.

Even sunburned, disheveled, and bruised to a fare-thee-well, she was younger and far prettier than he had imagined, with bright red hair and delicate features. Her hands and feet were tightly bound, and Pete had looped a noose around her neck.

Over the years, Matthew had collected several wanted posters and now knew each of the Sebastians on sight. Once she'd been dragged over to the fire pit, James and Charles, both staggering drunk, had entertained themselves with her. As if all the fight had drained out of her like water through a sieve, she sat, limp as a rag doll, staring into the fire, reacting to nothing they did. The blank expression on her oval face told Matthew that she'd moved outside of herself or was possibly in shock. *Sweet*

Jesus. He wanted to help her, but he needed to be smart about it. Eventually the men would pass out. When they did, Matthew would slip into camp and get her out of there.

He settled in to wait, his stomach rolling with nausea. They played with her like a bunch of little boys with a captured butterfly, fighting for a turn, not caring if they damaged their fragile prize in the tug-of-war. Pete was the most vicious of the bunch. Watching him, Matthew itched to kill the scrawny bastard, not swiftly and mercifully, but inch by slow inch. The little shit wouldn't think inflicting pain was so much fun when he was on the receiving end.

Matthew felt drained by the time the brothers grew tired and staggered off to their pallets. He watched them bed down with a bewildered frown pleating his brow. They had stopped short of actually raping the girl. What the hell was that all about? Without so much as a holey blanket to protect her from the cold, she lay curled in a tight ball near Wallace's pallet, her face drawn and pale in the flickering firelight. Studying her features, Matthew guessed her to be around twenty years old. Had they tortured her like this every blasted night? In his heart, Matthew knew they had.

As the men settled down to sleep, scratching their crotches and farting, Matthew kept his gaze fixed on the girl. The noose was still around her neck, the loose end of the hemp knotted around Wallace's wrist so she couldn't roll away or try to loosen her bonds without waking him. She drew up her knees to partially cover her breasts, her eyes glazed and staring at nothing. Matthew's heart hurt for her, and for a moment, his tender feelings tried to surface. He shoved them back down. Since Olivia's death, he had learned not to let himself feel much of anything strongly except anger. Anger was safe. No matter how hot it burned, it didn't hurt him in places so deep he couldn't even name them.

The Sebastians had drunk so much whiskey that Matthew doubted it would take long for them to lose consciousness. Soon, Pete was snoring and sputtering. Moments later, James joined in. Wallace was the last to fall into a booze-induced coma. Even then, Matthew remained in hiding. He would have a better chance of getting the girl safely out if he waited for the fire to die down.

When at last the flames flickered out and the camp was illuminated only by glowing embers, Matthew slithered forward on his belly, the Winchester at the ready in his left hand, his holster flaps unfastened in case he needed his Colts. If those snakes woke up, all hell would break loose.

Eden had just drifted off into a fitful sleep when a hard hand clamped over her mouth. She jerked awake to see the silhouette of a man hovering over her.

He bent low to whisper, "If you want to get out of here, don't move and don't scream."

Eden's heart caught. One of her brothers? She couldn't see his face in the darkness, and his gruff whisper made it impossible to recognize the voice, but who else would be crazy enough to enter this camp and risk his life to save her? She nodded ever so slightly that she understood the warning. The next instant, she felt him sawing at the rope around her neck. When the rough hemp fell away, he leaned over her to cut the rawhide that bound her hands and feet.

When Eden was finally free, he retrieved his Winchester and helped her to stand. Her legs had gone numb from lack of circulation, making it difficult to walk. When he saw she was having trouble, he shifted his rifle to his left hand, bent at the knees, looped a hard arm around the backs of her thighs, and tossed her over his shoulder. Still badly bruised from the pummeling from Pete's saddle horn that first day, Eden's stomach contracted against a stab of pain, and a knifing agony in her ribs quickly followed. It took all her self-control to stifle a scream.

This wasn't one of her brothers, she registered dimly. He wasn't as tall as Ace but was loftier than Joseph, David, or Esa. So who was he, and why was he helping her? She didn't dare ask for fear of waking the Sebastians. Not that she really cared what had inspired him to help her. She burned to get away. God existed, after all, and He had answered her prayers.

The man moved with amazing silence through the brush until he reached a tethered horse and pack mule some distance from camp. After lowering Eden to the ground and waiting for her to catch her balance on tingling legs, he fished in his saddlebag and handed her what felt like a shirt and sheepskin jacket. The canopy of the trees around them blocked most of the moonlight, making it difficult to tell for sure what he'd given her.

"Get those on and sit tight until I get back," he said softly.

Peering at him through the blackness, Eden still couldn't make out his face. She wanted to ask where he was going, but her vocal cords were so bruised from the noose, she couldn't get the words out.

As if he read her mind, he added, "I'll get you a horse and scatter the others."

Eden clutched the clothing to her breasts. Though this man was a complete stranger, she didn't want him to leave her. Her voice little more than a croaked whisper, she cried, "What if they wake up? They'll shoot you, sure as the world."

"They won't wake up until the horses take off. By then, I'll be riding back this way, hell-bent for leather."

He disappeared into the darkness. Eden donned the shirt and jacket he'd given her.

Then, clasping her throbbing ribs, she stood near the horse, terrified that she would soon hear shooting.

Matthew desperately wanted to open fire on the Sebastians when he got back to their camp. Only concern for the girl's safety forestalled him. He believed he could hold his own against the five men, but what if something went wrong? If he were hurt, she would pay the price. He couldn't take that chance, not with her life hanging in the balance. Once they reached safety, he would double back. If luck was on his side, he'd be able to pick up the Sebastians' trail again.

Hating that he couldn't kill the men he'd been tracking for so long, Matthew saddled a horse for the girl, counting on the rush of the night wind through the trees to drown out the sounds he made. Then he mounted up and followed the high line, slashing the reins that anchored the remaining equines to the tautly stretched rope.

"Hee-haw!" he yelled, slapping rumps and waving his hat.

The horses reared and then bolted every which way. To make sure they kept running, Matthew drew one of his Colts and fired three shots into the air. Goal accomplished. The animals would run now until exhaustion made them stop.

The ruckus brought the Sebastian brothers reeling to their feet. Still sloppy drunk, they staggered about for a second, clearly confused. All Matthew needed was that second. With a sharp dig of his boot heels, he urged the horse beneath him into a flat-out gallop, intent on reaching the girl and getting her out of there as fast as he could.

When he arrived at the clearing where he'd left her, she was trying to mount Smoky, who kept sidestepping so she couldn't get her foot in the stirrup. Anger surged through Matthew when he realized she was trying to make a run for it. If the horse had cooperated, she would be long gone by now.

At his approach, she whirled to face him, her eyes narrowed to peer at him through the shadows, her sunburned face pinched with fear.

"Where the *hell* do you think you're going?" he demanded.

She clamped a slender hand over her side. "You scared me half to death." Her voice was still hoarse and strained. "I thought you were one of the Sebastians. When I heard the gunfire, I thought . . . I thought they'd killed you."

Matthew swung down from the saddle. "It was me doing the shooting. I told you I needed to scatter their horses. Lucky for you, Smoky is a one-man horse and won't let anybody but me ride him. You'd be in a hell of a fix if you got lost out here."

He caught her at the waist and lifted her onto the back of the stolen gelding. She gasped as if his hold caused her pain, but there wasn't time to focus on that. He retreated a step and nudged his hat back to see her better. His sheepskin jacket nearly swallowed her. She'd rolled up the sleeves to free her hands, creating pillows of leather and fluff around her delicate wrists.

"One thing," he said softly. "If you want to make it out of this alive, you'll do what I tell you, when I tell you. Are we clear?"

"Perfectly clear."

With a curt nod, he climbed on Smoky, grabbed the mule's lead rope, and called softly over his shoulder, "Let's ride!"

He set out at a fast clip, glancing back

over his shoulder only once to make sure the girl was following him and could handle her mount. To his surprise, she rode as if she'd been born in the saddle. He thanked God for that, because it promised to be a hair-raising night.

Who was this man who had plucked her from the arms of death? As Eden followed him through the moon-washed darkness, she asked herself that question countless times. The howl of the wind made it difficult for them to talk, but he could have at least given her his name. His failure to do so worried her. She couldn't see him clearly enough to tell if he was clean-cut or a no-account. What if he was another outlaw? Maybe he had an ax to grind with the Sebastians, and stealing her from them was his way of getting even.

He set a bone-jarring pace that sent pain shafting through her body, especially her ribs, making her wonder if the toe of Pete's boot had fractured some bones. No matter. Broken ribs were painful, but they didn't usually prove fatal. All she could do was clench her teeth, hang on tight to keep her seat, and pray her rescuer didn't turn on her once they got safely away.

An hour into the journey, Matthew began to regret his harsh manner with the girl. God only knew what trials she had endured, and he'd had no business getting angry because she tried to run off. If he'd been in her shoes, he probably would have done the same. She didn't know him from Adam. She must have been scared half out of her wits when she heard the gunfire. He might have at least tried to reassure her.

When he noticed that she was lagging behind, he decided it was safe to slow the pace for a while. The Sebastians wouldn't be able to find all their horses until dawn, if then. Spooked equines could run for miles before they finally stopped to rest, and he figured the gang's horses, abused more often than not, had stronger reasons than most to go as far as possible. The way Matthew figured, he and the woman had a good head start. He also had a few tricks up his sleeve that would throw the Sebastians off their trail, most of which he'd learned from them, the rotten sons of bitches.

When the girl drew abreast of him, Matthew shifted in the saddle to look at her. Words had never come easily for him, and after three years on the trail with only his animals for company, they came harder now. He jerked off his hat, pushed his hand through his hair, and then plopped the Stetson back on his head again.

"I, um, shouldn't have jumped down your throat back there. It's just . . . I don't like anybody else messing with my horse."

Her voice wasn't quite as rough now. "If I hadn't heard the gunfire, I wouldn't have tried to run. If something had happened to you, what was I to do, wait there until the bastards found me? I'd rather take my chances in the wilderness."

Her language brought Matthew's head back around. It wasn't often he heard a lady use the word *bastard*. He'd met this girl's mother, if only briefly, and she'd been dressed like a queen. It took money, and a lot of it, to afford fine clothing and hats bedecked with gewgaws. This girl came from wealth, or his name wasn't Matthew Coulter. Hell, she'd probably even gone to one of those fancy schools where young females got finished, whatever the hell that meant.

As if she guessed his thoughts, she looped an arm around her middle and lifted her slender shoulders in a shrug. "I have four older brothers. They don't always keep their mouths clean."

A tension-packed silence fell between them. Matthew sensed that she was afraid of him, and he wasn't sure how to ease her mind. Telling her what a fine, upstanding fellow he was probably wouldn't work. She had no way of knowing whether his word was good, and he felt disinclined to talk himself blue in the face trying to convince her.

So far, she hadn't shed a single tear. One arm locked around her middle, she sat straight in the saddle, shoulders back, chin lifted. After all she'd been through, her behavior struck him as strange. He had a mother and sisters, and they were as strong as women came, standing fast beside their menfolk, no matter what. But in a situation like this, they'd be sobbing their hearts out. Not this gal. If he hadn't known better, he might have thought nothing bad had happened to her. Earlier, when he'd watched her by the fire, he'd figured her to be in shock. Maybe she still was. When things got too terrible to face, people sometimes slipped into a stuporlike numbness.

"You all right?" he couldn't stop himself from asking.

She cut him a sharp glance and then fixed her gaze straight ahead again. "Of course I'm all right. I'm alive, aren't I?"

She nudged her mount into a trot, forcing Matthew to increase his speed to stay abreast of her. Oddly, her avowal did little to ease his mind. Such steely self-control wasn't natural. He could only hope she didn't start thinking about what they'd done to her and suddenly fall apart farther along the trail. The last thing he needed was a hysterical woman on his hands.

In truth, Eden wasn't all right. The pain in her ribs exploded into agony every time she took a deep breath, and a horrible shakiness in the pit of her stomach made her feel as if she'd swallowed a handful of jumping beans. Tears burned at the backs of her eyes, and she yearned to cry. Only a fear that she might never be able to stop made her cling to her composure.

Besides, losing control in front of a total stranger went against her every instinct.

Never show weakness or fear to the enemy. Ace had driven that tenet of survival into her brain with merciless repetition. If she started to cry and couldn't stop, her rescuer might see her as a spineless, pathetic creature lacking the courage or strength to defend herself. If he was a no-account, such an opinion of her might encourage him to boldness and possibly bring out his mean streak.

Eden didn't like feeling so vulnerable, but facts were facts. Her body was about to give out on her. She'd been on starvation rations for five days. She felt fairly certain that Pete had broken at least two of her ribs. With her physical endurance tapped nearly dry, all she had left was her intelligence. She could *not* get weepy. She could *not* show weakness. Miscreant men were like dogs: If a victim rolled over on its back and showed its belly, they went for the jugular.

So she kept her gaze fixed straight ahead, endured the pain in her side, and held her emotions in check, ignoring the lump in her throat and the fear that sent shivers up her spine. What if? A dozen questions circled, all starting with those two words. What if the Sebastians' horses had returned to camp? What if the brothers were hot on their heels even now? What if her rescuer suddenly turned on her?

Feeling alone and frightened had come to seem normal to Eden over the last five days, but, oh, God, how she wished her brothers would suddenly appear up ahead of them. She imagined Ace's strong arms enfolding her in a hard hug, how she would love to hear David's deep, reassuring laugh. She would feel so safe with her brothers all around her. With the Keegan/Paxton tribe to defend her, no one would dare hurt her again.

But her brothers didn't appear, and though Eden tried, she couldn't conjure them up. She was alone with a man who might be a thief, murderer, and rapist, and more of his ilk could be closing in fast.

When dawn finally broke, Eden was appalled when she finally could see her rescuer. He had the look of a saddle tramp, his leather jacket stained with sweat and ground-in dirt, his tan Stetson battered and filthy. He also had a lean, razor-sharp look about him, as if he had survived for months on dried meat, death, and little else. He was edgy as well, glancing frequently over his shoulder and scanning the slopes at each side of the trail, as if he expected to be shot in the back at any moment. Clearly, danger had been his constant companion for far too long.

A scruff of sable brown whiskers covered the lower part of his face, telling her it had been days, if not weeks, since a straight razor had touched his jaw. A jagged scar angled from the shaggy line of his beard across his lean cheek to the outside corner of his left eye. Another scar bisected his left eyebrow. But what she found most frightening were his eyes. They were the deep azure of a summer sky on a clear, hot day, only they looked more like ice chips, chilling her blood when he stopped his horse and turned in the saddle to stare at her.

"This looks like as good a place as any to stop for a rest." He inclined his head at a frothy stream that flowed through a nearby cut of rocks in a stand of ponderosa pines. Rocky Mountain maple and sandbar willows peppered its moist banks. "The horses could use a drink, and so could we."

As he spoke, the left corner of his mouth

remained still, as if that side of his face had been paralyzed by the injury that had scarred him so badly. Ace had a similar affliction, compliments of a bone-shattering blow to his cheek from a rifle butt when he was only a boy, but never in Eden's recollection had her eldest brother looked so disreputable.

Clenching her teeth against the pain in her side, Eden twisted to look behind them. "I don't mind stopping for water, but I don't need to rest. What if the Sebastians are right behind us?"

He swung down from the saddle. "They aren't. And I don't care whether or not you need to rest. I'm stopping for the horses and mule. Unlike the Sebastians, I don't believe in running my animals to death."

"How can you be sure they aren't right behind us?" she asked.

"Because I scattered their horses to hell and gone, and we've been riding steady ever since." He drew off his hat to dust it on his denim pant leg. Had it been clean, his dark brown hair might have hung straight as an arrow to his shoulders, but instead it had separated into stiff, oily shanks, almost as greasy as his jacket. He glanced up at her. "We won't be staying here long, if that's your worry. I just want to get the weight off the horses' backs and let them take a breather. You need help down?"

Eden had endured being touched for five long days. She'd get down by herself or die trying. With shaky hands, she grabbed the saddle horn, using it for balance as she dismounted. Supporting her weight with her arms sent a white-hot pain lancing through her ribs that made her light-headed. When her legs felt steady enough to support her weight, she stepped away from the gelding. "You can't be sure their horses didn't return to the camp."

"After firing those shots, I'm fairly sure." He turned his back on her and began unsaddling Smoky. "Of course, nothing's certain in this life, unless you count being born and dying. Everything in between is a gamble, and anyone who thinks otherwise is a damned fool."

Just what Eden wanted to hear. She began loosening her gelding's saddle cinch.

"I'll get that," he said over his shoulder. "A little slip of a thing like you shouldn't be hefting a saddle."

Eden was tall for a woman and didn't

consider herself to be a "little slip of a thing." Even in San Francisco, Ace had insisted on having a stable, and he'd left Eden's and Dory's mounts behind when he moved to Colorado. She'd been saddling and unsaddling horses most of her life. Not on a regular basis, of course, because a stable hand usually did it for her. But in the event she had no help, her brother David had taught her how to swing the weight of her riding gear without much effort. Despite the fact that doing so now would set her ribs to throbbing, she was determined to handle the task by herself so she wouldn't appear helpless.

"I can do it."

He swung his saddle onto the grass and strode toward her. "I said I would get it. You're to do what I say, when I say it. Remember? The last thing I need right now is for you to hurt your back. If you can't ride, we'll be in a hell of a fix."

Unaccustomed to being treated like a child, Eden started to argue, then thought better of it. She knew nothing about this man. If she angered him, he might retaliate physically. "Fine, have it your way."

"I will."

She stood aside, watching as he unsaddled her mount. To her wary eyes, his hands looked as wide across the backs as laundry paddles, his fingers long and thick, his knuckles leathery from exposure to the elements. He moved with a catlike grace, his lean body powerfully muscled, each task executed with forceful strength, purpose, and an economy of movement. No stranger to work-hardened males, Eden knew without asking that he'd done grueling physical labor most of his life, developing the work ethic of a full-grown man long before puberty, just as her brothers had. Sadly, that knowledge didn't comfort her. Even no-accounts had to work in order to survive, especially out on the trail.

After unsaddling her horse, he unburdened the mule and then led all three animals to the creek. He moved upstream from them to get a drink himself and then splashed his face with water.

Coming up for air, he asked, "You thirsty?"

Eden hadn't had so much as a sip of fresh water in days. She walked slowly toward him, wishing she had a cup. Her ribs hurt so badly that the thought of lying on her belly in the dirt and drinking from her hands was daunting.

"Have you any utensils?" she asked.

His face and whiskers streaming water, he pinned her with a dark look. "Any what?"

"Utensils." Judging by his expression, he didn't know what she meant. "A cup?"

He glanced toward his saddlebags. "I have cups, but I'm not digging for one now. Just use your hands."

In the end, she found a fairly flat rock, lay across it with no small amount of discomfort, and drew in water, gulping repeatedly and still craving more. Never in her life had anything tasted better.

"Go easy," he warned. "Drink too much all of a sudden, and you'll be bent double with a bellyache."

Eden was already nearly bent double from the pain in her side. She forced herself to stop drinking and wiped her mouth with the leather sleeve of the jacket he'd lent her. It smelled of man, sweat, and horses. The odor almost made her shudder.

He apparently noticed her revulsion, for his expression hardened as he averted his gaze. "I've been on the trail for three years, tracking the Sebastians. If the jacket offends you, don't wear it."

Eden wasn't that offended by the garment's odor. At least the coat shielded her from the wind.

"Why?" she asked

"Why what?" One of his dark eyebrows arched in question.

"Why have you been tracking the Sebastians?" As she waited for his reply, her heart started to race. If he had an ax to grind with the gang members, stealing her away from them would be a perfect way to get revenge. "Three years is a long time to follow someone."

He wiped droplets of water from his shaggy beard with the back of his hand. "Let's just say I have my reasons. As soon as I get you to a large enough town where you'll be safe, I'll be back on their trail."

In Eden's estimation, only one town she knew of in Colorado was staffed with enough law enforcement officers to protect her from the Sebastians. "So you'll take me to Denver, then?" Hope welled within her. "My family is in No Name, only thirty miles south of there, and my brother has a telephone. I could call from Denver, and they would either come get me or arrange for me to take the train."

He squinted against the sun to meet her gaze. "Do you know how far away Denver is?"

Eden knew it was a goodly distance. "Quite a ways, I'm sure, but—"

"Wasn't the passenger train headed there?"

"Yes."

"Then the Sebastians will know Denver was your original destination and *expect* us to ride that way."

Eden got an awful sinking sensation in her stomach. "Who's to say I wasn't bound for one of the little towns along the way?"

He ran a burning gaze over her tattered skirt. "In clothing like that? You ever visited any of those towns?"

"No, I've only glimpsed them in passing."

"Well, judging from what I've seen, most of them were once tent cities that went bust during the gold rush. Now they're rough, tumbledown holes-in-the-wall with rutted streets, rotten boardwalks, and shacks that pass for houses. The ones that are a step up from that aren't much better. Why would a lady dressed in fine silk be going to a place like that?"

Eden could think of no reason. "Forget Denver then, and just take me straight to No Name. My family can protect me."

"If No Name is a few miles south of Denver, it lies in the same direction, and we'd still run the risk of bumping into the Sebastians."

"Where will you take me then?" Eden asked shakily.

"I have a place in mind."

He had a place in mind? Frustration welled within Eden, and she wanted to give him a hard shake.

Chapter Four

As Eden dried her wet hands on the dusty folds of her silk skirt, she tried to calm down and keep her imagination from running wild, but it didn't work. Any woman in her right mind would feel wary of a man who'd been chasing a gang of outlaws for three years and refused to tell her why. What drove him? Hatred? A burning need for revenge? She wished he would be more forthcoming with information. Anyone who stuck with something for so long must have a reason. She wanted—no, *needed*—to know what that reason was.

She also deserved to know where he intended to take her. At least then she would have something concrete to give her hope and help her make plans. Once in a town, she would need to contact her family. If they went to a community without telephone service, sending a telegram would cost money, and she hadn't a cent on her person. Did her rescuer have enough spare coin to wire her relatives of her whereabouts?

She yearned to press him for more information, but after all she'd endured the last five days, she was afraid of making him angry. A part of her desperately wanted to believe he was her salvation and that she was finally safe, but another part of her held back, keeping an iron grip on her emotions and schooling her every expression. Until she knew more about him and felt certain she was safe, she would be a fool to trust him.

Apparently oblivious to her growing alarm, he scooped up some dirt in the palm of his hand, added creek water to form a paste, and then, without warning, grabbed her wrist to make her kneel in front of him. Before she could guess his reason for that, he grasped her chin. The instant he touched her, Eden cried out and tried to jerk away, but he held her fast, the grip of his fingers relentless.

"Be still. I only want to protect you from the sun. Your face is already scorched to a fare-thee-well."

The mud felt cool and wonderfully soothing on her burned cheeks and forehead. Though Eden knew it would feel awful when it dried and started to crack, she released a taut breath, ceased struggling, and allowed him to slather her face with the paste. When he finished, he regarded her for a moment, as if her appearance displeased him somehow.

"I must look a fright."

"How you look isn't important. Much more sun on that fair skin of yours, and you'll be done enough to go on a supper plate."

"Do you have a name, sir?"

He gave her a deadpan look, a tendon ticking along his jaw. "Doesn't everyone?"

Eden searched his expression, wondering if he was still miffed because she'd found the smell of his jacket unappealing. "Yes, most people have a name, and I'd like to know yours, if you wouldn't mind."

"Why is my name important? I'm saving your ass. Seems to me that's all you need to know."

"How am I to address you? Yelling, 'Hey, you,' is impolite."

"After staring at the back of a horse's head for three years, I don't worry overmuch about what's polite. 'Hey, you' works fine for me."

Her wariness of him increasing because he was so reluctant to reveal anything about himself, Eden sighed in defeat.

He bent sideways to rinse his hands. Then, relenting with a sigh of his own, he said, "The name's Coulter."

Encouraged, Eden queried, "Have you a surname?"

"You are full of questions, aren't you? That *is* my surname. First name's Matthew." He wiped his hands on his dusty jeans. "I hail from Oregon." He angled an expectant look at her. "How about you? You got a name?"

"Doesn't everyone?" She let that hang there a moment. Then she said, "My name is Eden Paxton. I've lived in San Francisco most of my life."

"A city bird. I figured as much."

Eden could have told him that this particular city bird had a lot of country dust on her tail feathers, but caution held her tongue. The fact that she'd been taught wilderness skills and knew how to handle firearms might prove to be her only aces in the hole if Coulter was the scoundrel he looked to be.

"When the train was held up, my mother and I were traveling to No Name, where all my brothers now live," she settled for revealing. "She wants to be closer to them."

He pushed to his feet, collected the animals' reins, and led them back to where the saddles and packs lay. Watching him move, Eden couldn't help but notice the powerful contours of his thighs. With every step he took, muscle bunched beneath his jeans, snapping the denim taut.

"Are you always so reticent?" she called after him.

He glanced back over his shoulder. "Always so what?"

"Reticent," she repeated. Then, realizing he didn't know the meaning of the term, she added, "You don't talk very much."

His sky blue eyes narrowed on her face. "Not much point unless I have something to say, and most times, I don't."

Eden wondered if his economy of words was due to an inherent quietness or if he harbored secrets he didn't wish to reveal. Was he friend or foe, savior or tormentor? She didn't know, and the uncertainty made her insides quake.

As she followed him, the horses, and the mule, she pondered her predicament, trying to stay focused on the facts. Though prickly and stingy with information, he had treated her kindly thus far. She touched a fingertip to her mud-smeared cheek.

He ground-tied his animals, a method that worked only with well-trained and loyal beasts, because the ropes and reins dangled loose, anchored to nothing.

"I don't know if ground-tying is advisable for the borrowed gelding," she called out. "The Sebastians always tether their horses, even during rest stops."

"When you mistreat an animal," he replied, "you can't very well expect it to hang around when you turn it loose."

He stepped over to the bay, talking softly as he stroked its reddish brown neck and glossy black mane. The horse nickered in response, the sound plaintive and heart-wrenching. The poor creature had probably never been petted and wasn't sure what to make of it.

"I hate to get off on the wrong foot with him," Coulter muttered, to himself or to her, Eden wasn't sure. "If he wanders off, I'll tie him to a stake next time, but he deserves a chance to prove himself first."

She gave her rescuer a curious study. Her brothers held to the belief that an equine's intelligence and capacity for love should afford it the same regard that one would show to a human being. Not many men felt that way, though, only the ones with hearts that ran deep.

"That gelding has never had a chance to run," she warned. "If he gets one now, he may take it. I've seen Pete Sebastian work the poor thing until he was lathered and hanging his head. Then Pete would pistol-whip him to make him keep going."

Coulter touched a scar on the bay's forelock, then rubbed the spot lightly with his knuckles. "Pete Sebastian has a vicious streak a mile wide. That doesn't mean this fellow won't respond to a little kindness.

He's taking my measure right now." Cold amusement flickered in his eyes when he glanced her way. "Unlike fine-feathered city birds, horses don't judge a man by the condition of his clothes. Maybe he'll decide I'm not so bad."

The comment stopped Eden in her tracks. Heat crept up her neck and flooded her cheeks. She parted her lips to retort, but for the life of her, she couldn't think what to say. The truth was, she *had* passed judgment on him because of his clothing. Now, pinned by his sharp gaze, she felt small and petty for having done so.

The right corner of his mouth quirked. "The Sebastians aren't much for bathing or doing laundry. To keep up with them, I've adopted some of their bad habits."

Eden looped her arms around her waist and resumed walking. "I see."

She had just reached the saddles and packs when he stepped around to the other side of Smoky. The next instant, she heard him voiding. After being with the Sebastians for five days, she couldn't be shocked by much of anything, but she was disheartened, nevertheless. A man with any modicum of decency would have walked off into the trees to do his business in private.

Determined to maintain at least some semblance of propriety herself, Eden headed for the woods. It had been countless hours since she'd had an opportunity to relieve herself.

"Don't wander too far," he called after her. "If they show up and you're to hell and gone off in the woods, I can't protect you."

Eden stopped and turned to give him another wondering look. Was that why he hadn't sought privacy in the trees a moment ago—not because he was uncouth, but out of concern for her safety? As she continued toward the pines, she turned that possibility over in her mind, and then, heeding his warning, did her business behind the first large tree trunk she found.

Moments later, when she returned to the clearing, he was rubbing down the horses and mule with a burlap sack. After she sank onto the grass, he dug through his saddlebag and tossed her a piece of jerked meat. Eden was sick to death of the stuff, but looking on the bright side, she was lucky to be getting some breakfast.

She remained on the ground near the packs to consume the small meal, which she found to be more filling than usual because she'd drunk so much water. It was nice not to feel hungry for a change.

"It appears that your assessment of the bay was right on target," she said, observing the gelding as it munched on grass. "He doesn't seem eager to run."

"Maybe he recognizes decent folks when he sees them." Coulter finished rubbing down the animals and grabbed a piece of jerky for himself. Even under the scruff of whiskers, she could see the tendons in his lean cheek bunch as he chewed. "Nothing to fear, no reason to flee." He collected his canteen. "I'm going down to rinse this out and fill it with fresh water. Stick close."

While he was gone, Eden circled what he'd just said about the gelding recognizing decent folks. Was Coulter a decent man? His rough and filthy appearance indicated otherwise. She could only hope the bay gelding was a better judge of character than she was.

Shortly after Eden finished eating, Coulter started saddling the horses. He moved with the same blend of strength and masculine grace she'd noted earlier, handling the weight of the gear with practiced ease. He said nothing while he worked, and the silence made her nerves as taut as overextended rubber bands. She wanted to ask him what town he was heading for and when he thought they would get there, but his reluctance to talk made her hesitate. She didn't want to be told she was full of questions again.

He said nothing more, and soon it was time to go. As eager as Eden was to put the Sebastians far behind her, she dreaded having to mount up. Her nether regions were deeply bruised, her back ached from sitting erect, her inner thighs felt as if they'd been pounded with a hammer, and knifing pain shot through her ribs every time she took a deep breath. She couldn't recall ever having been quite so exhausted and wasn't sure how much longer she could keep going.

As if she'd spoken the thought aloud, Coulter angled a piercing glance at her over his leather-clad shoulder, his blue eyes locking on hers. "Come twilight, we'll make camp. You'll be able to get a good night's rest, and I'll even scratch together a hot meal."

"Will it be safe to make a fire?"

The brim of his battered Stetson shadowed his face as he nodded. "By scattering their horses, I put quite a hitch in their get-along. They're at least eight hours away, if not more."

Eden needed no further explanation. A horse could cover four miles an hour at a walk. That meant the gang was at least thirty-two miles away. In this hilly, wooded terrain, they wouldn't be able to see a fire or smell the smoke.

After Eden mounted her horse, her rescuer surprised her with another piece of jerky. When he wasn't looking, she tucked it into a pocket. If it became necessary for her to flee from him, bits of hoarded food might come in handy. Her gaze fixed on Coulter's back, she nudged her gelding to fall in behind the pack mule. Soft from wear, Coulter's leather jacket clung to his broad shoulders like a thick second skin. Each time he moved, she glimpsed a play of muscle. If he had villainous intentions, she was in big trouble, she thought dismally. Even six days ago, when she'd been physically strong, she would have been no match for him.

For most of what remained of the morning, they rode northwest through breathtakingly beautiful but ruggedly treacherous terrain, climbing ever higher into the foothills. Eden had inherited her mother's love of wildflowers, and at any other time, the multihued displays tucked here and there among buckthorn, wavy-leaf oak, and silver buffaloberry bushes would have made her sigh with pleasure. It was as if God had sipped too much wine and spilled splashes of color from His heavenly palette, sprinkling the slopes, draws, and gulches with touches of loveliness nearly everywhere she looked.

She drank it all in, much as she had the water during their brief rest stop. Maybe it was the distraction that she craved. Identifying the plants helped to take her mind off the mess she was in. She knew only that the sight of the delicate yellow-white blossoms of golden currant rubbing elbows with the deep purple spikes of silvery leadplant made her feel lighter of heart.

Matthew Coulter seemed not to notice

the riotous display of spring colors. He rode past the daisylike faces of fleabane without glancing their way and allowed Smoky to trample the star-shaped white blossoms of mouse-ear chickweed. Eden winced and began to tremble. For reasons beyond her, she felt an affinity with the chickweed, as if it were she and not the petals that were being crushed. Her reaction made no sense. It was silly to grieve over flowers. But when she suspected that he meant to destroy in the same careless fashion a patch of incredibly blue sugarbowl clematis, her heart gave a painful twist, and she couldn't hold her tongue.

"Mr. Coulter!" she cried.

He drew Smoky to a stop and whirled in the saddle to look at her. Eden was about to admonish him for his callous disregard of the beauty around them when she realized she was looking down the barrel of a Colt revolver. He'd drawn the weapon with such speed that she hadn't seen his hand move.

"What?" he asked, scanning the trail behind her. "Did you see something?"

Eden moistened her lips and tried to swallow. Her throat had gone as dry as parchment paper. If he wanted to destroy every wildflower in his path, who was she to argue? Had she learned nothing during her time with the Sebastians? The trick to surviving was to do as she was told and keep her mouth shut.

"Nothing, I saw nothing," she managed to push out weakly.

"Nothing? You scared the holy hell out of me."

"I'm sorry. I didn't mean to startle you. It's just—"

He holstered the weapon and reined Smoky around to face her. "Just what?"

Eden glanced at the clematis bells that his gelding's back hooves were brutalizing. "Nothing. It was nothing."

"You screamed my name. You must have had a reason."

"I didn't *scream*." Why was it so infernally difficult for her to keep quiet? Joseph often said her tongue was tied in the middle and loose at both ends, and Eden couldn't rightly argue the point. "I just wanted to warn you—" She broke off and tried to swallow again. "You, um, were about to let Smoky trample the clematis."

"Trample the *what*?"

Eden inclined her head at the beautiful

flowers behind him. "The sugarbowl clematis. They're so beautiful, like little church bells, and you were about to ruin them."

He glanced over his shoulder and stared at the flowers for a long, tension-packed moment. Then, meeting her gaze, he rubbed a callused hand over his face and blinked as if he hoped the picture might change once his vision came back into focus. "Are you saying that you screeched like that to save some *flowers*? Sweet Christ, lady, I could've shot you!"

Eden couldn't blame him for being angry. She didn't know what had come over her, only that something inside of her had twisted and snapped when she thought the clematis might be destroyed. An awful, choking sensation filled her chest, and suddenly she wanted to weep. His face started to swim, and she realized she was staring at him through tears. Even worse, her hands had started to shake so badly that she had to wrap them around the saddle horn so he wouldn't see.

His blue eyes narrowed on her face. "Are you okay?"

Eden had rarely felt less okay. She was miles from anywhere with a stranger, her life hanging by a thread, her body bruised, battered, and defiled. She wasn't sure why the trampled flowers had brought all of her suffering and shame roiling to the surface, but suddenly her emotions screamed for release. It took every shred of control she had to blink back the tears, squarely meet his gaze, and nod in response to his question.

He stared at her for another long moment. Then he glared at the flowers again. As he turned his horse back up the trail, she thought she heard him mutter, "Son of a bitch," under his breath. But at least he circled the gelding around the clematis instead of plowing right through it.

As Eden followed him up the slight incline, she struggled to regain her composure. Until she knew for certain that Matthew Coulter could be trusted, she had to bury her feelings deep, keep a clear head, and be ready to defend herself should it become necessary. She could have herself a good cry later, when she knew for certain she was safe.

As the endless day wore on, the craggy, snowcapped peaks of the Rockies sometimes looked so close that Eden felt as if she could reach out and touch them. To the casual observer, they appeared impenetrable, yet she knew firsthand that wagon trains, stagecoaches, horsemen, and locomotives had found passes through them. When the sun reached its zenith and began its slow, downward slide toward the west, she saw a timber wolf at the crest of a rocky ridge, its shaggy body outlined against the powder blue sky. Later as the horses picked their way down a treacherous, shale-strewn embankment, she glimpsed a cougar slinking along the tree line at the opposite side of a meadow.

Her focus on her surroundings ended when Coulter suddenly rode down a muddy bank into a creek. The rocky streambed was slick with moss, and Eden's mount had trouble keeping its footing. In order to prevent herself and the horse from taking a swim, she had to concentrate on shifting her weight to help the gelding stay upright. That made her ribs hurt worse, the pain so sharp she became dizzy. For a good five minutes, she wondered if Matthew Coulter had lost his mind, but then she decided he'd taken to the stream to hide their tracks, a smart evasive maneuver. Not that she found it all that reassuring. If Coulter had stolen her from under the Sebastians' noses to exact revenge, he wouldn't want them to be able to follow his trail.

Matthew fully expected his female charge to complain about his decision to ride in the stream. The footing was perilous, and having been raised in a city, she probably thought he was either crazy or a glutton for punishment. But as she had from the start, Eden Paxton surprised him. Instead of protesting, she slid from the saddle to lead her horse over the rocks. He hated for her to get her clothing wet. When the sun went down this evening, the mountain air would grow colder than a well digger's ass, and he didn't want her to take a chill. Nevertheless, he couldn't quarrel with her decision and soon followed suit, dismounting to help Smoky and Herman traverse the slick streambed.

Walking backward much of the time, he had an opportunity to watch Eden with her horse. She handled the bay with an expertise that struck him as odd for a San Franciscan. How the hell had she acquired such skill with four-legged critters? Even more bewildering was her steely strength of will. She met every challenge with grim resolve. She'd been in the saddle for going on thirty hours straight with only a brief break last night and this morning. She had to be beyond exhausted, but she hadn't asked him to stop a single time.

Even more telling, she still hadn't broken down and cried. She'd come close earlier, when Smoky had trampled the flowers. He'd seen the tears in her eyes. But she'd managed to blink them away and tamp down her upset, thank God. He was no good with weeping women. But the tight grip she kept on her emotions concerned him. A lot of men couldn't have endured what she had and kept a stiff upper lip. He wasn't sure he could have himself.

Although her impractical boots made it difficult for her to maintain her footing, she spoke softly to the bay gelding, coaxing him over the rocks and soothing away his fear with gentle strokes of her hands. The animal whickered and grunted, almost as if he were talking to her. Matthew nearly smiled, an urge that had come to him rarely over the last three years.

"Where'd you learn your way around

a horse?" he called, raising his voice to be heard over the rush of the water and the clack of shod hooves on wet stones. "There can't be much opportunity for a lady to ride in the city."

Sunlight glanced off her fiery curls as she angled her head to look at him. As their gazes locked, Matthew found himself thinking that he'd never seen prettier blue eyes. They struck such a sharp contrast to the mud he'd smeared on her face that he found it difficult to glance away. Olivia's eyes had been brown, so he felt no sense of disloyalty for thinking Eden's were uncommonly beautiful.

"My father was a Virginian and raised horses before the war," she called back. "I wasn't born then, but my oldest brother, Ace, carried on the tradition after Pa died and we settled out west. As a girl living on the outskirts of San Francisco, I spent a lot of time in the saddle. Ace insisted on it."

Matthew glanced at her skirts. Wetness had seeped above her knees. If he didn't get her out of the stream soon, she'd be soaked to the waist. "We'll be able to get back on dry land here in a bit."

Matthew started watching for a rocky

patch of bank where they might leave the creek without making any tracks. If possible, he wanted to prevent the Sebastians from finding their exit point.

The icy rush of water dragged at Eden's skirts, and her feet were freezing. Occasionally she saw Coulter scan the north bank ahead of them for an exit, but he kept bypassing places that looked perfect to her. It finally dawned on her that he was waiting to find rock so the horses wouldn't tear up the earth.

At one point, they came upon a deep pool that Eden guessed would hit her just below the breasts. Before moving through it, she took off the sheepskin jacket to keep it dry, knotting the sleeves around the bay's neck and draping the tails over the saddle. A moment later, she was glad she had, because the water came clear to her armpits. The iciness nearly sucked from her what little breath she could manage with her broken ribs. Despite the drag of her clothing and the lack of solid purchase beneath her smooth-soled boots, she managed to get through the pool without too much difficulty and scrambled up a shale shelf to a shallower part of the stream.

To her surprise, Coulter circled back and handed her Smoky's reins. Like her, he'd removed his jacket and tied it around the horse's neck. Without a word of explanation, he drew a short-handled net from his saddlebag and plunged back into the deep pool. At first, Eden couldn't imagine what he was after. Water shot up in a spray around him. It wasn't until the eddy cleared that she saw trout swimming around him, some of them a foot long and as thick as a man's forearm. Coulter leaned sideways, swung the net deep into the ice-clear depths, and came up with two flopping fish.

Climbing the shale shelf, he flashed a grin, his teeth glowing white in contrast to his dark whiskers. Now that the fish were out of the water, they didn't look quite so large, but they were each sizable enough to provide a fine meal.

"Supper!" he said as he looped the excess netting into a loose knot and hung the trout from his saddle horn. "I hope you like fish."

Eden pushed a shock of damp hair from

her face. Just the thought of eating something besides leathery beef made her mouth
water. "I do."

"Good. I don't cook fancy but I cook
plenty."

His wet clothing sucked tight to his skin,
revealing the virile contours of his lean yet
muscular body. Eden's gaze snagged on
his powerfully built chest, then trailed downward to his trim lower torso. When she realized she was staring, she forced herself to
look away and suppressed a shudder. With
the exclusion of her brothers, she wanted
nothing more to do with men for a good
long while, maybe never.

As before, Coulter reverted to silence
as he retrieved Smoky's reins and led the
way farther upstream. A few minutes later,
they happened upon a patch of shale on
the north bank and were able to leave the
water. By then, Eden was so weary she
could barely stand, let alone lift herself
and the weight of her soaked clothing back
into the saddle. Pain exploded in her side
with each attempt. After she gave it two
tries, Coulter dismounted and strode over
to help. When he reached to settle his
hands at her waist, she retreated a step.

The thought of his touching her filled her with revulsion.

"Don't," she said, her teeth clacking from the cold. "I can mount by myself."

He backed off and held his arms out to his sides. "I was just going to lift you up."

"I don't need you to lift me up." Eden stuck her wet boot back into the stirrup, bounced twice on her other foot, and made another valiant effort to swing up, but her quivering legs and arms wouldn't cooperate, and the agony in her ribs made her feel as if she might pass out. "I can do it by myself. I *can*."

He said nothing when her third attempt went just as badly. Too exhausted to try again, Eden looped her arms over the saddle and pressed her face against the side of the smooth leather seat. "I can't believe this," she said. "I've been riding most of my life."

"Under ordinary circumstances, I'm sure you'd do fine," he said in a low voice. "You're just played out and need to rest for a while. Unfortunately, we've got a lot of miles to cover yet before it'll be safe to stop for the night."

Not lifting her head, Eden nodded. "Just give me a moment."

He dug at the sandy loam with the heel of his boot. Through her lowered lashes, she noted the sharp, irritated jerk of his movements.

"How about I just give you a leg up?" He bent forward and interlaced his thick fingers to create a stirrup. "Grab hold of the saddle horn and I'll do the rest."

When Eden lifted her face from the saddle, she felt tears making tracks in the dry mud on her cheeks. She could only hope he thought it was water from the stream. As she met his gaze, she glimpsed what she believed was compassion in the blue depths of his eyes, but it vanished so quickly she couldn't be sure.

Grabbing the saddle horn with both hands, she placed her foot in the cradle of his fingers. With a powerful thrust of his legs and arms, he propelled her upward with such force that she nearly missed the saddle and went sailing off the other side. He caught hold of her arm at the last second to halt her flight but let go the instant she was safely seated.

Untying the sleeves of the jacket from around the bay's neck, he thrust the wad of sheepskin at her. "Put that back on. Soaked like you are, this mountain wind will cut you clear to the bone."

Eden was already chilled to the bone, but she lacked the energy to tell him so. He was even wetter than she was, water streaming from his jeans and seeping out through the seams of his boots. But if it bothered him, he didn't let on.

He waited until she'd donned the jacket. Then he handed her Smoky's reins. Jabbing a thumb over his shoulder, he said, "Take the horses and mule over yonder to the grass and wait for me. I need to brush away our tracks."

Eden did as he said and then turned to watch as he cut a long branch from a Rocky Mountain maple. With long, rhythmic sweeps of his arm, he feathered away the horses' tracks and his own until he reached her. He surveyed the results of his work, then nodded.

"They'll have to look sharp to know this is where we left the water." He tossed the branch into a copse of red-berried elder and remounted his gelding, swinging into the saddle with an ease that she envied. "You ready?"

Eden nodded and fell in behind him as he once again headed north.

In the minutes that followed, Eden's exhaustion took precedence over all her earlier concerns. She was so wet, cold, and miserable that she no longer cared if Matthew Coulter was a decent man or a horrible one. She just wanted to get where they were going so she could warm herself by a fire, devour one of the fish he'd caught for supper, and then sleep.

After a couple of hours, her weariness abated somewhat and her thoughts came clear again. Something wasn't right. She instinctively knew that, but as they rode up one incline after another and then dropped into the rocky draws on the other side, she couldn't pinpoint what was troubling her. The terrain hadn't changed except for the small copses of nine-brush, manzanita, and hawthorn that created a colorful understory in the stands of ponderosa pine. She saw the deep royal blue blossoms of larkspur, conical shoots of white blossoms called miner's candle, and wild geraniums lovelier and more delicate than any green-house variety.

As they topped yet another rise and the sun glared directly into Eden's eyes, she finally figured out what had been bothering her. Earlier they'd been riding north. Now he'd changed directions and was heading due west. If, as he'd claimed, he was taking her to a town where she'd be safe, why had he suddenly altered their course? All of her senses went on alert.

After what Eden guessed was about three hours, Coulter suddenly switched directions again and turned due south. She frowned in bewilderment but continued to follow him because she had no choice. Then, as daylight began to fade, they turned east and soon cut across their own back trail.

At the sight of their tracks from that morning, Eden's stomach clenched with fear. He wasn't riding toward a town to get her to safety. He'd spent the entire day going in a huge circle! *Oh, God*. Sharpening her gaze, Eden recognized landmarks from that morning. Why had he brought her back here? It made no sense. Yet there was no denying that he'd cut back to their starting point. Frightening questions took shape in her mind. Did he mean to return her to the Sebastians? What if he wanted something from them and planned to use her as a bargaining chip? Eden couldn't bear the thought of being mauled again by those horrible men, and she had no intention of allowing it to happen.

She fixed her attention on the Winchester in Coulter's saddle boot. If she could get her hands on that rifle, he'd be in for a big surprise. Battered and exhausted though she was, she wasn't helpless. Raised in San Francisco, yes, but not the bit of city fluff that Coulter clearly believed her to be. Her brothers had seen to that. She needed no compass to find her way through these rugged mountains, and with a gun, she wouldn't need Matthew Coulter or anyone else to help her reach safety, either.

Once the thought took root in Eden's mind, it wouldn't depart.

As the remaining light faded to a blue-gray duskiness, Coulter drew his horse to a stop at the bend of a stream and swung down from the saddle. "This is as good a place as any to make camp," he informed her as he loosened Smoky's saddle cinch. "I'll take care of the animals, and then go fetch us some firewood." He tipped his hat to her. "I promised you a hot meal, as I recall. I'll get a fire going, find you some dry clothes, and warm your innards with some coffee."

"That sounds wonderful," Eden replied woodenly.

She watched as he unburdened the animals. When he'd wandered off into the trees with a small hatchet to collect wood, she hurried over to his saddle. Propped against the cantle, the Winchester slipped easily from the leather boot. Eden's hands trembled as she checked to make sure the weapon was loaded. *Yes.* Relief flooded her. Holding the gun made her feel as if she'd been reunited with an old and trusted friend.

With a skill born of long practice, she jacked a cartridge into the chamber, pressed her back to the rough bark of a ponderosa pine, and waited for her lying, treacherous rescuer to return to camp.

Chapter Five

Matthew had his arms full of wood when Eden stepped into his line of sight. With her enveloped in the oversize sheepskin jacket and her sodden skirts hanging in thick folds around her hips, he didn't immediately notice that she was holding his Winchester to her shoulder and had the barrel trained on him. When realization dawned, he froze in his tracks. Though she was weak and shaky, her stance and the way she held the weapon told him she was as accomplished with rifles as she was with horses. She also looked ready to shoot if he gave her a reason.

Making no sudden movements, he dropped the firewood at his feet and held up his hands. "What brought this on?"

"What brought this *on*?" she cried, her voice high-pitched and tremulous. "What do you think brought it on, Mr. Coulter, if that's even your real name? Do you mistakenly believe I'm both blind and stupid?"

Matthew considered her questions, but even after making two passes, he was no clearer on what had upset her. "I'm sorry. I'm not following."

"Don't play dumb with me," she cried. "You've ridden in a circle all day, bringing me straight back to where we stopped this morning. We just crossed our own back trail!" Her voice cracked on the last word. She tightened her finger over the trigger. "*Bastard*. What's your game? Did you have a falling-out with your horrible friends? Is it your plan to use me as barter to get something from them, possibly your share from the train holdup? Well, whatever your game, I'm not playing! If they show up, they'll be dead men, and so will you."

The tension eased from Matthew's shoulders. "You're reading this all wrong, sweetheart."

"Don't call me sweetheart, you lying, worthless miscreant! You have no intention of taking me to a town where I'll be safe."

Matthew had no idea what a miscreant was, but judging by the way she spit the word at him, he figured it must be pretty bad. Earlier that day, he'd noted how beautiful Eden's eyes were and had comforted himself with the thought that his appreciation of her loveliness was no slight to Livvy, because the two women's eyes were so different. Now he realized that Eden was Livvy's exact opposite in other ways as well. His wife had been a timid little thing, more likely to curl her fingers over his belt and peer out at trouble around his arm than to face it on her own. Eden Paxton would stand beside a man but never behind him. Even with the .44 caliber Winchester trained on his chest, Matthew marveled at her pluck. If he made a wrong move, she'd shoot him. He saw it in her eyes. And she would place the slug precisely where she meant to as well.

"Like I said, you've got it all wrong," he tried again. "I'm not playing a game, and I have no intention of returning you to the Sebastians. I'm just not much of a talker."

She jabbed the barrel of the weapon at him. "Well, if you value your life, you'd better start talking now!"

A sudden itch took up residence in Matthew's right nostril, and he wanted to scratch so badly that his fingers twitched. The hell of it was, he truly wasn't much of a talker. After spending three years alone with only his animals for company, he'd lost his knack for stringing words together.

"I had my reasons for riding in a circle all day," he admitted. Damn, but it was hard for him to communicate when he couldn't gesture with his hands. Until that moment, he'd never realized how strong that trait of his father's ran in him. "I'm sorry I didn't explain those reasons to you. The truth is, I figured you'd never notice which direction we were going, so I didn't bother."

"Well, I did, so explain now, or I swear to God, I'll kill you."

Matthew almost reached to rub his damned nose. "The best way to lose someone who's following you is to circle around and get behind him." As explanations went, Matthew knew that one was sorely lacking. "That way, if anyone's going to get a nasty surprise, it won't be you."

Her hands relaxed a little on the rifle, but she still kept it trained on his heart. "Go on."

"That's it. God strike me dead if I'm lying."

"God won't have to strike you dead. I'll do it for Him. Keep talking."

What more could he say? To his dismay, he'd run out of explanations. Since the thought of dying didn't appeal, he decided to restate his case with a change of wording and a little more embellishment. "If I had headed straight for a town, they would have figured out where I was going and split up, some heading for the town, others staying on our back trail. They would have either caught up with us before we reached our destination or cut us off along the way. Circling around behind them and trying to cover our tracks seemed like the best plan." A mosquito landed on the fleshy heel of his hand and dipped its stinger for blood. The burn made Matthew's fingers curl. "That's why I took to the water and covered our tracks as we left the stream—because I hoped I could lose them if I suddenly changed directions." He inclined his head at the terrain behind her. "When we crossed our back trail a few minutes ago, did you happen to notice their tracks mixed in with ours? They're following our trail from this morning. If you don't believe me, at least have a look before you go off half-cocked and pull that trigger."

She shot a quick glance over her shoulder. Matthew could see that she was wavering.

"Once you confirm that they're following us," he continued, "ask yourself this: If they're up the trail somewhere, trying their damnedest to catch up with us, how can they possibly be anywhere around here? And if they aren't around here, how could I be plotting to return you to them?" Matthew searched her beautiful eyes, trying to determine whether he was getting through to her. "I'm not in cahoots with the Sebastians, and I had nothing to do with that train robbery, I swear. All I'm guilty of is being close-lipped when I should have been explaining my plans to you."

To his vast relief, she finally lowered the

rifle. Then her shoulders slumped and her arms went limp, as if the Winchester had suddenly become too heavy for her to hold. Matthew expected her to say something— that she believed his story, for starters— but instead her legs folded as if an invisible force had struck her across the backs of the knees. As she collapsed, the barrel of his Winchester rooted through the dirt, taking a snort of dust up the bore. As much as Matthew prized the weapon, the ragged sob that tore up Eden's throat concerned him far more. Like a prayerful penitent, she knelt on the ground, rested her rump on her heels, and hugged her waist as if she'd just swallowed a bucket of rusty nails. Her face contorted with pain.

For hours, Matthew had wondered at her stoic strength, but now, like a water-color sketch left in the rain, she seemed to dissolve before his eyes. Still hugging her waist, she began to rock back and forth. *Shit.* He never knew what to do or say when a female took to crying. When Livvy had gotten upset, he'd just held her close and stroked her hair, murmuring nonsensical words until she felt better, but Eden Paxton recoiled at his touch. So what the hell was he supposed to do? Talking sure as hell wasn't one of his strong points.

He thought about letting her have at it while he built the fire and started supper. *Coward.* But that was the truth of it. He could face all five Sebastians without a qualm, but a crying female made his skin go clammy with nervous sweat. He walked two circles around her, hoping she'd snort, gasp for breath, and stop sobbing. No chance. She was crying as if her heart might break.

Matthew had seen what those devils had done to her, and he didn't blame her a bit for falling apart. He just wished he knew how to make her feel better. He settled for hunkering down in front of her.

She cupped a quivering hand over her eyes, which were spilling tears like leaky water spigots to make trails in the caked mud on her cheeks. "I'm s-sorry," she squeaked.

"You've got no call to be sorry. You haven't done anything wrong."

Her shoulders jerked on another sob. The awful tearing sound that followed came from so deep within her that Matthew feared she might do some damage to herself.

"It's just—" She gulped and mewled like a kitten. "I'm so *ex-exhausted*."

Matthew didn't doubt she was worn-out, but he had a hunch it ran deeper than that. She'd clearly believed he was trying to trick her, that he was somehow in cahoots with the Sebastians, and now she was coming to believe that might not be the case. Still clutching her waist, she swayed back and forth, making him worry that she might topple. Hoping to steady her, he settled a hand on her shoulder. He wasn't surprised when she flinched and jerked away.

"*Don't*," she pushed out. "Please, *don't*."

He lowered his arm but not quickly enough to suit her. She scrambled unsteadily to her feet and reeled away from him, her steps as unpredictable as a drunk's. He gazed after her, wishing with all his heart he could think of something to say that might comfort her. But he wasn't even sure where to start. He groped for words, discarded those that came to him, groped again, and finally settled for barking, "Don't hare off too far!"

The warning no sooner left his lips

than he wanted to give himself a swift kick in the ass. *Damn.* Couldn't he have come up with something better than that? His mother, a devout Irish Catholic, often prayed to the Holy Mother for divine intervention. Matthew had fallen out of the habit of praying over the last three years, hadn't stepped foot in a church. But he was sorely tempted to send up an appeal now, something along the lines of, *Please, God, help me to stop being such a dumb son of a bitch.*

Eden staggered toward the horses, making his heart leap with every step she took because he feared she might fall. When she reached the animals, she homed in on Pete Sebastian's gelding, leaned against the beast as if her knees were about to buckle again, and looped her arms around its neck to hold herself erect. Even at a distance, Matthew could hear her broken sobs. Every hitch of her breath made him feel guilty as hell. She'd been with him now for almost twenty-four hours, and she'd spent every minute of that time uncertain of his intentions and not knowing if she could trust him.

He might have eased her mind a bit if he'd told her a little about himself, but, oh, no. Instead he'd gotten in such a snit when he saw her sniffing the sleeve of his jacket and wrinkling her nose that he'd balked at even telling her his name. Not because he'd had good reason, but because he'd been angry. What in tarnation had he been thinking? Truth was, the jacket stank, and he'd been embarrassed that she noticed.

He bent his head, staring at the backs of his hands curled over his knees. His attention was caught by the coat of grime on his jeans. Was it any wonder she'd taken his measure and judged him to be a no-account trail bum who might do her harm? Whether he wanted to face it or not, that was exactly what he'd become: a filthy, ill-mannered, rough-talking trail bum who'd been deprived of polite company for so long that he no longer even said *please*, *thank you*, or *excuse me*. This morning, instead of handing her the piece of jerky, he'd tossed it at her. Hello? You tossed food to a dog. And when she'd wanted a cup to drink water from the stream, why hadn't he gotten her one? It wouldn't have taken him more than a minute.

Matthew felt a little sick to his stomach. Being around Eden was making him see himself through her eyes, and he didn't like the picture. Since leaving Oregon, he had traveled as far south as Mexico and as far north as Canada to even get in the Sebastians' general vicinity, and somewhere along the way, he'd lost touch with who he was and where he came from. His father had always done filthy work from dawn until dark, and when he'd come into the house at night, sometimes he'd been too exhausted to want to eat. Yet Matthew had never seen him sit down at his mother's table without washing up and changing his shirt first, and he'd demanded the same of all his sons.

Matthew turned one hand palm up to examine his fingernails, but seeing that they were clean didn't make him feel much better. He had some fresh clothes at the bottom of his pack, and it didn't take all that long to jump in the creek for a bath. Yet he hadn't done that recently, because he'd stopped caring how he looked.

Matthew tried to remember when that attitude had taken root, and he realized it had happened slowly. Taking a bath in a creek after dark was damned cold business. His laundry didn't always dry by a fire before morning, either, so he'd had to pack it away damp sometimes, and then it soured. His horse and mule didn't give a hang whether he was clean or dirty, and he seldom saw people unless he visited a town. Over time, he'd started making excuses. He was too tired and hungry to bathe. One more day wouldn't matter. Why wash clothes if they wouldn't dry by morning, and he'd only have to wash them again? Who was going to see him, anyway?

When Matthew finally pushed to his feet and collected his rifle, he felt almost as exhausted as Eden looked. He needed to walk over there and assure her that she was absolutely safe with him, damn it. Only, when he played it out in his mind, he saw himself bungling it. He'd blurt out something stupid, sure as rain was wet. *You're safe*. Yeah, like that would be convincing. *I'm a decent man*. Same result. After Livvy's death, everything within him had locked up, almost as if a cell door had clanked shut, and he no longer had the key to disengage the bolt. What he felt—which was precious little, because he preferred it that way—was buried deep inside him.

Walking toward the tumble of dropped wood, he decided to be useful in the only ways he could be—by building a fire, caring for the animals, finding her some clean, dry clothes so she wouldn't catch her death, and then fixing a hot meal. His ma had always said that actions spoke louder than words. He could only hope that was true.

Eden kept her wet cheek pressed against the gelding's sweat-slicked neck. Her body vibrated with spasmodic shudders from the cold, her legs felt as useless as wet rags, and it was all she could do to remain standing. The starch in her spine had dissolved and leaked out the bottoms of her feet. *Exhaustion*. She couldn't recall ever feeling so drained. Part of it, she knew, stemmed from relief. After six days of living in fear, she finally felt halfway safe. Matthew Coulter was unkempt, sorely lacking in social graces, and she still wasn't sure how far she could trust him, but at least she now felt nearly certain that he wasn't connected to the Sebastian Gang. His explanation for why he'd ridden in a circle all day made sense, and something in his eyes—she wasn't sure what—had convinced her he was telling the truth.

Right now, he was little more than a shadow in the darkness. Lifting her head, she watched as he fetched the wood he'd gathered earlier and laid a fire. A moment later, he struck a lucifer, cupped a hand around it, and bent to ignite the handfuls of dry grass that he'd placed under a crisscross of kindling. With a bit of coaxing, flames soon leaped to life.

Like a moth drawn to lantern light, Eden steeled herself against the pain in her ribs and moved haltingly toward the fire, afraid with every step that her legs might fold. Once there, she warmed her hands, but the sodden folds of her skirt repelled the heat. Feeling like a muskmelon that had been hollowed out with a spoon, she was only vaguely aware of Matthew, who was now rifling through his packs. When he emerged from the darkness again, he pushed a roll of denim, a length of rope, and a pair of wool socks into her hands.

"The britches will be too big. I figure you can use the rope to cinch them in at the waist."

Eden hugged the clothing to her chest. "Thank you."

He nodded and gestured toward the horses. "I need to rub down the animals, take them to the creek for water, and give them some grain before I start cooking. While I'm doing that, you can change here by the fire. I'll keep my back to you. You've got my word on it."

Eden watched him disappear into the shadows again. He wanted her to strip naked by the fire where he might see? Not on her life. As reluctant as she was to move her aching body or leave the warmth of the flames, she sought privacy behind some bushes before she peeled off the jacket and shirt Matthew had lent her. With a quick sniff, she determined that the jeans were clean. They smelled of leather and soap, but no body odor clung to them. The socks were fresh, too.

Relieved that he hadn't given her filthy garments to wear, she set herself to the task of stripping off her torn dress, boots, and underwear. As quickly as possible, she put the shirt back on to shield her modesty, then buttoned the front with shaky hands. Just as Matthew had predicted, the jeans were too large, so she used the rope as a makeshift belt, then sat on the ground to roll up the cuffs. The oversize wool socks felt heavenly on her ice-cold feet.

"You decent yet?" he called from the darkness.

The question was telling. He truly had kept his back turned and obviously thought she was still by the fire. "Almost!" she called back.

She grabbed the jacket and put it back on, then stared at the vague outline of her discarded clothing. The thought of wearing the garments again filled her with revulsion. She never wanted to see them. They would always remind her of the Sebastians and dredge up horrible memories. The bloomers were badly torn, and the toe of Pete's boot had broken some of the whalebone in the corset. The skirt was still mostly intact, though, and her practical nature wouldn't allow her to leave it. Out in the wild, one never knew when extra cloth might come in handy.

She collected her boots and lifted the

skirt between her right thumb and forefinger, holding it well away from her body. She turned her back on the other clothing. For all she cared, birds and squirrels could make nests with the cloth, and varmints could consume the whalebone.

As she moved back toward the light, Eden glanced up at the limitless expanse of dark blue sky where the Rockies rose, craggy and coal black, to loom over the landscape. Their vastness made her feel tiny, insignificant, and completely cut off from everything familiar to her.

"I'm dressed now," she called out as she drew near the fire.

Coulter moved toward her, a dark blur that took on definition as he came closer to the flickering amber glow. He had the well-oiled, loose-hipped stride of a horseman, his broad shoulders shifting with every step of his lean, powerfully muscled legs. She saw that he held a whiskey jug in his hand. After pulling the cork, he extended the bottle to her.

"Bottoms up. It'll warm you from the inside out."

Eden accepted the jug, tipped its mouth to her lips, and took two generous swallows.

With a tremulous smile, she handed it back to him. "I'm sorry I leaped to conclusions and called you those awful names."

His white teeth flashed in a brief smile. "I've been called worse."

"Still, I hope you'll accept my apology."

"Like I said earlier, you did nothing you need to apologize for." The firelight played over his face, delineating with shadows the sharp bridge of his nose and the chiseled cut of his cheekbones above his beard. As he met her gaze, his eyes glinted like molten silver. "The whole mess was my fault, not yours. I should have told you I was riding in a circle and explained why." He rubbed his whiskery jaw. "Just didn't occur to me."

"Because you mistakenly believed I couldn't tell north from south?"

He shoved the cork back into the mouth of the jug and set it on the ground near her feet. "I guess that'll teach me never to judge a book by its cover." Gesturing at the whiskey, he said, "Help yourself to more if you'd like. I still have work to finish up. Then I'll get busy cooking those fish."

A few minutes later, when Matthew returned to the fire to erect a spit for the trout, he found Eden huddled on her side, sound asleep. *Good.* A nap might make her feel better. He went to get his bedroll, which consisted of a quilted pallet and a wool blanket. He hated to let her lie on the cold ground, but unless he woke her, he had no choice. Instead he carefully covered her with the bedding and then hunkered at the opposite side of the fire to stave off his hunger with some jerky.

He allowed her to sleep until his belly started to rumble again. Then he set to work on their evening meal, being as quiet as possible, no easy task when he was pounding on a stick with a rock. She stirred awake and blinked sleepily at him.

"Sorry I woke you."

Stifling a yawn, she hooked an arm tightly over her side to sit up. The gesture wasn't lost on Matthew. She'd been favoring her ribs all day, giving him cause to wonder if Pete Sebastian had busted a couple of them with the toe of his boot.

Hesitant to admit that he'd seen Pete kick her, because then she'd know he'd also seen everything else the bastards had done to her, he settled for asking, "You hurt?"

She winced as she shifted to get comfortable. "Just very sore. It'll get better with time. How long was I asleep?"

"Three, maybe three and a half hours. I figured you needed the rest, so I held off on cooking for a while."

"Thank you. I truly did need the rest."

Her gaze fixed on the flames, her expression grew distant. She barely glanced at him as he speared the fish and suspended them over the fire. It reminded him of the way she'd looked last night while the Sebastians had bedeviled her. He could only hope she wasn't recalling what they'd done to her. He wasn't sure how he would handle it if she started crying again. Not that he would blame her if she did. Most of the females he knew would be off balance for months after going through something like that. Even his mother, one of the strongest, most resilient women he'd ever known, might have had trouble coming to grips with it.

"You feeling okay?" he asked.

Her eyes still swollen and puffy from weeping, Eden met his gaze and nodded. "Better than I was. I'm sorry I fell apart that way."

"No worries. You were taken hostage by a bunch of brutes and mauled, most likely ever since they took you. If anyone has a right to fall apart, I reckon it's you." The instant the words left his mouth, Matthew wanted to call them back. "Sorry. I don't mean to remind you of things best forgotten. It's just that I think you're being a little hard on yourself. Most women and a lot of men couldn't handle what happened as well as you have."

She lifted her shoulders in a shrug, then watched as he drew the mixings for corn bread from a pack, measured out the dry ingredients, then added water. After giving the concoction a good stir, he spread some coals at the edge of the fire and set the pan on them. His campfire bread wasn't the best-tasting stuff, but it would be warm and fill their empty spots. Along the trail, that was about all a body could hope for.

Rocking back on his boot heels, he fixed Eden with a long look. She was gazing into the fire again. Under the remaining streaks of dry mud, her sunburned face still managed to look pale. His heart twisted at the pain in her eyes. He leaned forward to give the fish a turn and then sat back on his heels again, uncomfortable because she was unearthing emotions within him that he hadn't felt in a very long time.

"I'm sorry I didn't get you away from them sooner."

"How did you even know I needed to be rescued?" she asked.

Matthew wondered why his first reaction to a question was always a reluctance to answer. It was natural for her to ask what had led him to that camp and motivated him to risk his life getting her out.

"I had been following the Sebastians' trail for several days and happened upon the train shortly after it was robbed."

"You were *there*?" Her blue eyes quickened with sharp interest. "At the train, I mean?"

He nodded. "I followed the Sebastians' tracks straight to it. The conductor—at least, I'm guessing that's what he was—told me you'd been abducted."

"Did you . . . did you see my mother?" she asked. "An older, well-dressed lady with blond hair?"

"I did."

"Was she all right? Please tell me they didn't harm her."

"Aside from being very worried about you, she looked fine." Matthew turned the bread pan again. "I don't think they hurt her."

Eden released a taut breath and blinked tears from her eyes. "Thank *God*." Her mouth quivered at the corners. "And the others? Was anyone else killed?"

"The train fellow said they had three dead and one man wounded. His ribs got busted up during the collision."

Her shoulders slumped, and she pressed a hand to her mouth for a moment. "There were already three dead when Wallace Sebastian carried me off the train. I was so afraid his brothers might let fly with more bullets. Every time anyone opened his mouth, he got shot for his trouble."

Matthew hated that she'd witnessed the killings. He almost uttered a curse but managed to bite it back in the nick of time, knowing it was an unsuitable word to use in mixed company. The thought no sooner passed through his mind than he backed up to analyze it. How long had it been since he'd worried about or even considered what was appropriate to say in front of a lady? Three years, he guessed. No big surprise. He hadn't been around a real lady since leaving Oregon.

He turned the fish, feeling ill at ease. His social skills had become so rusty that a simple conversation made him feel as if he were treading on a thin layer of ice and might fall through into deep water at any moment.

"Thank you for coming to get me," she said shakily.

Matthew shot her a surprised look. He almost told her, flat out, that rescuing her had been forced upon him by circumstances, but for the second time in less than a minute, he managed to hold his tongue until his brain caught up with his mouth. "You're welcome. I'm just sorry I didn't get there sooner. They were pushing their horses way too hard, and I couldn't bring myself to do the same."

She shoved at her hair, which had come loose from its pins and lay over her shoulders, the copper curls gleaming in the firelight. "None of what happened was your doing, and I lived through it." She shivered and rubbed her arms through the jacket sleeves. Matthew made a mental note to add more wood to the fire as soon as their meal was cooked. "I was lucky, actually," she said faintly.

Lucky? Matthew tried to school his expression, but the statement bewildered him. After all that they'd done to her, how could she say that? Most people would be shaking a fist at heaven and crying, "Why me?"

She caught his questioning look and shrugged again. "They are terrible men."

Matthew knew as well as she did how terrible they were. He'd been coming upon their bloody leavings for three endless years. "Yes, they are," he agreed.

"It could have been much worse for me," she said, her voice so soft he almost didn't catch the words. "If not for Wallace's plan to sell me across the border to an old Mexican who will pay only for virgins, my trials would have been far more horrible. He allowed them to have their fun with me, and he participated as well, but he wouldn't allow them to rape me. He was afraid the old man would refuse to buy damaged goods."

Most of the women back home in Oregon

shied away from using the word *rape*, especially in front of a man. But Matthew was quickly coming to realize that plainspoken Eden Paxton didn't conform to all the usual norms. She was a woman of more contrasts than he'd ever encountered. "I wondered why the bastards stopped short."

She sent him a startled look. Then her eyes went bright with tears again—tears of humiliation this time. "You saw?"

In that moment Matthew wished he'd been born without a tongue. No wonder he didn't talk very much. He grabbed the square of leather he used as a pot holder and moved the pan of corn bread to the edge of the coals, where it wouldn't scorch.

"Yes, I saw some," he finally admitted. "After I found their camp, I had to lie low until they drank themselves stupid and passed out. Once I realized what they were doing, I stopped watching, though." It was the truth; he had stopped watching— not so much because he was a gentleman but because he hadn't been able to stomach it. "I wanted to shoot the sons of bitches, but I was afraid you'd get caught in the cross fire. I had to wait until it was safe to go in and get you."

Matthew realized, too late, that he'd let fly with a curse in spite of himself. For several minutes she said nothing. During the silence, he tried to imagine how he might feel in her position. It was one thing to endure such degradation and quite another to know someone else had witnessed it. He wanted to tell her that, despite all he'd seen, he'd come away with only high regard for her, but for the life of him, he couldn't put his thoughts into words. If he tried and made a mess of it, he might make her feel even worse.

When she finally spoke, her voice was pitched so low he could barely hear her. "While they did those things, I pretended I was somewhere else." She squeezed her eyes closed, her mouth quivering at the corners again. "I'd stare into the fire and imagine myself far away, walking with my mother to pick wildflowers or having good times with my brothers. It was the only way I could stay sane."

Matthew gave the spit a half turn. Anger as hot as the embers burned low in his belly. No woman should ever have to endure such treatment. That Eden had survived it and maintained her sanity was a miracle. It also gave testimony to her mettle. He wished he knew how to tell her that.

Instead, he settled for saying, "When I get you to a town, I'll double back and find them again. And when I do, I'll send every last one of them to hell."

A muscle twitched in the hollow of her cheek. She slowly lifted her lashes to meet his gaze. To his surprise, he saw that the tears he'd glimpsed had already burned away. "I wish I could be there to help send them off," she said, her voice hoarse with emotion. "Pete, especially. All of them are the scum of the earth, but he's the very worst."

"I know. I've seen his handiwork more times than I want to count."

She tipped her head to give him a questioning look. "Why have you been following them for so long? When I asked you earlier today, you didn't answer."

Matthew found it difficult to talk about Livvy and wanted to evade the question again. But the bruised look in Eden's eyes wouldn't let him take the easy way out. She had been honest with him, and he supposed she deserved the same frankness in return. "They raped and murdered someone who was very dear to me," he managed to say. "I swore over her grave that I'd hunt them down and make them pay. It's my bad luck that they're a slippery bunch. Except for once, when I ran one of the younger brothers to ground and sent him off to meet his Maker, last night is the closest I've ever come to catching them."

"And then instead of killing them, you had to rescue me?"

Matthew remembered how upset he'd been about that and felt ashamed. "I'll find them again. It's just a matter of sticking with it."

"Even if it takes you another three years?"

"Even so," he admitted. "There are some things a man has to do, no matter how long it takes." Other feelings pushed up from inside of him—as hot as lava from a volcano and just as eruptive, but he squelched them and only added, "Sometimes you can't turn your back, and for me, the Sebastians are a blight I have to wipe out. Until someone stops them, they'll just keep hurting people."

He drove two sticks in the ground near the fire and hung her boots over them to dry. Then he fetched his canteen, a dented washbasin, a bar of soap, and a towel so each of them could wash up before partaking of the meal. Eden knotted her long hair at the crown of her head and carefully washed the mud from her sunburned cheeks, which still bore purple bruises from the abuse she'd endured. When she drew the square of linen from her face, her delicate countenance caught his gaze. How a woman could still look so pretty after all she'd been through, he didn't know. He forced himself to look away.

After washing up himself, he tested the fish for doneness and fetched them each a plate. "Damn. I meant to make coffee and plumb forgot."

"We'll make two pots tomorrow to make up for it." She accepted the food that he handed across the fire to her, sniffed the fish, and made an appreciative sound low in her throat. "Yum. I haven't had a decent meal in six days."

"I don't know how decent it is by your standards, but it'll fill up your hollow spots."

"And just what do you think my standards are, Matthew Coulter?"

"Beats me, but they're bound to be more highfalutin than mine."

"Or so you think?"

Matthew felt off balance for a second. It had been so long since anyone had joked with him that he'd forgotten how to respond. She gave him a teasing look, once again making him admire her pluck. Eden Paxton was one hell of a lady. A rope burn marred her slender neck, and the vivid marks on her face told him that she'd endured punishing blows from the Sebastians' fists, but there she sat, less than twenty-four hours after escaping them, smiling slightly in the firelight.

She tucked into the meal, using her fingers without complaint and spitting bones into the fire with the expertise of a cowpoke who'd been spewing tobacco juice at flies most of his life. Matthew had forks and spoons in the packs, but fish and bread didn't call for either. Watching her eat, he nearly grinned. Considering that she'd asked for "utensils" earlier, he'd figured her to be fussy and prim; she was proving to be everything but.

"So tell me, how did you learn to handle a rifle?" he couldn't resist asking.

Cheek bulging with fish, she said, "My brother Ace taught me. He's of the opinion that women should be as proficient with weapons as men are."

"I agree," Matthew said. "It doesn't take a lot of strength to fire a rifle. A woman who knows her way around a weapon has a good equalizer at hand."

She wrinkled her nose in distaste, her expression reminding him of when she'd sniffed his jacket sleeve, which made him feel self-conscious and embarrassed again. "Ace took it to the nth degree, making me target-practice nearly every day after school. He also stood over me many a night after supper while I disassembled weapons, oiled the parts, and put them back together. Sometimes he even timed me."

The frustration that edged her voice made Matthew want to smile, which struck him as really strange. Normally he never felt like smiling anymore, but being in her company was rekindling the urge. "He's a smart man, your brother."

"Yes, well, at the time, I resented him for making me do all that stupid stuff. I was far more interested in becoming proficient at other things."

When she said the word *proficient*, Matthew thanked God his mother had insisted upon schooling him and his siblings at home after their formal education ended. At least he had a halfway respectable vocabulary. Eden had thrown only a couple of words at him today that had baffled him, *reticent* and *miscreant*. He'd known what *utensils* meant. He'd just never heard the term used in reference to a cup.

"Proficient at what other things?"

A pink flush crept up her neck. "Silly things—fixing my hair and kissing an imaginary beau in my bedroom mirror. When it happened for real, I wanted to do it exactly right. Boys may not worry about things like that, but most girls do."

His gaze caught on her sweet mouth. Any woman with soft, full lips like hers could get it exactly right without half trying. He shifted and rubbed the back of his neck. "Pardon me for pointing it out, but I think the target-practicing was more important."

"Yes," she agreed, her tone laced with regret. "Now that I'm older, I'm grateful for the knowledge and skill. If I'd been wearing my Colts when the train was held up, I might have saved several lives and spared myself a lot of heartache."

His gaze went to hers. "Did you say *Colts*?"

She took a bite of bread and once again spoke before swallowing. "My weapon of choice. Unfortunately, a lady in a silk traveling costume looks rather silly wearing a gun belt, so I packed my Colts and derringer in our camelback trunk. A lot of good the weapons were stowed away in the baggage car."

Matthew shook his head. "You truly are full of surprises. How good are you?"

"With a gun, you mean?" She shrugged slightly. "Good enough to get by."

"Which means?"

She graced him with another faint smile. "I'm not as fast as my brothers, but my aim is true. Why do you ask?"

"I've never met a lady who can slap leather. It's hard for me to wrap my mind around it, I guess."

"In my family, the oddity would be if I couldn't slap leather. Have you ever heard of Ace Keegan?"

"Most people have. He's a legend with a gun." He searched her gaze for a long moment, then narrowed his eyes. "No way. Your brother Ace is Ace *Keegan*?"

She nodded.

"You're having me on. How can that be? You have different surnames."

"He's my half brother. After his father died, our mother remarried."

"Well, butter my ass and call me a biscuit." He swept off his hat, stared into the bowl, and then settled it back on his head. With a low laugh, he said, "You truly must be good with a gun if Ace Keegan was your teacher. He's so famous, there were dime novels written about him. Is it true that he once took down six men with only five bullets?"

"The fifth bullet ricocheted, a freak accident actually, going through the first man, hitting a rock, and glancing off to hit the sixth man in the temple." She gestured with her half-eaten corn bread. "Ace says that ricochet was all that saved his hide that day. They never tell the whole truth of it in dime novels. They wanted it to sound as if he's so good he can fire his gun and kill two men in one swoop. He hates most dime novels, by the way. He says they glorify violence."

Still reeling from the discovery that he'd rescued Ace Keegan's sister, Matthew thought of the books he'd read about the man. "I suppose they do, at that. From what I gathered from the stories, though, Ace used his guns only to defend himself. It's not as if he went looking for trouble."

"No. Once he got a reputation with a gun, trouble came looking for him. That's how it goes for famous gunslingers. They can't have a cup of coffee in the town café without worrying about someone calling them out. He's married now and has two children. He straps on a gun belt only when he has no choice, his hope being that any upstarts looking to make a name for themselves will leave him alone." Her expression went suddenly sad. "This situation makes me feel terrible. I am sure that he and my other brothers are out there somewhere, trying to find me, and Ace is wearing his guns. You can bet on it. If he takes on the Sebastians and word gets out, his happy life with Caitlin and their children could be ruined."

Matthew helped himself to another piece of corn bread. He'd never thought about what it might be like for a man who had a reputation with a gun. "In the past, did a lot of upstarts go gunning for him?"

"So many that Ace lost count." She sighed wearily and set aside her half-eaten meal. "He told me once that most of those upstarts were little more than boys, that there's no way to describe how he felt afterward when he was the one left standing. It bothered him so much that he'd swear he wouldn't draw the next time, that he'd rather die than go through it again."

"But when it came right down to it, he always went for his gun?" Matthew had killed only one man, but even though he'd despised the bastard, he understood how Ace must have felt. "I'd do the same, I reckon. It's one thing to *think* about dying and quite another to actually do it when you're nose-to-nose with a revolver."

"I'm glad he could never just stand there and get shot," she said softly. "It wasn't as if he *wanted* to kill anyone. They gave him no choice."

"Before I left Oregon, I practiced with a

gun for three solid weeks to get good enough to take on the Sebastians. I'd read stories about your brother, and it was my aim to become just like him. Now, talking to you, I can only wonder what I was thinking. In the dime novels, they don't talk about the dark side of being a gunslinger. They just—"

"Glorify the violence?"

Matthew nodded. "Right before I set out after the Sebastians, I'd sold my spring calves for a goodly sum. After I hit the trail, I practiced damned near every night and spent a good deal of my cash to stock up on more ammunition."

"Did you accomplish your goal?" she asked. "Did you become as good as Ace?"

Matthew believed that he was pretty damned good, but being boastful didn't sit well with him. Instead he repeated her words: "I'm good enough to get by."

This time, the smile that touched her lips was full-blown and made her whole face seem to glow. In that moment as Matthew gazed across the fire at her, he decided that he'd never seen a more beautiful woman. Even sunburned, trail-worn, bruised all over, and swallowed by his clothes, she outshone every other female he'd ever clapped eyes on, including Livvy. Even as the thought moved through his mind, Matthew felt a stab of guilt. While his wife had been alive, he'd never looked at another woman. What kind of man was he that he could do so now, with her lying dead in a grave that his stupidity and carelessness had dug for her?

After cleaning up the supper mess, Matthew gave his only bedroll to Eden and got her settled near the fire for the night. With his saddle for a pillow and only his jacket for warmth, he would sleep in the darkness, where he wouldn't be blinded by firelight if the Sebastians came calling. Probably an unnecessary precaution, but he reasoned that Eden would feel more at ease if he kept his distance.

Right after stretching out on the ground, he sat back up again and lifted one side of his jacket to sniff himself. He detected nothing rank, which just went to prove that the old adage was true: After three days without bathing, a man could no longer smell himself. He had enjoyed talking with Eden tonight over the meal. Being around her, even for so short a time, was making him remember his other life—how it had felt to wash up before supper after a long day of hard work and laugh at the table over silly jokes, how good it had been to bow his head in thanksgiving before shoving food into his mouth, and what fine ladies his wife, mother, and sisters had been. After three years without dinner conversation, he realized not only that he'd lost his social ease, but also that he missed it and wanted it back. The first step, he decided, was to clean himself up.

Pushing back to his feet, Matthew went to rummage through his packs, praying the clothes he'd lent Eden weren't his only laundered ones. Toward the bottom, he found three pairs of fresh jeans and several clean shirts. He headed for the stream armed with soap, a towel, and his straight razor.

The water was colder than a witch's tit and nearly took his breath. He got used to it, though, and set to work scrubbing away the layers of grime and sweat on his skin and in his hair. After drying off and dressing, he laundered his soiled garments, cringing as he scrubbed. Now that he was clean, the stench of the clothing told him just how awful he must have smelled. *Damn*. He'd had no business taking a jab at Eden earlier that day for judging him by his appearance.

Matthew started to shave and then hesitated. His face was badly scarred, and the growth helped conceal some of that. Jesus had worn a beard, so it wasn't as if whiskers were unacceptable. Besides, Eden would be sure to ask what had happened if she saw his entire face, and he wasn't inclined to answer such questions. There was also the inexplicable fact that he didn't want her to see how ugly he actually was.

After returning to camp, Matthew stretched back out on the ground and contemplated the vastness of the starlit sky. Why did he care if Eden thought he was ugly? As soon as he could drop her off in a decent-size town, he would never see her again, so why did her opinion even matter? It didn't, he decided. It *couldn't*. He was a man, and he had eyes in his head, so he was aware of how pretty she was. But that was as far as it could go.

He drew his watch from his pocket and ran his thumb over the engraved words on the back. *Forever.* That had been his and

Livvy's vow to each other, to love each other forever. Now, after only twenty-four hours in the company of another woman, he was wavering on that promise.

No way. Matthew's word was his bond. He would never betray Livvy. *Never.*

Chapter Six

With the deepening darkness came a plummet in temperature that curled like icy fingers over the thick collar of Eden's jacket to send shivers down her spine. Even with the fire and Matthew's bedding to shield her, she grew so cold she couldn't sleep. Turning herself like the fish on a spit that Matthew had cooked earlier, she tried in vain to warm all parts of her body, but the heat of the flames failed to chase away the chill that had taken up residence deep in her bones. How on earth could Matthew sleep with only his coat to shield him?

Guilt lanced through her as she recalled

how Wallace had slept under two wool blankets while she huddled in misery on the icy ground with nothing to protect her from the cold. Now she was doing essentially the same thing to Matthew. Apparently, he possessed only one bedroll and had given it to her. Eden considered offering to share the pallet and blanket with him, but fear and revulsion held her back. If it came down to that, she would be the one to brave the elements, and he could have the bedding.

She'd just turned over again, hoping to warm her back, when his shadow fell across her. She squeezed her eyes closed in dread, thinking he meant to join her in the bed. She jumped with a start when he tossed more wood on the fire. Her body went limp with relief when he toed the pieces to get them burning and then returned to his own spot just beyond the firelight. *Thank you, God.* She was coming to trust Matthew to a degree, but what the Sebastians had done to her was still too fresh in her mind for her to trust any man completely.

Unable to drift off, Eden was aware that Matthew returned to stoke the fire several more times. With each of his visits, her guilt mounted. At this altitude, the night temperatures dropped to near freezing, even in the late spring. If she was shivering within a few feet of the flames, he had to be absolutely miserable.

Watching Eden toss and turn, Matthew was in a quandary. Keeping the fire built up hadn't helped. She was still shuddering from the cold and wasn't getting a wink of sleep. Tomorrow would be another grueling day, possibly twelve hours or more in the saddle. If she didn't get some rest, she might collapse from exhaustion. Only what could he do about it? As rusty as Matthew's social skills had become, he still remembered the rules of common decency. No matter what the reason, a man didn't share a bed with a lady who wasn't his wife, especially not with someone like Eden, who'd so recently endured sexual abuse. She panicked if he even touched her. How would she react if he slipped under that blanket and wrapped himself around her to share his body heat? He couldn't do that to her.

It was miserably cold, though. Even Matthew felt the chill, and he was accustomed to being exposed to the elements. He thought about giving her his jacket for extra warmth, but then he'd be tossing and turning himself, and the bottom line was, in order to save her life, he needed to be well rested and thinking sharp in the morning.

It was a hell of a pickle. As things stood, neither of them was getting any sleep. Matthew got up again to fetch more wood for the fire. Once the flames were reaching high, he returned to his chosen spot to sleep, but ended up staring worriedly at his charge instead. She turned one way, then another. He saw her chafe her arms through the jacket sleeves and rub her feet together, trying to chase away the chill. By morning, the poor girl would be an icicle. *Damn.* He didn't want to frighten her, but at least she'd recover from that. After all that she'd been through over the last six days, she might not survive if she caught pneumonia.

Still watching her, Matthew sat up. A lump that felt the size of a breakfast muffin had lodged at the base of his throat. She looked so fragile in the firelight. Despite her game attempt that evening to appear normal and chipper, she hadn't been able to eat all of her supper or hide how utterly worn-out she was.

For the last three years, Matthew had lived by the motto that a man had to do what he had to do. Right now, he regretted that, because what he had to do was not going to sit well with her. And that was putting it mildly.

Sometime later, Eden heard Matthew get up to throw more wood on the fire and then he startled her half to death by placing a hand on her shoulder. "I'm sorry, Eden. I meant to be a gentleman and let you have the bedroll, but I'm freezing my ass off. We'll have to share."

Share? Eden made fists in the wool blanket, staring up at his whiskery countenance. She'd come to believe that he was a decent man despite his ragged appearance, but that didn't mean she wanted to share a bed with him. "Pardon me?"

After setting his folded gun belt on the ground near her head, he drew off his Stetson, lifted an edge of the blanket, and slipped onto the pallet beside her. When he hooked an arm around her waist, she jerked as if she'd been stuck with a hat pin.

"Easy," he said near her ear. "I only mean to spoon with you, nothing more. If we share our body heat, maybe we can both get some rest."

Eden's heart leaped and then pounded against her sore ribs like a trip-hammer. "Spoon?" she echoed.

"Yeah, like two spoons tucked together in a drawer."

Eden was not an eating utensil, and as cold as it was, she had no intention of pretending to be. "Mr. Coulter, *no*, this is highly improper. If you need the bedroll, take it, by all means. But I'm not going to sleep with you."

"Why? You afraid the squirrels might tattle on us?" He tightened his arm around her waist, his broad hand heavy on the front of her jacket just beneath her breasts. When she stiffened and grabbed his wrist, he sighed, his breath stirring her hair. "That hand's not going anywhere. If you're thinking otherwise, get the thought straight out of your head."

Eden couldn't get the thought out of her head. She struggled against the steely circle of his arm, but he tightened his hold and slung one leg over hers to keep her from moving.

"Stop it," he said firmly. "If I meant to rape you, do you think I'd bother to be sneaky about it? All I want is to get you warm. You're on your last legs, Eden. You need sleep, and you can't get it when your teeth are chattering."

Eden couldn't bear to be touched, and it felt to her as if he were touching her *everywhere.* She tried to pry his arm from around her again, but it didn't budge. "Please, Mr. Coulter, don't do this. You can have the blankets. I'll be fine sitting up by the fire."

"I don't want the damned blankets," he said gruffly. "I want you to get some sleep. That's *all* I want. I'm not good with words, Eden. But this is about surviving. Do you understand what I'm saying?"

She tried to think of a response, but nothing came to her.

"Do you want to live?" he asked softly.

"Yes," she managed to push out, remembering that horrible moment when she'd chosen to eat rather than die.

"Then do what has to be done. You've

been on a horse for over thirty hours. You've been brutalized. Your body has needs, and right now, one of them is sleep. We can't make a bad situation better by catching pneumonia." He turned his hand despite her grip on it and enclosed her smaller fingers in his. "I could touch you anywhere I want. Am I?"

"No," she replied, hating herself for the squeak in her voice.

"Why do you suppose that is?"

Tears burned her eyes. She squeezed them tightly closed. "Because you don't want to?"

"Exactly. We need to stay warm. You need to rest. Until I get you somewhere safe, you're my responsibility. How will your brothers feel if I let you freeze to death? It's colder out here than a whore's tits in a snowstorm." He muttered something under his breath and in a louder voice said, "*Damn* it. Every time I open my mouth, I stick my foot in it."

He ran his thumb over her clenched knuckles, and the tears in Eden's eyes spilled over onto her icy cheeks, feeling hot against her skin.

His voice still thick, he added, "I've spent

three years alone, Eden, with only Smoky and Herman for company. The few times I rode with a posse, the other men were as rough around the edges as I was." He fell silent. "I haven't rubbed elbows with polite folks for way too long. I don't mean to sound like I was raised in a barn."

"I've spent five days with monsters," she replied, her voice shaking. "I don't mean to be difficult, but I'd rather go without sleep than do *this*."

"Your druthers don't play into it." He released an exasperated sigh and suddenly sat up. "Okay, fine, you win. There's more than one way to tree a coon."

She turned onto her back to stare incredulously up at him. With abrupt, frustrated jerks, he removed his jacket and flung it over her.

"*No*," she protested. "You'll freeze without a coat."

"I'll stay by the fire and be fine." He circled the pit and hunkered down. "Now, do me a big favor and go to sleep."

Wincing at the pain that danced over her ribs, Eden pushed to a sitting position. Now that he'd shed the jacket, she noticed that he'd changed into clean clothes and looked as if he'd taken a bath. Just the thought of getting in that icy water made her shiver more convulsively. To the left of the fire, he had erected a makeshift rack where wet jeans, a shirt, underwear, and socks had been hung to dry.

"I can't take your coat, Matthew. I felt guilty enough about hogging the bedroll."

"No choice. You can't sleep alone and you can't sleep with me. Maybe you'll be able to stay warm with the extra jacket. I can catch a few winks and be fine, but you've *got* to get some rest."

She knew he was right. She was beyond exhausted. "I appreciate the gesture, truly I do, but I can't take your coat."

"I *gave* you the coat. Remember the rule. You're to do what I say when I say it, and I'm telling you to go to sleep."

Eden sighed. "All right, *you* win. We can sleep together."

"You just said—"

"Forget what I said. I won't sleep a wink knowing that you have no jacket."

In the firelight, his incredibly blue eyes glinted like sapphires as he regarded her. "I won't take liberties," he finally said.

"I pray not."

"I've never forced myself on a woman in my life, and I'm sure as hell not about to start now."

"I didn't mean to offend you. It's just—" She broke off, searched for a way to explain, and in the doing, finally understood how frustrating it must be for him when he wanted to communicate a thought and couldn't. "I can't get them out of my head. The Sebastians, I mean. And when . . . when you touch me, even in impersonal places, I feel frantic."

He nodded his understanding and stared into the fire with a thoughtful frown. When he returned his gaze to her, he said, "Think of it this way. If I wanted to rape you, what's stopping me?"

Eden could only gape at him.

"You sure as hell couldn't stop me," he went on. "One second to pin you, three seconds to jerk those britches off, no contest." Propping an elbow on a bent knee, he rubbed a hand over his eyes and pinched the bridge of his nose. "Son of a *bitch*. I just did it again. If my mother was here, she'd wash my mouth out with soap."

Eden had a hysterical urge to laugh, a telltale sign that she truly was exhausted beyond all measure. Oddly, though, he had accomplished his goal with the bungled attempt to reassure her. She felt a little better. He was a strong man, could overpower her without half trying, and had had countless opportunities to do so if that had been his intent.

"Come to bed, Matthew."

He pushed slowly erect, looking nearly as weary as she felt. "You sure? I've lost sleep before and lived through it."

Pushing back a wave of apprehension, Eden patted a spot beside her. He retraced his steps around the fire pit, lifted the blanket, and joined her on the pallet. She rolled onto her side with her back to him, bracing herself for the weight of his arm around her. When it came, she flinched in spite of herself.

"You okay?" he asked huskily.

"No, but I'll live through it." Eden gulped and opened her eyes to stare blankly at the fire, willing herself to drift away into memories as she had so many times during her five days with the Sebastians, only she couldn't quite manage it. "Promise me. Promise me you won't touch me anyplace private."

He curled his hand over the throbbing place on her ribs, turned his face into her hair, and said, "You've got my word on it."

Eden still couldn't relax. Visions of what the Sebastians had done to her ricocheted through her mind. She gulped and tried to control a shudder that ran the full length of her body.

"I know you aren't much for conversation, Matthew, but could you talk to me for a while?"

"About what?" His voice rang with incredulity. "The whole idea here is to fall asleep."

"I know. I just need . . . a distraction so I can relax."

"A distraction?" His hand shifted slightly, and she jerked. "Easy," he whispered, using the same gentling tone that he'd employed with the abused bay gelding earlier that day. "What kind of distraction? I'm not a storyteller."

Eden didn't care what he said. "I just need you to talk. About anything. Tell me about Oregon. I've seen photographs, but I've never actually been there."

Silence. Finally he offered, "It's pretty there."

She waited expectantly, but he said

nothing more. Another crazy urge to laugh came over her. He hadn't lied. Words came very hard for him. "That's all you can say?"

"There are lots of trees."

"What kind?"

"Ponderosa pine."

Her eyes tried to drift closed and she blinked to stay awake, still too skittish to lower her guard completely. "Are there mountains?"

"Yeah, the Cascades."

Getting him to talk was as difficult as trying to scratch her own back. "Are they big mountains?"

"Yeah."

"What do they look like?"

"Like mountains."

Eden smiled sleepily. "Is there any snow on them?"

"Yeah, a lot of snow, even in summer. You can see them from the Lazy J."

"Is that the name of your family's farm?"

"It's a ranch, and yes, that's its name." He shifted to get closer to her, pressing his bony knees against the backs of hers. Eden stiffened at the more intimate contact. His scent surrounded her, a pleasant blend of clean skin, male muskiness, and faint traces of soap. "Never could figure out why my father named it that. Nothing about raising horses and cattle is lazy. We worked our asses off from dawn to dark, and then some."

Finally, he had volunteered a tidbit of information. "Who's *we*?"

"My pa, my brothers, and me."

"How many brothers do you have?"

"Eden, we *have* to get some sleep. We can't dawdle here tomorrow so you can rest up. The Sebastians would be on our asses like bears after honey."

"I know." Eden realized that she'd finally stopped shivering. Heat emanated from his big body, which was surrounding hers like a cozy blanket. "Just a little longer, Matthew, and then I'll shut up. How many brothers?"

"Three. Hoyt, Zedediah, and Gareth. I'm the oldest."

"Any sisters?"

"Breanna, Caira, and Dacey. Why does it *matter*?"

"It doesn't. I just need to hear your voice." Her eyes tried to close again. This time she didn't fight it. "Tell me about the Lazy J."

"Not much to tell. Just a ranch."

"Where is it in Oregon?"

"On the eastern side in the high desert. Pa found a grassy little valley with a running stream that keeps the meadows green and pretty. There's a lot of timberland around it for free-range grazing."

She could hear the yearning in his voice and blinked her eyes back open to say, "You miss it."

"Not as much as I used to."

"Will you go back after you've caught up with the Sebastians?"

"No. Nothing left for me there but sad memories."

Eden couldn't imagine never going home to see her family. "Where will you go then?"

"Not sure. Montana, maybe. It's damned pretty country, lots of elbow room. I'll find work. Save my money."

"So you can start your own ranch?"

"All I'm good at is running cattle and raising horses."

"What kind of cattle will you run?"

Eden never heard his reply. Between

one breath and the next, she dropped like a pebble into a black pool of exhaustion.

Eden awakened in the morning to the delicious smell of frying meat. To her surprise, the sun was already rising. She pushed up on an elbow and rubbed her eyes, then focused on Matthew, who was hunkered at the opposite side of the fire, the pinkish light of dawn playing like fireflies on his tousled dark hair. Though she couldn't be certain, the strands looked slightly damp, making her wonder if he'd already been to the stream to wash up.

"You should have wakened me. I can't be lolling around in bed all morning."

"I don't think the Sebastians have come in behind us yet, and you needed a good night's rest." At her bewildered look, he added, "Think of the circle we made as a racetrack. The horses all start at the same point, but the faster ones leave the slow ones behind. If the faster ones get enough of a lead, they eventually circle around and come in behind their competitors. *We* have a hell of a jump on the gang, so now I'm almost certain we're behind them, not the other way around."

Eden could picture a racetrack, and what he said made sense. "You must think I'm hopelessly obtuse."

It was his turn to look perplexed. "Dumb, you mean?" He shook his head. "You're not dumb, Eden, only exhausted."

Even after a bath and wearing fresh clothing, he had a lean, rugged look about him, but this morning, Eden found it more appealing than frightening. Studying his burnished countenance, she found herself wishing he would shave so she could see the rest of his face. She suspected that without the whiskers, he would be extremely handsome, with strong, masculine features.

Her boots had dried overnight. She struggled to pull them on over the bulky wool socks, which was no easy task and made her ribs feel afire with pain. When she finished fastening the footwear, she took a moment to catch her breath.

"My teeth feel as if they've grown a fur coat," she blurted.

He chuckled. "Want to borrow my boar-bristle toothbrush?"

"You carry a toothbrush?"

He narrowed an eye at her. "Of course. How else would I keep my teeth clean?"

He returned his attention to the frying pan. "I know using someone else's toothbrush sounds nasty, but you could clean it with some whiskey."

Eden was in no position to be picky. "Thank you. I may take you up on the offer. I've never gone six days without brushing my teeth or taking a bath in my whole life."

He flashed her a crooked grin. "When we make camp tonight, maybe we'll have time for you to get a good scrub. For now, you ready for a hodgepodge breakfast?"

Taking care not to jostle her ribs, which felt as tender this morning as they had yesterday, she turned onto her knees to roll up the blanket and pallet. He was full of odd terms to describe the trail rations he tossed together. "What exactly is a hodgepodge breakfast?"

"A little of this and a little of that. I don't want to fire a gun for fear the sound will carry, so I rigged up a spear this morning, using a long branch and my hunting knife. I got us a rabbit, a squirrel, and some frogs." He cut her a questioning glance. "You won't turn up your nose at frog legs, will you?"

Though Eden hadn't kept a running count, she felt fairly certain she'd never heard him string that many sentences together without being prompted. "Not as long as they aren't hopping in the pan."

"Truth is, they're actually pretty tasty, and I make sure they're all hopped out before I serve them." He gave a frog leg a prod with the fork as if to prove his point. "My Livvy was a finicky eater, and fussy about what she cooked. If I wanted frog legs, I had to fix them myself, so I got plenty of practice."

Eden heard a trace of sadness in his voice, and his use of the word *was* told her that the woman Livvy was probably dead. "She was your wife?"

He nodded. Then, as if he feared she might urge him to talk about her, he said, "I was serious about your being welcome to use my toothbrush. Anytime you want it, just holler, and I'll get it out of the pack."

"I'll wait until after I've eaten." She angled her head to look into the frying pan. "My goodness, that's a lot of meat."

"What we don't eat now, we can have for lunch. I don't know about you, but I get sick-to-death tired of eating jerky three times a day."

"Amen. I liked jerky a week ago, but now the longer I chew, the bigger it seems to get."

"I hear you. I've even used it in stew, believe it or not. Sometimes I don't have time to hunt."

Eden was about to stand up with the bedroll in her arms when she noticed a gun belt folded neatly on the dirt near where their pallet had been. The double holsters sported two Colt revolvers. She shot a bewildered glance at Matthew, thinking he might not have put his gun belt back on after rising, but he was wearing his weapons, leather thongs anchoring the twin holsters to his well-muscled thighs.

"They're yours on loan," he said, inclining his head at the weapons. "I figure any lady taught to shoot by Ace Keegan ought to be armed. I may be glad of the backup if the Sebastians take us by surprise."

Eden extended a trembling hand to touch the butt of one revolver. Tears sprang to her eyes. Men of the West prized their weapons and rarely let anyone else use them. For him to loan her his spare guns was a very generous and extraordinary gesture. Having her own sidearms would give her a fabulous feeling of empowerment. She would be able to defend herself now.

"Thank you, Matthew."

"Strap them on. Guns aren't very useful unless you're wearing them."

Peeling off the heavy jacket, Eden bent to pick up the gun belt. To her immense disappointment, it was too large for her waist, even with the tongue of the buckle in the very last notch. Matthew drew the meat to the edge of the fire and came around the pit, drawing his hunting knife from its scabbard.

"Easy fix," he said. "I'll just add another notch."

Eden shook her head. "You needn't do that. This is too nice a gun belt to poke holes in it."

"One little hole won't hurt it any," he insisted. "Pull it up tight so I can mark the spot."

Reluctantly Eden did as he said, making sure the belt rested over her hip bones. As he bent low to twist the tip of the knife in the leather, the side of his face lightly grazed her breast, and she instinctively jerked away. He straightened and met her gaze.

"I'm sorry," she said. "I just—"

"No need to apologize." He grasped the long blade in his fingers to turn the handle of the knife toward her. "You want to do it?"

Eden accepted the weapon. When she finished marking the belt, he sat by the fire with it draped over his lap to add another notch. Within seconds, the gun belt had been altered to fit her. As she strapped it on and leaned forward to knot the holster ties around her thighs, her gratitude was inexpressible. Friend or foe? She was coming to think she finally had an answer to that question.

She felt indescribably wonderful as she straightened with the Colts riding her hips. *Restored* was the word that sprang to mind. Yesterday, she'd felt like a shadow of herself, but now, wearing the guns, she was Eden Paxton again, daughter to Dory, sister to four wonderful brothers who loved her enough to die for her.

"Thank you," she said again.

She tested the pull of the leather on the revolvers. The weapons slipped easily from the holsters, just the way she liked. Next she began checking the cylinders.

"They're loaded," he told her.

Nevertheless, Eden gave each cylinder a whirl. Matthew inclined his head in approval. "Your brother trained you well. Always make certain your weapons are fully loaded."

She returned the nod. "And well-oiled and clean. You do a fine job of keeping your equipment in first-rate condition."

"Over the last few weeks, I've kept my weapons cleaner than I have myself, by far."

She settled both revolvers into the holsters and ran her fingers over the looped belt to be certain she had extra bullets. "If they show up now, I won't feel so afraid."

His expression turned suddenly solemn. "If they do show up and get the upper hand, save your last bullet."

Eden needed no further explanation. In hard country like this, a wise woman always saved the last bullet for herself. The long and short of it was, there were worse fates than dying, and for her, falling into the hands of the Sebastians again would be one of them. With the Colts at hand, she wasn't that worried about it, though. She'd never had to kill a man, and she would be pleased to keep it that way, but if left without a choice, she felt confident in her ability to hold her own. With Matthew standing beside her, her odds of success were even better.

He crouched back down by the fire and repositioned the meat over the flames. "So, Miss Paxton, show me your stuff."

She nearly laughed, and that felt absolutely marvelous. As recently as yesterday, she'd thought she might never want to laugh again. "My *stuff*?"

"Don't actually fire the gun, of course. A shot may bring them doubling back." He grabbed the fork to turn the quartered meat. As he sprinkled salt over the works, he glanced up. "But I would like to see you slap leather. I've never known a female fast draw."

"That's me, a bona fide Calamity Jane." Eden slipped the guns in and out of the holsters a few more times to get a good feel for them. Noting Matthew's expectant gaze, she began to feel self-conscious.

"I'd feel silly, drawing on nothing. And it's rude to show off."

"When your partner wants to know whether or not he can count on you to guard his back, it's not showing off. It's a necessary exhibition of your skill." He grabbed up the square of leather he used as a pot holder and sent it sailing. "Draw on that."

Taken off guard, Eden forgot to feel silly and snapped the Colts from the holsters.

"Holy hell," Matthew said, his voice pitched low in awe. "You're lightning quick, lady."

Eden's cheeks grew hot. In truth, she'd been slower than usual because of her hurt ribs. She slipped the guns back into the holsters. "Anyone can appear to be fast," she said. "But speed counts for nothing if you can't hit your target."

"You can hit it." Matthew's blue eyes held hers. Yesterday morning, Eden had judged his eyes to be cold, chilling her like ice. Today, a flick of his gaze warmed her skin like a physical touch. "I know good when I see it. You can probably draw that fast and knock a walnut off a tree."

"An acorn," she corrected. "At sixty-five yards."

He arched his dark brows. "A Colt's only dependably accurate at fifty yards, maybe sixty, at a stretch."

"Depends on who's firing it." Eden donned the jacket again, retrieved the square of leather, and joined him by the fire. "No brag, just information for my partner."

He flashed one of those crooked grins, the left side of his mouth remaining immobile. "Information appreciated. How did you become that accurate at such a distance?" He'd no sooner posed the question than he added, "Don't answer that. Ace, again, I suspect."

Eden returned the smile. "Ace, the bane of my existence."

Matthew filled a tin cup with coffee and handed it to her. "He was a hard taskmaster."

Eden took a sip of the scalding brew. It tasted so good she closed her eyes for a moment in pure pleasure. "He wanted me to be ready for anything—high wind, pistol grips slick with rain, swollen holster leather. You name it, he put me through it." She took another sip of coffee. "Our mother's second husband was murdered before I was born. Ace was about eleven and saw it happen. Being only a boy, he was powerless to stop it and couldn't protect Mama, either. I think it troubles him, even now, and I'm sure that's why he pushed me so hard. He needed to know I would be able to defend myself, no matter what."

Matthew checked the meat. "Makes sense." He angled her another thoughtful look. "I'm sorry about your pa."

Eden's throat went tight. She considered telling him that Joseph Paxton Senior had not been her father, but then she thought better of it. Matthew didn't strike her as being a narrow-minded, self-righteous man, but there was little point in putting him to the test by telling him the truth about her parentage. A lot of people looked down their noses at bastards, always had and probably always would.

"Losing him was much harder for my mother and brothers than it ever was for me," she settled for saying. "I never really missed having a father because I always had Ace. He was twelve years older than me, and by the time I came to realize that most other children my age had a pa, Ace was a grown man. I thought of him as my father and loved him as if he were." She gave the coffee a swirl and smiled. "Never mind that I wanted to shoot him more times than not for making me do all that infernal target-practicing."

Matthew threw back his dark head and barked with laughter. When his mirth subsided, he asked, "How on earth could you practice that often, living in the city?"

"It wasn't until Ace started winning big at cards and had made some lucrative investments that we moved into town. I was about thirteen. Even then, he dragged me to the country several times a week to target-practice."

"I have a feeling you must have been a handful as a girl."

"Headstrong," she confessed, "and cursed with a quick temper. I must have been a handful. Ace never lost patience with me, though. Joseph, the next oldest, was another story. We fought like cats and dogs."

In case he had only one cup, Eden handed it back to Matthew so they might share the coffee. He obliged her by taking a sip before returning it to her.

"You may meet my brothers, you know. I know they're looking for me."

"I'm sure they are. If someone took one

of my sisters, my brothers and I would be out for blood."

"Yes, well, if mine catch up with us, stand aside and let me do the talking. If my brothers think you were in on abducting me, they'll bury you first and ask questions later."

Matthew nodded as if that made perfect sense to him. Given the fact that he'd been dogging the Sebastians for three long years, probably to avenge his wife, Eden figured he understood how her brothers might be feeling even better than she did. She admired Matthew's stick-to-itiveness. Such tenacity showed the true nature of a man's character. He wasn't a coward or a quitter.

Eden realized that she'd told him quite a lot about her family and he'd said very little about his own. Setting aside the cup of coffee, she sent the square of leather sailing high into the air and cried, "Draw!"

Remaining in a crouch, he whipped around and drew both of his Colts with such speed that Eden barely saw his hands move. "Not bad," she told him. When he shot her a disgruntled look, she grinned and added, "Even Ace would give you high marks. All the practicing paid off."

"No fair. You gave me no warning."

"Neither will the Sebastians," she reminded him. "And you were still impressively fast."

He slipped the guns back into their holsters and returned his attention to their hodgepodge meal. "Four acorns, sixty-eight yards."

"No matter what the terrain or weather?" she asked incredulously.

"I practiced on the trail. I didn't have your brother to prod me, but the weather and terrain had a way of changing on a daily basis."

Eden took another sip of coffee. "As a partner, you'll do. You've got me beat slightly in distance, but I have you bested in acorns. I've emptied both guns and taken off an acorn with every bullet."

"Ha, now you tell me. Sounds like a tall tale to me."

"No brag, just fact." She sent him a teasing smile. "If we get out of this with our hides intact, I'm up for a shooting match. How about you?"

He bit back a smile. "You're on. Just don't be disappointed if I whip you."

Eden laughed. "Same goes. I would hate to bruise your male ego."

That earned her another lopsided grin. He dished up some meat for each of them, accompanied by some of the trail bread he'd made last night. Between bites, Eden said, "I'm guessing my brothers headed for the border after Mama told them what happened. Otherwise they would be here by now. They must have thought the gang would head for Mexico."

Matthew bit off a chunk of rabbit and pocketed it in his cheek. "Normal-thinking criminals would have. That's the trouble with the Sebastians. They never do what normal-thinking people believe they will. Since I've been tracking them, I've ridden with a few posses, and the Sebastians always gave them the slip. Every damned time, it was because the lawmen tried to anticipate their next move. With the Sebastians, you can't do that. They'll do the exact opposite of what I think they will every single time. In ways, they're dumber than stumps, but they're also wily as foxes and completely haphazard."

"They'll eventually head for the border. They spoke of a hideout somewhere in Mexico, and I got the impression it was near the Rio Grande. I also think it must be near a town because—" Eden broke off and averted her gaze. She preferred not to recount the gang members' conversations about the Mexican whores they looked forward to bedding. "Wallace said a few things that led me to believe there might be a cantina within easy riding distance of their hideout. A place called Margarita's."

Matthew frowned thoughtfully. "Thanks for the information. It may come in handy someday."

After finishing their meal, Eden cleaned up the mess while Matthew readied the animals for the trail. Then he set himself to the task of erasing all trace of their camp. After dousing the fire with water, he carried the charred wood into a copse and buried it. Then he threw dirt over the blackened earth and brushed away all their tracks with a leafy branch.

"Will that fool them, do you think?" Eden asked.

"Maybe, maybe not. I just don't want to leave them an engraved invite if they've somehow covered enough ground to circle around and come in behind us before we can get out of here."

"Do you think that's likely?"

He shook his head. "I doubt they got all their horses gathered back up until yesterday afternoon. Even if they rode all last night and managed to find our tracks where we left that stream, no easy task in the dark, we've still got at least a good eight hours' jump on them."

Before Eden knew it, she was once again in the saddle. At least this morning she felt more rested. "I forgot to brush my teeth," she called out.

He turned in the saddle. "Too late now. You'll have to wait until we stop for the night."

A few minutes later, he drew his horse to a halt and dismounted to examine some tracks. When he straightened, he was grinning. "Just as I suspected. This sign is still pretty fresh, twelve hours old, give or take a couple of hours either way. We're behind them."

Eden stared at the tracks. "What if they figure out we rode in a circle and double back on us?"

"They won't figure that out right away. We rode north, then west for a' ways. They may get suspicious when our tracks veer south, but they won't know for sure we rode in a circle until our trail cuts east. By then, they'll be so far into it, they'll keep going rather than double back."

He gazed eastward for a long moment. "Decision-making time, Eden. Do we make a beeline for a town, which is what they'll expect us to do, or do we ride in another circle?"

Eden followed his gaze, wondering what communities lay in that direction. The only towns in Colorado she knew much about were Denver and No Name, which weren't that far apart as a crow flew. But they were quite some distance away, to the southeast if she wasn't mistaken. She yearned to say they should head for help. Her ribs were paining her again, making it difficult to breathe, and though she'd slept well for a few hours last night, exhaustion was already returning.

Sadly, if the Sebastians were as wily about losing posses as Matthew claimed, they might be just as clever when it came to running prey to ground. As confident as she felt with two Colts riding her hips, she also had to factor in the possible element of surprise. If the Sebastians intercepted her and Matthew as they rode toward a community, catching them off guard, they would be at a disadvantage.

"I think we should do the unexpected," she pushed out. "At least for a few days. Who knows? Maybe we'll get lucky and my brothers will find us."

For an instant, she thought she saw admiration flash in Matthew's eyes. Then he adjusted the brim of his battered Stetson to shade his face from the early-morning light. "You sure? I know you must be exhausted beyond bearing after six days on the trail."

"I'm sure." And suddenly Eden was. Since last night, she was starting to trust this man in a way she couldn't rightly explain. "They'll expect us to head straight for help. The last thing they'll think we might do is ride around in circles out here."

"They'll really be confused if we take the same route today as we did yesterday."

Eden shifted to get more comfortable in the saddle. She appreciated his willingness to confer with her and take her opinion into account before making a decision.

"The trick to outsmarting them is to do the exact opposite of what they expect," he continued. "Following the same circle we made yesterday will accomplish that for today. They'll be scratching their heads, wondering what the hell we're up to. Their tracks are mixed in with ours now, too. That'll make it harder for them to follow us." He remounted his horse and grabbed Herman's lead rope. "Tonight we'll study a map. Come morning, we'll pretend to head for a town, then veer off course to head for another one, or make another circle in a totally new area. That's how they've escaped, again and again—by riding willy-nilly, first one way and then another."

It sounded like a good plan to Eden. She just prayed she could stay in the saddle. She fell in behind Matthew, keeping her bay in his tracks as much as possible. When they reached the stream where they'd stopped to rest the horses yesterday, he once again unburdened the animals and rubbed them down with burlap.

"May I ask you something?" she said.

"Shoot."

"Why do you remove all the gear from the animals and rub them down every time we stop?"

"Saddle sores. Normally, it isn't necessary, but these animals are being worked hard every day without a break. I worry that the constant rub of the gear will raise blisters. I like to get the sweat off of them and check them over. If one of them gets a sore, I'll catch it early."

That made sense to Eden. As much as she'd been around horses, she'd never lived on the trail, using a horse from dawn to dark every single day.

They dined on the leftover meat from breakfast. Before leaving, Eden smeared her cheeks with mud again for protection from the sun. When she returned to camp, Matthew handed her a weather-beaten and badly flattened straw hat with a long crack in the crown.

"I carry it for hot weather. Felt hats make me sweat in the late summer."

"Thank you."

"It hasn't held up very well, being stuffed in a pack, but it'll keep the light out of your eyes and help protect your skin."

He truly was talking more today than he had yesterday, Eden decided. Maybe being around another person was loosening his tongue. He still wasn't what she would call chatty, but she was grateful for a reprieve from the long silences.

As the day wore on, she took note of his skill at tracking. He often dismounted to hunker over the hoofprints and trace their edges lightly with a fingertip. He also toed the horse dung with his boot.

"How fresh do you think it is?" she asked.

"About twelve hours old." He graced her with a slow grin. "They truly did play heck catching all those horses. Would love to have been a fly on the wall—or maybe I should say on a pine tree. I'll bet the air turned blue."

Eden felt sorry for the horses. She'd seen how cruelly the Sebastians treated them. "If you belonged to those monsters, you'd run, too, if you ever got a chance."

He glanced up. Their gazes locked. An electrical feeling charged the air between them for a moment. Matthew's smile slowly faded and his jaw muscle started to tic. Once he had remounted his horse, he removed a gold timepiece from his pocket and thumbed the back of the case. Since he didn't open the watch, she wondered at the gesture, especially when she glimpsed the bleakness of his expression. *Livvy*, she thought. The watch had probably been a gift from her. At least three years had passed since her death, yet he still mourned her. Eden had once mistakenly believed that she'd found true love. Now, seeing Matthew's grief etched all over his dark face, she knew for certain that what she'd felt for John had been pale in comparison to what Matthew had felt for his wife.

The realization filled her with an inexplicable emptiness. When she recovered from this ordeal and could tolerate the opposite sex again, she wanted to find that kind of love. Not the paper-thin, superficial love that she'd shared with John, but the sort that ran bone deep and refused to release a heart even after death. To be loved that deeply—ah, it would be grand. Someday she wanted a man to pull his watch from his pocket, to trace the words she'd had engraved for him in the gold, thinking of her with heartfelt yearning.

Chapter Seven

That evening, Matthew stopped to make camp at the same place they'd stayed the previous night. Before building a fire pit or taking the gear off the animals, he crouched down to study the ground. Eden walked over to stand beside him.

"Are they making the circle a second time?" she asked.

He nodded. "Judging by the horse dung, they came through here about six hours ago."

Eden quickly calculated how many miles the Sebastians were from them and breathed a sigh of relief. *Twenty-four miles.*

That was a lot of distance on horseback. "They've lost time then."

"Probably lost our tracks for a while where we rode in the stream."

"Then your trick worked."

He nodded again and pushed erect. "Tomorrow we need to go into a totally different area, and I'll have to pull some other tricks from under my sleeve."

As Eden worked with him, caring for the animals and gathering firewood, she recalled how she'd trained the rifle on him the last time they'd been there and felt ashamed all over again. Over the last two days, Matthew had proved to be many things, but a scoundrel wasn't one of them.

Watching him as he groomed the horses, she felt her throat tighten with emotions she couldn't define. Against the magnificent backdrop of the majestic mountains and huge ponderosa pines, he looked as rugged and elemental as the terrain around him. Yet he touched the animals with such gentleness, his large, callused hands smoothing their manes and delivering scratches behind twitching ears. His voice carried to her through the twilight, deep and soothing. She couldn't catch the words he spoke, but his tone said it all. He truly cared for Smoky and Herman, and he was forging a fast friendship with the abused bay gelding as well. The horse nickered and grunted, clearly grateful for his new master's kindness. The equine's utterances made the horse sound almost as if it were trying to talk, and Matthew replied as if he understood every inflection.

After being with the Sebastians for so many days, Eden was as grateful for Matthew's kindly nature as the bay gelding was. Today on the trail, he had circled the clematis and other wildflowers that he'd allowed Smoky to trample yesterday—not, she felt certain, because he cared a whit about the blossoms, but because he knew they were important to her. That told Eden more about the man than he could possibly know.

When the animals had been tended, Matthew gathered rocks to build a small fire pit and then arranged the wood so they could enjoy another hot meal for supper. Eden was hungry and fantasizing about the concoction he might throw together when he began fishing through a pack and then approached her with an armful of bathing paraphernalia and a set of clean clothing.

"You first," he said as he thrust everything into her arms. "I'll get the fire going while you're gone so you can warm up when you get back. That water is bound to be ice-cold."

Eden accepted the armload and turned to go.

"Oh, wait a minute," he called. "Let me clean the toothbrush so you can use it. If it's all the same to you, I'd rather not spoon with a woman who's sprouted fur on her teeth."

The twinkle in his blue eyes made her smile, despite the bone-deep weariness that had her struggling to stand erect. "If I have fur on my teeth, you've undoubtedly developed a heavy winter coat on yours."

He winked. "Nope. I brushed last night and plan to again tonight after you have a go."

As Eden headed off toward the creek a few moments later, she marveled that she wasn't worried about Matthew sneaking peeks at her while she bathed. He wasn't that kind of man, and knowing that about him chased away the last traces of fear she'd been feeling for nearly a week. There were horrible men in the world, a fact that Ace had tried to drive home to her since childhood. But the goodness of humanity far outweighed the bad. She wouldn't spend the rest of her life being afraid of every stranger she came across. She *wouldn't*. Instead she would remind herself that there were far more Matthew Coulters in the world than there were Pete Sebastians.

As Matthew had predicted, the water was so cold that it nearly took Eden's breath away, but she determinedly immersed herself. After brushing her teeth and setting the toothbrush on a rock, she grabbed the bar of soap and began lathering up. At first, she felt almost lighthearted. She'd been denied the luxury of cleanliness for far too long, and finally getting to wash felt absolutely glorious. She had no sooner finished shampooing her hair, though, than her mood changed.

Filth. Images of the Sebastians filled her head. She could almost feel their hands on her. Overcome by a compelling need to rid herself of their touch, she waded into the shallows, returned the soap to the rock, and began scooping up handfuls of sand to scour her skin. To scrape off their scent, the lingering traces of their obscenity. At the edges of her mind, she knew the chafing passes should be causing her pain, but what little discomfort she felt seemed distant and unimportant compared to her need to feel pure again.

She wasn't sure how long she scrubbed, only that the sound of Matthew's low voice suddenly jerked her up short. "Eden, if you keep on that way, you'll rub yourself raw."

Eden whirled so quickly that her long hair swung over her face, the wet strands clinging to her nose and mouth. Then she remembered that she was naked, hugged her breasts, and dashed back into deeper water, where she could sink up to her chin.

Matthew stood on the bank, long legs braced wide apart, one knee slightly bent, his gaze fixed on the darkening horizon behind her. His jaw muscle twitched under the thick scruff of dark beard, and his larynx bobbed as he swallowed. Slowly, he drew his gaze back to her, his focus on her face. Shadows shifted in his eyes.

"You can't wash the memories away." He switched his weight from one leg to the other. "I wish you could, but scrubbing your hide off won't erase what happened." He passed the back of his hand over his mouth. "I'm sorry for interrupting your bath, but you were gone for so long I got worried, and I . . ." He swept off his hat, raked his fingers through his hair, then clamped the Stetson back on his head. "I didn't want you to take another chill, so I came to check on you."

Eden glanced down at the upper swells of her bobbing breasts and saw red tracks on her skin from the drag of her fingernails. For a moment, she felt dizzy and disoriented. Clawing at herself that way wasn't normal.

"I feel . . . so *dirty*," she pushed out, needing to explain her crazy behavior so he wouldn't think she was unhinged. "I need to get it *off*." A lump welled in her throat, and scalding tears filled her eyes. "Only no matter how hard I scrub, I don't feel clean."

Memories skittered around in her head like spiders. A low moan escaped her throat, and then, though she tried to stifle them, sobs erupted from her throat. Matthew cursed under his breath.

"Eden, you need to get out of that icy water. If I go back to camp, can I count on you to do that right away?"

She gulped and nodded, unable to speak. When he turned on his heel and walked away, she stared after him through a blur of tears until he disappeared from sight. Then, shivering from the cold, she waded toward the bank, grabbed the towel, and started drying off. Every time she looked at her scraped skin, she feared for her sanity. What had possessed her?

After dressing, she squatted beside the stream to wash the other set of clothes he'd lent her. If she hung them by the fire, they might dry by morning, and she'd have something clean to change into tomorrow night.

When she returned to camp, Eden felt embarrassed—over her inexplicable behavior at the creek, and also because Matthew had seen her naked. As she handed him the bathing paraphernalia, she couldn't look him in the eye. Fiery heat crept up her neck, and she turned away to drape her wet clothes over a bush.

As he cleansed the toothbrush in whiskey, he said, "After I take a bath, I'll hunt up a couple of forked limbs to make a clothes rack closer to the fire."

Her tongue felt as if it had been glued to the roof of her mouth. She pried it loose to reply, "That's, um, a good idea."

"The denim won't dry by morning, otherwise."

Still intensely uncomfortable and not wanting him to see how red her face was, Eden descended on the packs that had been removed from Herman's back. She quickly located the one that held the trail rations. "While you're washing up, I'll throw something together for supper," she said, glancing over her shoulder.

He inclined his head at the pack. "I've got spuds, carrots, and onions in there. If you cut the jerky into small pieces, it cooks up fairly tender. There are a few canned goods, too. Maybe you can make some stew."

"Stew it will be."

After washing and dressing, Matthew crouched by the stream to scrape the whiskers off his face. He'd skipped shaving last night because he was self-conscious about his scars, but he couldn't go on hiding them forever. Now that the rest of him was clean, the shaggy beard made him feel scruffy.

As he ran the straight blade over his jaw, he recalled what Eden had said to him when he'd caught her scouring her skin raw with sand. *I feel so dirty. I need to get it off!* He would never forget how she'd looked right then, her eyes dark with shame yet sparkling with tears. For an awful moment, he'd been tempted to wade into the water and scoop her up into his arms. He was damned glad now that he hadn't. She might have flown into a panic. Hell, no maybe to it—she *would* have flown into a panic.

When he was around Eden, he needed to step lightly and think before he acted. She was a courageous lady and had a strength of spirit he greatly admired, but even so, she wasn't steady on her feet yet and probably wouldn't be for many months to come. When a woman was sexually abused, it did something to her, way deep inside, and sometimes she never completely recovered. He hoped that wasn't the way of it for Eden. She was such a curious blend of vulnerability and mettle, of city sophistication and country charm. And pretty as a picture, to boot, with those delicate features, big blue eyes, and that glorious tangle of red hair. What a waste it would be if she never got over what had happened to her and missed out on all the wonderful things life had to offer—love, marriage, children, and happiness.

Matthew slapped some bay rum on his face, and then, following Eden's lead, washed his soiled clothing. Afterward, he collected all the stuff and headed back to camp, hoping with every step that Eden had started to feel better during his absence. He hated that he had embarrassed her so badly, but on the other hand, he couldn't regret that he'd gotten worried and interrupted her bath. She was in enough pain with those busted ribs. She didn't need the additional discomfort of raw skin.

Oh, yes, he felt certain that at least two of her ribs were broken. Right before she'd dashed back into the water, he'd seen her side. It wasn't only bruised, but also badly swollen. *Damn Pete Sebastian to hell.*

Matthew found Eden crouched by the fire, tending a pot of stew and a pan of trail corn bread. He didn't miss the way she kept her arm clamped tightly to her side each time she moved. He needed to do something about that, but only after he got some whiskey into her. Approaching her right now, so soon after the incident at the creek, would go over like rain at a Fourth of July picnic.

He draped his wet laundry over the bush where Eden had hung hers, then went to find limbs to erect a clothes rack. When he stepped into the light a few minutes later, she stared at him for a long moment. "You don't look like the same person," she said.

Feeling self-conscious, Matthew turned his back to her and drove the forked limbs into the ground. Without his beard, he felt exposed. "Sorry. I know I'm not much to look at. Pete Sebastian worked me over with a pistol butt." He strung a rope between the limbs and went to get their clothes. When he returned to hang them near the fire, he added, "I was never what you'd call a pretty boy."

His comments startled Eden even more than his appearance had. Without the whiskers to hide his face, he was one of the handsomest men she'd ever clapped eyes on. He had a disarming grin, the paralyzed corner of his mouth drawing down slightly to give it a crooked, boyish appeal that offset the chiseled cut of his features. In the flickering light, his blue eyes formed such a contrast to his dark skin that they almost mesmerized her. She barely noticed the scars. He thought he was ugly? In Eden's opinion, nothing could be farther from the truth.

"Smells good," he said as he hunkered down across from her. He raised one eyebrow when he saw that she'd put on a pot of coffee and hunted up the plates, spoons, and cups. "Been a long time since I've sunk my teeth into food I didn't fix myself. I'm surprised you know how to cook."

He was acting as if nothing had happened, which eased Eden's embarrassment. "Of course I know how to cook. Even people in the city have to eat."

"I figured maybe you had servants."

"We did have servants, but they had days off. And, as I said before, we haven't always had money. For years after my family got to

California, we lived in a tumbledown farmhouse outside of the city and scraped to get by."

"Tumbledown, huh? Somehow that's hard to picture."

Eden glanced up from the stew. "Trust me, it was tumbledown. The front porch was so rotten the overhang leaned sideways, and the roof leaked like a sieve. Ace and Joseph were constantly trying to patch it."

"You look like a lady to the manner born."

Eden shot him an incredulous look. "You've read Shakespeare?"

"No. Is that Shakespeare?"

"Yes. 'To the manner born' is from *Hamlet*." Eden lifted the spoon to her lips to taste the stew broth. "Anyway, back to my knowing how to cook. I was born in that old farmhouse and spent most of my childhood there. To keep food on the table, Ace swept saloon floors, and my mother did other people's laundry and cleaned houses. At the end of the day, she was exhausted, so I had to learn my way around a kitchen at a fairly young age."

He inclined his dark head at the pot. "I hope that tastes as good as it smells."

Eden couldn't help but smile. "I hope so, too. Right now it isn't bad, but I could still stub my toe as I'm adding the salt."

He chuckled. "You know the cure for too much salt?"

"Add more potatoes."

"You *do* know how to cook."

"Well enough, but it's been a while since I cooked over a campfire. There's a knack to it."

"Have you done it much in the past?"

Her mind drifted back over the years. "Not really. During the lean times, my brothers hunted to keep meat on the table, and I went along if Mama would let me. Then later, while visiting in No Name, I enjoyed helping round up cattle from the open range. When you're out like that, so far from a house, you have no choice but to cook the old-fashioned way."

He shook his head. "You truly are a marvel. You've worked with cattle?"

"Not as a job or anything, just for the fun of it."

"You actually thought it was fun?"

"Mostly. I stay away when they're branding and castrating—that part turns my stomach—but I enjoy the other stuff. It's relaxing to ride herd. I especially like the night shift. It's so peaceful in the dark and quiet. Out in the open, the stars are so beautiful, and the lowing of the cows is sort of like music."

"I've been on my fair share of cattle roundups. It didn't worry you to be so far from camp in the dead of night?"

She patted a holster on her hip. "Not with my Colts as backup. If there was trouble I couldn't handle alone, my brothers would have been there in a blink if I had fired three signal shots for help."

"I see." He gazed into the flames. Then he looked at her again. "So, you enjoy music?"

"I do. My brothers play string instruments. When we gather as a family, we have a lot of fun."

He pushed erect and went to the packs. When he returned, he had the whiskey jug and a small bag of sugar. After pouring them each a cup of coffee, he added a generous splash of liquor and a spoonful of sweetener to each mug. He stirred the drinks, handed her one of the cups, and lifted his in a toast.

"To a good night's sleep. There's nothing

better than a couple of stiff drinks to chase your cares away."

Eden wasn't sure she wanted her cares to be chased away. She no longer felt threatened by Matthew, but she didn't completely trust him yet, either. He was a man, after all, and if he got foxed, he might become amorous. That would land her in a fine mess, especially if she were foolish enough to get intoxicated herself.

Studying him surreptitiously, she took measure of the rugged masculinity of his face, the broad set of his shoulders under the leather jacket, and the bulge of thigh muscle that stretched the denim of his jeans taut as he crouched across from her. If he started making inappropriate advances, what on earth would she do? Her mother said a lot of men got lovey-dovey when they drank, and any woman, no matter how plain, looked good to them.

"I, um, appreciate your thoughtfulness, Matthew, but I don't care much for whiskey. I'll let you enjoy mine and have straight coffee."

He took a sip from his cup and grinned at her. "You haven't tasted whiskey fixed this way. Try it. It's delicious."

Reluctantly, Eden took a sip. It *was* delicious. She hadn't tasted anything sweet for so long that she wanted to guzzle it. "Mmm," she murmured appreciatively. "It is very good. Only one for me, though. I don't imbibe often, and I don't want to get silly."

"Who cares if you get a little silly?"

Eden cared. Matthew was undeniably handsome in a dark, dangerous way, but she wanted nothing to do with him physically. She appreciated how he pushed himself to find the right words just when she needed to hear them, his gentle manner with the horses, and how he had avoided looking at her naked body down at the creek. But that was as far as it went.

Ignoring his question, she served each of them some stew. They settled beside each other to eat, drinking the spiked coffee between bites. She started to feel warm from the pit of her stomach clear to her throat. Halfway through the meal, he fixed them both another drink. Eden eyed hers askance, determined not to touch it, but she found herself reaching for her cup anyway.

"This is lovely," she murmured. "The sugar adds just the right touch."

"It's my trail version of Irish coffee. Too bad I can't lace it with cream."

"It's wonderful just as it is." Eden meant that. The sweetness was difficult to resist. She took another sip and smiled at him. "I'm afraid I'm getting a little tipsy."

"No harm in that."

By the time supper was over and they'd cleaned up, Eden *knew* she was a little tipsy. When Matthew started to fix more Irish coffee, she held up a hand. "No more, Matthew. I don't want to get intoxicated."

"You won't. My aim is only to get you relaxed so you can sleep better tonight."

Against her better judgment, Eden accepted the third cup of coffee. He settled beside her to enjoy his own. Occasionally, his arm brushed against hers, making her acutely aware of how overwhelmingly masculine he was. If he got out of line, she would be in big trouble—only somehow, she no longer felt quite so alarmed by the prospect.

"Eden, about what happened down at the creek."

Heat inched up her neck. "I'm sorry about that. I don't know what came over me."

"Don't apologize. I think anyone who went through what you did might react the same way."

"Then why are you bringing it up?" Eden really, *really* did not want to talk about it. "If it's all the same to you, I'd rather drop the subject."

"I can't," he said softly. "What you said is still bothering me. You're not dirty, Eden. The Sebastians are. Dirty clear to the marrow of their bones." He looped an arm around her shoulders and drew her snugly against his side. Eden stiffened at the contact, but gradually she relaxed. "What you're feeling . . . it's all in your mind, and no amount of washing will make it go away. Instead, you just have to keep telling yourself that it wasn't your fault, that none of it was your doing. You hear what I'm saying to you? I know it's hard, but you've got to put it all behind you."

"I thought I had," she whispered, trying to keep her voice steady. "I felt so good when I first got in the water, and then, the first thing I knew, I was scrubbing with sand to get their filth off me."

He sighed and rested his chin atop her head. "Ah, Eden."

Those two words curled around her like warm tendrils of smoke, easing the ache in her chest and the tension from her body. Silence fell between them. Leaning against him, Eden listened to the rush of the creek and the twitter of birds as they roosted in the trees and copses for the night.

He finally ended the silence. "I hope you're not blaming yourself for what happened, Eden. You aren't, are you?"

"How did you . . . ?" She sent him a wondering look. "I never said a word about blaming myself."

"You didn't need to. I've been there, not in exactly the same way, but *there*, all the same. Crazy thoughts can go through a person's head after something terrible happens. You keep circling it in your mind, thinking of all the things you could have done different, of all the ways you might have changed it. I hope you're not having thoughts like that."

She rested her head on his muscular shoulder, wondering as she did how she could feel so at ease with his arm around her. The whiskey, she guessed. She never should have accepted the third drink. "Sometimes I do. When they came aboard the train, I called attention to myself. That was so stupid of me. Any sane woman would have stayed in her seat and kept her mouth shut."

"Why did you leave your seat?"

"They were shooting people, and the little boy behind us started to cry. Wallace threatened to kill him if his mother didn't shut him up." Eden closed her eyes. "When Wallace took aim at Timothy, I couldn't just sit there. I got between the gun and the child. Timothy is a darling little boy. I didn't want him to get hurt."

"And you think that was a stupid thing to do? Brave, maybe, but not stupid."

"They might not have taken me if I had stayed in my seat."

He sighed again. "Maybe, maybe not. But the little boy probably would have died. The Sebastians kill young and old alike. Down in Mexico, they slaughtered an entire family, including a baby. They don't know the meaning of mercy, and no life is sacred to them."

Eden shivered.

He tightened his arm around her. "You did what you had to do, Eden, and you paid a terrible price. But none of it was your fault." He shifted to get more comfortable. "The morning of the train robbery, I was following their tracks, like I told you. What I neglected to say is that I happened upon an old peddler in a clearing. They had slit his throat. Do you think it was the peddler's fault that he died—that he did something to deserve it?"

"No, of course not."

"Then stop blaming yourself for what they did to you. When thoughts like that enter your head, push them out. You protected a child. That was the right thing to do, and it took a lot of courage. If anyone should feel bad, it's the other passengers on the train who did nothing, especially the men."

Eden released a taut breath. "Feelings make no sense sometimes, Matthew. Rationally, I know none of what happened was my fault, but there are moments when I circle it, just as you said, thinking of everything I might have done differently. If I'd carried my Colts with me in a satchel, I could have defended myself and everyone else. If I'd stayed in my seat and just handed over our valuables, they might not have noticed me."

He rested his cheek against her hair, and she felt his lips curve in a half smile. "You'd be hard to overlook with that pretty red hair of yours."

It was Eden's turn to sigh. "Thank you for talking to me, Matthew. I feel better, and from now on, I'll try really hard to forget."

"Forgetting something like that is damned near impossible. Time will help. But what you have to do is make your peace with it and be okay even when you remember."

"I'll try."

"When it gets hard, think of how lucky you are to be alive. My Livvy didn't survive. After each of them had a turn with her, they went at her with a knife." His voice went thick. "Our baby died with her."

Eden lifted her head to search his expression. In the firelight, his eyes glimmered like polished silver. "And you blame yourself." She didn't pose it as a question because she heard the guilt ringing in his voice. "Why, Matthew? Doesn't everything you just said to me also apply to you?"

He puffed air into his cheeks and slowly released it through thinned lips. "It's different for me. It was my duty to protect Livvy, and I didn't." He gazed off into the darkness. "We'd been at the creek for a picnic. It was our special place. I asked her to marry me down there. We celebrated our wedding night and all our anniversaries there. So she chose that place to tell me she was finally in the family way. I didn't bother to take a rifle or revolver. We were on Lazy J land. There'd never been any trouble in the area. There aren't even that many rattlesnakes to worry about. So I went down there unarmed.

"As we were driving home, the Sebastians came out of the trees and surrounded the wagon. They wanted our valuables, and all we had with us was Livvy's wedding band, which wasn't worth very much. My gold pocket watch was at the shop for repair." He kept his gaze fixed on some distant place, his face tight with pain. "They were furious because we had nothing to give them, so they jerked Livvy out of the wagon to take it out on her. When I jumped in to defend her, two of them held my arms while Pete pistol-whipped me. After I went down, he started kicking me. Busted some of my ribs and fractured my hip. Then they dragged Livvy off a ways. I could hear her screaming my name, but I'd been beaten half-senseless, and no matter how hard I tried, I couldn't get up. Pretty soon, the screaming stopped."

"Oh, God, Matthew, how horrible for you."

"It was far worse for Livvy. The Sebastians go out of their way to inflict pain when they rape a woman. When they finished with her, one of them shot me in the chest. The slug barely missed my heart, and I guess they thought I was dead. I had blood in my eyes, so I couldn't see which one fired the gun. That's the last thing I remember, the blast of the gun. My parents got worried when Livvy and I didn't come home. They came looking for us. I was in a real bad way, and the doctor didn't think I'd make it. If not for my mother's efforts, I probably wouldn't have. When I woke up three weeks later, Livvy and my baby were already buried, and life as I'd known it was over. It was as if everything had been made of blown glass, and quicker than you can snap your fingers, it shattered. That's why I can never go back. I don't have it in me to try to glue the pieces together again."

"Oh, Matthew, I'm so sorry."

He cleared his throat. His voice was gravelly when he said, "I've never told anyone about that day—haven't been able to talk about it."

Eden rested her head on his shoulder again. "Well, I'm glad you were able to tell me. You need to have your own words repeated back to you. It wasn't your fault, and you shouldn't blame yourself. I didn't know Livvy, but if she loved you as deeply as you love her, she wouldn't want you to feel this way."

"Any man worth his salt protects his wife," he ground out. "She was a timid little thing, my Livvy. She believed in me and trusted me to keep her safe. Instead, I just lay there by that damned wagon and did nothing while she was raped and murdered."

"You were badly hurt. So badly hurt you couldn't get up. How can you blame yourself for that?" Eden touched a fingertip to the paralyzed corner of his mouth. "You were on your own land, Matthew, at a picnic spot you believed was safe. You had no way of knowing that you needed to take a weapon that day. You had no idea the Sebastian Gang was in the area, or that they'd trespass onto the ranch. What happened wasn't your fault. If someone else told you the story you just told me, would you blame that man for not saving his wife? Even if you'd been armed, it would have been one man against six, and at that time, you probably weren't very fast with a gun."

"No, but I should have been," he whispered gruffly. "Instead I waited until *after* my wife was dead to practice with a gun. How does that make sense? I should have been prepared for any kind of threat before I asked her to marry me. A man should make sure he's fit to be a good husband before he takes on the responsibility, and I didn't do that."

Eden felt so sad for him—and also for herself. Because of the Sebastians, they'd both endured terrible pain. Would either of them ever get past that, or would it haunt them for the rest of their lives?

"You know what, Matthew?"

"No, what?" he asked shakily.

"The way I see it, the two of us have a choice to make, probably the most important one of our lives. We can forget the terrible times in our lives and try our best to be happy—or we can live in the past and feel awful until the day we die. If we do the latter, the Sebastians win. Even if you finally manage to track them down and send them all to hell, they will still have won."

"Yeah, I suppose you're right."

"I don't know about you, but that thought doesn't sit well with me. They got the best of me once, but I can't allow them to get the best of me again."

He finally met her gaze. Her heart caught when she saw tears shimmering in his eyes. "You're quite a lady, Eden Paxton. And you're right. You need to put it all behind you. Just please understand that it's a journey I'm not able to make. It wasn't only me the bastards harmed. My wife and baby died. I'll never forgive myself for that, *never.*" He passed a hand over his eyes. "It's been so long now that I can't even picture Olivia's face anymore. Can't remember the sound of her voice. There have even been times when I've wondered what the hell I'm doing out here, chasing men that large posses have failed to catch. But even so, I can't turn loose of it. Keeping that promise is the one thing from my past that I can still hang on to. I have to finish it."

"And in the doing, punish yourself forever? Livvy wouldn't want that. If she's up in heaven, looking down on you—and I believe she is—her heart is breaking. She would want you to heal and be at peace. She'd want you to be happy. Imagine how painful it would be for you if the situation were reversed, and it was you looking down on her. Wouldn't you want her to have a good life?"

"Of course I would. If ever anyone deserved to be happy, it was Livvy. She didn't have a mean bone in her whole body."

"Neither do you," Eden told him. "I'm coming to believe that you're a fine man, Matthew Coulter, and you deserve to be happy, too. Don't let the Sebastians deprive you of that."

Eden straightened away from him and reached for her coffee. After taking a sip, she glanced over at him. He sat unmoving, his gaze fixed on the horizon, where ponderosa pines rose in black silhouettes against the darkening sky.

After a few minutes, he stirred, stood up, and went to one of the packs. After rifling through the contents, he came up with a shirt, which he began cutting into strips with his hunting knife. When he approached the fire, holding the lengths of cloth in one hand, Eden got a bad feeling as she met his gaze. *Purposeful* was the only way to describe the glint in his eyes.

"How tipsy are you feeling?"

Eden set aside the third drink, which was almost finished. "Why do you ask?"

"When we were down at the creek, I saw a big lump on those ribs of yours," he said without preamble as he hunkered down in front of her. "They aren't just bruised, Eden. Pete busted at least two of them, if not three. You should have told me."

"There isn't much to be done for broken ribs."

"True, but wrapping them tight will at least hold them steady. Without binding, if one of them is broken clean in two, you could puncture a lung if you took a tumble off the horse."

Eden angled a wary look at the strips of cloth he had started knotting together. "I don't think they're that bad."

He continued at his task. "Maybe, maybe not, but there's no sense in taking a chance. Besides, a tight binding will help ease the pain."

Eden wasn't about to strip down naked up top so he could wrap her ribs.

As if he guessed her thoughts, he said, "You can tie your shirttails snug under your protuberances. All I'll see is your belly and back."

His use of the word *protuberances* made her smile in spite of herself. She guessed he'd heard his sisters use the term. "Really, Matthew, the support isn't necessary."

"I say it is. Remember our agreement? I'm telling you to shed that coat."

Reluctantly, Eden took off the jacket and tied her shirttails snugly beneath her breasts. He motioned for her to stand up, his expression so grimly determined that she didn't know who felt more uncomfortable. As she gained her feet, she nearly lost her balance. He clamped a hand over her shoulder to steady her.

"You okay?"

"I think I'm a little drunk."

His eyes twinkled with humor. "That was my aim, to relax you. I knew this would be too unnerving for you otherwise."

It was unnerving for her anyway.

"Suck it in," he ordered, "and hold it until

I make a couple of passes. The tighter I
get it, the better."

It hurt to suck in her stomach. But she
held her breath until he'd wrapped the cloth
around her twice and told her it was okay
to relax. She felt self-conscious, standing
before him with her belly bared, but to his
credit, he made fast work of the job. Before she knew it, he had finished and told
her she could loosen the shirttails to cover
herself again. To her surprise, the tight binding did ease the pain in her side. It no longer hurt so much when she moved, and
she could take a deep breath.

"Better?"

"Much."

"Maybe that and the whiskey will help
you get a good night's sleep."

After spreading out the bedroll, he lay
down on his side. When Eden joined him
under the blanket, he looped his arm around
her waist and moved closer. This time, she
didn't flinch or grab his wrist. She suspected
it was because the liquor had numbed
her, and she didn't have the good sense to
feel panicky. Drifting in the alcohol-induced
haze, she relished the heat of his body,

vaguely aware that his hand remained anchored in one place. The realization made her smile sleepily. Maybe some men got out of line with women when they drank, but Matthew Coulter clearly wasn't one of them.

He reminded her of a gift her brother David had given her on her tenth birthday. It had been during the lean years, when they couldn't afford fancy paper or many presents, so he'd wrapped it in newspaper, one layer after another, because he had wanted to prolong the opening of gifts for her. Only somehow the newsprint had gotten wet and the ink had bled, creating a sodden, blackened lump that looked extremely unappealing. Not wishing to hurt David's feelings, Eden had pretended to be excited as she worked to pick away the tape, wondering all the while what awful thing he'd gotten her.

At the very center of that frustrating mess she'd found a beautiful little gold locket on a chain so fine and exquisite that it had felt like a strand of silk against her skin. David had saved back a portion of his wages every week for three months in order to buy it for her, and Eden had treasured it until the day of the train robbery, when she'd put it with all her other valuables in the knotted handkerchief.

She was coming to suspect that Matthew Coulter was very much like that locket in many ways. Before any of the layers had been lifted away, he'd looked extremely unappealing, but he'd cleaned up nicely, and tonight he'd revealed yet another surprise: that his feelings ran deep, strong, and true. If fate allowed them the time, she suspected that he might become a loyal friend.

That was her last conscious thought as she surrendered to exhaustion.

Chapter Eight

The next morning, Eden was dismayed to discover that the clothing they'd hung by the fire was still quite damp, especially the blue jeans. When she mentioned it to Matthew, he glanced up from where he was hunkered over the frying pan and said, "That's one reason I gave up on washing my clothes very often. When you pack them away wet, they can sour before nightfall if the day's halfway warm, and then you have to wash them again. That's a lot of work."

Scrubbing clothes on a rock *was* a lot of work, and Eden didn't want their efforts to be wasted. After considering the situation, she got an idea. "Is there any way we could drape the damp clothes over Herman's packs? They'll dry by evening that way, and we'll have fresh things to wear."

Matthew frowned thoughtfully. "How would we keep everything from falling off? Those packs rock back and forth when Herman's walking. Nothing's going to stay on them unless it's anchored down."

After breakfast, Matthew left the damp clothing on the drying rack while he got the animals ready for the trail. Once the gear was on Herman's back, he stepped away to regard the wooden pack frames. "If I string a line between one packboard and another, do you think tucking the clothes partly under the rope would hold them fast?"

"It's worth a try," Eden replied. "I can keep an eye on them. If they start to work loose, we can stop and tuck them back under the line again."

In minutes, Matthew had their wet clothes dangling from the packs. Eden couldn't help but laugh. "Poor Herman. He's become a walking clothesline."

Matthew chuckled. "He doesn't care

how he looks, and I think it's going to work."
He glanced at Eden with a smile. "Good
idea."

Before Eden knew it, she was back in
the saddle and struggling to keep the grueling pace that Matthew had no choice but
to set. They rode in another circle, but in
an entirely different area today, with Matthew yet again taking to a stream and
brushing away their tracks at other times.
Ever concerned for the horses, he stopped
for a breakfast break, again for lunch, and
also in the midafternoon, always removing
the gear from the animals' backs to rub
them down.

That evening, Eden was so spent that
Matthew announced that he would do all
the chores, which made her feel useless
and more than a little guilty. It wasn't in
her nature to lounge around while others
worked, but her ribs, though less uncomfortable with the binding, still hurt, and the
relentless pain seemed to have sapped
what little strength she had.

When she went to the creek to bathe, she
was once again assailed with an urge to
scour her skin. This time, she was prepared

for the irrational feelings that swamped her and was able to overcome them. The taint was all in her imagination, she assured herself. And Matthew was right: She couldn't wash away the memories. She simply had to deal with them.

After drying off, she was unable to rewrap her midriff tightly enough to do any good, so she stuffed the binding into a jacket pocket and washed her clothing without any rib support. Each time she rubbed the jeans over the rock, the pain in her side grew so intense that black spots danced before her eyes.

On the way back to camp, she wrestled with the knowledge that she would have to ask Matthew to wrap her ribs again, and this time she would have to endure the embarrassment without any whiskey to numb her sensibilities. That was not a pleasant thought, but she saw no way around it unless she wanted to ride all day tomorrow without the binding.

Matthew had soaked beans all day in a leather bladder of water suspended from his saddle horn, and after she'd draped her wet laundry over another makeshift drying rack, she saw that he already had the legumes cooking over a bed of red-hot embers. He'd tossed in pieces of jerky, chopped onion, and carrots to flavor the concoction, and when he gave it a stir, the aroma was divine. Eden winced as she lowered herself to the ground at the opposite side of the fire from him.

Matthew cocked a dark eyebrow at her, his amazing blue eyes locking on hers. "You need me to wrap your middle again?"

"If you wouldn't mind," she replied. "I tried to do it myself, but I can't get it tight enough."

"Of course I don't mind." He searched her expression and smiled slightly. "Knot your shirttails."

Eden's hands trembled as she removed the jacket and tied the shirttails beneath her breasts. As Matthew approached her, she got up, fleetingly met his gaze, and then averted her face, unable to bear looking at him when she felt so exposed.

"Honey, there's no reason to feel self-conscious. When it comes to partially unveiled ladies, I go blind in one eye and can't see out of the other one. Where's the binding?"

His use of an endearment startled Eden. "I, um, put it in my coat pocket."

He bent down to search for it. When he straightened, he spent a moment untangling the cloth. She stared at his big hands, remembering the warmth that radiated from them at night, but still dreading their touch.

"Suck it up," he said. "I promise to be quick about it. I've roped, thrown, and hogtied a steer in less than a minute and a half during rodeo competition. I guess I can make fast work of this."

If he could hog-tie a powerful steer that quickly, how long would it take him to overpower her?

"Eden, look at me."

She hadn't realized until then that she'd squeezed her eyes closed. She pried them open and stared at him through a blur of tears.

"You're wearing the Colts," he reminded her. "If I take liberties, you can shoot me."

It was true. She was armed. The stiffness drained from her spine. "Don't be silly, Matthew. I would never shoot you."

"That's good to know. I've never trifled with a lady who might put a bullet between my eyes."

Eden couldn't help but smile. He was trying to help her relax, and she appreciated that more than he could know. "How very wise of you."

As Matthew circled her, pulling the cloth tight over her ribs, he whistled a familiar tune under his breath, but she was too rattled to remember its title. As promised, he finished binding her ribs quickly, and Eden could finally breathe again without feeling faint.

He stepped back and held up his hands as if she had a gun aimed at him. "Am I safe now?"

She knew he meant it as a joke, and she was supposed to laugh, but she was so touched by his kindness that she found herself staring at him through another rush of tears. His smile faded, and his eyes darkened with emotions she couldn't name.

When he spoke, his voice had grown husky. "I think I'll mosey down to the creek and grab a quick bath now. Can you keep an eye on the beans while I'm gone?"

"Sure."

Loosening the knot beneath her breasts,

she quickly covered herself, then gazed after him as he walked away.

Matthew muttered curses under his breath as he waded buck-naked into the water and began lathering his skin with soap. *Honey?* What the hell had he been thinking to call her that? It had alarmed her. He'd seen it in her eyes. What was the matter with him that he couldn't control his own tongue? It was no excuse that he'd been raised by a father who used endearments with all females, young or old, whether they were members of the family or not. It had been a stupid and thoughtless slip of the tongue. No more endearments, period, and no more locking gazes with her, either. What was that all about, anyway?

Matthew was still upset with himself when he got dressed a few minutes later and crouched by the water to shave. With the first pass of the straight blade, he cut himself and let fly with another curse. As the word left his mouth and rang in the air around him, he resigned himself to the fact that he'd never be fit company for a lady again. He had a filthy mouth. He still wasn't remembering to say *please*, *thank you*, or *excuse me*. He needed a *complete* overhaul—that was what he needed.

The beans still weren't done when Matthew got back to camp. After hanging his wet clothes beside Eden's on the rack, he went to search through his packs. When he found what he needed and returned to the fire, Eden's gaze immediately caught on the silver instrument in his hand.

"A harmonica?"

Matthew nodded and crouched at the opposite side of the flames. The Sebastians were too far away for the sound of the instrument to carry to them, so he felt it was safe to provide her with some entertainment. "I'm a little rusty, but last night you said you enjoy music, so I thought I'd give it a whirl."

He blotted his lips on the back of his wrist, cupped his hands around the harmonica, and began playing "Oh! Susanna." Eden listened for a moment and then began singing along, her voice as light and sweet as a songbird's.

"'It rained all night the day I left, the

weather it was dry, the sun so hot I froze to death, Susanna, don't you cry!'" She beamed a glad smile at him. "'Oh, Susanna, don't you cry for me! I come from Alabama with my banjo on my knee!'"

Matthew broke off to catch his breath. Her smile was infectious, and he found himself grinning. He also caught himself gazing deeply into her lovely blue eyes again and immediately put the harmonica back to his lips, this time to play "Beautiful Dreamer." Again, Eden knew the lyrics and trilled along with the music, the words immediately making him wish he'd chosen another melody.

"'Beautiful dreamer, wake unto me, starlight and dewdrops are waiting for thee. Sounds of the rude world, heard in the day, lulled by the moonlight have all passed away.'"

She truly *was* beautiful, Matthew thought, as he watched her over his cupped hands. And it had been much too long since he'd eased his physical needs with a sporting woman.

"'Beautiful dreamer, queen of my song, list while I woo thee with soft melody.'"

Was that his plan, to woo her with music? The thought spurred Matthew into abruptly changing the tune to "Camptown Races."

Eden grinned impishly, began tapping out the lively rhythm on her knee, and gaily sang, "'Doo-da, doo-da! The Camptown racetrack's five miles long, oh, de doo-da day!'"

Safer ground. Matthew played that tune in its entirety.

When the song ended, Eden smiled at him across the flames, her eyes shimmering. "Thank you, Matthew. That was *lovely.*"

He tucked the harmonica in his jacket pocket. "I'm glad you enjoyed it." He checked the beans. "For now, though, supper's done, and then it'll be time for you to rest."

Eden had always loved beans. When she'd been a girl, legumes had been one of the main staples of her family's diet.

"You fix beans almost the same way Mama does. We ate them a lot when I was little, and she always added onion for flavoring, too. Meat as well, if we had any." She took a big bite and dimpled her cheek at him. "These are delicious."

He took a bite, too, and smiled. "Thank you."

"One time, David got a huge ham bone from the butcher shop, and Mama cooked it in our beans. Those were the best *ever*. She made corn bread to go with them, and we had a veritable feast."

As much as Eden was enjoying the meal, her appetite soon dimmed, and she had to set her plate aside half-finished.

"You didn't eat much," Matthew observed. "You're not feeling sick, I hope."

"No, just worn-out."

He finished his meal, and then went to get the bedroll. After spreading the pallet and blankets on the ground near the fire, he said, "In you go."

"But we haven't done the dishes yet."

"I'll do them. You get a head start on a good night's rest."

Eden sighed and handed him her plate. "I hate being a burden. I should be doing my fair share."

"Maybe tomorrow, but not tonight. You're too tuckered out."

As reluctant as Eden was to let him do all the work, she nearly groaned with relief when she lay down. *Tuckered* didn't begin to describe how weary she was. She dozed while Matthew washed the dishes, but a bit later, when he joined her on the pallet, she came wide-awake.

As if he sensed her uneasiness, he lay on his back instead of turning to put an arm around her. Gaze fixed on the starlit sky, he said, "Those mountains never fail to awe me when I look at them. They're so massive and intimidating, yet beautiful."

"The sky is amazing, too. Just look at all those stars. There must be thousands of them."

He joined her in admiring the sparkly patterns for a moment. "According to Shoshone legend, the Milky Way was created by a huge grizzly bear."

"Really?" Eden searched for the constellation. When she found it, she asked, "How does the legend go?"

"The grizzly climbed high into the mountains, getting clumps of ice and snow on its feet. As it crossed the sky, bits of white fell away from its paws, creating the Milky Way."

Eden gazed thoughtfully at the stars. "That's a cute story. Who told it to you?"

"I fell in with an old Shoshone named

Two Dogs who'd escaped a reservation. He rode the trail with me for about a month."

"Was he good company?"

"Like me, he wasn't much of a talker, but he did like to tell stories by the fire at night."

"I like to do that, too. On hunting forays with my brothers when I was young, I always begged for stories after supper. Joseph liked to tell spooky ones and scare me half-silly." Gaze still fixed on the Milky Way, Eden asked, "What happened to him? To Two Dogs, I mean."

"He just up and left one day. Said he needed to take a spirit walk."

"A spirit walk?"

"Yeah," Matthew said softly. "He never explained what a spirit walk is, but I'm guessing it's a prayerful time, maybe similar to a vision quest."

Eden's uneasiness had abated. Was that why Matthew had chosen to talk, because he'd sensed her nervousness? "Do you know any other Indian stories about the stars?"

"No, but Two Dogs did tell me that his people call the Little Dipper by another name, Little Bear."

Eden turned onto her side to face him. In the firelight, his chiseled profile looked as if it had been carved from polished teak. "I wonder why bears play such a large role in their lore."

He shifted onto his side as well. "I don't know. Maybe it's because bears are so big and strong. Most Plains Indians revere the buffalo, too, probably for the same reason. They're mighty powerful beasts."

Eden searched his gaze until he lightly touched a fingertip to each of her eyelids to urge them closed. "Go to sleep, Eden. You need the rest." He trailed the fingertip down the bridge of her nose, the caress so light that she wondered if she imagined it. "Sweet dreams."

"Sweet dreams," she murmured.

As Eden slipped away into the blackness of sleep, she felt Matthew curl his arm around her, and this time she didn't find it alarming.

Matthew lay awake long after Eden fell asleep, his thoughts in a tangle. *Eden.* She was so damned beautiful with that flame-colored hair and those gorgeous blue eyes, and he was finding it increasingly difficult not to be aware of that every time he looked at her. When he'd returned to camp earlier, he had been bound and determined not to lock gazes with her again, but he had. Something about the girl turned his brains to mush.

When he tried to think of something he didn't like about her, he came up blank. She was spirited, brave, and sweet, and he enjoyed her company far more than he should. Before meeting her, it had been so long since he'd laughed that he'd thought he might never want to again. Now he found himself smiling more times than not, talking more than he'd believed himself capable of, and searching for ways to distract her so she wouldn't feel nervous around him.

"Beautiful Dreamer." What had he been thinking to play that tune? When she'd sung the lyrics, he'd looked across the fire at her and thought, *Awake unto me.*

No more, he told himself firmly. He'd made a vow over Livvy's grave to find her killers and punish them, and even though he could no longer conjure up a clear image of her face, that was a promise he was honor-bound to keep. Perhaps, he thought groggily, Livvy had become less a real person to him than she was an idea that kept him going. Was that why he felt the need to draw his watch from his pocket occasionally, to strengthen his fading sense of connection to her? Without that sense of connection, was he afraid he would give up and go back on his promise to find her killers?

Matthew could no longer define his feelings for Livvy. He only knew she'd once been his whole world, and he felt obligated to continue tracking the Sebastians until he either killed them or died trying. He was almost asleep when Eden suddenly jerked and mewled in her sleep. He cracked open an eye, wondering if the weight of his arm was hurting her ribs.

"No!" she cried. *"No!"*

Matthew pushed up on an elbow and grasped her shoulder. "Eden? You need to wake up. It's a bad dream, only a bad dream."

She came awake with a vengeance, her hands clenched. Matthew didn't see the punch coming, and she nailed him right in the eye. Luckily the blow didn't blind him, and he was able to grab her wrists to stop her from hitting him again.

"Eden! It's me, Matthew. It's only a bad dream!"

She shrieked and tried to twist away from him. "Don't *touch* me. Get your *filthy* hands off me!"

She was thrashing so violently that Matthew feared she might do further injury to her ribs. To hold her still, he pinned her arms above her head and anchored her legs with his thigh.

"Eden, look at me. You're safe. It's me, Matthew. I'm not going to hurt you."

A breath hitched in her throat, and she gazed up at him, her eyes glassy with terror. He knew the instant when recognition began to dawn. The tension drained from her body, and with a tortured gasp, she burst into tears.

"M-Matthew?" she sobbed. "Oh, *God*. I'm s-sorry, so s-sorry. I hit you. I'm s-so sorry."

Matthew released his hold on her wrists, eased his weight off her, and drew her into his arms. "Shhh," he whispered. "Don't. I'm fine. It barely hurt."

She made tight fists on the front of his jacket and buried her face against the side of his neck. "The Sebastians. I dreamed they had me again."

Matthew curled a hand over the back of her head, threading his fingers through her thick, curly hair. "I know," he said softly. "I know. But it was only a terrible dream. You're with me now, and I'll never let them touch you again as long as I draw breath."

Her slender body jerked with the force of her sobs. She wrapped her arms around his neck and clung to him almost frantically. "It was s-so aw-awful. Th-the things they d-did to me were so *awful!*"

"It's over now, Eden. It's over."

"N-not in my dr-dream. It f-felt so real, Matthew. I c-could *feel* their h-hands on me."

Matthew tightened his hold. He'd seen the things they'd done to her, and he couldn't think of a single thing to say that might make her feel better. So he simply held her.

Later, Matthew couldn't say how long she cried. He knew only that when she finally fell into an exhausted sleep, her lush body was pressed snugly against him. The front of her jacket had fallen open and so had his. The tips of her breasts felt like hot embers burning holes in his chest. He tried to ignore it, but the softness of her felt so damned good that he couldn't. The next thing he knew, nature paid a call, and he had an erection throbbing against the fly of his britches. All he could do was clench his teeth and pray it would go away.

No such luck. At times like this, that part of his body seemed to be disconnected from his brain. He ached for release and yearned to find it in the hot, wet recesses of her body. But he knew it was madness even to think about it. When he could tolerate the torture no longer, he slipped cautiously from the bed, trying not to wake her. Then he grabbed his gun belt and the towel and headed for the creek, hoping the ice-cold water would cool his ardor so he could think straight again.

When Matthew returned to bed an hour later, his skin was as wrinkled as a dried grape, and he was chilled to the bone. He didn't know what idiot had come up with an ice-cold bath as a cure for male arousal. It had worked—eventually. But it wasn't something he looked forward to doing again. If he didn't catch pneumonia, it would be a miracle.

As he drew back the blanket and joined Eden on the pallet, she murmured something in her sleep and gravitated toward him. A warning bell jangled at the back of his mind. He was only human, and it had been several months since he'd scratched his itch with a woman. But when she snuggled close, he didn't have the heart to push her away. Instead he pressed his face against her hair and held her, hoping a certain part of his body would behave itself.

It was *not* his lucky night.

Matthew seemed out of sorts the next morning. Recalling her nightmare, Eden wondered if he was miffed at her for slugging him. She hadn't meant to. Well, that wasn't entirely true. She'd meant to hit him, but only because she'd believed he was someone else.

As they sipped coffee together in silence, the sun rose higher in the sky, and the birds started to sing. Eden listened to them for a moment and then said, "Isn't that a beautiful sound?"

Matthew scowled. "It's only a bunch of birds, Eden. You hear them every day."

She considered his disgruntled countenance. "Matthew, are you angry with me about last night?"

He gave her a sharp look. "What about last night?"

"About . . . well, you know . . . when I hit you. I never meant to. Honestly, I didn't. When I woke up from the dream, it took me a moment to realize where I was and who I was with."

His expression softened. "Of course I'm not angry with you. I knew when it happened that you didn't know who you were swinging at."

Eden let that stand for a moment. Then, unable to let it go, she asked, "What *are* you angry with me about, then?"

"I'm not angry with you about anything." He leaned forward to slosh more coffee into his cup. "I'm just grappling with a personal problem."

"Oh." Eden poured herself more coffee, too. "Would you like to talk about it? Sometimes that helps—getting another person's perspective, I mean."

His incredibly blue eyes lighted with what looked like amusement, and he appeared to be biting back a smile. "Thanks for the offer, but I don't think talking it over will help me out."

Eden set aside her cup to serve them each a plate of leftover beans, which they'd reheated for breakfast. As they ate, she said, "You've been such a good listener and have helped me so much. If you change your mind, don't hesitate to let me know. That's what friends are for, to listen and try to think of solutions."

Matthew regarded Eden with a confusing blend of amusement and alarm. She was not only coming to trust him, but now considered him her friend? When he searched her blue eyes, he saw no wariness, only a heartfelt desire to help him deal with a personal problem. She'd probably drop over in a dead faint if he told her what was wrong—namely that he no longer felt certain he could trust himself to sleep with her.

Matthew tried to tuck into his breakfast with enthusiasm, but his appetite was off, and he knew the reason was sitting across the fire from him. How in the hell was he going to get through another several days with her in his care? They had only one bedroll, and she shivered from the cold all night if he didn't join her in it. Until last night, he'd been okay with that, but now he felt like a short-fused stick of dynamite lying perilously close to a lit lucifer.

He couldn't possibly tell Eden that. This was his dilemma, and it was up to him to deal with it, even if it meant playing a little five-fingered stud in the bushes every night, a prospect that Matthew found unappealing. What he needed was a willing woman, preferably one of ill repute, who'd be happy to accommodate him in exchange for a couple of dollars. Unfortunately, there probably wasn't a saloon within a hundred miles, and even if there had been, he couldn't leave Eden to fend for herself.

Matthew chose to ride in a different pattern that day, in a zigzag this time, moving in first one direction and then another. At one point, he came across the Sebastians' tracks. He judged them to be at least a day old and felt confident that the gang wasn't still in the area, but seeing the sign still raised the hair on the back of his neck. He chose not to burden Eden with the discovery. She was managing to keep the pace, but he knew it was costing her dearly. They weren't in any immediate danger, after all, and she had enough on her plate.

By lunchtime, she looked as if she felt better, much to his relief. Then he heard her humming "Beautiful Dreamer." At first it didn't bother him too much, but after a while, he almost lost it and asked her to be quiet. Why that song, and *only* that song? Pretty soon, the tune had him grinding his teeth, the romantic lyrics drifting through his mind like a witch's chant. He vowed to play his harmonica again that night, regaling her with every song he knew *except* that one so she would hum something else tomorrow.

Feeling irritated and all-over grumpy, Matthew caught himself getting cross with her when they stopped for a break that afternoon. While he was at the creek, watering the horses, he gave himself a stern lecture. It wasn't Eden's fault they were in this fix, and it *definitely* wasn't her fault that his body had turned traitor. *Beautiful dreamer, awake unto me.* He was losing his mind; that was it.

By the time the light started to fade, Matthew's nerve endings felt as if they'd been rubbed back and forth over a cheese grater. Every time he contemplated sleeping with Eden again, his skin went clammy. What if she felt his erection and panicked? That would put both of them in a fine pickle. He couldn't let her sleep alone unless he gave her his jacket for extra warmth—and if he gave her his jacket, he'd be the one who stayed awake all night. Her life depended on his keeping his wits about him, and that would be nigh onto impossible if he got no rest.

Matthew was searching for a suitable place to make camp when Eden suddenly called out for him to stop. He jerked around on the saddle, heart in his throat. As grueling as this ordeal had been for her, she'd never once asked him to stop. His first thought was that she was about to collapse, a fear that had dogged him ever since he'd rescued her.

She dismounted, using only her right arm to suspend her weight as she swung from the saddle. Then, hugging her side, she walked a few feet from the gelding and crouched to stare at something. Matthew prayed it wasn't the gang's tracks she was studying. After the nightmare last night, knowing that they'd been in this area would have her trembling in her boots.

"What is it?" he called.

She sent him a glowing smile, her heart shining in her eyes. "Matthew, these are Shakespeare's prints!"

Though Matthew had never read any Shakespeare, he believed the man had been dead for over two hundred years. He dismounted and strode toward Eden, fearful that she might be delirious with a fever.

"Eden, Shakespeare couldn't have been out here. He's dead. Are you okay?"

She dimpled a cheek and shook her head. "Not *that* Shakespeare. I mean Ace's stallion. *Look*. See that notch in the shoe? That's Ace's mark."

Matthew hunkered down to examine the track. It had definitely been made by a horse with a notched shoe. "Why on earth does Ace mark one shoe?"

"Shakespeare is his pride and joy, a gorgeous and very expensive black stallion. If he's ever stolen, Ace will be able to distinguish Shakespeare's tracks from those of another horse so he can follow the thief."

Matthew hated to get her hopes up, only to have them dashed. "What if someone else came up with the same idea?"

"It's possible, I suppose, but on the other hand, we haven't seen a single soul out here. How many riders can be in this area on a horse with a notched shoe? I think my brothers are trying to cut across our tracks and find us."

Matthew examined the other hoofprints and started to feel a little hopeful himself. "There were four riders and a couple of pack animals carrying heavy loads," he said as he walked back to her. "The man riding the horse with a notched shoe is heavier than the other three."

"That's Ace. He's *huge*. Well, not fat or anything, but he towers over the others." She reached up to clutch Matthew's hand. He automatically reciprocated, wrapping his fingers around her slender ones. "It's them. I just *know* it, Matthew. They're looking for us."

Matthew could only hope she was right. Maybe they'd show up before bedtime and take her off his hands. He gazed off into the trees. "They're old tracks. I'd say they came through here two days ago. God only knows where they are now."

Eden drew her hand from his and struggled to her feet. Though her cheeks were pink with excitement, there was still an underlying pallor that worried him. "What matters is that they're out here. I feel so much better, knowing that."

When Matthew found a level place along a stream a bit later, Eden was bubbling over with enthusiasm. "Maybe we could follow their trail, Matthew, and find them instead of waiting for them to find us."

He considered that possibility, but decided it was too risky. The eager anticipation in her eyes made him rescind his decision not to tell her about seeing the Sebastians' tracks that morning. "I don't think we should do that, Eden."

"Why?"

"Because the gang has been in this area. I saw some sign today. In the morning, we need to ride to hell and gone west and then do another circle."

"I see," she said, her voice ringing with disappointment.

"We can't let our guard down. How do we know the Sebastians aren't heading in the same direction your brothers are? Their tracks looked about a day old, your brothers' two days old. If we try to follow them, we could run into the gang."

Looking crestfallen, Eden gazed off in the direction her brothers had gone, but after a moment, her resilient nature had her smiling again. "I'm still thrilled to know my brothers are somewhere close. They'll find us soon. Won't that be wonderful?"

A strange, twisting ache shot through Matthew's chest. He gazed solemnly at her lovely face, tracing the delicate slope of her dainty nose, the stubborn thrust of her small chin, the fragile angle of her cheekbones. When her brothers showed up and took her away, he would probably never see her again. He didn't know why the thought made him feel melancholy, but it did.

"It sure will be wonderful," he agreed.

And he meant it. He was one man against five ruthless killers, and he had to think of Eden's safety. He believed he could take the Sebastians, but what if he couldn't? She was too sweet and wonderful to put her life at risk simply because he dreaded telling her good-bye, which made no sense at all. He didn't want another woman in his life. He had other obligations, and he wouldn't rest easy until he fulfilled them.

But—and suddenly it was a big *but* in Matthew's mind—he had never met anyone quite like Eden Paxton, and he doubted he ever would again. She was amazing, and that wasn't saying it by half. He'd seen her keep going when she could barely lift her feet. He'd heard her laugh when her shoulders were slumped with exhaustion. He'd also witnessed her incredible courage and dauntless determination to survive that first night, when the Sebastians had gone after her like dogs after a bone. Somehow, she'd come through that and emerged on the other side—extremely wary and skittish at first, but becoming less so with each passing day.

She wasn't just a lady; she was one *hell* of a lady.

As a precaution, Matthew decided to keep the fire small that night even though he didn't believe it was necessary. As he laid the few pieces of kindling, he cursed the whole situation, wishing he could build a roaring blaze to keep Eden warm so he wouldn't have to sleep with her. Not that it would have worked. He'd thrown a lot of wood on the fire that first evening, and she'd still shivered and been unable to rest.

They dined on reheated beans again, which saved Matthew the bother of scrounging up something to eat. He added water to the pot and brought the legumes to a full boil for ten minutes, a trick his mother had taught him to make sure the concoction wasn't tainted. While it boiled, he mixed up some trail corn bread to complement the meal, but that didn't take much time, and after they ate, it was still barely dark. He settled by the fire and drew his harmonica from his pocket, determined to get "Beautiful Dreamer" out of Eden's brain. If she hummed that song again tomorrow, he was going to lose it.

She studied him across the fire pit as he cupped his hands around the instrument. "Is it safe for you to play tonight, Matthew? What if the sound carries?"

"In hilly, forested terrain like this, the sound of music and singing won't carry that far. They'd have to be almost on top of us to hear it, and in that event, we'd be in deep trouble, regardless."

Matthew positioned his mouth on the instrument, but before he could push out a single note, she said, "You play beautifully, you know. I can't believe you said you were rusty."

"I play now and again for Smoky and Herman," he confessed. "The music seems to soothe them." In truth, it soothed him as well. After days of silence, sometimes he got edgy, and the music eased that away. "I don't know many songs, though, only a dozen or so."

Tonight he began with "Blue Tail Fly." He expected Eden to sing along, and when she didn't, he decided maybe she didn't know the lyrics. He broke off to ask, "Why aren't you joining in?"

Her beautiful eyes went shadowy. "Because, to me, it's a very *sad* song. I don't think it ever should have been written."

"Why?"

"Because it's about a slave, glad that his master's gone. On the surface, it's a happy tune, but when I sing the words, it makes me think about how terrible enslavement was and how awful those poor people's lives were."

Matthew knew the words to the song—

had sung them a thousand times—but he'd never thought about them that way. She was right; it was a sad song. So he changed stride and broke into "The Bear Went over the Mountain." Eden laughed and started to sing, her voice ringing softly in the twilight.

Next, he started to play a Stephen Foster composition, "My Old Kentucky Home," and again Eden didn't sing. Matthew recalled the lyrics and didn't need to be hit over the head with a hammer. His charge had a tender heart, and she refused to sing songs and enjoy herself if the lyrics were about slavery. He respected that, admired it, in fact, and once again changed course, choosing a lighthearted and safe song, "Camptown Races." She sang out, clearly enjoying that one. He played it all the way to the end, and then he moved on to "Oh! Susanna," which was also about a slave, but apparently didn't offend her sensibilities.

When the notes from his harmonica fell silent, she gazed expectantly across the fire at him. Matthew tried to think of another song he might play that she would enjoy, but he was fresh out of selections.

"Play 'Beautiful Dreamer,'" she suggested. "It's one of my favorites."

When he met her shimmering gaze, he couldn't deny the request. He breathed experimentally into the harmonica to get his start, and then he began to play. Eden's gaze clung to his, and she sang the lyrics as if she meant them solely for him. He searched her rapt expression and got the awful feeling that she was *flirting* with him. Hello, no question about it, she *was* flirting, innocently and perhaps unconsciously, but her gaze clung to his as if he'd hung the moon. And it occurred to him then that perhaps in Eden's eyes he actually had, because he'd rescued her. Maybe she thought of him as her knight in shining armor. Wasn't that a fine how-do-you-do?

By bedtime, Matthew felt like a treed coon with hounds snapping at his tail. As he spread the bedroll, Eden said, "You know what, Matthew? I've been thinking."

"Oh, yeah, what about?"

"It seems to me it'd be a lot easier to share our body heat if we took off our coats and used them as extra blankets."

He stared up at her with mounting dismay. She wore no covering over her breasts but a wash-worn shirt, and that was what had gotten him into trouble last night. "I, um, don't think that's a good idea."

"*Why?* Your heat and my heat must radiate clear through two jackets the way we're doing it now."

And he wanted to keep it that way. Two layers were good, *excellent,* in fact. Only he couldn't think of one plausible reason to nix her idea unless he told her the unvarnished truth. "Haven't you been staying warm at night?"

"Yes, but it takes me a while to get there. I'd fall asleep much more quickly if I got warm faster, and we'd both still be fully clothed."

Matthew seriously considered leaving camp to bang his forehead against a tree. "Wearing our coats makes sleeping together a little more proper," he tried.

"Who's going to tattle on us, the squirrels?"

Matthew could remember saying that to her. He wished now that he'd had better sense. Looking into her guileless blue eyes, he couldn't bring himself to tell her that being near her had become a problem for him. It would frighten her, and right now, he was the only person she could count on.

"All right," he heard himself say. "Why not?"

It turned out that Eden was right. Without the jackets, it was much easier for them to share their body heat. In fact, her method was so much more efficient that Matthew felt on fire everywhere they touched. When he curled his arm around her to spread his hand over her midriff, her unfettered breasts lay against his wrist and thumb, so temptingly soft that he feared he'd cup one of them in his palm after he fell asleep.

As boys, he and his brothers had christened their peckers. Matthew couldn't remember now what his siblings had called theirs, but he'd named his Old Glory. Why, he had no idea. He only knew that Old Glory was already harder than a rock, and before the night was over, he'd be back in the creek. Pneumonia lay on his horizon.

"Ah," Eden murmured, "this is *lovely.*"

Matthew bit down so hard on his back teeth that he nearly broke a molar.

"I'm *much* warmer tonight than I've ever been before," she informed him. "Let the squirrels tattle all they like."

He smiled in spite of himself. Bless her heart, she had no idea how perilous this was, and he was endeavoring to keep it that way by maintaining some distance between her plump posterior and his groin. She wouldn't be quite so happy if Old Glory poked her in the butt.

"At home, I use a hot rock to stay warm on chilly nights," she murmured.

He had a hot rock that he'd be happy to share with her.

"Mama heats hers and mine in the oven and wraps them in towels."

Matthew wanted his hot rock wrapped in feminine wetness, and the thought almost made him come in his jeans. That damned creek was calling his name, *loudly*. "Eden, it's time to go to sleep. No talking tonight, okay?"

"Okay," she conceded softly.

He breathed a sigh of relief.

"It's just—"

When she broke off, he unclenched his teeth again to ask, "It's just what?"

"I like snuggling up to you a *lot* better than I do a rock. You're longer and make me feel warm from head to toe."

Jesus Christ. Was she *trying* to push him over the edge? Matthew went back to clenching his teeth, wanting her so badly that he was afraid he might start to shake. What would he do then, tell her he was sick? He was glad she'd come to trust him. He'd worked toward that. But he'd never considered how completely treacherous a beautiful, *trusting* female could be. She wasn't trying to seduce him. He knew that. But her lush curves were making short work of the task anyway.

When she wiggled her butt closer to his fly, he rolled over onto his back and lifted the blanket. "I've gotta go see a man about a dog."

"Oh. Be careful out there. Away from the fire, you might stumble in the dark."

The only thing Matthew feared he might trip over was Old Glory. Most men wanted to be hung like a horse. Right then, he would have been happy with a pecker the size of a thimble. As he strode away, he snatched their bathing towel from the rack he had erected, hoping Eden wouldn't notice. He had a very important meeting with snow-melt.

This time, Matthew stayed in the icy water so long that he figured chunks of his body could be used to make ice cream in a crank machine. When he was forced to get out of the water by convulsive shuddering, he looked down at his totally out-of-control member and cursed. Old Glory was still at half-mast.

As he dressed, he shivered like an aspen tree in a high wind. Then he went off into the bushes to play some five-fingered stud, praying to God that Father O'Flannigan, the parish priest in Crystal Falls, had lied when he'd said that such an activity made some men go stone blind.

Chapter Nine

Over the next three days, Matthew battled his demons while Eden was apparently conquering hers. She continued to snuggle close to him at night, no longer flinching when he put his arm around her. When he wrapped her ribs, she no longer grew pale and trembled until the task was completed. No more nightmares plagued her, either.

Conversely, with every step Eden took back toward normalcy, Matthew's problem worsened. It seemed to him that he spent more time in the creek at night than he did in bed. Playing five-fingered stud in the bushes eased the ache in his loins for only about an hour. Then it was back, and so was the erection. It got so bad that he almost wished Father O'Flannigan's warning had been true. A blind man wouldn't notice the tantalizing bounce of Eden's breasts under a wash-worn shirt or the tempting roundness of her posterior in the borrowed blue jeans. He wouldn't feel as if he were drowning in her beautiful blue eyes, and her radiant smile wouldn't make him feel as if he were basking in sunshine.

One evening as they returned to camp after laundering their clothes, Eden seemed withdrawn and distant. When Matthew's arm accidentally brushed against hers as they walked, she put more space between them. Then, back at the fire, she scowled as she stirred the stew she'd put on to cook before they left.

"What deep thoughts are putting that frown on your face?" he asked.

When she glanced up, Matthew leveled a solemn look at her and added, "If you're thinking about the Sebastians again, get them out of your head. That part of your life is over. Remember?"

Her lovely mouth tightened, and she

bent over the pot again. Worried, Matthew sat cross-legged near the fire, rested his forearms on his bent knees, and studied her downturned face. She hadn't been this quiet and remote for days. Had he said or done something to offend her?

"Eden, can you talk to me? What's troubling you?"

She finally met his gaze. "I've never been one to prevaricate, Matthew. Perhaps you shouldn't ask that question. You may not like the answer."

Prevaricate? There was a word Matthew had never heard, but he got the gist of its meaning. "If I don't like the answer, I don't like the answer. Something's bothering you. Maybe I can help."

She worried her bottom lip with small, pearl white teeth. "It's just—" She broke off and went back to stirring again. "I'm worried about the way I'm starting to feel about you."

"How, exactly, are you starting to feel?"

Clanking the spoon against the pot with each turn, she murmured something he didn't quite catch.

"Come again? I couldn't hear you."

She stopped stirring, met his gaze, and

swallowed hard before repeating herself. "I'm starting to feel attracted to you."

Trying to look perfectly calm and unruffled by her admission, Matthew shifted into a crouch and leaned around the fire to pour himself some coffee. Only he forgot to watch how full the cup was getting, and hot liquid spilled over the rim onto his hand. "Son of a *bitch*!" He dropped the cup, started waving his hand, and barely managed to set the coffeepot back over the flames without upending the whole works. *"Damn."*

Eden had spare water in a pan that she hadn't needed for the stew. She rushed around the fire. "Here, Matthew, put your hand in this. It'll lessen the burn."

He jerked away when she reached for his wrist. "Don't. I'm fine. My hands are tough as leather."

Eden had felt those hands on her bare skin—their rough texture, their strength and gentleness. Even after what she'd been through with the Sebastians, she couldn't honestly tell herself that she would dread having him touch her that way again. *Madness*. Deep down, she knew she wasn't ready for any form of intimacy. But the feelings were still there—and growing stronger. It was as if a tiny leak had sprung in a dike, and no matter how hard she tried to hold back the flow, the feelings seeped into her anyway. She guessed it was because Matthew was so nice. She'd started to think of him as a friend, and she trusted him now almost as much as she did her brothers. Being attracted to him felt right somehow, and natural.

She returned to her place at the opposite side of the fire and crouched back down. "I've shocked you. I apologize for that. My brother David says I'm the most plainspoken person he's ever known, and he doesn't mean it as a compliment. You asked me a question. I *knew* better than to answer it, but you insisted."

He rubbed a hand over his face and blinked. She'd seen him do that once before when she'd scolded him for trampling the clematis. She guessed it was a habit of his when something set him off balance.

Matthew surprised her by saying, "You're not thinking straight right now. That's all it is."

"What do you mean?"

He shrugged. "It's clear as rain to me. You've been through a terrible ordeal, I rescued you, and now your feelings about me are all mixed-up. It used to happen a lot to women taken captive by Indians. After all the mistreatment, they fancied themselves in love with the first brave who showed them any kindness. Sometimes they were so convinced of it that they resented being rescued and didn't want to be taken home to their families."

Eden considered that possibility and couldn't say for certain that he was wrong. Her emotions were in a tangle, no question about it, and she did feel profoundly grateful to Matthew, not only for saving her, but also for his kindness and understanding. When she stepped back from the situation and looked at it rationally, she had to concede that her attraction to him might stem from confusion and fade with time. On the other hand, it felt very real to her right now, and her feelings were her feelings, no matter what caused them.

He studied her for a moment and then drew his watch from his pocket to trace the writing on the back with his thumb.

"Don't take that to mean I'm not flattered," he told her. "Any man would be. You're a pretty lady, and I'd have to be blind not to notice that."

"Thank you."

He returned the watch to his pocket. "There's a problem, though. I'm not free to do anything more than look. I swore off marriage after what happened to Livvy. I failed to keep her safe, and if I took another wife, I might not be able to protect her either." He gestured limply with one hand. "Even if I could get past that, I can't get involved in another relationship until I've caught the Sebastians, and that may never happen."

Eden had come to understand that about Matthew, and she respected him for it. He'd vowed to love his wife forever, and he was a man of his word. That he'd honored a graveside promise for three long years, no matter how rough the going, was proof of that.

He picked up the dirt-encrusted tin cup and stared at it as if he'd never seen it before. Then he tossed it back on the ground and strode off into the darkness. A moment later, she heard him talking to the animals. She listened to the low thrum of his voice and sighed. Would she never learn to keep her mouth shut? David was right; honesty wasn't always the best policy. Now Matthew felt uncomfortable around her, and she couldn't blame him. It had been inappropriate to confess her feelings. When a lady felt attracted to a man, she was supposed to bat her eyelashes, simper, and blush prettily, not come right out with it.

The odor of scorched stew startled her into jerking the pot from the fire. She gave the contents a stir, and then tasted to see how badly it was burned. *Passable.* Maybe if she added more salt, he wouldn't notice.

He returned to the fire a few minutes later. After rinsing his cup and pouring more coffee, he hunkered down across from her again. Eden had grown accustomed to long silences between them, but this one was different. The air was thick with tension. When she could bear it no longer, she said, "I'm sorry, Matthew. I—"

"Let's let the subject drop. Okay?"

She glanced up at him. "I was only going to say that I burned the stew."

He had just taken a sip of coffee and almost choked on it when he laughed. "Oh."

Pleased that he was smiling again, Eden gave the contents of the pot another stir. "I don't think it's too bad. I caught it in the nick of time."

"I've eaten burned stew before. I reckon I'll survive as long as my belly gets full."

She moved the bread off the coals and went to the packs to get them each a plate and spoon. Minutes later, they settled down to eat, at first in silence, then with occasional exchanges of impersonal conversation. Eden knew Matthew's sudden uneasiness was entirely her fault. Down at the creek, they'd laughed and joked while they washed their clothes. Now it was as if he had erected a wall between them.

"I'm sorry for being so forthright about my feelings, Matthew. Truly, I am. I know it was inappropriate. I have a tendency to say whatever's on my mind. It's an unbecoming trait, I'm afraid."

"I don't find it unbecoming, just a little unsettling."

Judging by his tense behavior, Eden guessed that was an understatement. They cleaned up after supper and went to bed without speaking. Tonight Matthew didn't put his arm around her, and Eden fell asleep missing the comforting weight.

The following morning, Matthew said very little over breakfast, and whenever Eden tried to meet his gaze, he looked quickly away. While they readied the horses to ride, he avoided touching her. She also noticed that he frequently drew his watch from his pocket to trace the lettering on its back, almost as if it were a talisman to protect him against evil. At first that irritated Eden; then it began to amuse her, and finally, it made her feel sad. Any man who went to so much trouble to hold a woman at arm's length had to feel threatened by her. Given that Eden lacked the physical strength to overpower him, the only explanation for his wariness was that he must be as attracted to her as she was to him.

Poor Matthew. Living as he did wasn't natural. Didn't he realize that he had needs, not only physical ones, but emotional needs as well? He was a caring, gentle person. She had witnessed his kindness with the horses and mule, always putting their welfare before his own. During breaks and at the end of the day, the animals drank, ate, and were rubbed down before Matthew ever saw to his own comforts. He was a man with a deep capacity for love, and he was denying himself that to honor the memory of a wife who probably wept in heaven to see him leading such a lonely and joyless existence.

Midmorning, Matthew suddenly reined Smoky to a stop and then steered the horse sharply to the right before pulling to a halt again. At first Eden thought he meant to give the animals a rest, but when she saw the rigid set of his shoulders, she realized something was wrong.

"Stay back, Eden," he said in a low voice. "Don't move and draw attention to yourself. If he leaps, I want him to come for me."

Eden glanced frantically around, and then she saw the cougar, a huge male, crouched just above Matthew on an outcropping of stone. The cat was tensed to spring. An adult mountain lion had powerful jaws that could snap a man's spine with one crushing bite at the nape of the neck. It was also capable of disemboweling prey with one swipe of its claws.

Doing as Matthew had told her, she kept

her gaze riveted on the cat and didn't so much as twitch a muscle. *Matthew.* He had moved between her and the lion, and he meant to keep it that way so she wouldn't get hurt. In that moment, Eden knew she was falling in love with Matthew Coulter—hesitantly and warily, yes, but falling in love, all the same. He was putting his life on the line to protect her from harm.

She held her breath, praying that the creature would back off and leave them alone. Why on earth didn't Matthew grab his rifle? *The Sebastians*, she realized. He was afraid the sound of a high-powered weapon would carry and lead the gang right to them.

Just then, Herman smelled the cat and let loose with a frightened bray, sidestepping and jerking against the lead rope to get away. The shrill scream of the mule was all it took to spur the feline. A blur of speed, it leaped from the rock at Matthew, knocking him off his horse upon impact. Eden drew both her guns, but man and lion rolled over the ground in such a tangle that she couldn't fire her weapon. *Oh, God, oh, God.* Matthew was going to be ripped to pieces.

She slid off her mount and ran closer,

hoping to get a clear shot. She was trying to take aim when steel flashed in the morning sunlight. Matthew's hunting knife. He swung it out to the side and, with a powerful thrust, buried the blade in the cat's neck and then twisted the hilt. For a horrible instant, the lion kept fighting, but then it growled low in its throat and went limp with a whining sigh, pinning Matthew under its dead weight.

Holstering her weapons, Eden sprang forward. "Matthew? Oh, God, Matthew, how badly are you hurt?"

He pushed at the cougar to get it off him. Eden bent to help. Working together, they finally managed to roll the cat away. Eden dropped to her knees at Matthew's side. His blue shirt was in shreds and soaked with blood. His dark face glistened with sweat, and his blue eyes were glassy. Grabbing the front plackets of his shirt just below the open collar, she gave a hard jerk and sent buttons flying. The sight that greeted her eyes nearly made her pass out. Deep, crimson scores ran at an angle across his well-muscled chest.

"Oh, Matthew. Did he get you on the back, too?"

"Just the front," he pushed out. "I'm . . . lucky. Could've killed me." His larynx bobbed as he swallowed. "Get the . . . whiskey. Nothin' worse . . . to get infected. Gotta wash the cuts . . . as fast as you can."

Eden raced back to the horses. Herman was still braying and trying to break the lead. She took a moment to calm the mule so he would stand still while she dug through the packs. "It's okay, Herman. It's okay. It's dead, sweetie, and can't hurt you now."

When she finally found the whiskey, she hurried back to Matthew. As she tugged the cork from the jug, she couldn't help but think how badly the alcohol would sting. Matthew fixed her with a glassy gaze. "Don't hesitate. Do it . . . fast, and get it . . . over with."

She nodded and splashed the alcohol over his chest. He sucked in a sharp breath, clenched his teeth, and lay in rigid agony until the burn finally abated. Perspiration beaded on his face and ran into his dark hair. Struggling to stay calm, Eden examined the cuts.

"Oh, Matthew, some of these will need stitches. They're deep."

He closed his eyes at that news. Then, his voice gravelly, he told her where he kept his needles and thread. After finding what she needed, Eden jerked several strands of hair from Smoky's tail before returning to Matthew. After sterilizing everything with whiskey, she laid the spare strands of horsehair on Matthew's striated belly and threaded the needle.

"This is gonna hurt . . . like blue blazes," he told her haltingly. "While you're . . . sewing me up, talk . . . to me."

Eden's fingers were quivering so badly that she feared she would botch the job. She'd watched her mother stitch up her brothers, but she'd never had to perform the service herself. "What should I talk about?"

"Any . . . thing." He let his eyes fall closed. "Give me something . . . to think about besides . . . the pain."

Eden could think of nothing. The horrible task that lay ahead of her dominated her thoughts. She fixed her gaze stupidly on a scar near his heart, which she guessed had been put there by one of the Sebastians' bullets the day of the ambush at the Lazy J.

"There's a mark . . . on your left ring finger," Matthew said. "Tell me . . . about that."

Eden glanced at her left hand, and sure enough, John's ring had left a faint impression. "Would you like some swallows of whiskey before I start stitching?"

"Better save it for the cuts. Cat claws carry a lot of germs."

As Eden pushed the needle into his flesh, he clenched his teeth and knotted his fists with such force his knuckles went white. Frantic to distract him, she started talking, her voice trembling with regret at causing him such pain.

"Until a week before the train robbery, I was engaged to a man named John Parrish. The impression on my finger is from the ring he gave me five years ago."

Matthew unclenched his teeth to ask, "What . . . happened?"

Eden forced the needle through again. She had started to sweat almost as much as Matthew was. The needle was dull. She had to shove on it and could feel the resistance of his flesh with every pass. Knowing how badly she must be hurting him, she felt sick to her stomach.

"Keep . . . talking," he urged. "Don't

think . . . about what . . . you're doing. . . . Just talk."

"But I'm *hurting* you."

"I've felt . . . worse, and I'll . . . live through it. What . . . happened? Why aren't . . . you wearing the . . . ring anymore?"

"My origins didn't measure up to his parents' expectations." Eden pushed on the needle again and gulped to keep from vomiting. "Oh, Matthew, I'm so *sorry.*"

"Don't think. . . . Just talk, I said."

She swallowed again. "Where was I?"

"His parents didn't . . . approve."

Her hands shook as she tugged the needle through. "That's pretty much it. They disapproved of me, and John's father threatened to disinherit him if he went through with the marriage."

"So John . . . backed out?"

"Not for quite some time. Instead he stalled and made excuses to postpone the nuptials. Idiot that I was, I never suspected that he wanted out until he wrote me a letter to end the engagement."

"Bastard. What the hell's . . . wrong with your . . . origins?"

Eden had finished sewing up the first cut. While she rethreaded the needle, she told him about her real father, Connor O'Shannessy. "He was a horrible man, a liar, a swindler, a drunk, and a killer. He took cruel advantage of my mother, knowing he wouldn't spare her husband's life, no matter how she shamed herself. In short, Matthew, *I'm* the bastard. John's pedigree is without blemish. I don't suppose I can blame his parents for not wanting me as their daughter-in-law or as the mother of their grandchildren."

"Bullshit." He flinched at a stab of the needle. His lips had grown gray from the pain. "They should . . . have welcomed . . . you into the family with . . . open arms. Did you . . . love the . . . spineless asshole?"

Under any other circumstances, Eden might have smiled. She'd had the same thoughts about John a few times herself. "I thought I did, early on. I was young when we met, only seventeen—eighteen when we became engaged." Matthew had been wise to insist that she talk. It helped to take her mind off what she was doing. "Looking back on it now, I think I was more in love with the *idea* of being in love than I was with the man. At first, it was so exciting. Choosing my wedding dress, planning our honeymoon, poring over cookbooks so I'd be able to manage our kitchen staff, deciding what costume to wear when John took me to the theater or opera. I was so focused on all the fun things that I had very little time for soul-searching—and to be honest, at that age, I don't think I understood what true love felt like, anyway."

As she started to work on the last wound, she went on to tell Matthew how John's parents had vilified her reputation in order to protect their son's good name. "My so-called friends would no longer acknowledge me. If they saw me on the street, they pretended not to know me. My mother and I were turned away from homes where we'd been welcomed for years. The situation wouldn't have improved with time. People have long memories when it comes to a scandal. Bastards and the women who bear them are shunned. I didn't want to live that way for the rest of my life, and I certainly didn't wish to see my mother treated that way, so we decided to put the house up for sale and relocate."

"I'm . . . sorry."

"Don't be. Not on my behalf, at any rate. My mother loved living in the city, but I always found the strict social mores a bit stifling. Even though I went to finishing school and learned to say 'mercy me' instead of 'damn it to hell,' I was still the same old Eden, just a more polished and educated version. Knowing French and Latin doesn't change who you are inside."

That earned her a faint smile from him. "Ace taught you to say 'damn it to hell'?"

"No, I owe Joseph for that. When we were young, Mama had to work to help Ace keep food on the table. It fell to Joseph to watch after me most of the time. He used crass language in my presence, and I grew up not realizing there was anything wrong with it. When Ace started winning big at cards, Mama was finally able to stay home. She set to work polishing away all my rough edges and turning me into a lady."

With a sigh of relief, Eden tied the last knot and sat back on her heels. "There, it's done."

"Not quite. Douse 'em . . . with whiskey again, just for good measure."

She did as he said, but with no small regret. He hissed in air at the sting. Then she went to find him another shirt so the flies wouldn't get to the wounds. When she returned, Matthew appeared to be either fast asleep or passed out. As she worked to get the shirt on him, she decided it was the latter, for he didn't awaken as she tugged, pulled, and shoved to get his upper body covered. When that was done, she laid out the bedding and rolled him onto the pallet. Then she set up camp. By the time she had a small fire going, her injured ribs pained her greatly.

She yearned to rest, but first she needed to bury the cougar carcass. The smell of a fresh kill might bring in other predators. Using Matthew's spade, she hacked at the hard earth near the cat until she'd dug a deep enough hole. Her heart ached with sadness when she looked at the lion. Even in death, he was majestic. Why, oh, why hadn't he just run away? Instead, he had attacked and, in the doing, had sealed his fate. Moving him proved to be another daunting task, because he weighed far more than she did. By the time Eden had covered him with dirt, her legs were trembling and her knees felt as if they had turned to water.

Just then, Matthew stirred. Eden hurried

over to him. He fixed her with a bleary gaze. "How long have I been out?"

"A couple of hours."

He grimaced as he sat up. "We need to get the hell out of here."

Eden could scarcely credit her ears. "You can't ride in this condition."

"Damned thing didn't gut me. I'm just cut up a little. I can ride."

"You might break open the wounds!"

"They aren't *that* deep."

Eden watched helplessly as he staggered to his feet. It took him a moment to get his balance, but as soon as he did, he bent to roll up the bedding.

"I'll get it," she insisted.

He shot her a disgruntled look. "I'm not hurt that bad, Eden. Don't fuss over me."

Despite her protests, he helped to break camp and determinedly saddled the horses. When she tried to assist him, he shooed her away with, "You've got busted ribs, damn it. You're in a lot worse shape than I am."

When the horses were trail ready, he mounted up. Eden had no choice but to do the same. Falling in behind the mule, she glared at Matthew's back. *Foolish man.*

He sat the horse as if nothing had happened to him. What was he trying to prove, that he was invincible? Granted, the cuts weren't that deep, but they still had to hurt every time he moved.

At dusk, they stopped to rest the horses until darkness fell. Then, at Matthew's insistence, they rode for another two hours to make up for the lost time. Eden was so exhausted when they finally stopped that her feet dragged as she helped Matthew get the animals settled for the night. She couldn't eat her portion of jerky. Instead she only drank some water.

Evidently Matthew was as weary as she was, for as soon as he'd eaten, he unrolled their bedding, doffed his hat and gun belt, and gingerly settled on the pallet. By his movements, Eden knew his wounds pained him more than he let on. When she joined him under the blanket, she also realized that he had no intention of holding her close to share his body heat. Her admission that she felt attracted to him still hung between them, she guessed. That made her so sad. Matthew had far more wounds than those on his chest—wounds that ran deep and continued to fester.

They lay on their backs, gazes fixed on the heavens. Eden couldn't remember ever having seen so many stars. Even with inches separating them, heat radiated from Matthew's rangy body and cocooned her in warmth. Oh, how she hoped he didn't have a fever. What would she do if his wounds grew infected? They were nearly out of whiskey, and over the last two days, she hadn't seen an aspen tree, the bark of which could be boiled into tea for treating a high fever. If he fell ill, she guessed she would have to hide him somewhere and go in search of an aspen grove.

Eden tried to close her eyes and fall asleep, but her mind raced. There were things she wanted to say to him, things she felt he desperately needed to hear. "When I was a little girl, my mother would sometimes tell me that out of all her children, she loved me most of all." He said nothing, but Eden was determined to finish what she'd started. "It bothered me dreadfully," she went on. "I felt sad for my brothers and more than a little guilty. It seemed to me that she should have loved all of us exactly the same."

Eden rolled onto her side to face him.

His gaze fixed on the heavens, he smelled faintly of bay rum, the scent lingering from when he'd shaved last night. "One day when she said that to me, I couldn't stop myself from asking how she could love me more than she did my brothers. I told her it made me feel awful."

His jaw muscle started to tic.

Eden sighed, but she refused to allow his silence to discourage her. "Mama just laughed and hugged me tight. Then she told me about all the different corners of her heart and how each corner had one of her children's names on it. In Ace's corner, she loved him most all. In my corner, she loved me most of all. As she named off each of us, it started to make perfect sense to me, and I never worried again when she said I was her favorite."

Matthew finally turned his head to search her gaze. "Where are you going with this, Eden?"

"I think you know, Matthew. You have many corners in your heart. My name may never be on one of them, but the point remains: You *can* have a life with someone else without breaking your vow to love Livvy forever. She has her own special corner of your heart, and in that corner, you'll always, *always* love her."

"What woman on earth would ever feel right with me, knowing that I still love my dead wife?"

"What woman worth having would object?" she countered. "You loved Livvy and always will. Love isn't something we can simply decide to stop feeling. It stays with us all our lives. I admire your loyalty to her. It tells me that when you love, you love very deeply. That's a good thing, not a bad one, a very admirable trait."

He studied her for a long while. Then he turned his gaze back to the sky. Eden wished he would say something, but he didn't. And he stubbornly maintained a safe distance from her, even on the narrow pallet.

Eden said nothing more. She'd given him enough to chew on for one night.

Matthew lay awake long after Eden fell asleep. The soft whir of her breathing wasn't exactly a snore, but close. Corners of his heart. What a bunch of skimble-skamble. And unless he missed his guess, Eden was bound and determined to chisel her name on one of them. The very thought scared him half to death. She was a beautiful woman and a tempting package, no question about it, but he couldn't let himself love anyone again. Life was too full of risks. If that cat had attacked her this morning instead of him, she'd be dead. Tomorrow they might encounter another danger. This was harsh and perilous country. There was no guarantee that he'd be able to protect her a second time.

The long and short of it was that he couldn't let her get under his skin and then end up burying her. He just couldn't. Call him a coward, but he refused to live through that again. When she looked at him with those big blue eyes, he read emotions in them that made him feel as if he were standing at the edge of a cliff and she was about to give him a push. She had his thoughts all messed up. She was making him question convictions that he'd had for three years. Just looking at her gave him a hard-on. *Enough*.

From this moment forward, she could preach all she liked, but that didn't mean he had to listen. As for her being attracted to him, he would nip that in the bud, too.

He wasn't sure how just yet, but he'd figure out something.

Eden awakened before Matthew did the next morning. Hoping to lighten his workload, because she knew he was in more pain than he wanted to reveal, she strapped on her guns, donned her jacket, and traipsed off through the early dawn to gather firewood. Then she fished through the rations for ingredients for breakfast. Hunting for meat was out. She didn't think she'd be able to get anything with a crudely fashioned spear, and firing a gun would be too risky. She found a tin of beef and decided fried potatoes would accompany it nicely.

As she set to work, stoking the fire and peeling the spuds, Matthew stirred awake. When he saw that she already had a pot of coffee on to boil and was preparing to cook, he sat up and finger-combed his hair, looking so handsome that he nearly took her breath away.

What truly spoke to her were his eyes. They were so incredibly blue and clear, like the crest of an ocean breaker on a calm summer day, and, unlike when she'd first met him, they seemed so expressive to her now, twinkling with amusement when he was about to laugh, going warm when he studied her face, darkening to the color of storm clouds when he felt sad or worried. This morning they were stormy.

Studying him, Eden knew she was treading on perilous ground, in danger of losing her heart to a man who claimed he had nothing left to give her in return.

"How's your chest this morning?" she asked.

"Fine," he bit out. "The cuts aren't that deep. They'll heal fast as long as infection doesn't set in."

"I cleaned them well. Let's hope that doesn't happen."

He struggled to his feet and bent to roll up the bedding.

"I'll get that, Matthew."

"You're hurt, too, and a whole lot worse than I am," he retorted. "I'm fine, I said."

"My goodness, aren't we cheery this morning?"

"Maybe I'm cross more mornings than not. Did you ever think of that? You think you know me, but the truth is, you don't."

He strode down to the creek without fetching his shaving gear. Eden gazed thoughtfully after him. When he returned a few minutes later, she offered him a cup of coffee. He took it without saying thank-you. Then he ate the food in sullen silence.

When the remains of breakfast had been cleaned up, they broke camp without speaking. Eden was weary of riding. Last night, she'd grown so exhausted that she'd caught herself nodding off in the saddle. She didn't look forward to another long day, especially when her companion was in such a grump.

There was no help for it, though. If they made for a town too soon, the Sebastians might cut them off before they got there. Eden understood the danger, and she preferred to avoid a shoot-out. Target-practicing was a lot different from aiming her gun at a man and pulling the trigger.

While Matthew saddled the horses, Eden hurried down to the creek for a quick scrub. The water was icy, but she enjoyed the first bracing splash to her face to get the sleep out of her eyes. She used her reflection on the water as a mirror to do something with her hair. The wild mane of curls proved impossible to tame without a brush and pins, so she settled for combing it with her fingers and knotting it at the back of her head. At least that would keep it out of her eyes when the wind picked up later. She hadn't smeared mud on her face in days. Her sunburn was now healed, and the battered straw hat Matthew had lent her had a wide brim to help protect her from the sun.

Matthew was putting the packs on Herman when she returned. While he did that, she began erasing all signs of their campfire, as she'd seen Matthew do, and then she feathered away their footprints and all the hoofmarks. The binding around her ribs was a godsend.

She hoped that Matthew might say she'd done a good job when she finished erasing their tracks, but instead he swung up onto his horse, tipped his hat low to shade his eyes from the sun, and rode off before she'd even mounted up. She had to hurry to catch up with him.

That morning he headed northwest into the foothills, undoubtedly to make another circle. Since coming upon the Sebastians' tracks, he'd been extremely alert to their surroundings, either scanning the hillsides or searching for signs that the gang had

recently been in the area. She'd also noticed that he'd been keeping their fires
small at night, which told her he feared the
criminals could be somewhere nearby.

A few minutes later, when they came to
a meadow, he slowed his horse so she
could ride abreast of him. "Yesterday when
you were telling me about John, you said
his father threatened to disinherit him if he
went through with the marriage. Can I take
that to mean John will be a rich man someday?"

Eden nodded. "His father owns five
banks and several businesses."

"So John was quite a catch."

"I suppose you could say that, yes."

He drew his horse to a stop and looked
her directly in the eye. "The next time you
fancy yourself attracted to me, Eden, remember one thing: I'm *not* a good catch. I
have very little money and no way to make
a lot."

"Money isn't everything. You're not afraid
of hard work, and heaven knows you have
a determined nature."

"Big problem. I have no land to work,
remember?"

"You have the land in Oregon."

"Even if I decided to go home, which I have no intention of doing, the Lazy J is a family-owned ranch, and the profits are divided among everyone. My share was never large, and we're all a far cry from wealthy. My parents' house is livable, but there's nothing fancy about it. The cabin Livvy and I shared was nothing to shout about, either, squat and tiny, with only two bedrooms."

"I didn't always live in a fancy house, Matthew, and I have no overwhelming need to do so again. There's a lot more to life than that. I could be happy on a ranch with only the basic necessities."

"You think that now, but you might change your mind after the new wore off. On a ranch, you don't work with cattle only for the fun of it, and you can't avoid the unpleasant jobs just because they turn your stomach. Branding and castrating are part of the business. So is selling the steers for slaughter, no matter how fond of them you become. It's a hard, demanding life with few days off. No expensive honeymoons, no fancy dresses, no attending the opera or theater, no kitchen staff to oversee. You've got mettle, Eden; I'll give you that. But you're not made of stern enough stuff to be a rancher's wife."

He nudged his horse into a trot to leave her trailing behind him again. Eden wanted to shout a retort at him, but she could think of nothing to say. Why did he always sell her short? It made her so furious that she had to clench her teeth to keep from screaming. Yesterday, after the cougar attack, had she balked at stitching him up? No, not even once. How dared he say she didn't have what it took to be a rancher's wife!

For about five minutes, Matthew congratulated himself on a job well-done. A woman couldn't very well feel attracted to a man when he riled her temper at every turn. But then he started to feel guilty as hell. He'd seen the hurt, bruised look in Eden's eyes when he'd taken that jab at her, and now he wished he could take it back. She *was* made of stern enough stuff to be a rancher's wife, and he was a low-down, cowardly skunk for telling her she wasn't. Just because she was getting under his skin was no excuse for him to tell her a flat-out lie, and it was no excuse to injure her feelings, either.

Damn. Every time he looked at her, his brains leaked out his ears. He dreaded having to apologize, but he knew there was no help for it.

For lunch, they stopped by a narrow stream that meandered through a gorgeous stand of ponderosa pine. While they rested the horses and chewed on jerky, Matthew spread a map of the area over his lap. Though still miffed, Eden scooted close so she could peruse it with him.

"That's Holden Creek," he said, pointing to a small dot. "After the train was held up, I rode there for help. To say I wasn't impressed with the marshal would be an understatement. He's an old, paunchy drunk, and his pals were the same. They wouldn't offer much protection against the Sebastians."

"No," she agreed. "We should head for a town where there are a lot of people and enough lawmen to deal with gunslingers. Denver would be ideal." Squinting to make sense of the squiggles on the map, she asked, "Where are we right now?"

He indicated the spot, and when she followed the point of his finger, her heart sank. "Oh, *mercy*, Matthew. We're clear out in the middle of nowhere." She located Denver, and her heart sank even more. "Please tell me that isn't as far away as it looks."

"Not quite as far away as it looks, but a far piece all the same. I'd say it's a five- or six-day ride, maybe even seven. Not that it matters."

She shot him a bewildered look. "What do you mean?"

"We aren't going there."

"Where are we going then?"

He rubbed his jaw and glanced away. "Nowhere," he muttered.

"Pardon me?"

In a louder voice, he repeated himself. "Nowhere. I've been mulling it over, and I think we should keep moving into different areas and riding in circles. Your brothers are halfway decent trackers, right?"

"Right. David is a lawman, so he's especially good."

"We've seen their tracks. We know they're

out here somewhere. We just have to wait for them to find us."

"You're constantly riding in streams and covering our tracks. They may not find us for several more days, maybe even *weeks*." Eden gaped at him. "What happened to our plan to ride in circles for a few more days and then head for a town?"

"Well, that's just the thing. There are a number of towns, but this map doesn't tell their population, so I'm not sure how big they are or what kind of law enforcement they have. If you know something I don't about them, fill me in, because the way I see it, Denver is our only safe bet, and if I'm thinking that, so are the Sebastians."

"So you're afraid to go there?"

"If we go that way, they'll head us off, sure as rain is wet, and I'd rather avoid that if we possibly can."

"You don't think we can take them?"

He sighed and finally met her gaze again. "We're both pretty damned good with a gun, but so are they. In a shoot-out, it'll be two against five. What are our chances? If one little thing goes wrong, we're dead."

Eden's throat felt as if she'd swallowed flour paste. "But, Matthew, we can't ride around out here in circles indefinitely. We'll run out of supplies."

"I can hunt. I won't let you starve."

"I'm tired. I don't know how much longer I can do this."

"If you go down, I'll carry you in front of me on my horse."

Eden knew he would do exactly that—even with a lacerated chest. "I'm not a small woman, Matthew. Your arms would feel as if they were falling off after only a few hours."

"You're not that heavy. I've picked you up, remember? If it comes to that, I can carry you, no problem."

She started to make another protest, but he held up a hand to silence her. "I know it won't be easy, Eden, and I understand that the prospect seems overwhelming to you. But I can't in good conscience put your life at risk, not if I can help it." He puffed air into his cheeks and slowly released it. "The moment I carried you from that camp, you became my responsibility. I don't take that lightly, and I have to do everything in my power to keep you safe, even if it means riding in circles out here for weeks. Do you understand? With any luck, the Sebastians will grow tired of the chase and give up."

Eden understood his reasoning but wished she didn't. "Maybe we should change tactics and start tracking *them*," she suggested. "If we catch them by surprise, it'll increase the odds in our favor."

"It would still be risky. I say we should just keep outsmarting them until your brothers find us. When they do, it'll be six fast guns against five. At least then we'll have a decent chance. Maybe Ace will pull a rabbit out of his hat and take two of them with one bullet."

"Do I have a vote?"

He looked away again. "Not really, no. I have to keep you safe if I can, and this is the best chance I've got of doing it."

"We can take them, Matthew. I know we can."

He cut his gaze back to her. "You ever killed a man, Eden?"

"No."

"Well, I've only killed one. You know what that makes us? *Green*. We can talk big, but when it comes right down to pulling the trigger, what if one of us hesitates? Shooting acorns off trees isn't the same as drawing down on a man. The Sebastians may be the scum of the earth, but they're still human beings. Can you look me in the eye and tell me you won't think about that when you're about to shoot?"

"No," Eden replied shakily, "but I'm fairly confident I won't hesitate. It'll be them or us."

"Yes, but if you hesitate, it could be us. I'd have to be nuts to deliberately seek them out when I've got you with me."

"What if my brothers never find us?"

"They're searching for you, and they'll find us."

"But we've been brushing away a lot of our tracks to fool the Sebastians. If we've fooled them, what's to say we haven't fooled my brothers, too?"

"The Sebastians aren't that smart. Wily, maybe, and hard to predict because they don't think like normal folks, but if you put all their brains in a pot and gave them a stir, you wouldn't have a full ladle. They also drink themselves stupid every night, which makes them even dumber, because they're always hungover. We can outthink them if we use our heads, but the same can't be said of your brothers. They'll find us eventually. I'd bet my last double eagle on it."

"What if the Sebastians run out of liquor and smarten up?"

"They won't. When they start running low, one of them will ride to a town and buy more."

"How do you know that?"

"Because that's how I happened to get Eric, the youngest brother, and reduce their number to five. They sent him into Tucson alone to buy booze."

"How did you know for certain it was him?"

"I saw all of them the day Livvy died and a thousand times after in my dreams. When I hit the trail, I got wanted posters so I could put their names with their faces." He slanted her a steely look. "It was Eric Sebastian, no question. After we swapped lead, I hoped his older brothers would ask around in Tucson to find out who might have killed him. It would have suited me fine if they had come after me. I wouldn't still be out here, trying to find the bastards, if they had. But they evidently never figured out who shot him."

Eden could come up with no more arguments about remaining in the wild until her brothers found them. "How long have you known that you intended to ride around out here indefinitely?"

"Almost from the start," he said so softly she barely caught the words.

"Say that again?"

"Almost from the start," he repeated in a louder voice.

"So when you asked for my opinion that morning, it was all for show. Essentially, you were giving me a pat on the head."

He didn't deny it, and Eden felt her temper rising. Pocketing her jerky, she pushed angrily to her feet. Before stalking away, she whirled on him. "Don't *ever* play games with me again. I'm not some empty-headed female who appreciates being flimflammed."

"I wasn't playing games. I just didn't want to say anything too soon because I knew it would upset you."

"Discovering that you've lied to me almost from the start upsets me far more!"

"I didn't lie, exactly. And I wasn't patting you on the head when I asked for your input. I was counting on your good sense to help you reach the same conclusion that I already had. It seemed better to me, doing it that way, than shoving my decision down your throat."

So angry she was shaking, Eden strode over to her horse. *Not made of stern enough stuff to be a rancher's wife?* And now she discovered that he'd been hoodwinking her from day one. When she grabbed the saddle blanket, Matthew tucked the map into a pocket and struggled to his feet. "I'll take care of that. It's heavy work."

"A man's work, you mean?" She elbowed her way past him to grab the saddle. "I may not have what it takes to be a rancher's wife, Matthew Coulter, but I can sure as hell saddle a horse."

"Look, I know you're angry at me right now, and with good cause, but that's no reason to risk hurting yourself. You've got busted ribs. That's too heavy for you to be lifting."

"But you can do it with a stitched-up chest? I've been saddling horses all my life." In truth, one of the stable hands had often done it for her, but Eden was too mad right then to mention that. "I don't need a big strong man to do it for me."

"I am *not* letting you saddle that damned horse."

He wrested the gear away from her. His commandeering manner made Eden want to kick him. She was no hothouse lily, and it hurt to know that he thought she was.

"I said I'll do it!" she cried.

"And I'm saying you won't." He settled the saddle on the bay's back and then gave her a heated look. "I'm bigger than you are. My vote carries the day."

That cinched it. Eden stepped in close and shoved his arm to get him away from her horse. Matthew curled viselike hands over her shoulders and lifted her as if she weighed no more than a child to deposit her out of his way. She doubled her fists.

"Don't go there," he said evenly. "I'm saddling the damned horse, and that'll be the end of it."

"So help me, Matthew, don't be high and mighty with me."

He shot her another dark look. "I've seen stubborn, honey, but you take the prize."

"As if you have room to talk?" She thought she glimpsed a grin flirting at the right corner of his mouth. "Don't you dare laugh at me."

The grin won over, and he chuckled. "I'm not laughing at you, I swear. Not only at you, at any rate. I'm laughing at both of us. Here we are, two grown adults, acting like children." He turned toward her, resting one bent arm on the saddle seat. "If I let you do the rest, will that satisfy you?"

Eden wanted to stay furious, but his amusement was contagious. She truly had been acting like a child. She struggled not to smile, but his sheepish grin took the wind out of her sails. The next thing she knew, she was laughing with him. On some level, she knew it wasn't really funny and that she should still be angry with him, but she giggled until she was breathless and holding her injured side. Matthew laughed just as hard as she did, a hand clamped over his tender chest.

When their mirth finally subsided, he wiped tears from his cheeks, released a shaky sigh, and asked, "Are you always so impossible when you get your tail tied in a knot?"

"Sometimes I'm even worse."

He gave another weak chuckle, holding

up a hand so she wouldn't make him laugh again.

"Are you always so mule-headed?" she couldn't resist asking.

"Only when I get my back up."

"And how often does that happen?"

"Only every now and again, mostly when an empty-headed female challenges me. I'm the man, after all. I should be wearing the pants. Just because you've borrowed a pair doesn't mean they fit you."

Eden was over her snit, so she took the words as they were meant, as a teasing remark. While she tightened her horse's belly cinch, Matthew saddled Smoky with an economy of movement. As he worked, he said, "Eden, I owe you an apology."

Taken by surprise, she shot him an expectant look.

He ran a hand over Smoky's mane. "I didn't mean it when I said you aren't made of stern enough stuff to be a rancher's wife. You *are*, and it was a rotten thing to say."

It wasn't the most flowery apology that Eden had ever received, but when she searched his gaze, she knew it was heartfelt. "If you didn't mean it, Matthew, why did you say it?"

He sighed and shoved his hat back on his dark head. Then he shifted his weight from one long leg to the other, clearly uncomfortable. "You make me feel cornered," he confessed. "I look at you, and I want things I shouldn't. I think things I shouldn't. I've been walking one way for a long time, and now suddenly I feel like I'm at a crossroads. Does that make any sense?" He rubbed a hand over his face and sighed. "You yammer at me about corners in my heart, about how what happened to Livvy wasn't my fault."

"It *wasn't*, Matthew."

"There you go again, yammering at me. And those looks you give me with your heart shining in your eyes. You think I'm not tempted? That I don't want the same things other men want? If you believe that, you're dead wrong. I'm just not free to act on it right now. I have a score to settle, and until I've taken care of that, I can't make any commitments."

"So you took a mean shot at me to make me angry at you."

He looked sheepish. "It seemed like a good plan at the time." His gaze locked with hers. "You could have died yesterday morning, Eden. That cougar could have just as easily leaped on you."

"It didn't, though. You put yourself in harm's way to protect me."

"I may not be able to protect you next time. What then? I'll be burying you—that's what."

In that moment, Eden realized that Matthew was coming to have feelings for her, but he was fighting it. And now she finally understood why, as she hadn't before.

"Bad things happen, Matthew. We can't see them coming, and there's often nothing we can do to prevent them. But that doesn't mean we shouldn't all live life to its fullest."

"Life is a huge gamble—that's what," he replied. "And I always get dealt rotten hands."

He tightened Smoky's belly cinch and swung up onto the horse, his way of ending the conversation. Eden gazed up at him for a moment, wishing she knew something to say that might ease his mind, but there was nothing. They were in dangerous country and being pursued by conscience-less men. She couldn't promise him that nothing bad would happen to her.

Soon they were riding again, and Eden nearly groaned at the discomfort it caused.

"I'm sorry it has to be this way," he said over his shoulder. "I'd take you straight home if I thought it was safe."

Eden no longer had a home. After all that had happened, she would have to live in a town where no one knew her and lie through her teeth about her past. Women abducted by rapists and held for five days were automatically presumed to be defiled. Unmarried young ladies who spent weeks alone with a man, which might be the case for her before this was over, were considered to be compromised. The closest she might come to living near her brothers would be to reside in Denver, and right then, Denver seemed a million miles away.

"I'm fine," she called out. "Riding in circles is starting to grow on me."

Chapter Ten

Matthew drew rein again at midafternoon to give the horses another rest. Eden was unaccountably relieved. She was so *tired*. While he unsaddled the horses, murmuring his concerns about the possibility of their developing saddle sores, she found a spot on the grass in full sunshine, lay down, and luxuriated in the heat. It felt so lovely that she wanted to stay there for hours. Guilt nipped at her, though, and she pushed up to follow Matthew down to the creek, wanting to do her share. While the horses drank, he normally rubbed them down, and she could help with that. She knew his chest had to be hurting him.

The ground was rocky, forcing her to watch her step. As she neared the stream, she glanced up. What she saw made her heart freeze, and she jerked to a stop. *Snakes*. While the horses drank, Matthew had gone down on his belly among the rocks to drink himself. He lay perfectly still. A rattler was coiled about two feet from his bent left arm. He'd clearly heard it buzzing, knew it was close, and didn't dare move.

Normally Eden would have reacted instantly, but that one snake wasn't the only serpent posing a threat. Matthew and the horses were *surrounded*. She'd never seen so many rattlers in once place, *never*. To her frightened eyes, there appeared to be a hundred of them. *Impossible*. For a fraction of a second, she wondered if her sleepy mind had conjured them up. But no, they were real.

There wasn't time to think. Eden whipped a Colt from its holster, swung into a crouch, got the snake by Matthew's elbow in her sights, and fired. The rattler's head blew off.

And then she fanned the hammer, shooting at every slithery thing she saw.

The horses and mule went nuts. Matthew's animals had been conditioned to gunfire and trained not to bolt at the sight of a snake. But this wasn't just *one* rattler. Oh, God, if they were bitten, they might die. Eden had come to love both of Matthew's critters, and the stolen bay gelding as well. She'd gotten the snake closest to Matthew, so now she turned to protect the animals. Risky business, that. Matthew hadn't been moving when she killed the snake near him, but the geldings and Herman were. It required all her skill not to hit one of them in the leg.

After emptying all twelve rounds from her guns, she frantically started to reload, jerking bullets from her belt with hands that were amazingly steady, even though she was so afraid for Matthew she could barely think. As she shoved bullets into the cylinders, she heard his weapons going off and realized he was firing, too. As soon as she had six more bullets in a cylinder, she started shooting again, and when those ran out, she stuffed more ammunition into the gun. How many snakes had she and Matthew shot now? At the back of her mind, she still questioned her sanity. Was this real? It was only June. In the chilly climes of the high Colorado foothills, rattlers should not have been out in such numbers yet. At this elevation, even in August, their populations were scant. Where had they come from? How could this be happening?

But they were there. Unless, of course, she'd drifted off to sleep and was having a nightmare to end all nightmares. She kept shooting. Reloaded. Started firing again. When all the snakes that hadn't been blown to smithereens began slipping away into their hiding places among the rocks, she shuddered and dropped both arms to her sides, the revolvers dangling limply from her sweat-slick hands. She stared stupidly at Matthew, who stood much as she did, limp with relief. He regarded her blankly for a long moment, and then, slowly, one of those crooked grins she had come to love so much stole across his face, creasing his lean right cheek.

"Holy Mother, girl, you can shoot! That was a whole lot more impressive than knocking acorns off a tree."

Eden's eyes welled with tears. He could have died. She snapped her gaze to the horses and mule. All three were still quivering, but they'd stopped rearing and screaming now.

"Matthew," Eden said in a low-pitched voice, "move away. I think it's a snake den. I saw them go down only one hole, but there could be other exit points. Get the animals out of there."

He glanced around at the rocks that lined the stream. At the other side of the waterway, a shale cliff rose toward the sky, reaching as high as the trees. His blue gaze locked on hers. "I've never come across a den until now, thank God, but I must be standing on top of it, and so are the horses."

Eden nodded and swiftly reloaded both guns. When she'd done that, she dropped down to one knee, ready if she had to be. "Lead the horses and mule away. *Now*. I'll cover you."

He glanced around again. His jaw muscle started to work. "How many snakes are normally in a den?"

"I have no idea, but it's spring; they're venturing forth, and you have to get out of there."

He locked gazes with her. "If I'm on top of a den, the snakes could strike again. Horses are heavy and vibrate the earth with every step. I can't lead them and the mule away with a gun in my hand."

"You won't need a gun. I've got you covered. Trust me and *move.*"

He glanced around again. Then he stepped softly over to gather up all the dangling reins. "If it's a den and they bite the horses, our asses will be grass. We can't evade the Sebastians on foot."

The Sebastians were the least of Eden's concerns right then. She just wanted Matthew away from the danger that he'd unwittingly waded into. Her fingers were ready on the triggers of both guns. When the horses and mule started to move, sending vibrations through the earth, Eden scanned the ground all around Matthew and the animals. As she feared, there was more than one hole leading from the den. When serpents poked up their heads, flicking their forked tongues at the air, she took aim, fired, and killed them before they could come out.

When Matthew reached her, he dropped

to his knees, swiped his jacket sleeve over his mouth, and just sat there on his boot heels for a long moment. "You truly are the most amazing woman. I thought I was dead. I reached to cup some water in my hands, and there it was, right beside me. I was afraid to breathe, let alone move. It could have killed me, biting me that close to my heart. You blew the bastard's head off at thirty feet."

"Go on and get the animals out of here, Matthew. God only knows how many of them there are, or where they are."

He pushed erect and led the horses and mule back to the clearing. Eden remained where she was until he and the animals were safely away. As she hurried after him, she knew all of them were still at risk. When she reached him, she said, "We've got to get away from this place. I know nothing about snake dens, but I'm guessing not all of them are inside it."

He checked the horses and mule for bites. All three animals had escaped without injury. He picked up Smoky's saddle, then let it drop and stared at her. "You saved my life."

Eden was still standing guard, watching for snakes. "You would have done the same for me."

"I've never seen anyone shoot like that. I thought you might hit one of the horses, but you didn't. You're incredible, Eden, absolutely incredible."

"You didn't do too badly yourself."

He went back to work, moving fast so they could ride. Eden kept her guns drawn. So many snakes. Just thinking about them made her skin crawl. "Why are they out in such great numbers at this time of year?"

"Spring is the time of new life," he replied as he handed her the reins of the bay. "When I led the horses over the top of their den, I reckon I got a bunch of protective mamas all stirred up."

Ever conscious of her tender ribs, Eden held her breath as she swung up into the saddle. "We need to stay alert. I have no idea how far snakes wander from a den. This whole area may be infested."

"I'll keep an eye out."

He led the way, guns at the ready, and she followed, thanking God every step of the way that she hadn't lain back there in the delicious warmth of the sun and fallen asleep, as she'd yearned to do. Matthew would have been bitten, and the horses and mule as well. She would have been left alone out here, and on foot. But she knew her emotions were about more than herself. *Matthew*. When she'd seen that snake near his elbow, her heart had almost stopped. She cared far more for him than was wise—or even explainable. If something happened to him, she didn't know what she would do.

She drew in an uneven breath and slowly released it, trying to stop shaking. Now that it was all over, her joints felt as if they had dissolved.

Raising his voice to call back to her over his shoulder, he said, "I think we're probably far enough away now to stop worrying about snakes, unless we count the two-legged kind."

Eden's heart skittered with fear again. *All the gunfire*. "Oh, God, Matthew, do you think the Sebastians heard us shooting?"

"The sound can travel quite a distance. If they're anywhere in this general vicinity, they may have heard it. We need to ride, and ride hard, honey. Get as far away from this area as we can. Otherwise we're liable to get some unwanted company."

He urged Smoky into a fast trot. Eden's mount increased speed to keep up. Over the next several hours, they pushed the horses, alternating between a fast pace and a walk so the animals could have a breather. Eden knew they were covering a lot of ground. She could only pray it would be enough.

At dusk, they stopped to rest the horses, but as soon as full darkness descended, they lit out again and rode all night. Eden assumed they were going in another circle, but she became too exhausted to note which direction they were headed at any given time. She just kept her gaze fixed on Matthew and followed wherever he led.

At dawn, they stopped to eat, rest the horses for a few hours, and sleep. Eden was still bone-tired when Matthew awakened her. "I'm sorry, Eden. I know you're beat, but we need to get moving again."

They rode steadily for the remainder of that day, stopping only to give the animals rest periods. When twilight finally darkened the forest, Matthew deemed it safe for them to find a place to camp for the night. They built no fire and ate only jerky for supper. Immediately after the meager meal, Eden rolled out their bedding, lay down, and slipped into a dreamless sleep.

Eden awakened the next morning to full sunlight and the delicious smell of fresh coffee. Crouched over a tiny fire, Matthew grinned at her as she sat up.

"Mornin', sleepyhead."

As much as Eden looked forward to a cup of coffee, she glanced worriedly at the flames. "Is that safe? What if they see the smoke?"

"The little smoke this puts off won't be seen from afar. I also think we've put enough distance between us and that snake pit to relax a little now. If we got really lucky, the Sebastians stumbled onto it."

Eden loved the thought of that, snakes happening upon snakes.

"I kept the fire small just to be safe, but it probably isn't necessary. We cut so many loops getting here that they shouldn't be able to follow us."

"Does that mean we can go at a slower pace today?"

"It does."

That was welcome news. Every joint in Eden's body ached. She didn't look forward to being in the saddle again, let alone at a bone-jarring trot for much of the day. "I'm glad."

"You've done great," he told her. "I know this has been hard on you."

"It's been even harder on the animals."

Eden helped him fix a quick breakfast and do the dishes. Then they took turns going down to the stream to wash up. Though she knew it was silly, Eden kept a sharp eye out for snakes as she performed her ablutions. When she returned to camp, Matthew had already packed the gear and had the horses saddled. It was all she could do not to groan. Mounting back up was the last thing she wanted to do.

Blessed with a sunny nature, Eden had reconciled herself to another day in the saddle before the hour was out. Until her brothers showed up, she would be riding around in circles behind Matthew Coulter. There was no alternative. Moaning and groaning about it, even if only to herself, would just sour her mood and make an already difficult situation worse.

She decided to focus on the positive. First and foremost, at least she liked her traveling companion and enjoyed his company. Even when they quarreled, they ended up laughing. Eden was also well schooled in the edible flora of Colorado, compliments of her mother, so she didn't think she and Matthew were going to starve.

In hopes of adding to their food stores, she began keeping an eye out for plants they might eat. Over the course of the afternoon, she managed to collect a goodly number of groundnuts, a tuber that tasted a lot like sweet potatoes; cattail shoots, which would be delicious simmered; some false Solomon's seal, a great substitute for asparagus; and the makings for a salad— wild lettuce, amaranth, wild onions, and dandelion leaves. She even found some citrus oregano, a wonderful spice for meat, and a nice bunch of yellow morel mushrooms that would be lovely fried up with whatever meat Matthew got that night.

All the dismounting and remounting to collect plants took a huge toll on Eden's energy, but she insisted, despite Matthew's protests. He helped with the digging and picking, but it was still a lot of work. By evening, when he finally located a good spot to camp near a stream, she had to concede that he'd been right to discourage all her foraging. She was so tired it was difficult to put one foot in front of the other one, let alone contemplate cooking. Nevertheless, she couldn't allow the bounty they had collected in the folds of her traveling skirt to go to waste. After depositing the food on the ground, she began gathering rocks to build a fire pit, then searched for firewood while Matthew tended to the animals. By the time he'd finished his chores, Eden had a fire going, had washed all the vegetables, and was enjoying a cup of coffee.

"What kind of meat do you hope to get tonight?" she asked.

He went to a pack that he seldom opened and withdrew a bow and arrows she hadn't realized he had. "I don't know about you, but I'm ready for some real meat for a change. I've seen a lot of deer sign today. I think I'll go try my luck."

"Some venison would be delicious."

Just thinking about it made Eden's stomach rumble.

"Better than gnawing on jerky and rabbit bones. It takes me a little longer to find large game, but I think it'll be worth the effort."

"You won't go far, I hope."

"If you fire a shot, I'll be here in two blinks. Just keep your guns handy."

While Matthew was out hunting, Eden took advantage of his absence to bathe, wash her hair, and launder her clothes. Per his warning, she placed the Colts on a rock within easy reach. After entering the water, she was once again assailed with the compulsion to scour her skin, but she managed to talk herself through the moment. As she dried off, she made a mental note to wash the linen towel after Matthew finished using it later. The cloth was so thin that it would easily dry by morning if she draped it near the fire.

Binding her ribs tightly by herself once again proved to be nearly impossible, so she saved the long strip of knotted cloth, resigned to revealing her bare stomach to Matthew again before the evening was over. The extra support truly did help to ease the pain in her side, and now she was loath to go without it.

She was sitting cross-legged by the fire trying to dry her thick hair when Matthew rode back into camp. He'd removed his leather jacket, and in the twilight, she could see that his tanned, corded forearms were smeared with blood up to the rolled-back sleeves of his blue shirt. Behind him, an already gutted deer lay over Smoky's haunches.

"You got one!" As Eden walked toward him, she experienced a momentary pang of sadness for the deer, but it quickly passed. Without meat, and plenty of it, she and Matthew wouldn't survive a prolonged stay in the wilderness. "Good job."

As he dragged the dead animal off the horse, Eden noted that it was a small buck. Normally, fawns in this country were born in early June. She would have felt dreadful if helpless babies had been left alone in the woods to starve just so she might eat.

"I'm glad it's not a doe," she mused aloud.

"Wouldn't shoot a doe unless I was desperate. Even in deep snow when we were low on meat, my pa always brought in a buck, never a doe." He glanced up. "They keep the deer population strong."

Eden drew her jacket more snugly around her. The evening air had developed a bite. "Does it snow a lot on the Lazy J?"

"It snows so deep we have to jack up the cows to milk them."

Eden laughed softly. "That's pretty darned deep."

"You need to be long in the leg to wade through the stuff after a storm. We spend a lot of time shoveling paths—that's for sure."

He jabbed his knife through the sinew and tendons just above the buck's hocks, shoved a sturdy branch through the openings, and soon had the animal hanging head down from a tree. Watching him work, Eden couldn't help but notice the play of muscle in his arms and shoulders, the masculine taper of his upper torso to a narrow waist and lean hips, and the powerful contours of his thighs. He moved with fluid strength, everything about him so male and attractive that Eden's knees felt a bit watery. Exhaustion, she assured herself, but even as the thought moved through her mind, her gaze went to his big hands, which looked so capable and strong, yet always touched her with such gentleness.

Within minutes he'd skinned the deer and trimmed away some of the backstrap. Using a fallen log as a work surface, he wielded the knife with skill born of long practice and then handed Eden four butterflied steaks. She took the meat down to the creek to clean it. When she got back to camp, she started preparing their meal while Matthew finished cutting up the deer.

When he had washed up and joined her at the fire, Eden had a five-course meal ready—seasoned steak slathered with morel-mushroom gravy, pan-roasted groundnuts, mountain asparagus, simmered cattail shoots, and a mixed green salad. Matthew's eyes widened when she handed him a filled plate and a steaming cup of coffee.

"This is a meal fit for a king."

Pleased, Eden said, "My mother is fascinated by wild flora and passed her interest on to all of us. I learned a lot about Colorado's edible plants during my visits to No Name. We went on horseback rides and lots of walks. She's a font of information and has taught me most of what she knows." She swung an arm. "God's general store. If you know what to look for, there are all sorts of things to eat out here."

He took a bite of cattail, chewed for a moment, and then arched his eyebrows. "These are *good*. I won't complain tomorrow about you stopping to collect food." He murmured even more appreciatively when he tasted the groundnuts. "What are these?"

Eden chewed and swallowed. "Indian potatoes. My mother calls them groundnuts. They sprout underground from a vine with purple flowers. You can harvest them year-round, but they're best in the fall. My sister-in-law Caitlin gathers them every autumn to use over the winter. They're supposedly more nutritious than regular potatoes."

"Nutritious or not, they're flat tasty."

He made similar comments about the asparagus and salad, but he especially loved the tender venison steaks in mushroom gravy.

"I can't believe you put a meal like this together with stuff you found," he said.

"I didn't do it all by myself. You helped. My thought is to utilize as many wild plants as we can to make our rations from town last longer."

He nodded. Then he grew quiet, his expression solemn as he ate. When his plate was clean, he glanced up and flashed a crooked, decidedly sheepish grin. "I have to apologize again. I should never have said you don't have what it takes to be a rancher's wife." A twinkle danced in his eyes. "You've been dragged from pillar to post for so long I've lost track of the days, the last two of them pure hell. Yet, here we are, eating a meal you mostly put together by finding food along the trail."

"Well, all my trimmings would have tasted bland without your contribution of the fresh meat. Let's just say it was a joint effort and pat each other on the back."

"I definitely don't want to make the mistake of patting you on the head."

She gulped back a giggle. "Will I ever hear the end of that?"

"Probably not." He fell into another brief silence. "I don't really blame you for getting your back up that morning. I meant to tell you so that night, but we ran into the snakes, and I never got the chance."

She tried to speak, but he cut her off.

"It was high-handed and sneaky of me to make a decision and then put off telling you for so long. I honestly wasn't playing games, though. I just knew how exhausted you were, and I figured it wouldn't be news you'd be glad to hear, so I kept it from you for as long as I could."

Eden took a thoughtful sip of coffee. "I overreacted." She slanted him an apologetic smile. "It *wasn't* news I wanted to hear. I'd been comforting myself with the thought that I could do anything for a little while longer. When I realized that a little while might be extended into weeks—well, it was overwhelming. Your comment earlier about my not cutting the mustard as a rancher's wife was still bothering me, too. The combination of it all—my exhaustion, my stung pride, and facing weeks on the trail—well, it sent me reeling, I guess. The next instant, I'd moved from annoyance into a full-blown temper." She lifted her shoulders. "I have a quick temper, and when it gets the better of me, I'm not always reasonable. I insisted on saddling the horse to prove something. I'm not sure what, exactly, but it made sense to me at the time."

He chuckled. "I understood." He turned

the tin cup in his big hands. After gazing into the dregs of his coffee, he looked at her again. "I shouldn't have said that to you, Eden. It was a complete lie, and I really am sorry." He pushed up the brim of his hat and rubbed a hand over his eyes. "The truth is, you'd make any man a fine wife. You've got more grit than any woman I know, including my mother, and she has enough sand to smooth a rough-cut board."

"You just don't wish to be the unlucky fellow who gets saddled with me?" she asked with a lightness of tone that she was far from feeling.

Again, he took his time before speaking. His eyes shimmered like polished pewter in the firelight when he finally met her gaze again. "I'd like to be that man," he said, his voice gone gravelly. "And just having the thought in my head scares the ever-loving hell out of me. Does that make sense?"

It touched Eden that he would admit he felt afraid. A lot of men would rather bite off their tongues. "Perfect sense."

"Anyhow." He gestured limply with his hand. "Like I said before, I felt cornered that morning. When you look at me, I see tenderness in your eyes." He swallowed hard, his larynx diving and then bobbing upward again. "You make me feel in ways I don't want to feel—feelings I never thought I'd shake hands with again. So I took a shot at you. I'm just not ready to go there again, Eden, not yet anyway, and maybe I never will be."

Recalling her recurring urge to scour her skin when she bathed, Eden could sympathize with how he felt, perhaps better than he knew. "I guess that's two of us. As strongly as I'm attracted to you, Matthew, I'm not sure I'm ready to take it anywhere, either."

He tossed away the dregs of his coffee. "You'll get there, honey. You just need time and the right man to help you find your way."

Watching him refill his cup, Eden wondered, *What if you're the right man?* But it was a question she didn't voice. "I'm sorry I made you feel cornered," she told him softly. "I'll try never to do that again."

Cocking a dark eyebrow at her, he smiled slightly. "You want the truth? Meeting you has been one of the best things that's happened to me in a very long time. You take me places in my mind where I don't want to go and force me to look at my life from a new perspective. You've given me a lot to mull over."

"I have a lot to mull over as well." Eden pushed up on one knee to refill her coffee cup. As she sat back, she said, "Let's make a bargain."

"What kind of bargain?"

"To just be friends. No pressure, no expectations, and no disappointments if friendship is all we ever share." Resuming her cross-legged position, she hunched forward to rest her arms on her knees, the cup cradled between her palms. "You're a wonderful friend, Matthew, and hopefully, you feel the same way about me. Just friends. That way, neither of us will ever feel cornered. Things will just happen—or they won't."

"Speaking of things happening . . ." His voice trailed away, and his gaze chased off into the darkness. "Have you ever?"

Eden didn't understand the question. "Have I ever what?"

"Been with someone? With a man, I mean."

"In the biblical sense?"

He chuckled. "Where I hail from, the

Bible doesn't have a whole hell of a lot to do with it, but, yes, in the biblical sense, have you ever been with a man?"

Eden's neck went hot. "John and I kissed, but I always said no to anything more. A lady saves that for marriage. According to Ace, a man isn't inclined to buy the cow when he can get the milk for free."

"A very smart man, your brother."

He ended the conversation by starting the after-meal cleanup. Eden went to help, and they worked side by side in companionable silence. When Matthew spread out the bedroll, Eden felt drawn to it like a shaving of iron to a magnet. She sat on the pallet to remove her boots and jacket, then doffed her gun belt and hat.

"After I bathed, I couldn't get the binding tight enough around my ribs," she told him. "Would you mind doing me up again?"

"Not a bit. Knot the shirt under your protuberances and stand up."

Eden smiled to herself as she tied the shirttails snugly beneath her breasts. It was so like Matthew to attempt to ease her self-consciousness. "This is highly improper, you know. After all else that's happened to

me, I know it's absurd to fuss about propri-
eties, but the dos and don'ts have been
drilled into my head ever since my mother
started trying to make me into a lady. In
San Francisco, a *real* lady wears gloves in
public, and if the wind lifts her skirts and
shows her ankles, she's in danger of dam-
aging her reputation. Just think what people
might say if they could see me baring my
middle night after night."

Matthew's mouth tipped in an understanding smile. "I don't fault you for feeling
self-conscious. I'm a little uneasy about it
myself. Until now, all my friends have had
hairy bellies."

Eden nearly choked on a startled laugh.
He grinned lopsidedly at her and began
wrapping her ribs. When his fingers grazed
her skin, Eden snapped taut, not from fear
this time. A delicious, tingling warmth
moved through her and pooled like liquid
fire low in her belly.

As if Matthew felt it, too, he hesitated
and shot her a piercing look. She couldn't
be sure, but she thought his hands trembled slightly as he finished the task.

"Thank you, Matthew. It feels so much
better with the binding."

She'd snuggled down under the blanket and jackets when Matthew joined her. He looped a hard arm over her waist, pressed full-length against her, and toyed with her damp hair, his touch as light and airy as the brush of a bird's wing. Eden felt that fiery, tingling sensation again. She tried to analyze why she was suddenly starting to have such feelings, but she was too exhausted. Her eyes fell closed on a wave of blissful contentment. It felt so wonderful to have him hold her again.

The last thought that flittered through her weary mind before sleep overcame her was that perhaps she was more ready to make love with Matthew Coulter than she was prepared to admit, even to herself.

From that night on, Matthew and Eden began forging a strong friendship. With each passing day, she came to admire his wilderness savvy even more. He continued to keep them supplied with meat by hunting with a makeshift spear, or with his bow and arrows when they needed larger game. She was grateful for the food and continued to do her part—collecting wild roots and other edible plants to round out their meals, gathering firewood, helping to care for the horses, keeping the canteen filled with fresh water, and helping to cook and clean up, morning and night. In addition to so many hours each day in the saddle, the extra tasks exhausted her, but even when her feet were dragging, she forced herself to keep going. To survive, it would take both of their efforts, and she didn't want to let Matthew down.

Matthew's respect for Eden grew in equal measure. Ten days after the cougar incident, Eden removed the stitches from his chest. The wounds had nearly healed, and whenever he stripped off and saw the angry red marks, he had to give her credit for a fine stitch. She'd done a fabulous job of sewing him up, a lot better than the doc had done on his face. She'd already saved his life once, and it was never far from his mind that she might yet again. She also impressed him in other ways. Climbing off her horse to collect edibles clearly exhausted her, yet she continued to do it, day after day. On more than one occasion, he glanced back to see her nodding off in the saddle, so drained of energy that she couldn't stay awake. He knew how badly broken ribs could hurt, because he'd suffered with them himself, and he'd still been in agony after three weeks of bed rest. Yet Eden never complained. The only way he could tell she was suffering was when she held her side as she moved.

At night Matthew did all that he could to lighten her workload, but he quickly came to discover that Eden truly was one of the most stubborn females he'd ever met. If he took over the meal preparation, she found another chore to do, often one more difficult than cooking would have been. While he understood her need to contribute, her determination to do so became a constant worry for him. Now that her sunburn had faded, she seemed pale, and he thought she might be losing weight. Some evenings, no matter how tasty the food, she pushed it around on her plate and didn't really eat much.

At night after the work was done, they sometimes sat cross-legged facing each other, knees almost touching, to play checkers, using squares traced in the dirt and rocks as their game pieces. Because their board wasn't color-toned, it was challenging to remember which squares were supposed to be red or black, and their mistakes led to merciless teasing.

"You little *cheat*," Matthew accused.

Eden laughed. "I am not a cheat. I'm merely *creative*."

When checkers didn't appeal, they switched to hilarious bouts of tic-tac-toe or hangman, using the light of the fire to see their scratchings in the dirt. One night Matthew chose the word *utensils* to baffle his pretty opponent. When she finally gave up and he told her the word she'd been trying to guess, she gave him a sharp, wondering look.

"You are a complete *fake*."

"How so?"

"That first morning when I asked if you had any utensils, you pretended not to know the meaning of the word! Now I discover you not only know the meaning, but how to spell it, too!"

Matthew couldn't help but grin. "I never said I didn't know the meaning of the word. It's just that where I come from, we don't call cups 'utensils.'"

"What do you call them, then?"

"Cups."

Clutching her sore ribs, Eden chortled with laughter, tears of mirth streaming down her cheeks. When she caught her breath, she squeezed out, "I suppose there's something to be said for keeping things simple."

Some nights, instead of engaging in games, Matthew played the harmonica while Eden sang along. When the tunes he knew grew repetitious, she hummed some new ones for him, and he was able to play them by ear. Other times, they made up stories, some funny, others scary.

One evening, Eden launched into a spellbinding tale. "When I was still little, eight men who lived near us went out hunting and disappeared for weeks," she told him. "Search parties were formed, but no one could find them. Finally one of the wives remembered her husband mentioning a camp along Stillman Creek, so a group of searchers followed the stream up into the mountains to see what they could find."

"And?" Matthew asked. "Did they come across the men?"

Eden nodded. "All of them but one. They found seven men and eight horses, all dead."

"Dead?"

She nodded again, then shivered and looked over her shoulder into the encroaching darkness. "It was *strange*. So far as the searchers could see, there'd been no reason for the men and horses to remain in that camp. But they did. Rather than leave, they stuck fast until they starved and thirsted to *death*. Imagine that, with water only a few feet away."

Matthew bit back a smile because he'd heard this story before, only it had been four men who had disappeared in the mountains of Oregon. "So what happened to the eighth man?"

"That's the *really* scary part. They found him wandering in the woods, so thin he was skeletal. His hair, which had been black before he left, had turned as white as snow, and he was raving mad. The searchers determined that *something*—they had no idea what—had surrounded the camp, making all the men and horses terrified to leave. So terrified that they preferred to stay in that place and starve to death rather than face the horror that awaited them in the woods. Only one man had the courage to run, and he paid for it with the loss of his reason."

"Did he ever get better?"

Eden's expression went sad, and she shook her head. "He never came right again, and he was never able to tell anyone what had happened. To this day, hunters who venture up Stillman Creek still disappear. Only now no search parties will go looking for them. They're too afraid."

Matthew strove to keep his expression solemn. "What do you think is up there?"

She shivered and rubbed her arms through the jacket sleeves. "There are evil forces in the world, Matthew—forces we can't see or feel until it's too late. That's what I think is up there, something unspeakably *evil*."

He finally allowed himself to grin. "It's impossible for a man's hair to turn white in a few weeks. Human hair only grows a half inch per month. It has to turn white at the roots and grow out, little by little, to become snow-white."

Her cheek dimpled in an impish grin. "I know, but isn't it a deliciously *scary* story?"

Matthew threw back his head and guffawed. "You little minx! You sat there, pretending to look over your shoulder. You don't believe a word of that tale."

"No, but it's still fun to tell it."

A little later, as they prepared for bed, a loud snap resounded through the woods near their camp, the report rivaling that of a high-powered rifle. It wasn't an uncommon occurrence in a forested wilderness area. Limbs suddenly broke loose from trees all the time. Matthew had no fear that it was the Sebastians moving in on them. Those scoundrels would approach like snakes, quietly slithering through the bushes to catch them by surprise. Even so, Eden started so badly that her feet nearly parted company with the ground. Matthew found himself smothering another laugh. She hadn't managed to scare him with her story, but she'd definitely frightened herself.

When they got into bed, she snuggled close to him, clearly feeling edgy and in need of his nearness. *Sweet torture*. He couldn't hold her like this without growing aroused. It just happened. Old Glory had a mind of his own. Only tonight, with a shock of wonderment, Matthew realized

Old Glory wasn't the only recalcitrant body part under the blanket. His wrist accidentally grazed one of Eden's breasts, and her nipple was as hard as a little rivet. He hadn't touched her there to cause that reaction. Which meant what? That she was as inflamed as he was?

Shit. He tried to close his mind down, to evict the thought from his brain. But now it was *there*, with roots that ran stubbornly deep. She wanted him. And, God help him, he wanted her. But she wasn't ready for that yet, and he wasn't either. Eden wasn't a woman to use and then discard. If he took her, he had to be prepared to take their relationship to another place—the forever place. That was ground Matthew didn't want to tread.

Before the night was over, he was back in the creek, freezing his ass off and cursing Old Glory, who refused to give up the ghost.

Despite her unnerving effect on his body when they went to bed each night, Eden proved to be an engaging companion otherwise, always ready to tease or laugh no matter how weary she was. For

Matthew, who had been alone on the trail for so long, her presence became something he prized. He limited their entertainment time each evening to only an hour so she would get plenty of rest, but he enjoyed himself so much it wasn't always easy to call it a day, especially when he knew he'd end up back in the creek at least once during the night.

Despite her obvious exhaustion, Eden still awakened before he did some mornings, and he'd crack open his eyes to find her already cooking their breakfast. More than once, Matthew thought to himself that she was the damnedest woman he'd ever met, but he didn't mean it in a derogatory way. Eden faced all challenges with her shoulders straight and her chin up. She had an indomitable spirit.

He found it impossible to picture her in some fancy drawing room with a bunch of stuffy society types, serving tea and pretending she had no thought in her head beyond her next dressmaker's appointment or charity ball. It was equally impossible to imagine that she'd have been happy living that kind of existence.

During their long rides during the day,

they sometimes broke up the monotony by sharing stories about their lives and families. She laughed at some of his tales, and he laughed at some of hers. In the sharing, the friendship they had agreed to forge deepened to a level of intimacy that was everything but physical, which Matthew regretted every damned night and was coming to suspect that she regretted as well. He came to care about her in a way he'd never have believed possible when he first met her. Maybe people truly did have different corners in their hearts.

Eden, on the other hand, found herself experiencing those fiery tingles more often than not. Just the brush of Matthew's fingertips on the back of her hand sent a jolt up her arm, and at night when he held her close, she was filled with yearning. Sometimes she ached to have his hands on her breasts. Other times she felt a peculiar wetness at the apex of her thighs. At first, she wondered if she was developing a female ailment, because her sensitive places felt almost feverish and throbbed with every beat of her heart. But no. She finally decided that the new sensations stemmed from desire.

After what the Sebastians had done to her, Eden hadn't expected to be physically aroused by a man, ever. But having Matthew's arms around her made her feel safe in a way that nothing else did, not even wearing the borrowed Colts.

As their weeks in the wilderness moved toward a month, Matthew started to get the whim-whams now and again while they were riding in circles. That worried him, because his hunches rarely proved wrong, and he feared the Sebastians might be somewhere in the general area. He didn't believe they were close enough yet to pose an immediate threat, but he needed to determine where they were and what they were up to. Not wishing to alarm Eden unnecessarily, he decided a few days later to ride out and do a little scouting. To that end, he stopped to make camp early one afternoon, telling Eden that he needed to go hunting.

"I haven't seen much deer sign in this area," he said. "In order to get something, I may be gone until well after dark."

Eden nodded and glanced toward the trees. "I'll spend the time looking for edibles."

Matthew wished she would just rest, but he knew telling her that was a waste of breath. She was already heading into the nearby woods when he rode out. Recalling the circles they'd ridden in and the directions they'd gone over the last couple of days, Matthew decided to ride east for a few hours, keeping an eye out for tracks. *Nothing.* He crossed old back trails of his and Eden's a few times but saw no sign that the Sebastians had been in the area.

He was breathing a sigh of relief when he came to a narrow gorge, commonly called a defile where he hailed from. As he rode along the west rim to find a way across, he finally saw what he'd been praying he wouldn't—churned earth. His heart jerked in his chest when he hunkered down to examine the hoofprints. They couldn't have been any fresher if the horses had still been standing in them.

The hair at the back of his neck prickled. A cold sweat broke out on his forehead. *Shit.* Glancing at his watch, he determined that he had been riding for only two and a half hours. Pulse starting to hammer, he swung back up on Smoky and followed the trail. *No mistake.* He recognized the odd paddle gait of Wallace Sebastian's gelding. The gang was way too close for comfort.

Matthew longed to stay on their trail to see where they were headed, but another part of him wanted to get back to Eden as fast as he could. While it was important that he learn what the Sebastians were up to, he didn't want to leave his partner alone for too long.

Matthew felt pulled in two different directions and couldn't think what to do. *Damn it*. He had just decided to turn back when he heard voices. He dropped to the ground as if he'd been shot from the saddle, then slunk in a crouch to a copse of tall brush, pulling Smoky along behind him.

"When we find that bastard and kill him, I'm gonna take my time with the woman. No more playin' by the fire at night. I'm gonna rape the little bitch."

The deep male voice rang as clear as it would have if the speaker and Matthew had been standing face-to-face. He cupped his palm over Smoky's muzzle, a signal for the horse to be quiet. If the gelding so much as snorted, the Sebastians would hear him. Perspiration ran into Matthew's eyes. He didn't dare draw his hand from the horse's nose to clear his vision.

"About time you smartened up, Wallace," another man said. "To hell with sellin' her across the border. I never thought it was a good plan, anyway."

"Me, neither. Makes me mad that we didn't enjoy her proper while we had her."

"Oh, shut up, all of you! I done what I figured was best. She'd still bring a fine price. I'm just too riled right now to care."

"You're riled?" another man cried. "It was my damned bay that got stole. It ain't you who's stuck with a draft horse. When we stop at night, I feel like I been split clean in two. I ache from my gonads clear up to my gullet. I've never seen a horse this wide across the back."

"Oh, stop your bellyachin'. At least you got somethin' to ride."

The men had come abreast of the copse where Matthew was hiding. Peering through the branches, he was afraid to even breathe. He could have lobbed a pebble and hit any one of them. They were just that close. If Smoky blew or fidgeted, Matthew would be in a fine fix. He wasn't afraid to swap lead with the five men. He wanted to. But he couldn't put his life at risk when Eden was counting on him.

Using the arm with which he held the reins, Matthew wiped the sweat from his eyes with his jacket sleeve so he could see more clearly. Pete was the one riding the draft horse. Even at a distance of several feet, Matthew noted a gray tinge on the man's skin—the kind that came from months of not bathing. The stench of unwashed bodies drifted to Matthew on the afternoon air. The smell was so bad it burned his nostrils and gave him an urge to sneeze. He swallowed hard and held his breath. If he sneezed—well, he just couldn't—that was all.

Pete continued to complain about the discomfort of riding such a huge horse. "I hate ridin' bareback. His goddamn backbone is crushin' my balls. When we catch up with that son of a bitch, I'll be too sore to dip my pecker in that little whore's honeypot. Why can't we stop for a break?"

No, Matthew prayed. They had to move on. He wasn't sure how long he could keep Smoky quiet.

"Confound it!" Wallace cried. "I swear,

Pete, you've gone softer than a down-filled mattress. We took a break two hours ago."

"Only for a few minutes. You try ridin' this sunbuck and see how you like it."

A few yards beyond the copse, the brothers dismounted, tethered their horses, and sat in the shade of a tree. James drew a jug of whiskey from his saddlebag before joining the others. They passed the bottle, each of them swilling the liquor as if it were water. Matthew had little hope that they'd drink themselves into a stupor so early in the day, and his heart jumped inside his chest like a child playing hopscotch. Smoky was bound to snort or whinny sooner or later.

"So which way you reckon we oughta go next, Wallace?" Pete asked.

"My gut tells me they're west of here." Harold wiped his mouth with the back of a grimy hand and returned the bottle to James. "I think we should go that way again."

"They ain't west of here." Wallace snatched the jug from his youngest brother and took another slug of booze. "We went that way yesterday and didn't see any fresh tracks."

"I think that Coulter fella is rubbin' 'em out," Harold retorted.

Matthew was startled to hear the man call him by name. Except for the night when he'd rescued Eden, he'd seen only one of the Sebastians in the flesh, and that brother hadn't lived to tell the story. How the hell did they know his name? The answer came to Matthew straightaway: He'd gone into a number of towns over the years and asked questions about where the gang had last been seen. The Sebastians must have visited some of those places and been told that a man named Coulter was tracking them.

"He couldn't have rubbed 'em *all* out." Wallace snorted in disgust. "I swear, Harold, if I looked in your ear, I'd see daylight out the other side. After riding cut for a few days, we're headin' south. No more tryin' to follow the son of a bitch. He's goin' in circles, no rhyme or reason to it. The only way to find him is to ride every which way ourselves until we cut across fresh tracks."

"Why would he go south?" Pete asked.

"'Cause that's the way he has to go before turning east for Denver," Wallace answered. "That's the only town big enough in these parts to have any law enforcement that's worth a fart. His big concern right now is protecting that fire-haired little bitch, and she has to be played out by now. If he sees no sign that we're still following him, that's where he'll head soon enough, Denver. All we need to do is park ourselves in one place, ride cut a few times a day, enjoy ourselves, and wait for the fool to make a run for it. When we see sign that he has, we'll be on him like flies on shit."

Pete held up his hands. "Yesterday you said he wouldn't make a try for Denver because he knows that's what we'd expect him to do."

"That was yesterday." Wallace took another swig of whiskey. "I got a feelin', and I always listen to my gut. If he gets that woman to Denver, this is finished and we lose. You wanna catch him and get your horse back or not?"

"I wanna do a whole lot more than that," Pete grumbled. "Ain't nobody gets the best of the Sebastians and lives to tell about it. Same goes for taking my horse. I'm gonna do some fancy work with my knife on that son of a bitch and shove his dick down his throat while he's still alive to choke on it."

Matthew listened to them discuss his agonizing demise, each of their suggestions more creative than the last. He wished they'd stop yammering and leave. When they didn't, he decided he had to get moving himself. Staying there in the bushes with a restive horse was too risky. Better to make a run for it and ride like hell.

The son of a horseman, Matthew had worked with Smoky from the time he was a foal. The gray not only knew when to keep quiet, but also how to walk backward. Matthew had originally taught him that in case he ever needed the horse to pull him out of a bog by the reins. A rancher never knew what might happen when he was off somewhere alone. A well-trained horse could save his life.

Now Matthew needed Smoky to walk backward for an entirely different reason. They had to get out of this copse, and going forward wasn't an option. Keeping his palm cupped over the horse's muzzle, Matthew whispered, "Back." Smoky dipped his head, then brought it up. "Back," Matthew commanded again. The gelding's withers twitched, but he finally started moving.

"You hear something?" Pete asked, interrupting Wallace.

Silence. Matthew drew Smoky to a sudden halt, his body so taut with tension his legs ached. He knew the gang members had their ears cocked.

Finally, Wallace said, "It was just one of the horses, is all." Then he guffawed. "What you thinkin', Pete, that Coulter's got brass balls or somethin'? He'd have to be crazy to sneak in on us in broad daylight."

"I heard something, I tell ya."

"You heard somethin', all right. It was them rocks rattlin' around inside your head."

Matthew got his horse moving again, hoping that the drone of conversation would drown out the sound of Smoky's hooves. No such luck.

"There it is again!" Pete cried.

Matthew heard the men scramble to their feet. He swung up into the saddle, reined his horse sharply around, lay forward over Smoky's neck, and dug in with his heels. The gray leaped forward, plunging through the tall bushes as if they weren't there. Once they cleared the tangle of branches, the gelding broke into a full gallop. Behind them, Matthew heard shots ring out. A bullet whizzed by, coming so close it almost parted his hair. Grasping a rein in each hand, he angled his head closer to Smoky's ear.

"Go, boy, *go.*"

The horse had always been fleet of foot, but never had Matthew believed him capable of the speed he exhibited then. Maybe it was the gunfire, with dirt kicking up all around them like geysers. Matthew expected to take a bullet in the back at any moment.

He gave Smoky his head, and the horse came through for him, zigzagging through the trees, streaking across clearings, never slowing the pace. The gunfire continued, telling Matthew that the Sebastians had given chase. At one point, he felt something hit his upper arm. *Not a slug.* It felt more as if a man's bunched fist had plowed into him. A rock, possibly, that had been kicked up by a bullet.

Smoky raced like the wind. Matthew had always prized the gray as a trusted friend. Now the horse was giving him everything he had. Matthew hated to run him this hard, but he had no choice. Soon the gelding's neck was flecked with lather, and Matthew heard him blowing. A loyal horse would go until he dropped. When that happened, he was a goner. *Not Smoky. Please, God, not Smoky.*

Matthew lost all sense of time, but he guessed someone heard his prayer, because the gunfire finally petered out. Smoky had outrun the Sebastians' mounts. Knowing that he had to slow the pace before he killed his horse, Matthew nearly whooped with relief when they came upon a stream. He drew Smoky to a brief stop, took stock of the situation, and circled back to ride south for a bit until he came upon some shale-strewn ground where the gelding would leave no hoofprints. Once on the other side, Matthew cut a bough from a pine tree. Leading Smoky on foot, he stopped every few yards to go back and feather out their tracks. He continued to erase all evidence of their passing until they reached the stream again.

He led the gelding into the hock-deep water, waded back onto the bank to feather away the last few yards of prints, and then, keeping hold of the bough, remounted the horse. He hated to go downstream in an easterly direction, which would take him farther away from Eden, but he had no choice. If he headed west and the Sebastians followed him, he might lead them straight to her. He had a hunch this was the same stream that meandered past their camp.

Smoky was blowing hard. His gray coat had gone white with lather. Matthew wished he could stop to let the animal rest, but walking was the only safe way to cool him down. He was glad of the rushing water. Maybe the sound would drown out the clap of the gelding's hooves on the rocky streambed. Pete apparently had sharp ears, and noise could carry quite a way if the wind was just right. Matthew had no desire to meet up with those bastards again. He tossed the branch away on the north side of the stream into a thick stand of brush.

Minutes ticked by, and the tension slowly ebbed from Matthew's body. He felt uncommonly tired, as if he'd been the one who'd done all the running. He guessed the bad fright had sapped his strength. He even felt a little light-headed. Just then he glanced down and saw something red all over his left hand. *Blood*. Drawing Smoky to a stop, Matthew stripped off his coat to see where he was hurt. His shirtsleeve was soaked with crimson from the shoulder down.

Incredulous, Matthew realized that the punch he'd felt on his shoulder hadn't been from a rock, after all. He'd been shot.

Chapter Eleven

Matthew had warned Eden that he might be gone until well after dark, so she didn't start to worry until it grew really late. Where on earth was he? She'd waited until after the sun went down to cook, hoping to keep the food warm for him, but now it had gone stone cold. She had no watch to check the time, but she suspected it was close to midnight. He never would have stayed gone so long by choice. Something had happened. She felt it in her bones.

She thought about saddling the bay and trying to find him, but in the dark it would be next to impossible to follow his trail. If he didn't come back, she would have to wait until morning to head out after him.

Far too worried to sleep, Eden sat by the fire waiting, her ears pricked for the sound of his horse. When she finally heard hoofbeats, she pushed erect, her first impulse to run out to meet him. She quickly thought better of it. The approaching rider was most likely Matthew, but what if it wasn't? She slipped behind a tree, hands curled over the handles of the Colts. She heard the horse plod into camp, then the squeak of saddle leather as whoever it was dismounted.

"Eden? Where are you?"

Relieved to hear Matthew's voice, she stepped out from behind the tree. "Right here. I wanted to make sure it was you before I showed myself."

"Good thinking."

She moved toward him and grasped his forearm. "I've been worried half-sick. I never expected you to be gone so long. What in heaven's name kept you?"

He moved away from her into the sphere of flickering light. "I met up with the Sebastians."

As he related the afternoon's events,

Eden joined him by the fire. "Oh, God, Matthew, you might have been killed!"

"Came close." He held up his left hand, which was covered with what looked like blood. "One of the bastards shot me."

"What?" Her heart started to pound. "Where? How bad is it? Get your jacket off so I can see."

As he peeled off the coat, he said, "It's not that bad, honey, just a flesh wound. I got a little light-headed from the bleeding at first, but once I got that stopped, I was fine."

He had cut off the sleeve of his shirt at the shoulder seam and bandaged the wound with the length of cloth. With shaking hands, Eden untied the material to assess the damage. The slug had dug a furrow through the flesh of his upper arm, but the wound wasn't deep or in need of stitches. She was glad of that. She didn't want to perform that service ever again.

"We need to clean it," she told him.

When she returned to the fire a few minutes later with what remained of the whiskey, Matthew took a hefty swallow before allowing her to douse the cut. He hissed air through clenched teeth at the sting.

Eden decided not to rewrap his arm. "The cut isn't that deep. As long as it doesn't start bleeding again, I think we should let it breathe."

She went to find him another shirt and brought it back to him.

As he slipped the garment on, he looked out into the darkness. Eden followed his gaze. "Are you afraid they may have followed you?"

"I don't think so. Smoky ran his heart out for me and lost them. Then, after laying a false trail, I rode east in a stream for about three hours before turning back."

If he wasn't worried that he had been followed, Eden wondered why he looked so concerned. She decided to let it go, though. He would tell her what was bothering him when he was ready and not before.

"Would you like me to take care of Smoky for you?" she asked.

He shook his head. "I'm starving. I'll get the horse if you'll heat up my dinner."

While Matthew rubbed Smoky down and fed him, he recalled the conversation he had overheard among the Sebastians.

They'd figured out his game, changed tactics, and were now riding in a straight line in one direction and then another, much as Matthew had done today, hoping to cut across fresh tracks. It was only by the grace of God that they'd failed in the endeavor yesterday.

He and Eden needed to light out in the morning and ride like hell to get completely out of this area, then erase their tracks to lose the gang before they headed south for Denver. He wished they'd finally cross paths with Eden's brothers. He and Eden could use the backup manpower. So far, she'd been great about keeping up without complaint, but Matthew doubted she could maintain the pace if he pushed her any harder. And he would definitely have to push with the Sebastians closing in on them.

After eating supper, Matthew cautiously broached a subject that he knew would prick Eden's mercurial temper. He smoothed the dirt near the fire with the palm of his hand to draw a rudimentary map with a stick.

"We're about here," he told her, trying to lead into the subject slowly. "And when I ran into the Sebastians, I was about there."

She threw him a startled look, her blue eyes wide with alarm. "That's not very far away."

"No, it isn't." He told her about the conversation he'd overheard. "We're damned lucky they didn't cut across our tracks yesterday and come in on us."

"I had no idea they were so close."

"I suspected it. That's why I rode east today."

Her gaze sharpened on his. "So you weren't really hunting."

"Oh, I was hunting, all right, just not for deer." He tried to think how he might explain. "I get feelings sometimes—hunches, I guess you'd call them. Over the last few days, I've been getting the whim-whams for no reason, and once I thought I smelled campfire smoke that I didn't believe was our own. If the wind is just right, the smell of smoke can travel quite a distance, so just to be safe, I needed to check it out."

"So you didn't accidentally run into the Sebastians. You were trying to find them."

"And I was a little more successful than I wanted to be."

"You could have been killed, Matthew."

"Thanks to Smoky's speed, I wasn't.

All's well that ends well. Now we just have to figure out what to do."

"Have you any ideas?" She glanced worriedly over her shoulder.

In order to get out of this mess, Matthew felt that they would have to ride hard in an unpredictable pattern, possibly without rest for a prolonged period. He knew Eden wasn't strong enough yet to endure that kind of punishment. Her ribs had nearly healed, but she was still too pale for his liking and growing thinner by the day. He explained what he felt needed to be done and then gently informed her that he didn't believe she had it left in her to ride that hard without rest.

"I'll just have to do it, that's all," she said. "If they've changed tactics, we have no choice but to get out of this area and lose them."

Actually there was one other choice, though he feared what her reaction might be when he told her. Nevertheless, he had to share what he was thinking, and soon. He didn't want to be accused of playing games with her again.

"There is another way," he said carefully. "I can load up the bay gelding with some stuff from Herman's packs to make it look as if the bay is carrying your weight. Then I can find a safe hiding place for you and make the ride by myself. When I'm sure I've led them a merry chase and have them heading to hell and gone in the wrong direction, I can circle back to you."

Eden's chin shot up, which Matthew was expecting. "You plan to stash me behind a rock, in other words, while you take all the risks in order to save me."

That pretty much described his plan, but Matthew tried his best to soften the blow to her pride. "Honey, you're already played out, and with good reason, after all you've been through. This will give you a chance to rest for a few days. I'll leave you plenty of meat and find you a hiding place near water. You can eat, sleep, or just lie around. When I get back, you'll be fit as a fiddle again and ready for anything."

"No." She locked her arms around her bent knees and glared at him. "It's bad enough that you went looking for them today without taking me. I won't hide while you play hero. We either do this together, or we don't do it at all."

"Eden, you don't have the strength left

in you to ride hard enough or long enough to lose them. I do."

"You've been shot!"

"I'm fine. It's only a flesh wound. Both of our lives depend upon you being rational about this. If we stay together, you'll slow me down, and we'll run a much greater risk of the Sebastians catching up with us. You need to let me do this—only this once, because you're so tuckered out—and then, from here on out, we'll stick together, I swear."

"You'll be one man against five, Matthew. As exhausted as I am, I'm still a good shot. What if you can't outdistance them, and they catch up with you? You'll stand a better chance if I'm there to help take them on. You seem to see me lolly-gagging around a fire and sitting on my tuffet when I'll actually be worried sick the whole time you're gone. Not only for myself, but for you, too!"

The disagreement escalated, each of them tossing in arguments to prove his or her point, and by bedtime, the situation still wasn't resolved. Eden huddled on her side with her back to Matthew. Her anger and frustration charged the air with tension. Staring gloomily at the stars, he tried to put himself in her shoes, and as much as it griped him, he understood how she felt. It wouldn't sit well with him to be left behind in a hiding place while his partner went out and took all the risks.

"All right, you win," Matthew said softly.

She stirred to look over her frail shoulder at him. And it had become frail, Matthew realized. He hadn't been imagining the weight loss. The feisty girl he'd rescued a month ago was now little more than skin and bones. Something twisted in his chest as he looked at her, and a deep, bone-chilling fear quickly followed, moving through him like a rush of ice water. If she died on him . . . Well, it didn't bear thinking about.

"What do you mean?" she asked.

"I mean that you win. We'll go together. If you get too puny to ride, I'll carry you in front of me on my horse."

She settled beside him on her back to join him in stargazing. After a long while, she said, "If that isn't the dumbest idea I've ever heard."

Matthew cast her a startled look. That

was the last thing he'd expected her to say. "What do you mean, dumb? It's what you've been angling for all evening."

"I don't always angle for what's good for me, Matthew." She squeezed her eyes closed. "Your plan is the best one. If you take me, I'll only slow you down." Her slender throat worked as she struggled to continue. "It's true that I can't make the ride. I don't know why I'm so played out. I keep thinking I'll perk up, but I don't. Maybe you're right, and a few days of rest will do the trick."

Matthew got that awful twisting sensation in his chest again. "Are you sick, honey?"

"Not sick, just not myself. Normally I'm full of energy and have a good appetite. But now I go to sleep exhausted and wake up exhausted, and even when I feel really hungry, I lose interest in the food after only a few bites. I don't know what the problem is."

Matthew could make a good guess. "You've been on a horse at least twelve hours a day for over a month, five days with the Sebastians and more than four weeks with me. Add to that the physical beatings you took, plus two or three busted ribs, and I reckon you've got call to be feeling off plumb. What you need is a lot of rest and feeding up. I'd take you to a town if I could, set you up in a hotel with a feather bed, and let you sleep for about a week."

"I'll get plenty of rest if you go without me."

Matthew listened for a forlorn tone in her voice, but all he heard was determination and resolve. Typically of Eden, she'd made up her mind to stay behind, and now that she had, she wouldn't whine about it.

"You're quite a lady, you know it?" he whispered.

No answer. Matthew tucked in his chin to look at her. She was sound asleep. A tender smile touched his mouth. He turned onto his side to gaze at her profile. When, he wondered, had every curve and angle of her face become engraved in his heart? Hesitantly, he reached to trail a fingertip along the bridge of her saucy little nose. Next, he traced the soft fullness of her lips and the stubborn jut of her pointy chin. In that moment, he said a silent prayer that a few days' rest truly would cure what ailed her, because, whether he liked it or not, she'd come to mean a lot to him.

The following morning, Matthew's sole occupation was to find a safe hiding place for Eden. While she fixed breakfast, he saddled Smoky and rode out to go scouting. Within an hour, he came across a small cave, the inner chamber about six feet wide and twelve feet deep. He unearthed no critters when he went inside. A stream flowed within easy walking distance. Ponderosa pines and undergrowth provided plenty of cover. If he was careful to erase all tracks leading to this place, and Eden built only small fires, the Sebastians would play hell ever finding her here.

When Matthew got back to camp, Eden had their breakfast sitting in pans at the edge of the fire and was busy sorting through the packs, setting aside a few tins of food, some perishables, and cooking tools. Implements, she called them. Now that he'd come to know her better, he realized that she used a lot of fancy terms to describe ordinary things. She could probably balance cake and tea plates on her lap in a velvet-lined parlor, yet she could shoot the heads off rattlesnakes like a hired gun.

As he swung off Smoky, she glanced up and smiled. "Hope you don't mind. I'm trying to set myself up to camp alone for a few days."

Matthew was taken aback by her cheerful attitude. Not many people he knew would happily embrace being left behind in the wilderness without even a horse. But if Eden was worried, not a flicker of concern showed in her expression.

"I won't cut you short," she assured him. "I can make do much of the time with plants that I can find. The main thing I'll need is meat."

His throat went tight. He couldn't help but think of Livvy, how she would have clung to him and begged him not to leave her. Not that he faulted his wife. She'd been as sweet and dear as a woman could be, and he'd loved her more than anything. She simply never could have faced this situation with the same jaunty fortitude that Eden was.

"I'll get you a deer before I head out." Matthew hunkered down across from her, noticing that she was taking precious few of the tinned goods for herself. "Honey, you'll need more than that. What if something goes wrong, and I can't get back as quick as I think?"

She shrugged. "I'll manage. If I have a whole deer, what more will I really need?"

The thought went through Matthew's mind that she might need someone to hug her at night. It was a lonely business, being out in the middle of nowhere. In his early days on the trail, he'd gotten spooked after dark himself—more times than he cared to admit. "Will you be afraid? After dark, I mean."

She glanced off into the trees, her expression thoughtful. "No. Darkness is merely the opposite of daylight. Monsters don't come out just because the sun goes down."

True, but bears and cougars did. Matthew picked up a twig and drew squiggles in the dirt. "It can still be spooky out here at night when you're all alone."

"I won't be alone. God will be with me." She caught his gaze and smiled. "Would you stop worrying, Matthew? I'm a full-grown woman. I'll have the revolvers and plenty of ammunition. I'll be fine for a few days—safer than you will be, by far." Her expression clouded. "That's the only thing that bothers me, you going out alone and taking all the risks while I huddle up, comfortable as can be by a fire with my belly full. I hate the thought."

Matthew knew he'd feel the same way if their roles were reversed.

"But never mind that," she went on. "I'm exhausted; I admit it. It can't be helped. Let that be the end of it." An expectant look came into her eyes. "Did you find me a good camp spot?"

"Perfect." He described the cave and nearby stream. "If the weather turns bad, you'll have shelter. At night, you'll be protected on three sides so nobody can sneak in on you."

"It truly does sound perfect." She brushed her hands clean on the knees of her pants. "Will we go there after breakfast, or do you plan to hunt first?"

Matthew half expected her to say, *Here's your hat, and what's your hurry?* He found himself wanting to grin. Just when he thought he understood this lady, she surprised him again. "I thought I'd get you settled and then try to get a deer. No point in packing the meat from here to there."

"True." Hugging her side, she pushed to her feet. "Breakfast is ready, venison steak and fried potatoes with trail bread."

"Sounds good enough to eat."

The sun hung at its zenith in the sky when it came time for Matthew to leave Eden behind at her hideout. She walked with him to his horse and spent a moment saying her good-byes to the bay gelding before she turned toward him. When Matthew searched her wide blue eyes, he saw no trace of apprehension in their depths. She truly wasn't afraid to stay alone. He guessed he was worried enough about it for both of them.

"After I leave, if you see a lot of smoke, don't be worried," he told her. "I'm going to build a huge fire where we camped last night and then dump some water on it. I want the Sebastians to see it."

"So they'll be sure to find the place and come after you?"

"That's right. I'll leave a trail a blind man could follow to lure them north."

"You'll feather away your tracks as you leave here, though?"

Matthew nodded. "They won't find you. They'll be too focused on following me." He swept off his hat and ran his fingers through his hair. Now that the moment had come to leave her, he was no longer so sure it was the right thing to do. "You positive you're going to be okay?"

She shoved playfully at his good arm. "Get out of here, you silly man. Of course I'm going to be okay." Her smile suddenly faded, and she curled her slender fingers over his to give them a hard squeeze. "Be careful, Matthew. Promise me?"

"I'll be careful." He shuffled a boot in the dirt, feeling as if there were still unfinished business but uncertain what it might be. "I've been doing this for a while, you know, never before with them cutting my trail, but with me cutting theirs. I've learned from them over the years. They might be cunning, but that's not the same as smart."

Matthew mounted up. The bay and mule were tethered single file behind him, the gelding's lead rope anchored to his saddle. He nudged Smoky into a walk. He'd covered several yards when he drew his horse to a stop and glanced back. Eden stood alone among the trees, her arms wrapped around her waist. When she saw him looking at her, she smiled and waved, plucky as always. *Damn. Unfinished business doesn't say it by half.*

Cursing under his breath, Matthew swung back down off the horse and strode toward her. She gave him a wondering look.

"Did you forget something?"

He nudged up the brim of his hat as he stepped in close to her. "You remember all those damned corners of the heart you told me about?"

A tiny frown pleated the flawless skin between her finely arched eyebrows. "Yes."

"Well, a pretty little redhead with a fiery temper and a sassy mouth sneaked past my guard with a pick and chisel."

Her frown deepened. "Pardon?"

Matthew rubbed a hand over his mouth. "You heard me," he ground out. "She sneaked into my heart and went to work, chipping away, day in and day out, until she hollowed out a corner all for herself, and then, as if that wasn't enough, she went and carved her name on it."

Tears sprang to her eyes, glistening in the sunlight like diamonds. In a quavering voice, she said, "Oh, Matthew."

"And now I'll be damned if I can just ride off. What . . . what if something happens, and I never make it back? It's not likely, but the possibility is there. If I don't muster up the courage to tell you how I feel before I leave, I'm afraid I'll regret it."

"How do you feel?"

He swallowed hard. "Mixed-up, mostly."

Despite that tears were now spilling over her burnished lower lashes onto her pale cheeks, she laughed, a light, tinkling sound that warmed him all the way through.

"You think this is *funny*?"

She shook her head and wiped her cheeks. "No, of course not. You've chiseled out a corner for yourself in my heart, too, Matthew. It's good to know I'm not the only one feeling that way."

"Well, now that I've said it, I can leave with no regrets." He turned to go, but he'd barely taken a step before he felt as if an invisible hand had clamped over his shoulder to stop him. He halted, pivoted on his heel, and said, "Just one more thing."

It had been a very long time since Matthew had kissed a woman—so damned long that he'd forgotten all his moves. Sad-eyed whores in the rooms above saloons didn't welcome such intimacies. He took off his hat and then wondered why, so he plopped it back on his head. He leaned slightly toward her and then rocked back to scratch beside his nose. *Son of a bitch.* He was acting like a green kid. He was almost thirty-one years old. If he didn't know how to kiss a lady by now, he was a sorry excuse.

To hell with his moves. They probably hadn't been all that slick, anyway, and kissing was sort of like riding a horse: A man never lost his knack. He seized her by her arms and pulled her against his chest. He would just kiss the woman, right and proper, and be done with it.

Only, as she had from the start, Eden surprised him once again. Instead of being shy and hesitant, she melted against him like a pat of butter on a hot biscuit and went up onto her tiptoes to wrap her arms around his neck.

"Matthew Coulter, you are one of a kind," she whispered, and proceeded to press her lips against his. *Problem.* Her mouth was clamped tightly shut. When Matthew nudged at the part of her lips with his tongue, she jerked as if a bee had buzzed up and stung her on the butt. Arms still hooked around his neck, she reared back to look up at him in startled bewilderment.

And in that look of uncertainty, Matthew found his confidence again. "Darlin', remember all that practicing on a mirror? Clenched teeth don't cut it."

He saw her jaw muscles relax. "John never—"

"I'm not John," he whispered fiercely as he lowered his head, "and don't you forget it."

As Matthew slanted his mouth over hers, he forgot all about making fast work of this task and riding away with a clear conscience. *Honey and silk.* As he dipped his tongue into her mouth, he could have sworn that his toes curled in his boots, and from that instant, he was lost in the sweetness of her. *Eden.* She was vinegar, spice, and sugar, all rolled into one. Stubborn, feisty, impossible to understand sometimes, and yet—she had become his everything.

He wished he had the words to tell her that. In her special corner of his heart, she had become *his* rescuer, not the other way around. She had dug deep and searched out all of his hurting places to soothe away the pain, giving him hope where he'd had none, forgiveness for his mistakes when he'd wanted to blame himself forever, and the ability to laugh again without feeling guilty. Most important of all, she'd taught him that his love for Livvy would never be diminished if he allowed himself to love someone new. He didn't have to say good-bye to Livvy in order to say hello to Eden.

And this kiss, so deep and dizzying, was definitely a hello. Matthew wanted to sweep her up into his arms, carry her to the cave, and make love to her. Instead he had to leave, not knowing for sure if he'd ever make it back. The thought made him tighten his arms around her, and he never wanted to let go.

When he finally came up for breath, he felt dizzy, and Eden's beautiful blue eyes looked like cobalt glass that had been melted with a torch and given a brisk stir. She made fists on his jacket as if her legs might not hold her up.

"Oh, *my.*"

Matthew thought, *Oh, shit*, because in that moment, he knew for sure that he loved her. He just prayed to God he could lead the Sebastians on a ride that would have them so confused, they'd wonder which *country* they were in, and then he'd find his way back to her. A sense of urgency driving him, he kissed her again, wishing with all his heart that he could stay. Only he couldn't. Forcing himself to break contact with her sweet, generous mouth, he shuddered for breath, loosened his hold on her, and fell back a step. His purpose hadn't changed but his motivation had. To see Eden again, that was his goal.

"I'll be back," he whispered gruffly. "If I take longer than expected, don't worry. I swear I'll be back, no matter what, even if I have to crawl every foot of the way."

She nodded. "You'd better come back, Matthew Coulter. If you don't, I'll hunt you down."

He couldn't believe she could make him smile when his heart felt as if it were being torn from his chest, but she did. He stared at her for a moment, taking in every detail about her. Then he found himself with his arms around her again, which made no sense at all. He had to get going. Her safety depended on it.

"Eden," he said gruffly, "on the off chance that something does happen, figure out a way to lead your brothers in to where you're hiding. They're out here somewhere, looking for you. I know they are. I just wish to God we'd met up with them sooner."

"I don't want to think about anything going wrong, Matthew."

"It's not likely, but there's always a possibility. I need to know you'll be okay."

"You're coming back. Understand?" As he pulled away, she cupped his face in her hands, her eyes smiling up at him through sparkling tears. "I mean it, Matthew Coulter, and don't think I don't. I'm twenty-three years old, and I'm not even green-broke yet. I want my first time to be with you."

She truly was the damnedest woman he'd ever run across. "I haven't asked you to marry me. What about a man not buying the cow when he can get the milk for free?"

Her cheek dimpled in an impish grin. "If I waited around for a proposal of marriage from you, I'd be an old maid before you got the words out."

Matthew figured she had a point. He'd sort of sidestepped when he'd been trying to tell her that he cared about her, and chances were good he'd sidestep again.

"Besides, I'm not all that interested in a ring and promises anymore."

"You aren't?"

"Heck, no." She crooked her little finger under his nose. "I want your heart wrapped around my pinkie. If I have that, Matthew, I'll have *everything*."

Well, the lady definitely had his heart wrapped around her pinkie. As Matthew rode out, his thoughts remained with Eden at the cave, and it took all his strength not to double back. She was a feisty little package, but she was also a battered, exhausted, and fragile lady right now. Leaving her alone in a wilderness area thick with grizzly bears and cougars was one of the hardest things he'd ever done. Had he hung the meat high enough from the tree and far enough away from her camp? *Shit.* A bear could smell a fresh kill from over a mile away. So could a cougar. What the hell was he doing?

Doggedly, Matthew continued forward. When he narrowed it all down, the biggest threat to Eden's safety didn't come from bears or cougars. The Sebastian boys were the real danger. They weren't accustomed to being bested. Out from under their noses, Matthew had stolen a woman who would have brought them a fine price across the border, taken one of their horses, and made fools of them as well. They were men with small minds who'd come to expect things to go their way. They rode in, they conquered, they spilled blood, they looted, and then they rode off, priding themselves on how clever they were. *No one* ever caught them. *No one* ever messed with them. No one *ever* turned the tables on them.

Right now, they were hopping mad. It was no longer about the price that Eden might have brought them across the border. It wasn't about the bay gelding that he'd snatched out from under their drunken noses. They were still on his and Eden's trail because they couldn't let him get away with besting them. If they allowed that, they would have to face themselves as they really were: stupid, no-account snakes who would eventually get caught and strung up.

Matthew had to ride and ride hard, diverting their attention from Eden's hideaway. And yet, after watching her shooting skill, he felt a spark of hope flame in his heart that, given enough warning, she'd be able to put a bullet right between the eyes of each one of those lousy scum. She'd find tubers and shoots to survive on if the meat ran out. Or she'd figure out a way to hunt. And Matthew had every confidence that her brothers would eventually find her. Even if he ended up getting his ass shot full of lead, she would be all right.

A quarter mile from the cave, Matthew dismounted to cut several branches from an elm. He tied the limbs with rope to trail them behind Herman, travois-style. After saddling up, he looked back every few feet to make sure the brush was obliterating all his tracks, and was relieved to see that it was working.

Once back at last night's camp, Matthew threw the green branches onto the bonfire he started. When he doused the flames, smoke mushroomed into the sky, sending up a signal he knew wouldn't go unnoticed. He left some of the wood still burning so the smoke would continue to flow upward. Then he headed north, not really caring where he went, just as long as the day's ride took him miles away from Eden. The Sebastians would follow him.

He felt sure of it. They would be expecting him to ride in a circle, as he'd been doing for weeks. *Not this time*. He would zigzag first one direction and then another to confuse the hell out of the sons of bitches.

Eden missed Matthew dreadfully that first night. She cooked her supper well before dark, because there was less chance of her fire being seen when it was still daylight. She'd chosen a spot among the trees for the tiny pit, hoping that the thick canopy of pine boughs above it would cant the smoke, sending it off in angles that would thin out and hopefully vanish before it reached the sky. Matthew believed the Sebastians were somewhere close, so she had to be extremely careful.

As soon as her meal was ready, she kicked dirt onto the flames, the only way she knew to smother them without causing an upward spiral of gray. She didn't look forward to being alone in the dark without a fire to see by, but it was better than sending the Sebastians an engraved invitation to pay her a visit. She had assured Matthew that she wouldn't be afraid out here at night, and that had been the truth. On cattle drives, she'd been left alone at camp a number of times. Only then she'd always had light. Tonight would be a whole different kettle of fish. Oh, well. As Ace would say, if she couldn't tote it, she shouldn't have picked it up. Tomorrow night would be easier. By then Matthew would have led the Sebastians well away from this area, and it would be safe for her to keep a small fire burning.

As she consumed her supper, she thought of Matthew with every bite. He would like the meat and gravy, she thought, and he'd be making appreciative sounds as he wolfed down the groundnuts. She wished she had his appetite. Normally she ate quite a lot for a woman, but lately she got full really fast and couldn't force down another bite. She knew she was losing weight at a fast clip. Over the last few days, more than once she'd had to cinch in the rope that Matthew had given her to use as a belt.

When she'd eaten all that she could, she buried what remained on her plate so as not to attract long-toothed predators. After cleaning up the pots and dishes, she went into the cave to figure out where she would sleep. As she moved toward the back of the enclosure, her gaze caught on a familiar shape, and she missed a step. *The bedroll.* Matthew must have sneaked it in here when she wasn't looking. Tears burned in her eyes. It pricked her temper that he'd left behind his only blanket, but the gesture was so sweet and thoughtful she felt as if he were sending her a hug. He would freeze his behind off tonight. Unlike her, he'd be out in the open, vulnerable to the wind and weather. *Stubborn man.* He was bound and determined to play hero, whether she wanted him to or not.

The pallet and blanket smelled of him—a wonderful blend of leather, sweat, soap, and bay rum. As she huddled at the back of the cave, trying to drift off to sleep, she buried her nose in the wool and pretended he was there beside her. *Matthew.* She grinned as she recalled how he'd told her that he was coming to care for her. *A pretty little redhead with a fiery temper and a sassy mouth sneaked past my guard with a pick and chisel.* As a girl, Eden had dreamed of how a man might someday tell her that he loved her. Her favorite scenario had been of a handsome fellow in a suit who went down on bended knee and spouted romantic avowals of devotion as he handed her a bouquet of flowers. *Bah.* John had finally fulfilled that girlhood fantasy, but when she remembered back, it hadn't been nearly as fantastic as she'd thought it would be. Now, instead of a well-heeled Beau Brummell, she'd tied up with a dusty cowboy who wasn't much of a talker, but she wouldn't have traded him for a thousand San Francisco dandies. Matthew's proclamation had come straight from his heart. She'd seen that in his eyes. Even more important, he'd had to push out every word. Even though he had never actually said that he loved her, the message had come through loud and clear.

Thinking of how delicious it had felt when Matthew kissed her, Eden knew for certain now that she'd never really loved John. His kisses had never made her feel the way Matthew's did; nor had she ever felt so deeply moved when John held her in his arms. Earlier in her relationship with Matthew, Eden had cringed at the thought of physical intimacy. Her experiences with the Sebastians had made her dread being touched again, and if what they'd done to her even remotely resembled what went on between a man and a woman in the marriage bed, she'd wanted no part of it.

That feeling had left her now. Remembering the glow of happiness on the faces of her sisters-in-law, Eden knew it *wasn't* like that between two people who loved each other. More important, she'd come to trust Matthew completely. He would never do anything to hurt her. She felt certain of that. Drawing the blanket more tightly around her shoulders, she tried to imagine what it would be like if he touched her body, not in the impersonal way he had a few times before, but as her lover. Instinctively she knew that every light stroke of his hands over her skin would feel absolutely wonderful. If he ever issued her an invitation to lie with him, she would not hesitate to say yes.

As Eden drifted off into an exhausted sleep, she said a prayer that God would keep Matthew safe. If he died out there, trying to protect her, she would never forgive herself. *Never.* Having that thought helped her to understand Matthew's guilt over Livvy's death in a way she'd never been able to before. Eden was glad of that. Matthew

Coulter deserved a woman who understood him—a woman who would love him, support him, and stand beside him.

If given the chance, Eden would do everything in her power to be that woman.

Chapter Twelve

Matthew sorely missed Eden when he stopped for the night. Though he'd brought along some of the deer meat, what he cooked up didn't taste half as good as what she would have fixed. He'd also left her the coffeepot, and the coffin varnish that he boiled in a tin can was so strong it almost made his pant legs roll up and down like a window shade. After eating, he tried entertaining himself by playing the harmonica, but it wasn't nearly as much fun without Eden to sing along. He ended his repertoire with "Beautiful Dreamer," and as the last note trailed away, tears made his vision blurry.

Feeling foolish, he smothered his fire to make an early night of it. With Eden along, he'd always waited until after daybreak to hit the trail, but now that he was alone, he could light out in the dark if he wanted, and stop to rest the animals during the early dawn, when the dim light hampered their vision.

Using his saddle as a pillow, Matthew stretched out on the ground with only his jacket to shield him. It was so chilly, he could envision waking up with a crust of frost coating him. He didn't really mind the lack of a bedroll, though. He'd slept with Eden to keep her warm, not the other way around. After three years on the trail, he was used to the cold.

Sighing, he stared at the stars. For a while, he thought about the Sebastians, wondering how far behind him they were. Tomorrow he'd ride in a zigzag pattern again. When he had lured them far enough away from Eden, he would take to a stream, travel a goodly distance, and then break for shore, feathering away his tracks as he went. If he rode far enough north before circling back to the cave, maybe it would be safe for him to take Eden to Denver. Her recent weight loss and pallor truly concerned him. She needed not only to rest and feed herself up, but also to see a doctor. He had a bad feeling those busted ribs weren't healing right. So far as he knew, there wasn't much a sawbones could do about that, but maybe there was an elixir to build her strength back up.

Remembering the time when she'd been so mulish about saddling her own horse, he smiled in the darkness. She'd been bound and determined to prove to him that she was as tough as a woman came, and damned if she hadn't succeeded. If he lived to be a hundred, he would never forget that day at the snake den, how she'd fanned the hammers of those guns. He'd known stouter and sturdier females, but none of them had ever possessed Eden's pluck.

A funny, achy sensation settled in Matthew's chest as he recalled their good-byes that afternoon—how she'd clasped his fingers and how her eyes had sparkled so prettily with tears. He'd done a poor job of telling her that he cared for her, and re-gretted that now. He expected to see her again, but what if he didn't? He hadn't said the one word he knew she'd wanted to hear, and he felt like a chicken-livered coward. *Love.* Why was it so hard for him to spit that out?

Matthew guessed it all circled back to Livvy—that feeling way deep inside that he was betraying her. He'd fallen in love with her when he was still in knickers, and he still loved her now. He always would. It felt strange to be having such strong feel-ings for Eden at the same time, like he'd become a philanderer or something. Yet rationally he knew that wasn't so. A man couldn't be unfaithful to a dead woman, only to her memory, and Matthew knew that wasn't the case with him. He would always treasure his memories of Olivia. He would always hold her in high regard. Never would a word come out of his mouth to malign her character or criticize her in any way.

He was just ready to move on now, to say good-bye and get on with his life.

For the first time in a very long while, Matthew was able to picture Livvy's face clearly again—the gentleness of her smile, the innocence in her big brown eyes. For so long, he'd remembered only her final moments and never thought about all the good times they'd shared, because it hurt too much. Now, suddenly, the hurting had stopped. He remembered once when he'd tried to carry her through the snow from the cabin to his folks' house and lost his footing. They'd both ended up buried in a drift. Livvy had been wearing one of her nice dresses, and he'd expected her to get in a grump. Instead, she'd shrieked with laughter, grabbed a handful of snow, and rubbed it in his face. He had retaliated, and the snowball fight was on. They had arrived for supper at his parents' place rosy-cheeked, soaking wet, and weak in the knees from laughing so hard.

She'd always been such a sweetheart, fussing over him constantly. One year, she'd burned his birthday cake and cried her eyes out over ruining his party. Nothing he said had comforted her. She had wanted it to be a perfect day. Another time she'd scorched his Sunday shirt with the iron and had spent every spare second all the next week making him a new one. And when she'd failed to become pregnant, she fretted because she knew how much he wanted children.

In short, the most important thing to Livvy had always been his happiness, so how could he believe that she would want him to be unhappy now? If she was up there in heaven, like Eden said, Matthew knew she was rejoicing that he'd found someone else. Livvy wouldn't want him to be alone. She wouldn't want him to feel guilty or sad. It was time to let her go.

Matthew took a deep breath and slowly released it. *Letting go.* For so long, he'd clung to his sorrow with an iron fist, refusing to turn loose of it. And he'd felt as if a constant, heavy weight rode his shoulders. Now he suddenly felt light as a feather, and *free*. No worry about betrayal, no sense of guilt. He'd been the best husband to Livvy that he'd known how to be. It wasn't his fault that the Sebastians had come onto Lazy J land that afternoon. It wasn't his fault that they were murderous bastards. It wasn't his fault that they'd beaten him senseless and he hadn't been able to get up to defend his wife. None of it, absolutely none of it, had been his fault.

The acceptance added to his relief. He had dragged the guilt around with him long enough.

All day, when he'd started to think about how it had felt to kiss Eden, he'd shoved the thoughts from his mind. And deep down, he knew why. Though it pained him to admit it, Livvy's kisses had never made his blood heat the way Eden's had. When he recalled how she'd melted against him and how intoxicating her mouth had tasted, his throat went as dry as a preacher's sermon.

It wasn't that he hadn't thoroughly enjoyed kissing Livvy. It was just that the two women were very different. Livvy had been so shy and overly modest that it had been months before he ever saw her nude, and she'd balked the first few times he'd tried to taste the recesses of her mouth when he kissed her. In bed, he'd tried to be a gentleman about it, never pressing her to do anything that made her feel uncomfortable. Even after five years of marriage, their lovemaking had been pretty tame. He doubted it would be that way with Eden. As soon as he'd convinced her to unclench her teeth while they kissed, she'd held nothing back. He expected she would do the same when they made love. She was an all-or-nothing kind of lady.

There were other differences between her and Livvy. Eden would never cling to the back of his belt and peer out at trouble around his arm. She'd be more inclined to step out in front of him and take a bullet. The thought scared him half to death. He didn't want her to protect him. It was supposed to be the other way around, but he had a feeling he would play heck ever convincing Eden of that. If trouble knocked, she would answer the door and take it on. He had to respect that, because he would do the same himself, but loving a woman like her was going to be a challenge, and he'd probably be worried about her more often than not.

Before drifting off to sleep, Matthew drew his watch from his pocket to thumb the inscription on its back. *Just this one last time.* The gold case winked in the moonlight, the flash as yellow as sunlight. That was odd. Normally the timepiece looked like tarnished silver in the darkness. It was probably pure silliness, but he took it to be a sign, a last little message from Livvy that she had given him her blessing. He could almost hear her say, *Stop being such a goose, Matthew. Eden is wonderful. Love her with all your heart and don't look back.* Maybe he was just conjuring up the words he wished he could hear her say, but whether they were all in his imagination or not, it felt good to have them play through his head.

Now that he'd made a commitment to Eden, the watch had to go. He couldn't expect her to put up with his carrying it. She would know every time he checked the time that he was thinking of Livvy. When he got back to the cave, he would stow it in one of the packs. Someday when he and Eden settled down somewhere, he'd find a special place for it, maybe stored at the bottom of a drawer for safekeeping. He knew without asking that Eden wouldn't expect him to throw the timepiece away.

Tucking the watch back into his pocket, Matthew tipped his hat down over his eyes. His last thought as he went to sleep was that he wished Eden were there beside him.

Over the next three days, Eden gathered edible plants to supplement her stores of food, collected firewood, cooked, cleaned up, took leisurely baths, laundered her clothes, and rested. She couldn't believe how much she slept. The first morning, she'd lain down again right after breakfast and slept until late afternoon, but even so, she had still been ready for bed when darkness fell. On the morning of the second day, she felt a little less lethargic, but still took long naps in between her chores, and once again slept like a convalescent all night. By day three, she was starting to feel more like her old self. She wolfed down breakfast and then wished she'd cooked more. When she went walking through the woods in search of groundnuts and mushrooms, she felt a bounce in her step again. When she breathed deeply of the fresh mountain air, she felt a pang in her ribs, but the pain no longer nearly bent her double. Matthew had been right: All she had needed was some uninterrupted rest.

She worried about him constantly. Where was he? Was he safe? Was he heading back toward her yet? Sometimes she envisioned him holed up behind rocks, shooting it out with the Sebastians and running low on ammunition. Other times she pictured him at his campfire, cooking or washing dishes. She prayed for his safety. Oh, how she missed him. It was strange how she'd so quickly come to feel lost without him. She yearned to hear the deep, silky tenor of his voice or the bark of his laughter. She wanted to feel the hardness and heat of his big body stretched out beside her at night. She ached for the touch of his hand on hers.

On the fourth day, her concern mounted. He had hoped to be gone for only two or three days. What was taking him so long? What if he was dead? All that afternoon, she kept an ear pricked for the sound of a rider approaching, but the thump of hooves on the forest floor never came, and she went to bed with an ache in her heart. Something had gone wrong. She was sure of it.

By day five, Eden knew she had to come to grips with the fact that Matthew might never return. When the sun began to dip toward the western horizon late that afternoon, she sat beside her small fire, arms locked around her bent knees, face buried in his jeans, and wept. *Oh, God*. She would never see his crooked smile again, never feel his arms around her, never hear his voice. Why had she allowed him to go without her? She could have kept the pace if she'd really tried.

When Eden had cried herself empty of tears, she smothered the fire and went to bed with a sharp ache in her chest that kept her awake for hours. *Matthew.* If he was dead, she would always blame herself. Partners were supposed to stick together.

In the morning, Eden sat by the fire and had another good cry. *Six* days. Something had happened. She had to face it: Matthew never would have stayed away for so long by choice.

So now what? Before leaving, Matthew had asked her to look after herself, and though she hadn't said she would do that, the promise had been implied when she kept assuring him that she would be fine. She also remembered how she'd harangued him for giving up on life after losing Livvy. Now her own words came back to haunt her. Matthew wouldn't want her to sit here at the mouth of this cave and die. He'd want her to pick herself up, brush off her britches, and turn her mind to how she was going to survive. She had no horse. The deer he'd left suspended from the tree would soon start to sour, and she'd have no meat. Her brothers were looking for her. She needed to think of a way to signal them so they might find her.

Eden forced herself to her feet. If Matthew was up in heaven, watching her right now, she wanted him to be proud of her.

Her first order of business was figuring out how to preserve the deer meat. She unfastened the rope that suspended the partially consumed carcass from the tree limb and lowered it onto a bed of pine needles that she'd gathered. Then she set to work with a knife to trim away all the meat from the bones. Once again, her torn traveling dress came in handy. Saving back some of the meat to cook later, she laid the rest on the spread cloth, knotted the material into a bundle, and used her rib cage binding as a rope. The creek was ice-cold. Constant submersion in water would turn the meat white on the surface, but the chill would preserve it for a few more days. In the meanwhile, she would have to determine a way to get more meat by herself without firing a gun.

Mindful of attracting bears and cougars, Eden carried the cut-up deer downstream from her camp until she found a sapling along the bank that would provide adequate anchor. She tied one end of the rib cage binding around the bundle's knot and the other around the slender base of the alder. Soon the meat was floating in the stream. She crouched at the edge to wash her hands. Cutting up meat was bloody business.

When she got back to camp, she realized it was time for lunch. She had to eat to maintain her strength, so she prepared a midday meal and then forced herself to eat every last bite. After washing the dishes, she found a small slab of shale to use as a spade and dug a hole so she could bury the deer bones. She was sweating like an overworked horse by the time she finished the excavation, but surprisingly, she wasn't so tired that she wanted to collapse. All that sleep truly had put her right. Her ribs still hurt, but not as much as they had. She didn't get light-headed. No knifing pains. She was on the mend.

So what next? She decided she should fashion a spear for hunting and a pole for fishing. Sitting by the fire, she used a rock to sharpen the knife with which she'd cut up the deer. When it had an edge like a razor, she found a fairly straight branch and went down to the stream to slice off strips of the skirt to use as binding. Soon, she had the meat back in the water and had fashioned a halfway decent spear. Practice at hunting would begin first thing in the morning. She probably wouldn't get anything for a few days, so she needed to learn that skill while she still had the deer meat to sustain her.

The sunlight was starting to fade by the time she got around to making a fishing pole, no easy task. It was simple enough to find a limber branch, and she'd salvaged a couple of her hairpins and stowed them in her pants pocket. She could use those to fashion hooks. But she had no fishing line.

If she unraveled one end of the wool blanket, the strands would be thick and visible to the fish. She needed horsehair, or something like that, but she had no horse's tail handy. What she did have was her own mane of hair. She didn't relish the thought of plucking herself half-bald. It would hurt, for one, and she'd have to triple-strand the line to make it strong enough, but needs must. Her hair was coarse enough to work.

She sat by the fire and set herself to the task, jerking long strands of hair out by the roots, her scalp smarting with every pull. When she had several lengths, she began working three strands together into a thin braid. It took a lot of tugging to braid a line that was only four feet long. She needed it to be long enough for casting. She truly might be half-bald by the time this project was completed. Her hair would grow back, though. If she starved to death before her brothers found her, there would be no second chances. Clenching her teeth against the sting, she began plucking more strands from her head, determined to have a fishing line made before she started supper.

"I knew you'd be worried, but I didn't think I'd find you in such a state that you'd be pulling out your hair."

Eden jumped with a start and jerked her head up. *"Matthew?"*

He stood at the opposite side of the fire, his long legs braced wide apart, his big hands riding low on his narrow hips. The battered Stetson shadowed his eyes. He wore no jacket, and his clothing was coated with reddish brown dust.

"You were expecting someone else?"

Eden shot to her feet, raced around the fire pit, and launched herself at him. When his hard arms closed around her, she let loose with a sob.

"It's really you!" she cried. "Thank God, thank God. I thought for sure you were dead."

He tightened his embrace, pulling her more firmly against him, and began to sway back and forth, his face pressed against her hair. "You aren't going to get rid of me that easy. The Sebastians just proved to be a little wilier than I thought, and losing them took me longer than planned."

Eden wrapped both arms around his neck and stepped up onto the toes of his boots to hug him tightly. A tangle of emotions coursed through her: relief and joy mingled with a rush of desire. "I'm so glad to see you. So very glad!"

"I'm glad to see you, too," he murmured. "I've missed you so much."

"I've missed you, too." Eden leaned back to gaze up at his dark face through a shimmer of tears. "Did you lose them, then?"

"They're as lost as last year's Easter eggs. Let's just hope they stay that way. I'd like to get you to Denver before they figure out the trick."

Eden no longer cared about reaching Denver. As long as she had Matthew, she had everything. Her happiness welled so huge that her heart felt as if it might burst.

He bent to kiss her. The brim of his hat bumped against her temple and toppled from his head. He paid it no mind as he slanted his mouth over hers. Eden's heart truly did almost burst with happiness then. *Matthew.* As the kiss deepened, she felt as if every nerve in her body started to hum. She couldn't feel her feet, and the pleasure made her dizzy.

When he finally came up for a breath, he flashed one of those lopsided grins that she'd come to love. "Have I ever told you how very beautiful you are?" he asked.

"That's a compliment that I will happily hear more than once."

"You are so beautiful that my tongue sticks to the roof of my mouth when I look at you."

"It felt to me as if your tongue was stuck to the roof of mine."

He gave a startled laugh. "Complaining?"

"No. I hope it takes up permanent squatting rights."

He chuckled again. "Will you settle for occasional visits? I won't get much done if I'm kissing you constantly."

Keeping her fingers intertwined at the nape of his neck, she leaned back the length of her arms to gaze up at him. She loved every line and angle of his face. "You are a sight for sore eyes, Matthew Coulter."

"So are you, Eden Paxton. I tried to get back sooner. I knew you'd be worried sick. But I couldn't shake the bastards."

"You're here now. That's all that matters."

He glanced to where she'd been sitting by the fire. "I know it's probably a stupid question, but why were you yanking your hair out?"

"To make a fishing line." She told him about her day's activities. "If you were up in heaven watching me, I wanted to show you that I *do* have what it takes to be a rancher's wife."

He grinned again. "If I had been in heaven, why would that have mattered?"

"I wanted you to be proud of me."

He searched her gaze. "I am. It's good to know that if something ever happens to me, you will be okay." He arched an eyebrow. "How are the ribs?"

"Much better. You were right: All I needed was a lot of rest. I'm feeling good, and my appetite is coming back. Speaking of which, you're probably hungry. I'll go down to the stream and get some meat for supper."

He loosened his hold on her so she could step away. Then, before she could, he grabbed hold of her hand to give it a hard squeeze. "Don't be long. I swore all the way back that I'd never let you out of my sight again."

"It's not that far away."

"I'll tend to the animals while you're gone. Then I'll help fix supper."

While Matthew unburdened the horses and mule and then set to work rubbing them down, his thoughts remained on Eden. He wasn't sure which he wanted more, a bite of food or a taste of her. She was so damned beautiful. After all she'd been through with the Sebastians, though, he didn't want to rush her. He decided he'd be smarter to just eat supper and keep his hands off her. She didn't seem wary of him, but with Eden, it might be hard to tell. She had a way of pretending she was stronger and braver than she actually was.

After watering the animals and giving them each a bit of grain as a well-deserved treat, Matthew went to the creek for a much-needed bath and shave, washed his clothes, and then joined Eden at the fire. He peeled potatoes while she floured the steaks, put them in the skillet to fry, and started making a salad.

As he worked, visions of her body ricocheted through his head. Though he'd tried not to look that night when he'd interrupted her bath, he'd taken in details in spite of himself. Her skin was the color of fresh cream, pale and silky-looking. And she had beautiful breasts, small but plump, and tipped with strawberry pink crests. Her narrow waist flared out to temptingly full hips that made his hands itch to stroke them and knead her soft flesh.

Thirty minutes later, the meal was finished and Matthew was already in need of another dunk in the creek. The realization both frustrated and amused him. As much as he loved being with Eden, it was sweet torture, too.

Determined to get his mind off sex, Matthew sat beside her and went after his food like a starving man. The lady could flat cook. "I missed your steaks and salad while I was gone. Nothing I fixed tasted half as good as this."

She smiled softly. "I hope you missed me for other reasons as well."

"Lots of other reasons. Playing hangman by myself was boring as hell."

She rolled her eyes. "You're such a romantic."

Matthew remembered how much he had regretted not telling her that he loved her before he left. "I may not be much of a romantic, but that doesn't mean I love you any less."

Her gaze shot to his. "What did you say?"

"I said that I love you. You got cotton in your ears?"

Her eyes went sparkly. "No cotton. I just didn't think—"

"That I'd ever get up the guts to say it?"

She smiled tremulously. "I thought you'd get around to saying it eventually, in your own time and in your own way."

Matthew looked at her expectantly. "Well?"

"Well, what?"

"Aren't you gonna say it back to me?"

Her cheek dimpled in an impish grin. "I love you, Matthew Coulter. Now that we've both said it, what are we going to do about it?"

Matthew circled that. "Sweetheart, it pains me to say this, but I reckon we should just sit on it for a while, give ourselves time to get used to the idea."

She set aside her plate and mug. "I'm already used to the idea. Now I think it's time to make it official. Don't you want to make love with me?"

He almost choked on a half-chewed chunk of meat. When he finally got it swallowed, he stared at her, not sure how to answer that question. At last a reply popped out. "Of course I do."

"Well, then?"

He gave the last of his spuds an agitated stir. "Well, then, what?"

"Don't you think you should . . . do something about it?"

He gave up on eating what little was left

on his plate and set aside his meal. "But we're not married yet."

"If you don't marry me as soon as you can, I'll tell Ace to get out his shotgun."

Matthew shook his head. "I think you delight in shocking me, Eden Paxton. Maybe your mama never got around to explaining things to you, but this isn't how it's supposed to go."

"Ah. I suppose it's unseemly for a woman to confess that she wants to make love. How improper of me. So how is it supposed to go, Matthew?"

He rubbed the back of his neck. "I test the water and decide when the time is right. Then I—" He broke off and shrugged. "You've been through one hell of a lot. What kind of man would I be if I pushed you before you're ready? You're also a lady, through and through. If we do anything, you may regret it in the morning."

"Nobody pushes me to do anything I don't choose to do, Matthew. And I'm as ready as I'll ever get. I won't regret anything in the morning."

She rose lithely to her feet and disappeared into the cave. When she returned, she carried the bedroll in her arms. After laying it out beside the fire, she straightened to take off her jacket. Her hands went to the buttons of the shirt, and Matthew's heart started to pound in his chest like the hooves of six runaway horses.

"What are you doing?" he croaked.

"Taking my clothes off." Her lovely blue eyes found his. "A lady has no choice when a man won't do it for her."

Matthew sat frozen as her slender fingers worked their way down the front of the shirt. When the last button came free, he was on his feet without realizing that he'd even moved. He circled the fire pit to grasp her wrists.

"I prefer to unwrap my gifts myself."

She relaxed her arms. "Then I'll leave you to it."

"Have I ever mentioned that you're the damnedest woman I've ever met?"

"I do believe you have." Her chin came up. "When I thought you were dead, I had two terrible regrets. The first was letting you go without me. The second was that I had missed my chance to know what it would be like to make love with you. Now you're back, hale and hearty. I'm not a person who likes to make the same mistakes twice. We can't predict what lies in wait for us around the next turn, Matthew. I don't want to die without ever being with you that way. Call me bold, but I want to experience it at least once, and, if I'm lucky, many, many times. No need for promises, no need for a ring. I was joking about Ace and the shotgun. I know a huge part of your heart still belongs to Livvy and that you may not be quite ready for all of that. It doesn't matter. All I ask is that you make love to me."

Matthew had never in his life wanted a woman as much as he wanted Eden. When he thought of all the times he'd stood neck deep in ice-cold water trying to squelch his desire for her, he almost laughed. Instead he cupped her sweet face between his hands and lightly brushed his lips over hers.

"That is a request you won't have to make twice."

Chapter Thirteen

Eden expected Matthew to immediately peel away the shirt, and she *wanted* him to. After lying awake so many times in his arms, yearning for him to touch her breasts, she was eager for it to finally happen. No fears slipped into her mind. No waves of dread crashed over her. This was Matthew, her dearest friend, and now he was about to become her lover.

She was disappointed when he left the shirt alone and gently pushed her down to sit on the bedroll. Then he hunkered in front of her and set to work unlacing her boots. With two tugs, the boots were gone, and her socks went next. Shifting forward onto one knee, he removed his gun belt and put it aside. Then he settled his big hands over her shoulders.

"Before we do this, there's one thing I need to make clear."

"What's that?" she asked, wishing he would just get on with it.

"There's only room in my heart for one woman," he said huskily. "Livvy still has her own little corner, but all the other corners have your name on them now. While I was gone, I said my good-byes to her, and I've come to believe she would want it that way. It's time for me to let go and move on. Not to forget, just to move on."

"Oh, Matthew." Tears gathered at the back of Eden's throat. She'd naturally yearned to hear him say it, but she hadn't been sure if he ever would. "Your name is on all the corners of my heart, too."

"I know," he whispered. As he pressed her back into a reclining position on the pallet, he trailed his silken lips over her brow and then kissed her eyes closed. "I love you, Eden. Just you, only you, and as soon as we reach Denver, I'm going to marry you, if you'll have me."

"Do you really need to ask?"

He settled that fabulously talented mouth over hers and kissed her so deeply her head went muzzy again. Between one breath and the next, Eden felt as if the world were spinning off its axis. This was Matthew, her trusted friend, and she loved him in a way that she'd never loved anyone. There was no room between them for hesitation or shyness, no room for silly last-second doubts. He trailed his lips from hers to trace tantalizing paths to the sensitive place just under her ear. Then he teased the column of her throat with the tip of his tongue. By the time he'd worked his way down to her breasts, the shirt had drifted away somehow. She couldn't remember him removing it; she knew only that it was gone.

When his hot mouth closed over one of her nipples, the shock of sensation that rolled through her body had her arching against him. *Matthew*. His name became like a gentle song in her mind. Every moist touch of his mouth on her breasts, every brush of his work-hardened hands over her skin, felt indescribably wonderful and absolutely right. Eden couldn't think. She could only feel, and every sensation was just as beautiful as she'd imagined.

As he teased her breasts, urgency grew within her to touch him, too, and she fumbled with the buttons of his shirt, frustrated when her fingers kept losing hold of the fastenings. Freeing one hand, he helped her, and she moaned when her palms finally connected with the warm, well-padded contours of his chest. Eager to learn every line of his body, she slipped her hands to his shoulders. She felt the healing line of the flesh wound on his upper arm and veered away. The layers of roped muscle under his skin were so thick and vibrant that she had to search for bones. With eager fingertips, she discovered his clavicle and traced its shape. But soon that didn't satisfy her, and she twisted to trace the angular ridges with her lips, her taste buds delighting at the male muskiness of his skin.

Hungry for more of him, she trailed her mouth lower, and he moaned. "Whoa, honey. Slow down, or this will be over before it starts."

Eden barely heard him. She *wanted*. All of him, she wanted all of him. She felt his heart pounding against her tongue, its fast rhythm echoing her own. The hard ridge of his manhood pressed against her thigh through the denim of his jeans. As if of its own accord, her hand went there. He jerked and sucked in a sharp breath. Then he moaned again. She realized dimly that her touch was as arousing to him as his was to her, and she slid her fingers under the waistband of his pants, frustrated by the belt buckle that interfered with her aim.

"Sweet Lord." His breath came hard and fast near her ear. She felt him fumbling with his belt and unfastening his jeans. "You're gonna be the death of me, girl."

A rush of delighted satisfaction went through her when her hand could finally curl around his hard, pulsating shaft. He jerked at her touch and muttered a curse under his breath, his voice thick and throaty with pleasure. Then he went after the rope at her waist and was soon jerking off her jeans. When his fingers found the hot, wet center of her, Eden's whole body snapped taut at the thrill of sensation that jolted through her. She didn't think anything could feel better, *nothing*, but Matthew proved her wrong with light, repetitive strokes over a sensitive place. Soon, way low in her belly, a quivery, electrical feeling began to build within her. Eden knew she was moving toward something, that Matthew was determined to take her there.

"Matthew?"

"It's okay," he whispered. "Trust me, sweetheart. Hold on to my neck and just let it happen."

Eden did as he asked, trusting him with all her heart, but the feeling that mounted within her was so intense it was almost frightening. He knew just how to touch her. With expert strokes, he pushed her over the edge, making her gasp and then tremble. She couldn't see, could barely think. It was the most wondrous experience of her life.

When she lay spent and quivering in the aftermath of orgasm, Matthew rose over her, his arms braced next to her shoulders, his chest a rippling bronze canopy above her, the healing wounds from the cougar attack barely visible. In the firelight, he looked like a carving of seasoned oak, and as she gazed mistily up at him, she knew God had fashioned every line of him just for her. He parted her thighs to get his knees between them. Eden had been on horse ranches enough to know what came next, and she knew this first time might be painful for her. But she wasn't afraid.

Suspended in position, Matthew hesitated. In the swirl of firelight and descending darkness, his blue eyes locked on hers. "Damn, honey, I don't want to hurt you, but there's nothing I can do to prevent it."

"It's okay, Matthew. I don't think it'll hurt that much."

He shoved forward with his hips, and Eden gasped at the knifelike pain.

"Shit," he said.

"It's . . . okay." Afraid he might pull away, she locked her arms around his neck again. "It's over, Matthew. It's okay."

Tension eased from his body like water being poured from a cup. "You're sure?"

Eden nodded, amazed that she was telling the truth. The pain had been horrid, but he'd done it so quickly that it had ended almost before it started. Inside she felt hot and full, but it no longer really hurt. She hooked her calves around his thighs, aware as she did of the rub of his denim pants against her heels and ankles. When she pushed up with her hips to meet him, his muscles bunched in his shoulders, and his chiseled features contorted, his lips drawing back on the right side of his mouth to reveal a white blaze of clenched teeth. A shock of dark brown hair fell over his forehead, gleaming in the firelight.

Finally succumbing to the needs of his own body, he began to move within her. Eden braced for more pain, but instead a ribbon of pleasure streaked through her. She pushed with her hips to meet his thrusts, inexperience setting her off rhythm at first, but she soon moved in unison with him.

"Come with me," he whispered raggedly.

This time, Eden wasn't surprised as urgency and delight started to mount within her. She accepted his invitation and went with him, knowing their destination would be heaven on earth.

Afterward they lay exhausted in each other's arms, too breathless to even talk for a while. Feeling content in a way she'd never imagined possible, Eden snuggled close to him and listened to the crackle of the fire.

When they had finally recovered enough to speak, Matthew broke the silence. "I wanted your first time to be perfect."

"It *was*," she protested, unable to comprehend how he could think otherwise.

"I made love to you wearing my damned boots."

He sounded so disgruntled that Eden pressed her face into the hollow of his shoulder to stifle a giggle.

"You think that's funny. I never got my dad-blamed britches all the way off. The first time is supposed to be slow and easy."

"Why?"

"Just because, that's why. I never should have let you take me there."

Eden smiled sleepily. "Do I get a vote?"

"No, I'm bigger than you, and my vote carries the day. It was my job to make sure your first time was perfect."

"It was, at least for me. Wasn't it perfect for you?"

"Pretty damned close," he finally admitted. "I've just never made love to a virgin with my belt buckle clanking on my knee."

Eden burst out laughing, and soon he was laughing with her. When their mirth subsided, she said, "When we settle somewhere, I want that belt, Matthew."

"What for?"

"So I can frame the buckle as a me-

mento of the most wonderful night of my life."

He rolled over to hold her close. With the heat of their passion fading, they had become vulnerable to the chill evening air. He fumbled for the blanket and drew it up.

"Maybe the most *memorable* night of your life," he told her, "but not the most wonderful; I promise you that. Next time, I'll make love to you slow and proper."

It was a promise that Eden wholeheartedly hoped he would keep. As it happened, she didn't have to wait long. After they rested, he made love to her again, this time without his boots and jeans on. What he did to her and what he taught her to do to him was so sweet and indescribably intimate that Eden knew she was going to blush every time he looked at her tomorrow, but that didn't stop her from enjoying every sensation or glorying in the climactic conflagration that followed.

Afterward, they slept the exhausted sleep of small children who'd played too hard, arms and legs entangled, bodies pressed close for warmth. When Eden awakened, it was early dawn, and Matthew was nibbling at the underside of her breast. She became instantly aroused, and they made love once again in the rosy pink glow that streaked the eastern sky. Eden wished this time between them would never end, but she had to settle for cherishing the moment, which was once again beautiful and immeasurably sweet.

Later they fixed breakfast together, and then she cleaned up the mess while Matthew prepared the animals for the trail. Far too soon to suit her, he'd fetched their meat from the stream, hung the bundle from a pack frame, and was erasing all sign of the camp. Sadness swamped Eden, because this had become their special place, and now they would never see it again.

"What?" Matthew asked.

She explained why she felt sad. Matthew grinned. "We'll find a new special place."

"Never one as special as this."

"Oh, yes, we will. I plan to make love to you in a lot of different places, and every single one will stand out in your memory. Give me a year, and then you can decide which spot is your favorite."

After he'd feathered away all their tracks, he strode over to Herman. Eden saw him take his watch from his pocket and stow it away in one of the packs.

"What are you doing?" she called.

"It's time for it to be put out to pasture," he said.

Eden's heart caught. "*No*, Matthew. You get that watch out of there and put it back in your pocket."

"I don't need a watch out here. I use the sun. And I shouldn't be carrying an engraved timepiece from my first wife."

"Why not?"

"Because it isn't right."

"Who says? Livvy was a huge part of your life. That watch is very special to you. I'm serious. I want you to carry it."

"And be reminded of her every time I look at it?"

"Yes." Eden turned her horse so she could meet his gaze. "She *deserves* to be remembered. I don't feel threatened by that, and I'm going to be very upset if you start hiding everything that reminds you of her."

"But—"

"No buts. Get the watch back in your pocket."

"I think it'd be better if I just tuck it away."

Eden recalled her wish to be loved someday the way that Matthew had loved Livvy. If she encouraged him to forget his wife, she wouldn't deserve to be remembered herself. There had to be room in their relationship for his memories of Livvy, and it was her job to provide that room.

"Please, Matthew. It's difficult for me to explain how I feel about the watch, but it's important to me that you carry it in your pocket."

He sighed and retrieved the timepiece. As he slipped it into his coat pocket, he said, "You happy now?"

"Yes. That's where it belongs."

He searched her gaze, his eyes going dark with emotions she couldn't name. Then his throat worked as he struggled to speak. "You're crazy, you know it? If you had something special from some man you once loved that you carried around in your pocket, I could never handle it."

"Call me crazy if you like, but it's how I feel."

When they were well away from the cave area and Matthew had erased their tracks, they rode their horses side by side across meadows that nestled like lush green carpets between stands of trees. On the grass, they didn't have to worry so much about leaving a trail, and Matthew relaxed. Reins grasped in one hand, he drew out the watch to check the time, then slipped it back in his pocket without touching the engraved lettering.

"I have to ask you something," he said huskily. "When I was gone, I had this bad moment one night, thinking how upset I'd be if I thought for even a second that you still loved John. I think knowing that would make me crazy, and it's hard for me to wrap my mind around the fact that you feel so different. I thought you'd be pleased if I stopped carrying the watch, and I can't understand why you weren't."

Eden struggled to explain. As the words came pouring out, she knew she was making a mess of it, talking in fits and starts and never really completing a thought. She finally gave up on making any sense and just plunged into it.

"It's just this feeling I have." She fisted her hand and pressed it over her heart. "Love is a miracle, Matthew, a precious gift from God. When we receive that gift, even if it's for only a short time, as happened to you and Livvy, it's no less wonderful and precious. If I encourage you to toss it away or hide it—well, if I were instrumental in causing you to do that, I'd feel as if I'd committed a terrible sin, not murder, exactly, but almost as bad. You *loved* her. With all your heart. She was carrying your child when she died, so a part of you died with her, and a part of you lies with her in that grave. I think it's important that we *both* remember Livvy."

"Both of us? You never met her."

"No, but I feel a connection with her because now I love you the same way she does."

"She's dead. You talk about her as if she isn't."

"Dead, yes, but none of us ceases to exist when we die. At least, I don't believe we do. Livvy still loves you, and now so do I. Love that ends isn't really love. Maybe I'm all confused in my head, but it seems to me that everything we now have between us will somehow be less if I allow you to forget her. I never want you to forget me, that's for certain. Does that make any sense?"

He took off his hat to run his fingers through his glossy dark hair. "Honey, I will *never* forget you. If you died today, and all God gave me was the little bit of time we've had together, I'd still never forget you. How could I ever?"

"Then don't pretend to forget Livvy and the child you lost, Matthew. I'm uncomfortable with that."

He rubbed a fist over his scarred cheek. "I've always wondered if it was a girl or a boy. We tried for so long, almost five years, and I had started to think one of us had something wrong. I wanted kids—I wanted them really bad—but if we hadn't been able to have them, I would have loved Livvy anyway. I figured, coming from such a big family, that my brothers and sisters would eventually give us plenty of nieces and nephews to love. But she would have none of that. She wanted to give me my own child, and she was in a constant dither about it. Every time she got her curse, I'd come in from work to find her face all puffy from crying."

Eden swallowed hard. She could sympathize with how Livvy must have felt. It was up to her to make Matthew happy now. He wasn't a hard man to please. Livvy must have felt so miserably inadequate when she had failed, month after month for so many years, to get with child.

"I'd tell her it didn't matter, that I didn't want my own child that much, that we needed to focus on all our blessings, but having a baby was really important to her. That day, right before she died . . ." His voice trailed away. "Well, she was so damned happy. She kept her pregnancy a secret from me, telling only her mother, and she planned the picnic at our special place so it would be a memorable moment when she told me. I have to admit I was just as excited as she was, and we couldn't wait to get home to tell my parents that they would soon have a grandchild."

"And then the Sebastians came." Eden had long been able to picture that horrible moment. "Oh, Matthew. If it had been a girl, what would you have named her?"

"Hattie, after my mother, and Marie, after hers."

"And if it had been a boy?"

"We weren't sure. We already had two Matthews in my family, so we were leaning toward naming him after her father." He shrugged and released a deep breath. "On the headstone, it just says, 'Olivia Coulter, beloved wife of Matthew Coulter Junior, and Baby Coulter.' Our folks couldn't think how else to mark the stone."

Eden would never regret that Matthew had been free to love her when she met him, but there was also a place within her that would always ache with sadness when she thought of Livvy and Matthew's child that had died.

"I'll give you children, Matthew. I come from good breeding stock."

He slanted her a glance. "I'll hold you to it. But if it doesn't happen that way, don't be silly about it like Livvy was. Okay? If you don't get pregnant, there are a lot of orphans who need solid, loving homes."

Eden laughed softly. "There you go! But not all boys, Matthew. I'll need at least one girl, and whether she's born to me or plucked out of an orphanage, we'll name her Olivia. We'll call her that in memory of the first Livvy."

They locked gazes for a time, and then Matthew nodded. "I'd like that. And if we ever visit my folks in Oregon, we'll go to the grave together, have our time with them, and pull away all the weeds."

"You understand how I feel?"

He nodded. "I do. Talking about it has helped me understand the business about the watch. If you'd lost your husband and still loved your memories of him, I wouldn't get my tail tied in a knot about it. Just understand this. If I ever get wind that you love a man who's still drawing breath, I'll make him a memory right fast."

Eden laughed. "I love no one but you, Matthew, alive or otherwise. You don't need to worry."

"It's a good thing, because he'd be a dead man."

Eden smiled and reined the bay in closer to Smoky. "And if you *ever* so much as look at another woman, I will commit violence."

He grinned. "Will you now? Finally, you're talking halfway normal. Seems to me that a woman who truly loves a man ought to feel just a little green at times."

"Oh, not green, never that." She pushed at a stray tangle of curls that lay over her cheek. "I'm far too hot-tempered. I'll just see red. And it won't be your lady fair that I'll go after."

"It won't?"

"No, I'll go after you."

He threw back his head and laughed. "I consider myself warned."

He took out his watch again and gave it to her. Eden accepted the thick sphere of gold with reverence. When she read the inscription on the back, her eyes stung. She knew that Livvy had once held this watch and then had slipped it into Matthew's hand with limitless love. As she returned it to him, she smiled.

"Forever. I was right on target, Matthew. Forever is a very long time. It is only right that you always carry that watch."

He nodded as he tucked the timepiece back into his pocket, then sighed and tossed her another grin. "Now that I've met you, forever doesn't sound quite long enough."

"Oh, forever will do us," she assured him. "Even a month will do us, Matthew. It's not about quantity but quality, and last night was very fine."

He looked ahead and narrowed his gaze. "I feel pretty confident that I lost those bastards. When I find a secluded spot for lunch, would you consider dallying with me in broad daylight, Miss Paxton?"

Eden felt no sense of shyness with him. He was the other half of her heart. "Is there anyplace out here that *isn't* secluded?"

"Does that mean yes?"

"That's for me to know and you to find out."

They made love along a creek bank, which was glorious, but also ended with Matthew cursing the sand because they hadn't thought to lie on the blanket. The granules found their way into her private places and clung to his. When the abrasion interfered with their pleasure, Eden caught his face between her hands, smoothed away his fierce scowl, and said, "You've always said I've got more sand than any woman you've ever met. I guess I just proved it."

He was still laughing when they waded out into the creek buck naked to wash away all of the grit. Seeing his sculpted, muscular body shimmering with droplets of water made Eden want him again, and she waded slowly toward him, her gaze never leaving his.

"What about lunch?" he asked with a knowing twinkle in his eye.

"I don't care if I eat."

Eden reached him, looped her arms around his strong neck, and pressed herself against him. He groaned, the sound a low rumble coming up from his broad chest. She smiled with feminine satisfaction as they lost themselves in a deep, mind-numbing kiss.

Late that afternoon, after watching for the tracks of other horses for several hours, Eden heaved a frustrated sigh and called to Matthew, "I know my brothers are out here, so why has it taken them so infernally long to find us?"

"We've been covering our tracks," Matthew hollered back, his voice ringing with confidence. "If Ace Keegan is half the man he's made out to be in those dime novels, he'll find us. Just give him time."

Eden no longer felt frantic to see her brothers, but they would still be a welcome sight. When they finally showed up, she wouldn't pretend that nothing had happened between her and Matthew. It would be too difficult to hide, anyway. She'd thought long and hard about that all day, and it simply wasn't her way. She'd tell them straight out that Matthew was the love of her life, and she would not be ashamed of where that had taken her.

That night, after a simple supper and a bath that ended with them making love in the stream, Matthew settled beside her at the fire, pulled out his harmonica, and began playing "Beautiful Dreamer."

"You haven't played that for me in *ages*," she complained.

He drew the instrument from his mouth and gave her a smoldering look. "I couldn't. The first time I realized I was starting to fall in love with you was when you sang that song."

"And?"

"It scared the ever-loving hell out of me."

Eden giggled and playfully slugged his arm. "Coward."

He only grinned.

"What about the song made you realize your feelings?" she asked.

His larynx bobbed as he swallowed. "Because *you* are so damned beautiful.

I looked across the fire at you, and I wanted you to awake unto me."

Tears stung Eden's eyes. "Oh, Matthew, I've awakened unto you now."

"Thank God. You have no idea what it's like for a man to lie in bed with a woman, wanting her so bad. I can't count the times I hightailed it to the creek after you went to sleep."

Eden frowned. "What on earth did you do at the creek?"

"I stripped off and stood in the ice-cold water. It was the only way I could keep my hands off you."

Eden hugged his arm and rested her cheek against his shoulder as he played her favorite song. At the appropriate spot in the lyrics, she tipped her head to gaze at him and softly whispered, "Awake unto me."

He broke off, tucked the harmonica in his pocket, and gathered her into his arms. The kiss that followed made Eden's senses spin. The next thing she knew, Matthew was carrying her to bed. As he peeled her clothing away, he whispered huskily, "I'm thinking of a word that describes how I feel when we make love. Eight letters."

While he nibbled his way up from her toes to the bend of her knee, driving her half-mad with longing, several words swam through her mind, but none of them had the right number of letters. She thought of *bliss, perfect, sublime, unforgettable, indescribable*, and then Matthew was inside her, and she forgot everything but him. As he hammered home and brought her close to climax, the word finally shot into her brain, making her wonder what had taken her so long to think of it.

Paradise. That was it. If they'd been playing hangman, she would have trounced him. Only she was very glad that they weren't. If she never played hangman with him again, it would be too soon. She preferred to show him how much she loved him, only she was too breathless to say the words out loud and too lost in passion to care about anything except bringing Matthew with her into a realm of pure ecstasy.

Chapter Fourteen

Over the next three days, as Eden and Matthew rode toward Denver, he kept his promise to make love to her in many different places, and he made each spot memorable. Though they spent most daylight hours in the saddle, they still stopped to rest the horses, and during those breaks he always took her into his arms, and she went willingly. One afternoon, they came upon a gorgeous waterfall, and Matthew drew her behind the foamy curtain of cascading water. The thunderous noise made it impossible to talk. Matthew compensated by mouthing the words, *I love you,* as he entered her. Another time, he spread their pallet over sun-warmed rocks and took her with craggy mountain peaks and eagles soaring above them. Not even inclement weather deterred him. On an unforgettable morning that would be forever etched in Eden's memory, he stripped her naked as clouds gathered in the Colorado sky, and then tantalized all her senses in a warm mist of gentle rain.

The wondrous sweetness of their lovemaking filled Eden's mind, dimming her memories of the Sebastians. She had never been so happy.

They fell into the habit of riding side by side and talking whenever they came to open areas. Matthew told her more about his parents, family, and Oregon. Eden, eager to learn everything she could, soaked up the information like moss did water.

"Will we go there someday for a visit?" she asked one morning.

He took a moment to reply. "How would you feel about living there?"

Eden's heart caught. She sent him an incredulous look. "Are you serious? I didn't think you wanted to."

He smiled slightly. "My memories of home aren't so sad anymore."

It was a warm morning, so they'd both removed their jackets. Fearing that his watch might fall from his coat pocket, Matthew had slipped the timepiece into the left breast pocket of his shirt. Eden was pleased that he had decided to carry it.

"For a long time," he went on, "I thought only about the attack, never about the good times in Oregon. Knowing you . . . Well, you've helped me to get beyond that." He recounted a few stories about Livvy that made Eden laugh. "Anyway, I think I could go back now. The question is, would you be happy there? I know you love your mother and brothers. Crystal Falls is a long way from Colorado."

"I can return for visits." Excitement welled within Eden. "And for my mother's sake, my not living in or around No Name might be a very good thing." She'd already told Matthew the truth about her father, Connor O'Shannessy. "People look down their noses at bastards, and my resemblance to Caitlin is too striking to be overlooked."

"That is so small of people. As if it's your fault your mother was raped."

"She wasn't exactly raped. She offered her body to O'Shannessy in exchange for her husband's life."

"It's still rape. She didn't *want* to be with the man. He coerced her and then went back on his word. He should have been horsewhipped."

"I agree. He took heartless advantage of Mama's love for her husband. But that's beside the point. Anyone who sees me will immediately know Caitlin and I are closely related. Over time, someone is bound to put two and two together and realize I'm Connor's bastard daughter. People may snub me and my mother as well. If I only go there for visits, I may be able to prevent that by staying at one of the ranches and not going into town."

"You're sure you won't feel . . . I don't know . . . cut off from your family?"

"I'm *positive*. Oregon, here we come!"

Matthew chuckled. "I do have one request."

"What?"

"When we visit No Name on the train, remember to carry your Colts."

Eden burst out laughing. When her mirth subsided, she began spinning dreams about their future together. *Oregon*. She plied Matthew for information—details about the cabin that she would soon call home, what kinds of flowers grew wild on the ranch, if they could keep chickens, and if he would object to her having a dog. She'd always wanted another dog after Sam died, but they'd been so poor that her mother had said no. Later, while living in the city, she had never acted on the desire because she felt that dogs needed lots of open space to run and play.

"I'm not up on the names of all the flowers," Matthew confessed, "but we have a lot of them growing wild in the spring, summer, and autumn. And of course we can keep chickens. You can also have as many dogs as you like," he assured her. "There's lots of space, after all. As for the cabin, we'll make our home there at first, but eventually I'd like to build a larger house."

"I don't need a big house, Matthew. Really, I don't."

He winked at her. "You will when we start having babies."

"We'd better start thinking about the

design layout then, because I have a feeling I may get with child rather quickly."

He grinned. "If you don't, it won't be for lack of trying."

A few minutes later, Matthew got a bad feeling. He couldn't say precisely why. It was a beautiful, sunny morning. Birdsong filled the air. He was with the woman he loved and had never been happier. Why, then, did he suddenly have the whim-whams? He began scanning the terrain. He saw nothing, but his sense of foreboding remained strong. Better to be safe than sorry. He drew a Colt from its holster.

"Eden," he said softly, "unfasten your holster flaps."

She sent him a startled look. As she freed her revolvers, she, too, began scanning the forest. "Did you see something?" she whispered.

"No," he replied. "I just feel itchy all of a sudden, like someone's watching us. It's probably nothing, but I—"

The explosive report of a gun rent the air. Matthew felt the bullet hit him on the left side of his chest, the impact so powerful that it knocked him off his horse. Dimly he heard Eden scream. Then a cacophony of gunfire erupted. For a moment, Matthew was so stunned he just lay in the dirt, unable to move. Memories swirled through his mind of another sunny day when he'd been rendered helpless and had heard the woman he loved calling his name. *Not again.* He pushed up on his elbows and then to his knees. When he glanced down, he expected to see blood all over his shirt, but the pocket was only torn. *The watch.* A hysterical urge to laugh came over him. Had the slug struck the timepiece?

"Matthew?"

He glanced up to see Eden standing behind her horse and returning the Sebastians' fire over the seat of her saddle. She didn't spare him a glance.

"How bad is it?" she cried.

He retrieved his revolver, which he'd dropped when he fell, and sprang to his feet. "I'm okay."

"But you were hit!"

Matthew couldn't take time to explain. "Trust me. I'm fine."

Scanning the area, he saw a fallen log

about twenty feet away. He grabbed Eden's arm, spun her around, and yelled, "Run for it! I'll keep them busy!"

Crouched low to the ground, she sprinted toward the fallen pine. Matthew whirled back and snapped his other gun from its holster. Scanning the forested hillside, he saw nothing. Homing in on the direction from which the shots seemed to be coming, he returned fire, hoping to keep the bastards' attention.

"I made it!" Eden shouted from behind him. "Hurry, Matthew. I'll cover you!"

Matthew hated leaving the geldings as open targets. He could only hope the Sebastians would want the horseflesh for themselves. After snatching his rifle from the boot, he slashed at the lead rope with his knife so Smoky could flee with the bay. Then he grabbed Herman's halter and started to run. The packs on the mule's back held all his extra ammunition. Before this was over, he and Eden would need every bullet.

It felt to Matthew as if he were trying to slog through waist-deep water. He could feel his feet moving and hear his lungs rasping for breath, but the log didn't ap-

pear to be getting any closer. Twenty feet seemed more like a mile. Running, running. With each footfall, his teeth snapped together and he felt the jolt all through his body. *Eden.* He had to reach her. If he went down, she'd be left alone.

He glimpsed her red hair as she popped her head above the log to fire her Colts. Stupidly, he wondered what had happened to her hat. *Please, God, please, God, don't let her take a bullet.* When he finally reached her, he dived over the log without thought for how he might land. Herman, terrified by all the bullets that kicked up dirt around his legs, sailed over the barrier after him. Rolling swiftly onto his knees, Matthew slashed at the bindings that held the packs on the mule's back. When the load fell to the ground, he slapped the animal hard on the rump to get him out of there, then dropped to his belly beside Eden. Herman let loose with a frightened bray and trotted off into the woods, heehawing with every step.

"Are you sure you're not hit?" Eden cried.

"Pretty sure. I think the bullet struck my watch." He hadn't had time to look at the timepiece. Gold was soft metal and normally wouldn't stop a slug. "I guess it glanced off or something. I felt the impact, and it stunned me, but near as I can tell, I'm not hurt."

"Thank God!" Eden laughed a little hysterically. "And thank you, Livvy!"

"Thank *you* for insisting I keep the watch on me." Matthew turned to look over the log. "Have you spotted them yet?"

"Up there on the slope behind those rocks." She sank behind the downed tree to reload. "I have no more rounds in my belt!"

"There's more in the pack." Matthew brought the butt of the Winchester to his shoulder, settled the barrel on the rough bark, and watched for movement behind the rocks. When he glimpsed the crown of a hat, he tightened his finger over the trigger, took careful aim, and fired. He heard a deep-throated wail, which was quickly drowned out by a volley of retaliatory shots. "Keep your head down, Eden."

"You son of a bitch!" one of the brothers yelled. "You got James! You're a dead man, Coulter!"

Matthew hoped to take as many of them with him to hell as he possibly could.

Eden slithered on her stomach to reach the packs. When she crawled back moments later, she had the large leather pouch that held his spare ammunition. Matthew dropped behind the log to reload. While he shoved bullets into the cylinders, Eden returned fire. Stealing a quick glance at her, Matthew's admiration for her grew. She watched for movement, took careful aim, and pulled the trigger without hesitation. *Glorious* was the only word to describe her. She was absolutely *glorious*.

He heard another Sebastian cry out in pain. "Good job, partner!"

She grinned but kept her gaze fixed on the hillside. "Two down, only three to go." She sighted in and fired again. "Damn, I missed by a mile."

Matthew turned to hunker beside her. "They're a little too far away for a Colt."

"Bite your tongue. If I got one of them, I can get another one."

Matthew drew in on the rocks with his rifle again, but the Sebastians had two men down now and were being more cautious. Taut with tension, Matthew never took his eyes off the boulders. In order to shoot, the Sebastians would have to show themselves, however briefly, and he meant to be ready.

Wrong. Steel flashed in the morning sunlight, and bark exploded on the log just under Matthew's chin. He ducked his head. "Holy hell." His heart hammered like a fist against his ribs. "Keep down!"

A spray of bullets hit the other side of the fallen pine, the vibrations jolting through Matthew's shoulder. He waited for a break in the volley, pushed up, and returned fire, not because he saw anything, but because he hoped to discourage the Sebastians from leaving the protection of the rocks. If one of them made a run for it and managed to circle around behind him and Eden, they'd have lead flying at them from two directions. When he shared that concern with Eden, she slanted him a worried look.

"We can't keep firing indefinitely, Matthew! We'll run out of bullets!"

He had already thought of that. He carried a goodly amount of spare ammunition, but it wouldn't last forever. "When you see we're running low, save one round. Promise me."

She locked gazes with him. "I won't let

them take me alive, Matthew. No need to worry."

He nodded. "Same for me. If it comes to that, we'll both be better off dead."

Her eyes sparkled with tears. "I love you, Matthew Coulter. No matter what happens, remember that."

A tight, choking sensation filled Matthew's throat. "I love you, too."

They returned their attention to the rocks. After a while, Matthew lost track of time. He knew only that he'd fired the Winchester so often his trigger finger ached and the barrel was fire hot. Eden was probably tiring, too, but they had no choice except to continue shooting. Their lives depended on it.

The sun was sinking toward the western horizon when Eden said the words Matthew had been dreading to hear. "I just put the last of the forty-five bullets into my Colts, and you have only six rounds left for the Winchester."

"Save one round," he reminded her.

Face pale, her lips pulled thin against her teeth, she nodded. "This is it, isn't it?"

Matthew bit down hard on his back teeth. "I'm sorry, Eden."

"Sorry for what? This isn't your doing, Matthew, *none* of it."

She shot toward the rocks again, and he heard her say, "One," under her breath. He felt sick. *Eden*. She was going to die out here. He'd done everything in his power to keep her safe, but sometimes a man's best just wasn't good enough. God, she was so young. She should have a long life ahead of her. He wanted her to live to have babies, even if they couldn't be his. He wanted her to know the joy of waking up every morning beside the man she loved, even if that man couldn't be him. He had to do something. He just wasn't sure what. Then suddenly it came to him.

"Eden, I'm gonna circle around and get on the slope above them. That big ponderosa will give me some cover."

"*What?* You're nearly out of ammo. You can't go up there."

Matthew sank down behind the log and met her tear-filled gaze. "I have to. When I get there and draw their fire, I want you to run. Try to find the horses. Smoky knows you now. I think he'll let you ride him. Head south. When you start seeing oaks, turn east for Denver."

"No! You can't do this. Please. You said we'd stick together, Matthew. You promised."

Sometimes promises had to be broken. She was too precious and dear for him to lie here behind a log and let her die. If he did this, at least she would have a fighting chance.

Matthew jerked his gaze from hers and belly-crawled toward some brush about thirty feet behind the log. He ignored Eden's pleas for him to come back. Whether she understood it or not, this was something he had to do.

Heartsick, Eden held off on returning the Sebastians' fire, saving her ammunition so she could help Matthew once he circled around. *Run?* If he thought she would do that, he had another think coming. He would never leave her behind, and she wasn't about to leave him. They'd do this together. If that meant she had to die with him, so be it.

She kept her eyes peeled for any movement higher on the slope above the rocks. How long would it take Matthew to circle around? All she could do was pray that God would keep him safe.

Finally she glimpsed a flash of blue. Matthew, zigzagging through the ponderosas. Like a baseball player running for home plate, he turned his feet sideways to brake and slid on his hip to the base of a thick tree. She saw the barrel of his Winchester flash in the fading sunlight.

"Drop your guns!" he yelled. "I've got you dead in my sights! Drop them *now.*"

Instead of dropping their weapons, the Sebastians turned on him and opened fire. Eden let loose with two rounds, hoping to get the attention of at least one of them. *Three.* She had only three bullets left, and one of them had her name on it. Tears nearly blinded her as she popped off another shot. *Matthew.* He'd gone up there to die for her. She wished he'd stayed beside her. If she had to use the gun on herself, she wanted his face to be the last thing she saw.

It wasn't to be. She saw a head appear above the rocks, fired, and missed. She was now down to her last round. She slumped behind the log. That was it. She could do nothing more to help Matthew. Only, when she looked down at the revolver, she couldn't bring herself to put it to her head. Life was precious. She'd wait until the last second—when she saw the whites of the Sebastians' eyes. Miracles could happen. By her count, with the six cartridges she'd given him, Matthew still had about ten left. Maybe he'd pull a rabbit out of his hat and make at least three of them count.

The hillside erupted with even more gun-fire. Eden had become inured to the sound after so many hours. Then her numb brain finally registered that some of the shots were coming from off to the right of the rocks. She twisted onto her knees to peer over the log. Sure enough, she glimpsed a flash of denim on the slope where no one should be. Afraid she was seeing things, Eden rubbed her eyes and looked again. *There! Another man.* She could scarcely believe it, but someone had come to their rescue.

Dodging the hail of bullets that now pep-pered them from two directions, the three remaining Sebastians scurried from behind the rocks, running from tree to tree for cover. Before Eden could blink, they had disap-peared into the forest. A moment later, she heard the unmistakable tattoo of galloping horses' hooves receding into the distance. *Gone.* Just that quickly, it was over.

Matthew emerged from behind the pine. He tossed down the Winchester and put up his hands. "Don't shoot! I'm not one of them."

A tall man emerged from some bushes to the right of the rocks. *Ace.* Eden nearly shrieked with joy. Her brothers! They'd finally found her. Mindless prayers of thanksgiving bounced around in her brain as she scrambled over the log. And then she was running, at first toward her siblings, and then, with a sudden change of mind, she veered toward Matthew, who still stood on the slope with his hands up.

"Don't shoot him," she cried out. "He's a friend!" Her lungs screamed for breath. The slope was steep, and it was all she could do to keep her legs churning to scale the incline. "Matthew? It's all right."

She reached him, threw her arms around his neck, and held on for dear life, even though it took him a moment to lower his hands to return the hug. Eden was shaking so violently that the tremors rocked both his body and hers.

She heard footsteps approaching.

"Eden?"

It was Joseph. She released her frantic hold on Matthew to turn and face her brother. He stood a few yards away, his legs spread, his Colts dangling loosely in his hands. His stance was unthreatening, but Eden knew his tension ran high, and Joseph was lightning fast with those guns. The breeze caught his shoulder-length blond hair and the straight strands drifted across his blue eyes. He never blinked.

Hoping to defuse the situation, Eden stepped forward to hug Joseph's neck. "I've never been so glad to see anyone in my whole life! How on earth did you find us?"

Joseph holstered his weapons and returned her hug, but he never took his gaze off Matthew. "We heard the gunfire late this morning and followed the sound all afternoon. Looks like we got here none too soon."

Ace finally reached them, and Eden flew into his arms. He embraced her fiercely and pressed his face against her hair. "You," he whispered huskily, "gave me a lot of sleepless nights. We had about lost hope of finding you."

"Thank God you didn't stop searching." Eden leaned back to grin up at him. "I saw your tracks and knew you were out here somewhere."

"We've been all over God's creation looking for you for five weeks. Initially we headed for the border, hoping to cut across the gang's tracks. When that turned up nothing, we went to the scene of the train robbery and finally found their trail. At first we followed the gang, hoping to run them to ground, but then we determined you were with someone else. The two of you have led us a merry chase."

Eden hugged David and Esa when they arrived. Then she returned to Matthew's side and took hold of his hand. "This is Matthew Coulter. He saved my life." She turned her gaze to Ace. "He's become a very good friend."

"Looks to me like he's more than just a friend," Joseph observed dryly. "I've never seen you hug anyone but a family member like that, not even that faithless bastard John."

Eden had been through too much over the last several hours to deal with Joseph's temper, so she cut right to the point. "You're right. Matthew *is* more than a friend. I love him with all my heart."

Joseph's gaze shot to Matthew. "Well, now, that's just fine and dandy. Question is, does he love you?"

Ace and David flanked their brother. Esa stood off to the left. Ace, the tallest, looked like a mismatched bookend compared to his shorter siblings, but in some strange way, despite his greater bulk, he didn't seem all that much bigger. He'd raised his younger brothers to be strong men who stood tall regardless of how many inches they measured in actual height.

"Joseph, keep your temper," Ace warned.

"Yes, Joseph, please do," Eden inserted. "For the last several hours, Matthew and I have been through hell. We're tired and need to recuperate before we're subjected to the third degree."

"Keep my *temper*?" Joseph's blue eyes blazed. "I guess I have a right to demand some answers when it appears my baby sister has moved past the handshaking stage with a man I've never clapped eyes on."

To Eden's dismay, Matthew moved down the slope to stand directly in front of her brothers. "As Eden told you, my name's Matthew Coulter. I hail from Oregon, and unless Eden changes her mind, I mean to marry her."

"Without asking one of us for her hand?" Joseph curled his lip in a sneer. "In our family, that isn't how it goes. One of us will decide if you're going to marry her or not."

"Oh, for heaven's sake." Eden stepped down to stand beside Matthew. "I'm a grown woman, Joseph. That's a decision I'll make for myself."

"Eden, let me handle this," Matthew said, an edge in his tone that was new to her. "I've never hidden behind a woman's skirts, and I don't plan to start now."

"I'm not wearing any skirts." Looking from one man to another, all she saw was stony anger or foolish male pride stamped on their faces. She couldn't believe this was happening. "Stop glaring, Joseph. He's my *friend*. If you hurt him, I'll never forgive you!"

"Eden," Matthew said softly, his voice filled with warning.

She clamped her mouth shut, her worried gaze fixed on Joseph, whose temper was the most volatile. David, who was slower to reach a boil, spoke then.

"Forget all the handshaking bullshit. I want some plain answers. Have you taken liberties with our sister, Coulter?"

"She's a consenting adult, and we love each other," Matthew replied. "Don't make something dirty out of it. That's an insult to her, and I won't have it."

"*You* won't have it?" Joseph's voice had gone low and silky.

Eden braced herself. This wasn't going well. Joseph was about to blow. She glanced frantically at Ace, but all he did was smile slightly and rub his jaw.

"I think this is a conversation we should have in private," Matthew said, not backing down an inch. "Eden's been through enough for one day. If you want a piece of me, Joseph, you can have a go, but not in front of her."

Joseph tensed and stood ready. "I don't recollect any introductions. How do you know I'm Joseph?"

"Your brother called you by name, and Eden painted a pretty clear picture of all of you in my mind. Joseph, the hothead. Doesn't take a genius to figure out who's who." Turning toward her, Matthew said, "Sweetheart, go back down to the log. We'll be along in a few minutes."

Eden gaped at him. Didn't he understand how dangerous her brothers could be?

"Go," he insisted, his tone brooking no argument.

Eden doubled her hands into fists and started down the slope. When she came abreast of her brothers, she said, "I mean it. Harm a hair on his head and you'll answer to me."

"Eden," Matthew said, his voice sharp. "Enough said. Go."

She went, but it was the longest walk of her life. As she passed the rocks, she saw that Pete had been the second Sebastian to die. The realization that it had been her bullet that had killed him almost sent her racing into the bushes to empty her stomach. But the nausea soon passed, followed by a sense of rightness. Of all the brothers, he'd been the cruelest to her. Maybe this was God's way of giving the horrible man his just deserts.

Chapter Fifteen

Matthew waited until Eden was well out of earshot. Then he met Joseph's gaze. "I'm only going to say this once, Paxton, so listen sharp. Your sister is one of the finest people I've ever known, and a lady through and through. What happened between us was my doing, not hers."

"She had no choice in it? What are you saying, Coulter, that you forced her?"

"Of course I didn't force her. I'm just saying it was more my fault than hers. I'm older and more experienced. If I'd kept my britches fastened, nothing would have happened. I don't blame you for being mad, but don't make her suffer for it."

Joseph worked his mouth and spit in the dirt. "You've got bigger balls than a whiteface bull, Coulter, and only half the brains."

"I may not be the smartest man who ever walked," Matthew replied, "but I love that girl. Say whatever the hell you want to me, but not in front of her. That's all I'm asking. She was abducted by monsters and held for five days. Beaten, kicked, treated like a dog. She's been to hell and back. When I left her behind that log to come up here, she had only three bullets left. She was down to her last round and probably about to shoot herself when you showed up. I think that's enough for her to deal with in one day."

Joseph hung his head, staring at the dirt with his hands hovering over his Colts, but the starch had gone out of his spine. The tallest brother, dark of complexion, with coffee brown eyes and black hair, was the one Matthew figured to be Ace. He looked a little older than the other three. Shifting his stance, he folded his arms across his chest. "It sounds like a fair request to me, Joseph. Coulter here got the cart before the horse, no question about it, but that doesn't mean Eden should pay the price for it."

Joseph glanced at him. "Have you taken a good, hard look at him, big brother? He's not cut from fine enough cloth to be our sister's husband. More along the line of a saddle tramp, if you ask me."

"It's not the clothes that make the man. You know that as well as I do." Ace stepped forward and thrust out a hand to Matthew. "I'm Ace Keegan. If what Eden said is true and you saved her life, I reckon we owe you our heartfelt thanks, not a kick in the teeth."

"He dallied with our sister!" Joseph cried. "Shake the bastard's hand if you want, but I'll be damned if I will."

"That's up to you," Ace said. "The way I see it, Eden's not a child anymore. She's made her choice, and we have to accept it."

"Not that long ago, her *choice* ended their engagement, defamed her reputation, and broke her heart. Now I'm supposed to believe she knows what's best for her?"

"John Parrish isn't a pimple on this man's

ass," Ace replied. "That citified mama's boy wouldn't stand up to you like Coulter has. He'd be pissing his pants right now. I'll also point out that our sister would probably be dead if she'd had to count on John to rescue her from those low-life skunks."

Matthew grasped Keegan's outstretched hand. "I apologize for getting the cart before the horse, Ace. Feelings took over, and there was no preacher handy."

Ace searched Matthew's gaze. "I like your grit, Coulter."

"Just know this," David interjected. "If you don't do right by her, we'll hunt you down and see that you do."

Matthew smiled. "I'll do right by her."

Joseph spun on his heel and cut across the incline to where he and his brothers had left their horses. Esa and David stood there for a moment and then decided to follow him. Clearly Ace had the final say over Eden's future.

Over his shoulder, Joseph yelled, "If you marry her, you'd better treat her good. Lay a violent hand on her, and I'll kill you."

Matthew bit back a grin. He and Joseph Paxton hadn't yet seen eye to eye, but he had a feeling he'd one day like the man. He was loyal, loved deeply, and valued his family. Those were Coulter traits, ones Matthew understood and admired.

"Do you know how close you just came to getting your ass shot off?" Ace asked. "Joseph isn't all bluster."

"I'd rather risk getting shot than marry into a family of men who have no respect for me."

Ace chewed on that for a moment and finally nodded as if he understood the sentiment. "How did you happen along to save our sister?"

"The Sebastians killed my first wife, and I've been tracking them for three years. Eden was the one who happened along."

"Most men don't talk about a first wife unless they've already got a second one. Please don't tell me you're married, or I may have to kill you myself."

Matthew shook his head. "I've never been threatened so much in my life." Noting the murderous glint in Ace's eyes, he quickly added, "For all intents and purposes, I do have a second wife now. She's sitting on that log down there."

Ace glanced down the hill at Eden.

"She's not a woman a man trifles with if

he's got a shred of decency," Matthew went on. "I knew from the start that she needed a ring and promises, and that's what I aim to give her, God and Joseph willing. Maybe you don't see it the same way, but to me, the wedding will be nothing more than a formality. The actual marriage took place the first time I touched her."

Ace smiled slowly. Matthew noticed then that one side of his face was scarred and that the corresponding corner of his mouth didn't move. It was like looking in a mirror. "I like you, Coulter. Don't take that to mean I've given you my blessing. Before that happens, I need to know more about you— what kind of folks you come from and how you plan to provide for my sister, but now isn't the time for that discussion."

Matthew wholeheartedly agreed. He was too exhausted and worried about Eden right then to think straight, let alone present himself in a favorable light to the head of her family.

When the youngest of Eden's brothers reached the log where she sat, David and Esa immediately took charge of the horses and went hunting for the creek, which could be heard but not seen. Eden suspected that was a calculated gesture to give her and Joseph some privacy. She was in no mood for a quarrel, but she could tell by Joseph's body posture that he might not be in the same frame of mind.

He said nothing at first. He just sat beside her, jerked off his hat, and ran the brim through his hands. "I'm sorry for going off half-cocked."

That was the last thing Eden expected him to say. "Did I just hear you apologize?"

He sent her a disgruntled look. "When I'm wrong, I'm wrong. You've been through hell. I should have been thinking about that. Instead I lost my temper."

Eden smiled and looped her arm around his to rest her head on his shoulder. "It's a flaw of ours. When the day comes that you don't go off half-cocked, Joseph, I'll think you're sick and check you for a fever."

He pressed a kiss to the crown of her head. "I'm afraid for you, sweetheart. You can't know that fellow very well, and I don't like the looks of him."

"He cleans up nice, and I know everything I need to know about him." She hugged his arm. "How long did it take for you to fall in love with Rachel, Joseph?"

"How is that important?"

"How well did you know her?"

"Well enough. I don't see how that has anything to do with anything."

"As I recall, you only knew Rachel for a month or so. You got married so fast that Mama and I couldn't make it to the wedding, but as far as I know, it's worked out well. You're both very happy, right?"

"Right."

"Well, then? Don't stand in judgment of me for falling in love with a man I've known for a little over a month."

"I married Rachel *before* we—" He broke off. "I didn't take a bite of the bread before it was buttered. Coulter did. What if you're with child, and he backs out?"

"He won't."

"How can you be sure?"

"I just am. Countless times during the past weeks, he's put his life at risk to keep me safe. Do you think a man like that would break his word to me and back out?"

Joseph sighed and slipped his arm free of hers to hug her shoulders. "No, I guess not. Sounds to me like I owe the bastard an apology."

Eden curled her arm around his waist. "Yes, but Matthew probably doesn't expect that. He loves his sisters as well. In the same situation, he might have lost his temper, too."

"What other times besides today did he risk his life for you?"

Eden told him about that first night when Matthew had entered the Sebastians' camp and carried her out, about how he'd then returned to steal the bay and spook the gang's horses. "He's been risking his life for me every day since. The Sebastians are crazy. The fact that they've hunted us so relentlessly proves that. Sane men would have cut their losses after a couple of days and fled for the border. Not the Sebastians. Perhaps it was a matter of pride to them, but they couldn't allow Matthew to get the best of them and let it go."

"I'm going to kill them, you know."

Eden tightened her arm around him. "No, Joseph. Matthew has already wasted three years of his life trying to catch them. You have a wife and a beautiful future waiting for you. Don't allow a misguided need for revenge to rob you of that."

"Misguided? They hurt you. I can't let them get away with it."

"I'm fine now. They'll be caught, and when they are, they'll hang. Let the law deal with them. You have more important things to worry about."

Joseph said nothing. Like Matthew, he had a score to settle with the Sebastians now, and he wouldn't turn loose of that easily. Eden knew nothing she said was likely to change his mind, so she fell quiet, too.

Matthew and Ace arrived a moment later. Joseph pushed to his feet. Apologizing had never been easy for him, so he made fast work of it. "I was out of line earlier, Coulter. Thank you for protecting our sister."

"No thanks are necessary."

The two men shook hands.

Eden yearned to go to Matthew. She wanted to be near him, to feel the strength of his arms around her again. The time wasn't right for that, though. Her brothers were trying their best to accept that she'd been intimate with a man they didn't know.

It would be a mistake to press the point and rub their noses in it by clinging to Matthew. So instead she left the three men to get better acquainted while she went to find the creek. Her throat was as dry as parchment paper.

At the stream, she found both her younger brothers, David sitting on a rock, Esa sprawled on the bank to get a drink. The six horses, two loaded with packs, were downstream from them, slurping water.

"You got Joseph's hot fanned down to warm yet?" David asked.

Eden smiled at the question. "Yes. Now I've come to work on you." She crouched beside Esa to cup water in her hands. After drinking her fill, she dried her palms on her pants and joined David on the rock. After telling him the same things she'd just told Joseph, she said, "I know it isn't easy for you, David, but I hope you'll give Matthew a chance. He's a fine man. I think you'll like him once you get to know him."

"He's got guts. I'll give him that," Esa said. "Not many men will stand up to Joseph when he's riled."

David sighed and nudged up the brim of his hat to look her in the eye. "If he saved your life, like you say, I reckon I'll have to give him a chance."

That was all Eden needed to hear. "This morning, when the Sebastians ambushed us, Matthew cut the horses and mule loose. I don't know how far they may have wandered."

"You want us to go look for them?" Esa asked.

"Would you, please? I'm sure Matthew's worried about them. It's been a long day, and I'd hate to see him go searching for them on foot."

Matthew expected Ace to take him aside so the two of them could talk privately, but instead he drew a flask of whiskey from his saddle pack, passed it around, and began asking Matthew personal questions with Joseph present. Matthew answered each query candidly, telling the two men about his home, his family, and his financial prospects, which he feared might count against him. The Coulters were honest and hardworking people, but they weren't rich by any stretch of the imagination.

To his surprise, Ace shrugged. "Money doesn't guarantee happiness. All that matters to me is that you can keep a roof over my sister's head and plenty of food on the table, and make her happy."

"I can do all that. You have my word on it."

Ace smiled. "Then you have my blessing."

"Does Eden know you want to take her to Oregon?" Joseph asked.

"We've talked about it. I was worried she might not want to leave Colorado, but she says living in Oregon will be better all around." He glanced at Ace. "Her resemblance to your wife poses a problem. Eden's afraid someone will figure out that she's Connor O'Shannessy's daughter and that people will shun your mother because of it."

"She may be right," Joseph said. "Most of the folks in No Name have good hearts, but that's no guarantee. People can be quick to judge about things like that."

"When will you leave for Oregon?" Ace inquired.

"As soon as I can," Matthew replied. "I have some unfinished business to take care of first. Once that's settled, I'll come back for her."

"Unfinished business?" Joseph arched his eyebrows. "The Sebastians, I take it."

Matthew nodded. "They murdered my wife and put Eden through pure hell. I can't let that go."

"We have a score to settle with the bastards, too," Joseph said. "Once we get Eden safely to Denver, we'll ride along with you."

"I appreciate the offer, Joseph." Matthew looked the other man directly in the eye. "And I understand how you feel, but this is something I need to do alone."

Joseph's jaw muscle started to tic. Ace curled a hand over his brother's shoulder. "Joseph, we have to give our sister safe escort home. That can be our only concern right now."

"You can get her safely home with Esa and David riding drag. It'd be three against three, with Eden as backup."

"No," Ace said firmly. "We'll all escort her home. I'm not taking any chances with her safety, period, not with the Sebastians at large."

"Damn it, Ace."

"Grumble all you like, but I won't change my mind. You've also got a wife at home with a bun in her oven. You can't go haring off after outlaws and get yourself shot."

Joseph looked startled. "What?"

"Rachel's expecting. She told Caitlin right before we left."

"Why the hell did she tell Caitlin and not me?"

"Women whisper to each other about things like that. Rachel planned to tell you, but then we got word about Eden, and she decided to wait until you came home. She didn't want to worry you or make you feel guilty about leaving her."

"She's *pregnant*?" Joseph looked as if he'd just been poleaxed.

"Yes. You're about to become a father. If something happens to you, what will Rachel do? She can't operate that ranch on her own. I know you want to kill the sons of bitches for what they did to our sister. I feel the same way. But this is something we should let the authorities handle." Ace settled his dark gaze on Matthew. "The same goes for you. Taking the law into your own hands isn't the answer. Eden loves you. You've been intimate with her. What if it turns out she's pregnant? If you're bent on going after the bastards, I'll understand it, but you'll at least marry her first. I won't have my sister giving birth to a child out of wedlock."

"Fair enough," Matthew said. "Is there a town near here where we might find a justice of the peace? If I take the time to ride clear to Denver, the Sebastians' trail will get cold."

"We'll look at a map this evening."

David and Esa returned with the horses just then and heard the last of the conversation. "If you're going after the Sebastians, cut us in," David said. "Nobody harms our sister and lives to tell about it."

Ace held up a hand. "None of us are going after the Sebastians. If Coulter chooses to, that's his business, but the rest of you are going to use your heads for something besides hat racks. We have to get Eden home in one piece."

"But we should all go after them," Esa objected.

"No. This is something for the law to handle."

"I'm the law," David inserted.

"Yes," Ace retorted, "and the people of No Name pay you a good wage to protect them. You've already been gone for over a month. You have responsibilities there, not here. It's not your jurisdiction."

"We can't just let them go!" Esa cried.

"Yes, we can. You have a ranch to run. Joseph has a pregnant wife. David has a job to do. I have a wife and kids to think about. As the head of this family, I'm making the call. The law doesn't condone vigilante activity, and self-appointed doers of justice can end up in jail. You want to hang for killing a bunch of white trash? We're going to keep our heads and let the proper authorities handle it."

David muttered something unintelligible under his breath.

"No more discussion." Ace rummaged in his saddlebag and drew out a spade. "Right now we've got graves to dig."

"Graves?" Joseph shook his head. "I'll be damned. Let the buzzards have at them."

"No," Ace said quietly. "We'll do the decent thing and bury them. No matter what they did in life, they're still human beings."

"That's debatable," Joseph retorted.

"You can argue the point with me while we dig."

Joseph threw up his hands.

"Esa and I need to hunt up Coulter's horses and mule," David said.

"If you'll lend me a horse and some bullets for my revolvers, I'll go find them," Matthew inserted. "My gelding, Smoky, doesn't take kindly to strangers. He may not let you catch him."

Eden never intended to eavesdrop. She'd just been following her brothers up from the creek and had come within earshot to hear the last of Matthew and Ace's conversation. What she heard stopped her dead in her tracks. Matthew still meant to go after the Sebastians? *No!* The very thought made her start to tremble. They'd come so very close to dying today. It had been a miracle that her family had shown up when they had. A *miracle*. Against all the odds, she and Matthew had gotten another chance to build a life together, and now he meant to toss that away to go after three men who might very well kill him.

She couldn't let that happen, *wouldn't* let it happen. She'd always understood Matthew's determination to avenge Livvy, and in the beginning, she never would have dreamed of trying to stop him. But things had changed now. She loved him so much she ached. How would she live without him? It was time for him to stop living in the past and look toward the future. It was time to let go of the hatred and yearning for vengeance. He had Eden in his life now, and she had needs and desires and dreams that only he could make come true. Going after the Sebastians after their close call today was not only crazy but reckless.

Trying to stop trembling, Eden stepped around a tree and into view of the five men. "If you don't mind, Matthew, I'll go with you to find the horses. I think we need to have a talk."

He gave her a questioning look. "About . . .?"

"I'll tell you as we ride."

She went to collect two of her brothers' horses.

Once Eden and Matthew were away from the others, she couldn't think how to tell him what was on her mind. What she said and how she said it might make all the difference. Somehow she had to convince him not to leave. How could any woman who loved a man calmly watch him go on a mission that could end with his death? She didn't have that strength. The mere thought sent her into a panic.

Scanning the ground ahead of them for horse or mule tracks, Matthew asked, "What do you need to talk to me about, honey?"

She took a deep breath and slowly released it. "I heard the last of your conversation with Ace and Joseph, Matthew."

"And?"

"I'm very upset. We nearly *died* today. Do you know how close I came to putting a bullet in my brain? I feel so blessed that we were given another chance, so grateful to God for looking out for us. And now you intend to put yourself in harm's way yet again to go after men who will shoot you on sight?"

"It's something I have to do. I've never lied to you about that, Eden, and I thought you understood."

"I *did* understand, Matthew, but things are different now."

"Different how?"

Eden couldn't believe he'd asked her

that. Wasn't it obvious to him? He had *her* in his life now, and if he truly loved her, how could he think about leaving her and possibly never coming back?

"It's time to let go of the past, Matthew. You've already been after the Sebastians for three years. If you go after them again, you could be gone another three, or never return at all. Can you imagine how terrified that makes me?"

"I'm sorry it frightens you, honey." He drew his horse to a stop and turned to her. "You just have to have faith in me. This is unfinished business for me. I can't let it go. What kind of man could turn his back on what they did to you, not to mention Livvy?"

"I'm fine, though, Matthew. I lived through it and came out on the other side with my sanity. What more can either of us ask? I *love* you. What if I'm pregnant, and you're not there to see our first child born?"

He gazed off into the trees behind her. After what seemed like an eternity, he said, "I'll see the baby when I get back. If I head out after them right away, I probably won't be gone long. We took out James and Pete today. That leaves only three. My odds are a lot better now. I'll take care of it and come back for you before you even know I'm gone."

She already felt as if he were gone, and it made her desolate. "You can't promise me that. You could be killed. Where will that leave me, Matthew? And what will I tell our child, that his father had unfinished business that mattered more to him than anything else?"

"That isn't fair. I made a vow, Eden."

"To Livvy?"

"Yes, and to myself."

"Livvy's *gone*, Matthew. If you love me, truly love me, you'll let go of your need for vengeance and build a life with me."

"I want nothing more than that, but first I have to do this. If you love *me*, truly love me, you'll try to understand that."

His sun-burnished face suddenly swam in Eden's vision, and she realized she was looking at him through tears. She shook her head. "I truly do love you, Matthew, but I'm not willing to live a life overshadowed by hatred and revenge. Sometimes people have to let go and move on. The authorities will eventually run the Sebastians to ground. They'll pay for all the terrible, evil things they've done. It isn't *your* job to punish them."

"I feel that it is." He jerked off his hat and raked his fingers through his hair. "I love you, honey. Please don't do this."

"I guess you don't love me quite enough."

"Don't say that. My need to get the Sebastians has nothing to do with how much I love you. I even plan to marry you before I head out. Would a man who didn't love you do that?"

"I won't marry a man who doesn't love me with his whole heart, Matthew. I settled for something less than the genuine article once. I learned from it."

"Don't compare me to John."

"How can I not? For him, money came first. For you, it's revenge. Either way, I end up taking second place." Tears spilled onto her cheeks and went cold in the evening breeze. "I can live with your love for Livvy and always will, Matthew, but I can't live with your putting her first. If you do this, then you're telling me, loud and clear, that a promise you made to her is more important than your promises to me."

"That isn't so." He frowned at her. "What promises?"

"That we'll stick together. You *promised*, and now you're talking about leaving me again."

"Eden, you're the most important thing in the world to me."

"More important than your vow to avenge Livvy's death?"

When he didn't immediately reply, Eden had her answer. She felt as if a cruel fist were squeezing tighter and tighter around her heart. She stared at his dear face, knowing that he did love her in his way. But for her, that wasn't enough.

"If you're bent on going, Matthew, go," she managed to push out. "Just know this. I won't wait for a man who puts me second, and if you leave, that's what you'll be doing."

She turned her mount then and rode back toward her brothers. With every breath she drew, she prayed that Matthew would come after her, but he didn't, and when she reined her horse around to glance back, he'd disappeared into the forest.

When Eden got back to the stream, her brothers had already finished burying the two Sebastians and were setting up camp near the water for the night. Ace, who was laying a fire, took one look at her face and pushed to his feet.

"What's wrong?"

Struggling not to cry, Eden shook her head. She swung off the horse and went off by herself into the woods. When she found a fallen log, she sat down and buried her face in her hands. *Matthew*. She loved him so much, so *very* much. After John had broken their engagement, she'd wondered at herself for feeling more anger than pain over his betrayal. There was no anger in her this time, just a huge ache in every part of her body that made it difficult to move or breathe.

She started erect when she felt a hand settle on her shoulder. For a wild moment, she thought Matthew had changed his mind and come looking for her, but it was only Ace.

"What is it, Eden?"

"Matthew and I . . . well, we've had a terrible fight."

Ace frowned, and his voice went up a decibel in volume. *"What?"*

"He's going after the Sebastians even though I begged him not to. It's over between us."

He stared at her. "*What?* An hour ago, both of you were professing your undying devotion to each other."

"If he really loved me, Ace, he'd stay with me and build a future with me. Instead, he's honoring a promise he made to his dead wife and going after those animals, even though he knows he may end up getting killed."

Ace sighed and pushed to his feet to pace in agitated circles. "This is crazy. You either love the man or you don't."

"I love him," she said tremulously. "So much I can barely breathe when I think about losing him."

"Then grow up!"

Eden felt as if Ace had slapped her. She sent him a shocked look.

"I love you, Eden, always have and always will, but that doesn't make me blind to your faults. When you get upset or angry, you lose all perspective, letting fly with whatever words shoot through your brain and doing things you regret later. Pardon me for saying so, but you're a little spoiled around the edges."

"*Spoiled?*" Eden shot to her feet, fists

clenched at her sides. "How *dare* you say such a thing to me! I am *not* spoiled."

"Spoiled, headstrong, hot-tempered, stubborn, and as unpredictable as the weather. Those traits do *not* go over well in a relationship." He swung his arm in the direction she and Matthew had ridden a while ago. "You told me that man has put his life on the line for you countless times. How can you think for an instant that he doesn't love you with all his heart? I'll tell you how—because he made the fatal mistake of refusing to let you have your own way."

"That is *not* what this is about! I *love* him, and he's . . . he's determined to go after those skunks and get *shot*! He promised never to leave me again, and now he's going to break that promise! He should honor his word and *stay* with me."

Ace sank back down onto the log. With a ragged sigh, he said, "Eden, wanting a man constantly at your side isn't a reasonable expectation."

She didn't want to be reasonable. She wanted Matthew to love her as much as she loved him.

"Sometimes a man has to leave, and sometimes he has to put his life at risk. That's just the way it is. A mature woman who truly loves a man may not like it, but she understands and gives him her blessing."

"Since marrying Caitlin, name me one time, *one* single time, when you've hared off and put your life at risk!"

Ace looked Eden dead in the eye and said softly, "Five weeks ago, when I took off after a dangerous gang to find my sister."

She stared at him through a burning mist of tears, her mouth quivering, her hands still knotted into fists. "That's unfair. I was in danger, and you came to rescue me. Matthew has no one to rescue. He's just got a maggot in his brain about getting even with Livvy's killers."

Ace gave her one of those relentless looks she knew all too well. "Have you stopped to think his anger at them for what they did to *you* may be first in his mind right now? Did he specifically *say* this will all be for—what was her name?"

"Livvy! And it goes without saying."

"He never mentioned that he also feels a need to avenge you?"

Eden bent her head. "I *hate* you some-times."

"Ah." Ace laughed, stood, and put an arm around her rigid shoulders. "Can I take that to mean he *did* toss your name into the mix when he was trying to explain his reasons for going after them?"

"Yes, but I was secondary."

"Bullshit." Ace hooked a hand under her chin and lifted her face. After brushing away her tears, he said, "I spoke with the man. I saw the love he has for you in his eyes. They hurt his dead wife, and now they've hurt you. Matthew can't turn his back on that. Maybe he's thinking wrong, and maybe he'll change his mind, but if he doesn't, it's your job as the woman who loves him to understand and support him. Instead, it sounds to me as if you threw a temper tantrum."

"I do *not* have temper tantrums."

"Really? I guess you've changed since I saw you last."

Eden wanted to slug him.

Ace sighed. "Sweetheart, I know it scares you to death knowing he may get hurt or even killed, but don't castrate him with your love."

Eden couldn't believe he would say such a thing. *"What?"*

"You heard me. The man loves you. You have the power to bring him to heel and have him following you around like a well-trained bull with a ring in its nose."

Eden could only wish. "No, I don't. He made it clear, in no uncertain terms, that I come second to his need for vengeance."

"He'll think about it and change his mind. You've given him no choice. He either stays with you, or he loses you."

Eden's heart soared with hope, but Ace immediately dashed it. "Problem is, he'll be giving up on something he truly needs to do, and he'll never again feel the same about who he is or what he stands for. Is that what you want, to keep him at your side, even if it means he loses his self-respect?"

He bent to kiss her forehead, then turned to walk back to camp. Over his shoulder, he said, "Brat. But you're still my favorite sister."

"I'm your *only* sister!" she shouted after him. "How about giving *me* some support?"

"Not when you're making the worst mistake of your life."

Eden watched him go and then sank back down onto the log. *Spoiled?* That was absolutely not true. She didn't expect to get her own way all the time. And she was *not* trying to castrate Matthew with her love.

Was she? It bothered Eden deeply to think she could ever be that selfish. But even so, she couldn't forget that moment when she'd asked Matthew what was more important to him, her or a promise he'd made to a dead woman. His silence had pierced her heart. She needed some time to wrestle with that.

Eden's brothers had brought along an extra bedroll for her. She slept near the fire that night, closer to Joseph and David than to Matthew. Over supper, he'd tried to catch her gaze several times, but she refused to look at him. The pain she felt when she did went indescribably deep. *Second-best.* Why was she always tossed only crumbs when she wanted the entire loaf? Why could a man never love her with his whole heart and soul? Was it some horrible flaw within her that she wasn't objective enough to see?

She yearned to curl into a ball and cry herself to sleep, but her pride wouldn't allow it. Matthew might hear and come to her. If he so much as touched her hair and spoke to her in that low, silky voice, she would fall apart. If he meant to go, she wouldn't cling and cry or beg. It was his decision, and she would accept it with her head held high. She would never let him know how small he'd made her feel out there in the forest, or how deeply he'd hurt her. When she recalled their lovemaking, she cringed. She'd given him all of herself, holding nothing back, and she'd foolishly believed he had done the same. But the entire while he'd kept a part of himself walled off, not loving her completely and absolutely, the way she loved him.

Eden slept that night in fits and starts, and was awake when the first pink streaks of early dawn brightened the sky. Tired of lying there on the hard ground, she dealt with her bedding and then went to the creek to wash the sleep from her eyes. She wasn't really surprised when Matthew spoke from behind her.

"Sweetheart, can we talk?"

Maintaining a crouch, she turned to look

up at him. Her heart squeezed with pain because she'd come to love every plane and angle of his face, every wisp of dark hair. Shaking her hands dry, she asked, "About what?"

He wore his jacket to shield him against the morning chill. "I lay awake all night, feeling heartsick." He rubbed a broad hand over his jaw, then scratched beside his nose. "I *do* love you with all my heart, Eden. If I'm going to lose you over this, I won't go. Nothing is more important to me than you, *nothing*. I'm sorry I made you feel like you come second with me. You don't."

She could barely see him now through the blur of her tears. Ace had nailed it right on the head. Matthew loved her enough to change his mind and let go of something that was extremely important to him. Only, what would that do to him in the end? When he looked in a mirror, was he going to hate himself for the rest of his life? Eden didn't want that.

She never felt her feet move, but suddenly she was in his arms, clinging to him with all her might. "Oh, Matthew, I'm sorry. Ace is right; I'm a spoiled brat."

"What?"

"Ace," she said with a tearful laugh. "He laced me up one side and down the other, telling me I'm spoiled, headstrong, and hot-tempered. Oh, and I mustn't leave out that I'm as unpredictable as the weather."

"You aren't spoiled." Matthew's voice throbbed with anger. "What was he thinking to say things like that to you? A little headstrong, maybe, and you do have a temper. But I love those traits in you."

Eden tightened her arms around his neck and squeezed her eyes closed, searching for the words she knew she had to say, even though uttering them would break her heart. As Ace had so crudely put it, she couldn't castrate Matthew with her love. She had to let him be the man he'd been raised to be. If she didn't, he would never be quite the same.

"Matthew," she pushed out. "I was wrong to say those things yesterday. Whether I understand it or not, going after the Sebastians is something you need to do. You won't lose me if you go, I promise. I'll wait for you—forever if I must."

He buried his face in her hair and hauled in a shaky breath. "Ace is right. You are as unpredictable as the weather."

Eden laughed wetly. "Well, at least you'll never grow bored."

He found the sensitive place just below her ear and kissed her there. "Do you mean it? About me going, I mean? You'll wait for me, no matter how long it takes?"

"How can I not, Matthew? You're the other half of my heart."

He swung her around in a circle and then kissed her, long and deep. When he raised his head, his eyes looked suspiciously moist. "You're the other half of mine, too. I'm sorry I feel this burning need to go. If I could turn loose of it, I would."

Eden leaned back to trace each line of his face with her gaze. "If you could turn loose of it, Matthew, you wouldn't be the man I fell in love with."

They were married that afternoon by a justice of the peace in a ramshackle little town called Big Water. The JP, who performed ceremonies in his sitting room, also raised goats, chickens, and pigs, and when Eden stepped inside the dingy foyer, she wrinkled her nose at the stench. Evidently the livestock and poultry wandered indoors on occasion.

Matthew's grip on her hand tightened. Under his breath, he said, "I swear to you, Eden, when I get back, we'll have a proper wedding with a preacher and all the trimmings."

She nodded and smiled shakily, her horrified gaze fixed on the sitting room rug, which appeared to be peppered with chicken droppings. She and Matthew looked at each other, and it was all Eden could do not to giggle. This was *awful.* "That, Matthew Coulter, is a promise I expect you to keep."

He grinned and led her to stand before the old man. Eden's brothers stood behind them in a half circle, hats in hands, to witness the nuptials. The JP scratched his head, and flakes of dandruff parted company with his white hair to drift down onto the book he held open in one hand.

"Dearly beloved, we are gathered here today . . ."

That was all Eden heard until the elderly officiate intoned, "Do you, Matthew James Coulter, swear before God to love, honor, and cherish this woman until death do you part?"

Matthew squeezed Eden's hand. "I do."

"Do you, Eden Dorelle Paxton, swear before God to love, honor, and obey this man until death do you part?"

Eden wasn't certain she liked the "obey" part of her vows, but she set aside her reservations and said, "I do."

She sneaked a glance at Matthew and saw him bite back a grin. They both became solemn when the moment came for Matthew to slip the ring on her finger. He'd purchased it at the general store only thirty minutes earlier and told Eden he was afraid the gold would peel off. But in that moment, she didn't care about the quality of the ring, only about what it represented: never-ending love.

As Matthew bent his dark head and struggled to get the band over her knuckle, she knew she truly would love him forever, and in her heart, she knew he would love her with the same steadfastness.

When they were finally pronounced man and wife, Matthew leaned down to settle his lips over hers. As the kiss deepened, Joseph cleared his throat. At the sound, Matthew straightened away and squeezed her hand again before they signed the necessary papers and paid the justice of the peace for his services.

Once outside, Eden gulped the fresh air, smiling at Matthew. "I was afraid a chicken might parade through the sitting room!"

"I was afraid you were about to call the whole thing off when he said, 'Love, honor, and *obey*,'" Matthew told her with a laugh. "The look on your face was priceless."

Ace stepped forward to shake Matthew's hand. "Welcome to the family," he said. "Make her happy, and you'll never have a quarrel with me." Then he turned to Eden. After searching her gaze for a long moment, he winked at her. "My little sister, all grown up. I can't believe you're a married woman."

Eden grinned. "You didn't seem to think I was all grown up yesterday evening."

Ace chuckled. "And I've never been happier to be proved wrong."

Eden's other brothers followed Ace's lead, welcoming Matthew into the family and then hugging their sister.

"The chicken shit was a nice touch," Joseph said as he looped an arm around Eden's shoulders. "I'm just glad no goats attended the ceremony."

David laughed and lightly punched Matthew's shoulder. "Most men get married knowing the wedding day may be the high point of their lives. You're a lucky fellow. Things can only get better from here on out."

"It wasn't *that* bad," Eden protested. She patted the papers in her jacket pocket. "At least we got the deed done, and I've got proof that he's made an honest woman of me."

David settled his hat back on his blond head and bent to kiss her cheek.

After stocking up on supplies, including whiskey, Matthew rode with Eden and her brothers to the outside of town, where they'd set up a temporary camp. He knew Eden expected him to hit the trail the moment they arrived, but Matthew had other plans. He hadn't been able to give Eden the ring or wedding ceremony she deserved, but he could sure as hell give her a wedding night she would never forget.

To that end, he made camp some distance from her brothers, then went back to collect his wife. She laughed when he swept her up into his arms. "What are you doing?"

"Carrying you across the threshold."

"We don't have a threshold."

Matthew strode with her in his arms toward the other camp. "That's a moot point. I'm still determined to do this right." When he reached the fire pit he'd just built, he settled his bride on the pallet near the flames and began making them each a cup of Irish coffee. As he stirred in the sugar, he settled a smoldering gaze on her and said, "I'm going to make love to you until you're weak, and then I'm going to make love to you again. When I ride out in the morning, you'll have memories of tonight to hold close the entire time I'm away."

That sounded good to Eden, *very* good.

"Is that Irish coffee you're making?"

Both Eden and Matthew jumped with a start. They exchanged bewildered glances as Joseph joined them by the fire. "I wouldn't mind a cup of that. You got plenty?"

Matthew looked long and hard into his new brother-in-law's eyes. Then he said, "Sure. I got another jug in town. But we've only got two cups."

Joseph grinned and held up a tin mug. "I came prepared."

Before Eden knew quite how it happened, all four of her brothers had joined them, and Ace brought another jug of whiskey. Clearly they meant to stay a while. After two rounds of drinks, Matthew looked at each of her brothers and said, "Gentlemen, this *is* our wedding night."

"We know." Joseph passed Matthew his empty cup. "That's why we're here, to celebrate with you."

David bent his head and tugged down his hat to hide his grin.

Matthew mixed Joseph more Irish coffee. "Celebrating is fine. But this is Eden's and my last night together for a good long while, and as much as we enjoy your company, we had . . . well, you know, other things in mind for the evening."

Joseph raised his cup in a mock toast. "To getting the cart before the horse," he said with a smile. "You're not the only man in this family who likes to get revenge."

Matthew looked nonplussed for a second, and then he threw back his head and guffawed. Everyone else laughed with him, and the wedding party began. Soon Matthew had his harmonica out, and Eden was dancing around the fire with each of her brothers. When Matthew insisted on a waltz with his bride, no one else knew how to play the instrument, so he and Eden hummed the tune of "Beautiful Dreamer." As they whirled in the darkness, Matthew moved toward the trees. When they were far enough away not to be seen, he bent his head to steal a kiss.

"Ach!" Ace yelled. "None of that when you've still got guests."

Matthew groaned and rested his forehead against hers. "I'm going to kill them."

Eden shared his frustration, but at the same time, she could see the humor. "They'll leave soon."

"Promise?"

"If they don't, *I'll* kill them."

It was late by the time Eden's brothers left and Matthew could finally be alone with his bride. Fulfilling his promise, he made slow, passionate love to her until she lay weak and trembling on the pallet, her glorious hair fanned out around her head, the curls gleaming like polished copper in the firelight. In that moment, Matthew knew he'd never seen any woman more beautiful. Her body put him in mind of strawberries and cream, and every place he kissed tasted just that sweet.

Bracing himself on one elbow, he gazed solemnly down at her. "I love you," he told her, his voice throbbing with the intensity of his feelings for her. "God help me, Eden, I don't know how I'll be able to leave you in the morning."

She gazed drowsily up at him. "And I don't know how I'll let you go." She reached over to intertwine her fingers with his. "But I have to love you enough to do it."

Matthew bent to trail his lips over her cheek. "I'll come back to you, Eden. I swear it."

"You'd better, Matthew Coulter, or I'll hunt you down."

He smiled at the memory of when she'd voiced the same threat right before he left her at the cave and then made love to her again. Afterward they slipped into an exhausted sleep, wrapped in each other's arms.

The following morning, they arose bright and early, breakfasted together in weighted silence, and then it was time for Matthew to go. Eden walked beside him to his horse, her whole body trembling. Saying good-bye to him was going to be the hardest thing she'd ever had to do. She could only pray that God would give her the strength to get through it.

Matthew slipped his Winchester into the rifle boot and fiddled unnecessarily with the saddle cinch, his jaw muscle pulsing in his lean cheek. When he finally turned to look at her, he had tears in his eyes.

His voice gravelly, he said, "Don't say good-bye. I don't think I can handle it. Just tell me you'll see me soon."

Eden couldn't speak past the lump in her throat. She swallowed hard. "Can I say one other thing first?"

He nodded.

"I *love* you, Matthew. With my whole heart and soul, I love you."

He hooked an arm around her shoulders and drew her against him, his body so taut it was like being hugged by a board. "I love you, too, more than I can ever say with words. I'm a damned fool for leaving you, Eden, but I'm afraid if I don't go, it'll haunt me for the rest of my life."

She clung to him for a moment, and

then she found the strength to step back and smile up at him. "I know. Promise me you'll be careful?"

"More careful than I've ever been. I've got you waiting for me now."

"Godspeed, Matthew." Eden pressed trembling fingertips to her lips and then blew him a kiss. "I'll see you soon."

"Soon," he whispered.

Then he mounted up. Eden gazed after him, not allowing herself to cry until he was out of sight.

Chapter Sixteen

As her brothers broke camp and saddled the horses, Eden tried to focus on the journey ahead. She was unsuccessful. By now, Matthew would be hot on the trail of the Sebastians, and chances were good that he would find them. When he did, he would be one man against three. She couldn't stop thinking of what might happen to him. Unless God worked another miracle, he could die. The very thought made her heart hurt. How would she live through it if she lost him?

The southward journey home to No Name passed in a blur for Eden, one endless day of riding after another. Though Matthew had once shown her Denver on a map and told her they were several days northwest of there, she hadn't expected the community to still be so far away. It drove home to her just how vast this country was. She and her brothers were tiny specks of humanity in mountainous and hilly terrain that seemed to stretch forever ahead of them. Even worse, so was Matthew, and he was all alone.

On the sixth day, they finally began seeing oak on the hillsides and turned west for No Name. It was just turning dusk that evening when they finally reached the Paradise, Ace's ranch. Dory Paxton flew out the door and down the steps, her silk skirts flapping behind her like a flag. Eden dismounted and stepped wearily into her mother's outstretched arms.

"Oh, God, you're a sight for sore eyes," Dory cried. "I thought you were gone for good. Are you hurt? Talk to me, darling."

"I'm fine, Mama. I lived through it."

Caitlin came down the steps, carrying a baby in her arms. Eden pretended to be an excited and loving aunt when she saw her niece for the first time, but in truth, she felt dead inside. At the edge of her mind, she knew little Dory was beautiful, a more perfect reflection of both her and Caitlin's faces, but she felt nothing when she looked at her. Little Ace still looked the same, a bit taller and less chubby than when she'd seen him eight months ago, but still darling. Showing no trace of the shyness with strangers that many children his age exhibited, he clung to Eden's legs until she bent to pick him up.

His small face creased in bewilderment, he studied Eden for a moment, and then said, "Mama?"

Everyone laughed, even Eden, though for her it was forced. "No, sweetie, I'm not your mama. I just look like her."

Little Ace still looked mystified, but in the way of children, he seemed to accept the inexplicable: that a dead ringer for his mother had just appeared in his front yard. While David and Esa took the horses to the stable, Caitlin beckoned everyone else into the house, put baby Dory in the cradle, and hurried into the kitchen to don her apron.

"Lands, you must all be starved! Dory, will you help me get a meal on the table?"

Ace followed his wife into the kitchen, bent her back over his arm, and gave her a deep kiss. When he came up for air, he said, "I've been gone over a month, and you ignore me when I finally get home?"

As he released her, Caitlin blushed and pushed at her mussed hair. "I'll attend to you later, Mr. Keegan."

"Don't cook for me, sis," Joseph said. "I need to get home to Rachel." He hugged Eden, Caitlin, and his mother good-bye, then strode for the door. "We'll drop by tomorrow for a visit."

"See you then," Ace said.

After Joseph departed, Eden, under her mother's direction, located her trunk in one of the bedrooms, took out a nightdress, and slipped into the water closet for a much-needed bath. Ace had plumbed the house, so the tub was soon filled. She stripped off the clothes Matthew had given her, stepped over the porcelain side, and sank up to her chin in hot water, her eyes squeezed tightly closed against a rush of tears. Matthew's shirt, Matthew's jeans. She remembered the night he'd lent them to her and started to sob. Oh, God, where was he? She could only send up fervent prayers that he was safe and eventually would make his way back to her.

Over the next few days, Eden frequently sneaked away to be alone so she could weep, and after she wiped away her tears, she prayed for Matthew's safety. She kept remembering how she'd told him she wouldn't wait for him. At the time, she'd felt justified, but now, looking back, she only felt foolish and immature. How could she have said such things to him? She loved the man with all her heart, and she'd meant it when she told him later that she would wait for him for the rest of her life. She had no choice. Never would she love another man the way she loved Matthew. *Never.*

She often wondered if he recalled that horrible afternoon, if those words she'd said while in a temper still haunted him as they did her. If only she could write to him. Oh, how lovely it would be to pour her feelings and thoughts out onto paper and know that he would read them.

The days passed as slowly as cold molasses dripping from a spoon. Eden lost her appetite again. She had difficulty sleeping. One morning when she looked in the mirror, she saw darkening circles under her eyes. She needed to get a grip on her emotions, but she couldn't seem to do it. Matthew might die out there somewhere, and he'd draw his last breath all alone. Why hadn't she offered to go with him? He might have accepted. Then she'd be with him now, for better or worse. That was what marriage was all about, after all, sticking by each other, no matter what. What had she been thinking to let him leave without her?

Dory sought Eden out one afternoon and found her sitting on a hay bale in Ace's barn. "Would you care to take a walk with me, dear? It's a gorgeous day, and the flowers are so lovely at this time of year. I thought we might gather a bouquet for Caitlin's table."

"I'm sorry, Mama. Maybe another time."

Dory sighed and sat on the bale beside her daughter, her skirts rustling as she got situated. "Can you tell me what's troubling you so, darling? Maybe I can help."

"Nobody can help. Oh, Mama, I love him so much. What will I do if he dies out there?" In a jumbled rush, Eden told her mother about the awful things she'd said to Matthew when she first learned he meant to continue his search for the Sebastians, and how Ace had dressed her down for being so selfish and inconstant. "I deserved every awful thing Ace said to me. Matthew loves me, he *does*. Going after them is something he needs to do. I knew that from the start and understood how he felt. How could I have lost sight of that and become so focused on my own needs and wants? Even though we made up and I sent him away with my blessing, I worry that he'll remember those things I said. What if he dies, and those words are the last things he thinks of?"

Dory curled an arm around Eden's shoulders. "Silly girl, you are not selfish and you are *not* spoiled. I suspect that your brother just realized you were all caught up in your feelings and making a horrid mistake. Ace thinks very highly of you, in truth. Behind your back, he sings your praises, saying you're strong, loyal, and steadfast."

"He *does*?"

"He helped raise you, didn't he? He's proud of you."

Eden no longer really cared what Ace thought. Her whole being was consumed

by the danger Matthew was in and her
fear that she might never see him again. "I
can't lose him, Mama. I'll just die if something happens to him."

"No, dear heart, you'll only think you're
dying."

Eden realized she was talking to a woman
who had lost two men whom she'd loved.
She fixed a bewildered gaze on her mother.
"How on earth did you survive, Mama?"

"By putting one foot in front of the other
and focusing on my children, which is exactly what you will do if Matthew never
comes back."

"I won't have any children. I'll have
nothing."

Dory smiled softly. "Hmm. I think you
may be wrong about that. I've heard you in
the water closet of a morning. It sounds to
me as if you have a bad case of morning
sickness. You're also picking at your food.
I think you're pregnant."

Eden gaped at her mother. "I'm just upset. You know how I am. I get sick to my
stomach when my nerves are strung taut."

"Yes, but not only in the morning." Dory
gave her a hard hug. "Mark my words: We

have a baby on the way. How long has it been since you got your curse?"

Eden hadn't had a cycle since leaving San Francisco. "I, um, can't really recall, exactly. I should have had one when I was with Matthew, long before we ever made love, only I didn't. I'm sure that was due to all the physical hardships I went through."

"Possibly, at least at first, but you're not enduring any physical hardships now. Your body should have come right again. Has it?"

"No, but I'm so worried, Mama. I can't sleep for thinking of all the things that may happen to him. Couldn't that mess up my cycles?"

"Possibly. Nevertheless, I intend to get busy on a layette. I believe it's time to get out my crochet hooks."

Eden curled her hands protectively over her tummy. As worried as she was about Matthew, incredulous joy moved through her. Even if he never came back to her, maybe he'd left part of himself behind. She smiled at her mother through tears.

"Do you really think . . . ?"

Dory chuckled and pushed erect, smoothing her skirts as she met her daughter's disbelieving gaze. "Darling, I was evidently neglectful when we discussed the birds and the bees. Every time I failed to use a bit of sponge soaked in vinegar when I made love with either of my husbands, God rest both their dear souls, I got pregnant. Joseph used to tell me he could get me with child by hanging his britches on the bedpost. You're my daughter, and if I failed to mention that you probably inherited a propensity to conceive at the drop of a hat, I failed as a mother."

Eden laughed tearfully. "Mama, you *never* talked with me about the birds and the bees."

"I *didn't*?" Dory frowned and straightened her ruby brooch. "Surely I did. You're just misremembering."

"No. Ace told me. He did it with all the boys, so I guess he felt it was his responsibility to talk with me, too."

"Oh, dear." Dory continued to frown. "What did he tell you?"

Eden hadn't felt like laughing since she'd blown a farewell kiss to Matthew. But she rocked back on the hay bale now, hugging her middle as she gave way to bone-melting mirth. "He said if I fell in love, I should always carry a penny in my bodice."

"Whatever for?"

Eden giggled. "If my beau grew amorous, I was to hold that penny tight between my knees."

"Dear God." Dory cupped a hand over her eyes and sank back down on the hay bale to laugh with her daughter. "*Men.* God love him, he meant well." Another frown stole over Dory's lovely face. "I can't believe I failed to talk with you. Where was my head at?"

"You were so worried about teaching me which fork to use for my salad, I think you forgot."

Dory dissolved into laughter again. "You're probably right. I hadn't been intimate with a man for so long, I could barely remember what it was like." A dreamy expression moved across her countenance. "Well, that's an overstatement. I remember very well. It was just a joy that I'd lost, so I guess I chose not to dwell on it." Her face seemed to glow as she thought back. Then she turned to look questioningly at Eden. "Does your Matthew . . . well, does he make you feel as if he just handed you a handful of stars?"

Eden smiled and lightly rubbed her hand over her stomach. "He makes me feel as if he has handed me the moon as well, Mama. Maybe the whole universe."

Dory chuckled and patted Eden's knee. Standing again, she turned, her smile gone, her expression compelling. "From this point on, Eden Coulter, it is no longer about only you and Matthew. You must force yourself to eat. If you can't sleep at night, you must take naps during the day. And when your thoughts grow gloomy, you *must* find a way to cheer yourself up. Babies in the womb don't thrive when their mothers are upset. It is *your* responsibility to make sure Matthew Coulter's child grows strong within you, makes it into the world, and lives to adulthood. If you can't do that for yourself, then do it for Matthew."

"I just can't believe I may be pregnant."

Dory rolled her eyes. "I'll see how you feel about that in the morning when you're feeling nauseated again."

After that conversation, Eden spent a lot of time sitting on Ace and Caitlin's veranda swing, watching the horizon for a horse and rider in the distance. One week became two, and two became three. Following her mother's advice, Eden tried to cheer herself up by writing Matthew letters. She poured her heart out onto the paper, telling him how very much she loved him, about the possibility that she was pregnant, and how eagerly she awaited his return. She addressed each letter to him in Crystal Falls, general delivery, and asked Ace to mail them for her. If Matthew returned—and she clung to the belief that he would—he could read the letters someday when they moved to Oregon.

Matthew had been on the Sebastians' trail for over three weeks when he settled under a juniper tree one afternoon while resting the horse and mule. *Eden.* God, how he missed her. Sometimes he found himself selfishly wishing that he had invited her to come with him. She wouldn't have hesitated to accept. He knew that. But then he might have been instrumental in getting her killed. He had no idea how this would end, only that he was losing his enthusiasm for the chase and starting to question his sanity.

As always, the Sebastians were as unpredictable as a bunch of brainless hens being chased by a fox, flitting in first one direction and then another. Matthew remembered telling Eden that he'd run them to ground, lickety-split, and be back before she knew it. She hadn't believed him, and now he had to admit maybe she'd been right. He might be tracking those bastards for another three years. Hell, so far as he knew, possibly even six or seven. In seven years, Eden would be thirty. Her dreams of having lots of babies might never happen if she waited that long for him, and deep in his heart, he knew she would.

If he was gone for years, a part of him hoped she would have him claimed legally dead and get on with her life, but another part wanted so much to be the man she woke up with every morning. And therein lay the dilemma for Matthew. He no longer felt certain he should be out here. *Damn it.* Maybe Eden had been right about everything else as well, and he'd just been too blind to see it. When they'd been ambushed by the Sebastians, they'd both come close to dying. Matthew would never forget his startled amazement and incredulous relief when he realized that help had suddenly appeared out of nowhere. A miracle? He'd gone up on that slope to die, praying Eden would do as he said and run, but bless her brave heart, she'd stayed to spend her last spare bullets in an attempt to save him.

God truly had granted them both a second chance, and he was an idiot to be throwing it away. Why wasn't he with the woman he loved, making the most of the opportunity God had given them? Instead, he was riding toward possible death. As Eden had said, nothing he ever did would bring Livvy back. Nothing he did would wipe out what had happened to Eden, either.

So what was he *doing*? He was on a fool's mission—that was what. He'd said his good-byes to Livvy. She'd even made his watch glint gold in the starlight to tell him he had her blessing. Or so he would always believe. Yet here he was, still chasing her killers. Matthew sighed and leaned his head against the tree. His hat knocked forward over his eyes, creating a blind from the sun. Pictures swam through his mind of the night when he'd rescued Eden, what he'd witnessed before slipping into the Sebastians' camp to free her. When he thought about what those animals had done to her, he couldn't help but want to spill their blood. Eden believed his sole purpose for being out here was to avenge Livvy's death, but that was only partly true. Yes, the bastards needed to pay for what they'd done to his first wife, but more important to Matthew now was stopping them from hurting anyone else and punishing them for what they'd done to Eden. She was still alive. She had to live with the memories. Livvy was up in heaven, singing with the angels, not down here, going through hell.

He would never forget when he'd stood on a creek bank one night and watched a beautiful young woman scour her skin raw with sand. *I'm fine, Matthew. I lived through it and came out on the other side.* And God love her, she had. Maybe he'd helped her in some small way, but mostly Eden's recovery gave testimony to her incredible strength of spirit. She had been determined not to allow the Sebastians to ruin her life, and she'd won the battle.

Now she wanted to enjoy that life, grab hold of it with both hands and live it to the fullest. And she needed him beside her to do that. So what was he doing here, chasing men who were as difficult to catch as fruit flies? Eden wanted him there to hold her in his arms. She wanted him there to give her his babies. She wanted him there so they might build a future together.

A pent-up breath shuddered from Matthew's chest. His body went limp. He needed to get his head on straight and go home to his wife. Any husband worth his salt stayed around to provide for his family. Right now, Matthew was so down on his luck he could barely provide for himself, let alone for a woman and possibly a child. He needed to get his ass back to work.

Since the day of the ambush, Matthew hadn't had the heart to examine his timepiece. He knew the bullet had damaged it beyond repair. But he removed it from his coat pocket now, his intent being to bury it. Eden's heart had been in the right place when she had insisted that he continue to carry it on his person, and he'd come to understand her reasons, but he was having no more of that. His memories of Olivia would always be there, buried deep like the watch soon would be, but there'd be no room from now on for memories of her to be a part of his everyday life.

As Matthew drew the mangled gold case from his pocket, he gave in to habit, thumbing the back to feel the inscription he'd memorized. He winced and drew his thumb away. The watch cover had been badly mangled by the bullet, the metal jagged and sharp, the fine lettering obliterated. He turned the timepiece over, and what he saw made him smile. The only words left now were *Love* and *Matthew*. No more about forever. Livvy's name was gone. There remained only a simple command from one of heaven's most special angels, *Love, Matthew*.

Oh, God, seeing that watch, mangled into a twisted mess with only those two words winking up at him, set Matthew absolutely free. Eden was right again. More than one miracle had occurred the day of the ambush. He knew that for certain now. For as long as he drew breath, he would believe that Livvy had guided his hand that morning to put the timepiece in his breast pocket, that she'd been trying to protect him so he could live to know the joy of loving again.

He was finished with chasing the Sebastians. He was finished with letting them ruin his life. *If we let that happen, Matthew, they win*, Eden had told him. And it was true. The bastards would maraud and murder until they were stopped, but it wasn't his job to bring them to justice.

He was going home to his wife.

Late one afternoon about a week later, Eden was sitting on the porch swing, watching Little Ace for Caitlin, when she saw a lone rider top the horizon. Time after time, she had seen someone approaching and allowed herself to hope it might be Matthew, but it had always been one of her brothers instead. She refused to do that anymore. The disappointment hurt too much.

Only this time, despite her determination not to get her hopes up, a strange, tingling sensation moved over her skin, similar to how she felt during the calm right before a lightning storm, when the air fairly snapped with static electricity. Eden pushed slowly to her feet, her gaze fixed on the rider. As he drew closer, she saw that he was leading a pack animal, and the horse looked as if it might be a gray. A thrill of excitement shot through her. She picked up Little Ace, threw open the front door, and settled him back on his feet in the sitting room.

"Caitlin, it's Matthew. I think it's *Matthew*! I have to go meet him."

Coming from the kitchen, Caitlin beamed a smile and made a shooing motion with the skirt of her apron. "Go! I've got Little Ace. *Go*."

Eden slapped the door closed and hurried down the front steps. *Matthew.* It was definitely him. The gelding was indeed a gray, and she recognized the way Matthew sat in the saddle, broad shoulders relaxed, upper body swaying with each movement of the horse. Gathering her skirts and petticoats into her fists, Eden broke into a run.

"Matthew!" she cried out, even though she knew he probably couldn't hear her yet. "Matthew!"

He must have seen her then, because he nudged Smoky into a trot. Eden never broke stride. She streaked down the road, out through the entrance gate, and into an open field, so overjoyed she never spared a thought for the wagon wheel ruts and gopher holes that might trip her. She ran until she grew breathless and got a stitch in her side that brought her staggering to a stop. But Matthew kept coming. Soon she could see his dark face clearly. He was grinning—that wonderful, heart-stopping grin that she'd thought never to see again.

Smoky skidded to a stop about twenty feet from Eden. She broke into a run again as Matthew swung down off the horse. They met in a collision of bodies, Eden flinging her arms around his neck with such force that she knocked his hat from his head, Matthew locking her in his hard embrace. For several seconds, they were both too overcome with emotion to speak, so they simply clung to each other. Then when the words finally came, they both spoke at once, saying the same thing.

"I love you so much!"

They both laughed, tears slipping down their cheeks as they swayed together in the wind that blew across the flats.

"Did you get them?" Eden finally found the presence of mind to ask.

"I gave it up," Matthew whispered, his voice gravelly with emotion. "To hell with finding the bastards. I had to come back. You're the most important thing in the world to me, Eden. Nothing, and I do mean *nothing*, matters more to me than you do."

"But, Matthew, it meant so much to you. I don't want to be the reason you give up on catching them. If you need to go after them, go. I'll wait. No matter how long it takes, I'll wait."

Matthew turned his face into her glorious hair and breathed deeply of her scent. She smelled like rosewater, which was new, but beneath that was her own special essence, the one he'd dreamed of so often over the last month.

"I'm not going anywhere. From here on out, we're sticking together. I'll never willingly leave you again, *never.*"

Matthew told her the story about the watch and how he believed Livvy had sent him one final message—to move on with his life and love Eden with all his heart. When he finished talking, Eden drew back to look up at him.

"You buried it in southern Colorado?"

"It seemed like the right thing to do. There's no room in my life for Livvy now, sweetheart. No room in my heart for her, either. I'll always have memories of her, but that's all they are, memories." He bent his head to trail his lips over her finely arched brows. "If I'm going to carry a watch engraved with words of love, I want it to be one from you. Maybe it can be your wedding gift to me. I promised you a proper ceremony, remember, with a preacher and all the trimmings."

Eden smiled up at him, her blue eyes dancing with amusement. "Without any chickens in attendance?"

"Definitely no chickens, or goats, either."

She pressed her palms to his lean cheeks, drinking in every detail of his face. "You're freshly shaven."

"And clean from head to toe. I stopped at a creek for a bath before coming here."

Her cheeks grew warm with excitement. "I have wonderful news, Matthew. I think I'm expecting."

"Expecting what?"

She wrapped her arms around his neck again, pressing as close to him as she could get. "I think I'm pregnant. I've missed my curse only once, but that isn't normal for me. I think we have another baby Coulter on the way."

Matthew whooped with joy, tightened

his arms around her waist, and twirled across the grass with her. Then his heart caught and he stopped. "I didn't hurt you, did I?"

She giggled. "I'm not made of spun glass, Matthew, and neither is the baby. Of course you didn't hurt me."

He kissed her then—deeply and thoroughly. She melted against him, parting her lips and holding nothing back. As he tightened his embrace around her, he knew he'd made the right choice.

He held the whole world in his arms.

Before they went to the house, Eden and Matthew sought a private place where they could talk and plan their second wedding. They ended up sitting under the gnarled old oak where Joseph Paxton Senior had been hanged so many years ago. After seeing the tree and learning from Eden what had happened in this peaceful place, Matthew recalled the story she had told him about Ace's long-ago obsession with exacting revenge and clearing his stepfather's name. It was good that Ace had let go of that and married Caitlin instead. Matthew had learned the hard way that there was a lot more to life than setting wrongs aright. When a man allowed himself to be consumed by hatred, he missed out on all the sweetest things life had to offer. Sitting there in the shade with Eden, seeing her lovely face again, was very, *very* sweet, a moment he would always remember. To think that she might be pregnant with their first child was even sweeter.

"I want to have our second wedding right away," he told Eden. "I need to get back to work and provide for my family, and I can't do that until we get to Oregon."

"I love the sound of that word, *family*," she said softly, her palm curled protectively over her middle. "Just think, Matthew. We may soon have a child."

Matthew lifted her hand and pressed a kiss on her palm. "You've already made me the happiest man alive. If you're not pregnant, it won't matter to me. If you are, it'll be the icing on the cake."

Eden closed her fist around the kiss and then hugged his arm. "Are you sure you won't regret not going after the Sebastians?"

"Absolutely positive. It's over for me. I'll never look back, only forward."

She rested her head on his shoulder and sighed in contentment. "I hope it's a girl, Matthew. If it is, I still want to name her Olivia."

"You aren't going to be mulish about that, are you? I'd rather name her after someone in one of our families."

Eden told him how she felt about naming children after people who were still alive. "I think it's confusing for everyone, and embarrassing for the child later in life. When Ace's son grows up, he'll probably still be called Little Ace. I don't want to do that to our children."

Matthew had grown up being called by both his first and middle names much of the time because he was a junior. He had never minded it all that much, but he could see Eden's point. "We could name her after one of our grandmothers then."

"We'll have other daughters, Matthew. I want our first to be Livvy's namesake. It's important to me."

Matthew recognized that tone in Eden's voice and knew she had her mind set on it. *Olivia.* He'd always loved the ring of it, and he thought the nickname Livvy was cute. It definitely wasn't an important enough issue to butt heads with Eden over it. He had a feeling they'd do enough head butting over the years without quarreling over little things.

"What are you grinning about?" Eden asked, her tone laced with teasing accusation.

Matthew chuckled. "You don't want to know."

"Yes, I do."

"I was just thinking that I've tied up with a sassy, headstrong lady who'll probably need to be reminded on a daily basis who wears the pants in this family."

She giggled. "It's true that you wear the pants, Matthew, but always bear in mind that I wear the bloomers."

"Why is that important?"

"Because you'll never get them off of me if you're bossy and overbearing."

Matthew threw back his head and barked with laughter. Then he set himself to the task of getting the damned bloomers off her so they could make sweet, passionate love. He feared she might feel shy. It was broad daylight, after all, and they weren't far from the house. But as always, Eden settled in his arms without hesitation. He teased the sensitive spot just below her ear, then feathered kisses downward, unfastening her bodice as he went. She gasped and shivered when his mouth closed over her nipple. Then she made fists in his hair as if she feared he would stop.

Because they might get uninvited company, Matthew decided he should probably leave the bloomers alone, and her dress as well. He satisfied himself with slipping a hand under her skirt to find the slit in her underwear and brought her to climax without disrobing her. When the moment came to bury his shaft in her moist sheath, he only opened his fly.

Then he hesitated. "If you're pregnant, is it safe to do this?"

She smiled dreamily up at him. "Women can make love all through their pregnancies. It's fine, Matthew."

Nevertheless he entered her carefully and gentled his thrusts. Even so, the pleasure they shared was intense and indescribably beautiful. *Home*. He realized now that home wasn't a place. Home, for him, was in this woman's arms.

Afterward, as they lay spent in the shade of the oak, Matthew gazed up at the gnarly branches, thinking that a life had once ended here.

And now another one had begun.

Eden and Matthew's second wedding ceremony took place the following afternoon in Ace and Caitlin's sitting room. Hannibal St. John, the preacher at No Name's community church, officiated at the ceremony. Only family members were in attendance.

As she and Matthew exchanged vows, Eden gazed up at his dear face, thinking that, in a different way, both of them had closed the door on their pasts. Matthew had left behind a host of terrible memories, and she was finally laying her real father, Connor O'Shannessy, to rest. In Oregon, her striking resemblance to Caitlin would no longer matter. Her flame red hair would no longer mark her as a bastard. She would never have to worry again that someone might discover her secret or that her mother might suffer for it.

After the ceremony ended, Eden and Matthew cut the cake that Dory and Caitlin had slaved half the night to bake and decorate. Ace brought in a container of ice cream that he'd purchased in town and kept frozen in a tub of ice. When everyone had enjoyed the sweets and toasted the newly-weds with champagne, Eden and Matthew opened their gifts and then exchanged personal ones that they'd purchased for each other. He'd gotten her a locket. On the inside of the cover, he'd had the jeweler engrave the words, *To Eden, the love of my life, Matthew*, followed by the date.

With specific instructions, Eden had sent David to town to select her gift for her husband. When Matthew opened the small package and saw a gold pocket watch, he smiled. Then he turned it over, read the inscription, and got tears in his eyes. Eden had duplicated the words on his other watch, now buried somewhere in the wilds of southern Colorado. But the date and the name now following the promise were different. *Love Always, Matthew. Forever Yours, Eden, 1890.*

He ran his thumb over the words, looked deeply into her eyes, and then slipped it into his pocket. "I'll carry it with me always."

Eden knew he truly would, but he'd never feel sad when he checked the time. She planned to be around until he was a very old man. She hugged his waist and thanked him for the beautiful locket, knowing he'd spent money for it that he could ill afford.

David spoke up just then. "I know I gave you table linen, but I brought along another wedding gift I think both of you will appreciate even more."

Leaning against her husband, Eden smiled at her brother. "The table linen is gorgeous, David, and it must have cost you dearly. Whatever else you bought, please take it back."

David grinned. "It's not a gift I bought, little sister. It's news I received early this morning by telegraph. The Sebastians were caught by a posse three days ago in southern Colorado. They'll go to trial in two weeks."

Eden glanced up at Matthew. A stunned expression had settled on his dark face. "You're sure?"

David nodded. "Came straight from the marshal who apprehended them and is holding them in jail. I wired him back to see if your testimony as witnesses will be required at the trials. He says that's entirely up to you." David directed his gaze to Eden. "If you want the satisfaction of having them tried for the acts of kidnapping and assault that they committed against you, then you'll have to file formal charges and testify at each trial. If you prefer not to do that, there are so many other counts against them and innumerable witnesses to ensure a guilty verdict that they'll probably be hanged. If not, they'll be in prison for life. No matter what you decide, their reign of terror is officially over."

Eden looked questioningly at Matthew. "What do you think I should do?"

Matthew grinned. "You heard your brother. They're finished. I think you should put all of it behind you and start living the rest of your life—with *me*."

Eden laughed and went up on her tiptoes to hug Matthew's strong neck. "Of all our beautiful wedding presents, that one is the very best! They've been caught, Matthew! They've been *caught*!"

He wrapped both arms around her and buried his face in the lee of her neck. "Thank God. I can scarcely believe it. I was starting to think this day would never come."

"It's high time," Ace said, lifting his champagne glass. "A toast, Matthew."

Matthew loosened one arm from around

Eden to pick up his flute. Joseph stepped over to refill it. Throat working, his eyes warm on Eden's, Matthew said, "To justice. They're finally going to pay for their sins. I'll sleep better at night, knowing that."

Eden smiled as Matthew touched the crystal rim to her lips. "To justice," she murmured. "I'll sleep better at night, too, Matthew. They'll never harm anyone else." As her husband set the flute aside, she went up on her tiptoes to hug his neck again. "Another miracle," she whispered. "God has sent us another miracle."

As Matthew returned her embrace, she sighed and leaned into him, knowing without a doubt that she was exactly where she belonged and where she always hoped to be: in Matthew Coulter's arms.

Epilogue

Oregon
June 12, 1891

The afternoon sunlight warmed Eden's shoulders. The scents of wildflowers and field clover drifted on the gentle breeze that tousled the curls at her temples. Holding her three-month-old daughter, Olivia, in the crook of one arm, she crouched to tug weeds from the first Olivia's grave. As she worked, she smiled softly, thinking of Matthew. He was happy now and loved their little girl so much that he could barely focus on work. Several times each day, he abandoned his chores and returned to the house to play with the baby. Eden scolded, but didn't really mean it. It was wonderful to see the joy on his face when he took their child into his arms.

Eden trailed her fingertips over the words chiseled into the granite headstone. *Baby Coulter.* It made her sad knowing that Matthew's first child had never gotten a chance to experience life.

When Livvy's resting place was tidied, Eden moved through the small cemetery to pull weeds that had sprouted up around Matthew's grandparents' headstones. *Family.* In this place, Eden felt a sense of connection with the Coulters that ran bone-deep. During the time she'd been in Oregon, she'd come to love Matthew Senior and Hattie. They were kind, honest, and hardworking people with keen minds and good senses of humor. Eden had also forged strong relationships with Matthew's sisters and brothers. Though she sometimes missed her own family, the moments were fleeting. She and Matthew planned to visit Colorado in September, when Olivia would be old enough to travel by train. Eden looked forward to the trip, but she would be just as glad to return to Oregon. It was home to her now.

"What are you doing?"

Eden started erect. "Matthew, you scared me out of ten years' growth."

He stood outside the iron gate, booted feet set wide apart, arms crossed. Though they'd been married for many months now, Eden's heart still caught when she looked at him, and it probably always would. He was, without question, the handsomest man she'd ever seen.

"You wouldn't scare so easy if you spent less time in this graveyard."

Eden brushed her hand clean on her apron. "I thought you were working."

His blue gaze held hers. The mischievous grin that touched his firm mouth made her pulse start to race. "I finished up and decided to take the rest of the afternoon off. It's a gorgeous day. I'd like to spend what remains of it with my beautiful wife and daughter. I thought we might go for a picnic at the creek."

"A picnic? I have no food prepared."

He extended a hand to her. "I'll help. It doesn't have to be fancy."

Eden moved toward him. When she reached the gate, he bent his head to settle his mouth over hers. The kiss was long and deep, filling her with contentment and yearning, both at once. "Say yes," he whispered.

With a laugh, Eden said, "Telling you no is the challenge."

He collected his daughter from the crook of her arm. "Come on, then. Let's go up to the house and fill the picnic basket."

Settling Olivia in the bend of his left arm, he unlatched the gate, took Eden's hand, and drew her from the enclosure. She looped her arm around his waist as they crossed the field, loving the way his lean leg bumped against her hip as they walked. The chickens clucked and scattered when Matthew and Eden reached the front yard. Eden hadn't gotten a dog yet, but a neighboring farmer had puppies almost old enough to wean, and Eden had been promised pick of the litter. She had her eye on a darling coal black male with a white spot on its forehead.

Once inside the cabin, she and Matthew set to work filling the basket. When Matthew drew a bottle of homemade corn whiskey from the cupboard, Eden regarded him with upraised eyebrows. "What's the occasion?"

He winked at her. "That's for me to know and you to find out."

After hooking up the buckboard and parking it out front, Matthew came back in the house to strap on his gun belt. He also fetched his Winchester. Whenever they went to their special place along the creek—a different location from the one he'd once shared with Olivia—he never failed to take his weapons.

"Grab a couple of blankets," he said, lifting the baby from her cradle.

"A couple?"

"One for Livvy and one for us." He sent her a teasing look. "After we eat, I want to hold my wife in my arms and watch the clouds drift by. Think of it as my own special kind of dessert."

Eden laughed. "Apple pie isn't enough?"

"Not when I can hold you."

The wagon ride to the creek was lovely. Eden held Olivia in her right arm so she could lean into her husband as he drove the team. When they reached the bend in the creek, Matthew reined the horses to a stop, set the brake, and leaped from the wagon. He took the baby and then helped Eden from the conveyance.

Within minutes, they'd spread one blanket in the shade of an old oak and created a soft pallet for the sleeping baby with the other. As Eden sat beside her husband, she dragged in a deep breath of the warm summer air, enjoying the scents that drifted on the breeze—the piney ponderosas and the sweet alfalfa and wildflowers. The stream gurgled merrily as it surged over rocks. Birds twittered above them in the branches of the tree.

Hugging her knees, Eden sighed. "Oh, Matthew, what a great idea this was. I'm so glad you brought me."

He plucked the whiskey from the basket and set to work pulling the cork. Eden fished for the pot of coffee and cups she'd thought to bring. As he mixed them each a drink, both laced with cream, she studied his expression.

"It's not often that you quit work early and indulge in spirits. I'm dying of curiosity. What *is* the special occasion?"

He grinned and drew a thick fold of paper from inside his shirt. "I have something to show you. Nothing set in stone. You'll probably want to make changes. But I've been working on the plans for our house."

As he spread out the paper and smoothed away the creases, Eden leaned close to study the drawings. "A parlor?" she asked incredulously.

"Of course."

"And a *study*? Matthew, we can't afford anything so grand as this. Six bedrooms? It would be huge."

"I plan to fill those bedrooms, and I want to give my wife the home she deserves."

Tears stung Eden's eyes. "I don't need a grand house, Matthew. If you add some bedrooms onto the cabin, I'll be perfectly happy."

"I won't be, though." He took a sip of his Irish coffee and then gestured at the endless stretches of ponderosa pine that surrounded them. "It'll be a log structure, honey, and we have plenty of trees. Next week, Hoyt's going to help me fell them. They'll be seasoned enough by next spring to start construction." He searched her face. "I thought you'd be happy."

Eden held her cup aside to lean forward and kiss him. "I *am* happy. It'll be a lovely house. I just don't want you to think you have to build it."

"I know I don't have to, honey. I *want* to." He tapped the drawing. "Study the layout. Put your own stamp on it. I want it to be a house that suits you in every way."

Eden set her cup on the blanket to better peruse the plans. "Oh, Matthew, it's perfect just as it is." She glanced up at him, imagining their children growing up within those walls, Olivia and several brothers and sisters. She wanted a large family and so did Matthew. "I love it."

"Not as much as you love me, I hope."

"Never. I love you more than anyone or anything."

He smiled and lightly touched their daughter's curly dark hair. "In my special corner of your heart?" His smile deepened. "I finally get that, you know. I love our baby so much that it almost hurts." His gaze shifted to Eden's. "And yet I love you more than life itself. It's a mystery, isn't it, how limitless our capacity for love can be?"

Eden cupped a palm to his scarred cheek. "It *is* a mystery," she agreed. "A profound mystery."

He dipped his head to kiss her. Corn

whiskey slopped over the edge of his cup. They broke apart and laughed. Then their smiles faded as they looked deeply into each other's eyes as only lovers do.

"Meeting you was the best thing that's ever happened to me," he whispered.

"Same for me."

"No, I mean it. You gave me a reason to want to live again."

He set his cup beside hers. The spirits forgotten, they lay back, wrapped in each other's arms. Dappled sunlight played over them. The creek sang in the background. The music of the birds played through Eden's mind. Breathing deeply of the flower-scented air, she could think of nowhere on earth she'd rather be. Even lovelier, she could think of no better way to spend the rest of her life.